HISTORICAL

Your romantic escape to the past.

The Viscount's Christmas Bride
Bronwyn Scott

One Night With The Duchess
Maggie Weston

MILLS & BOON

THE VISCOUNT'S CHRISTMAS BRIDE
© 2024 by Nikki Poppen
Philippine Copyright 2024
Australian Copyright 2024
New Zealand Copyright 2024

First Published 2024
First Australian Paperback Edition 2024
ISBN 978 1 038 94183 1

ONE NIGHT WITH THE DUCHESS
© 2024 by Maggie Weston
Philippine Copyright 2024
Australian Copyright 2024
New Zealand Copyright 2024

First Published 2024
First Australian Paperback Edition 2024
ISBN 978 1 038 94183 1

This is a work of fiction. Names, characters, places, and incidents are either the
product of the author's imagination or are used fictitiously, and any resemblance to
actual persons, living or dead, business establishments, events, or locales is entirely
coincidental.

MIX
Paper | Supporting
responsible forestry
FSC® C001695
www.fsc.org

Published by
Harlequin Mills & Boon
An imprint of Harlequin Enterprises (Australia) Pty Limited
(ABN 47 001 180 918), a subsidiary of HarperCollins
Publishers Australia Pty Limited
(ABN 36 009 913 517)
Level 19, 201 Elizabeth Street
SYDNEY NSW 2000 AUSTRALIA

Cover art used by arrangement with Harlequin Books S.A.. All rights reserved.

Printed and bound in Australia by McPherson's Printing Group

The Viscount's Christmas Bride

Bride

Bronwyn Scott

MILLS & BOON

Bronwyn Scott is a communications instructor at Pierce College and the proud mother of three wonderful children—one boy and two girls. When she's not teaching or writing, she enjoys playing the piano, traveling—especially to Florence, Italy—and studying history and foreign languages. Readers can stay in touch via Facebook at Facebook.com/bronwyn.scott.399 or on her blog, bronwynswriting.blogspot.com. She loves to hear from readers.

Books by Bronwyn Scott

Harlequin Historical

The Art of Catching a Duke
The Captain Who Saved Christmas
Cinderella at the Duke's Ball

Enterprising Widows

Liaison with the Champagne Count
Alliance with the Notorious Lord
A Deal with the Rebellious Marquess

Daring Rogues

Miss Claiborne's Illicit Attraction
His Inherited Duchess

The Peveretts of Haberstock Hall

Lord Tresham's Tempting Rival
Saving Her Mysterious Soldier
Miss Peverett's Secret Scandal
The Bluestocking's Whirlwind Liaison
"Dr. Peverett's Christmas Miracle"
in *Under the Mistletoe*

Visit the Author Profile page
at millsandboon.com.au for more titles.

Author Note

Julien's story was inspired by Washington Irving's Christmas essays found in his work *Old Christmas*, which is a collection of essays he wrote as he traveled through England at Christmastime. Notably, Irving did as much for Christmas in America as Dickens did for Christmas in England. If you know Tristan's story (*The Captain Who Saved Christmas*), you know that Dickens's essay "Christmas as We Grow Older" inspired his homecoming, just as Irving's essays inspired Julien's homecoming. As I wrote every chapter, I found a line from each of his essays that spoke to facets of that chapter, whether it be a reflection on the feelings of home evoked by the holidays or a recollection of old holiday traditions.

Particularly, the feelings of home and friendliness are important to Julien and Aurelia's story, which is a tale of broken hearts, trust, second chances, leaps of faith and forgiveness, all important elements at the heart of the holiday season.

This story is for the Reed family and Jordan,
who helped brainstorm the duck-boxes.
Merry Christmas.

Chapter One

Hemsford Village, Sussex—
November 27th, 1850

There was no place like home for Christmas. Especially when home was Brentham Woods, just outside Hemsford Village, on a crisp, dusky evening in early winter. Julien Lennox, the newly minted Viscount Lavenham, drew his horse to a halt at the fork in the road and inhaled deeply of the fresh night air. To the left was Heartsease, home of his infant niece and rumbustious three-year-old nephew, home of his brother, Tristan, and his wife, Elanora, a place aptly named because of the love it was wrapped in. He would be welcome there. Or he could continue on to the right, to Brentham Woods, the Lennox family home where his parents expected him, where supper would be waiting for him punctually at seven of the clock.

Julien smiled to himself. His father was as well known for his appreciation of punctuality as his mother was for always setting a table with a full complement of silver and china. And he loved them for it. He chuckled and turned his horse, a big, pure-bred Cleveland Bay, to the right and headed for Brentham Woods. Far be it from him to upset the clockwork precision of his father's house. *His father's house*. A place where he was welcomed, but a place that was not quite his. Just like the town house, which was also not his, but his father's.

Well, that at least would change. He smiled a little to himself at the thought. This time next year, he would have his own place not far from here. He'd closed the deal right before he'd left town. His stay would be punctuated by several visits to the estate. There would be renovations to plan. He would need to enlist his mother's and Elanora's help on decorating. He could hardly wait to show them the property.

A mile later, Brentham came into view, soft lamplight emanating from each of his mother's lace-curtained windows, each lamp casting its golden glow into the indigo night like the welcoming beacon of a lighthouse calling ships to the safe harbour of home. This was the home he'd come of age in. They'd moved to Hemsford when he was thirteen and Tristan, ten, his father in search of a more genteel life for the family than the one they'd lived in Bloomsbury amid the bustle of London. That house, the house of Julien's extreme youth, was long gone now. Traded in by the Lennoxes for their country estate and a more upscale town house in Mayfair where Julien spent most of the year carrying out the family investment business.

Julien paused just beyond the gate to privately savour his homecoming before announcing his return. He let his gaze rove over the house with its many lamp-lit windows, let his lungs breathe in the cold, fresh country air, let his mind admit to the bittersweetness of the homecoming. The sweetness was in Christmas, in them all being together, celebrating the end of another year full of achievement: his father's aspirations for the family were alive and well. The coffers were full, business was growing, as was the family's name.

Julien had seen to it, devoting his time in London not only to business but to philanthropy. He'd seen a new foundling home established, a new school opened, and he socialised with the likes of the Dukes of Cowden and Creighton and their sons. Earlier in the year, he'd been bestowed the title Viscount Lavenham in recognition of his philanthropic efforts. It should be enough for any man—official recognition, wealth, a sense of purpose, a family who cared for him. Therein lay the bitterness. It should be enough, but he wanted more.

Specifically, he wanted a home of his own, a family of his own. The viscountcy had not come with any land, which was why it had been bestowed on him—the son of a banker. The family—his parents, his brother, his brother's wife and children—was not Julien's own. Whenever he saw his young nephew and little niece, the craving for family grew.

Once, he never would have dreamed he'd attain his thirty-eighth year without a wife and family beside him. Yet, despite the best efforts of his sister-in-law and the relentless matchmaking of the *ton*, here he was—thirty-eight and *sans* wife. He had only himself to blame for that, he supposed. He'd given his heart away in his youth and never quite got it back.

The sound of a dog's far-off bark drawing nearer cut through Julien's thoughts, recalling him from his ruminations as the dark blur of a black-and-tan hound barrelled towards him. Julien gave a joyful shout and dismounted to greet it, the hound's exuberance nearly knocking him to the ground. 'I'm home, boy. I'm home.' He laughed and ruffled the dog's short fur, to which the dog gave a happy, deep-chested bark. The house would surely be alerted to his arrival now.

Still, Julien lingered in the dark, playing with the hound. Benjamin was his in a way no one or nothing else was. When Julien had found him, Ben had been a stray puppy barely twelve weeks old, wandering the Hemsford countryside lost, alone and on a collision course with death, the little pup gallantly struggling to hunt and feed himself. The same desire that prompted Julien to fund orphanages and found schools had prompted him to scoop the pup up and warm him in the folds of his greatcoat.

Now Benjamin was five, the best hound in the field when it came to the Hemsford Hunt Club, and loyal. That's what Julien liked best about Benjamin. When he was home, Benjamin followed him everywhere. Ben slept on the floor beside his bed and lay at his feet, waiting patiently while he worked, or ran beside him when Julien went riding. Julien knew the rarity of such devotion and he did not take it lightly in animals or in people.

Julien gathered the reins of his horse in one hand and ges-

tured for Benjamin to fall in beside him for the short journey
to the house. The head groom, Joseph, waited for him there to
take his horse. No sooner had the horse been led away than the
front door opened, his mother and father coming out to welcome him. A sense of peace fell over him as his mother hugged
him and his father asked the usual questions: How was the trip
down? Was the train on time? What did he think of the new
branch line straight into Hemsford? Didn't it make the trip from
London so much more efficient?

Amid the questions and conversation of homecoming, he
was ushered into the cosy front parlour, a drink pressed into
his hand, Benjamin lying at his feet, a fire in the grate to take
off the evening chill. Julien let the peace engulf him, let the
sweetness of arrival sweep over him, and he pushed away the
sadness that lingered on the edges. There was no place for it
when one was home for Christmas.

The sweetness of homecoming sustained him right up until
the cheese plate was served at the end of supper—a meal which
had featured all of his favourites. His mother and Cook had
no doubt deliberately laboured over the menu quite intention-
ally to please him, and Julien had been effusive in his thanks.
'Food always tastes better at home.' He smiled at his mother,
who beamed with pleasure. She was a born hostess who could
put even a stranger at ease in her home and who loved nothing more than her grown sons at her table even if only in tem-
porary doses.

'Are you not happy with your cook at the town house?' she
asked. 'I could make enquiries.'

'Cook is fine, I think it's the eating alone that gets tiresome,'
Julien confessed. If he wasn't eating alone at home, he was eating out in the company of others for business or for pleasure and
he'd learned that the joy of eating at home was only in part the
food one ate. The other part was whom one ate the meal with.
In London he seemed unable to put those two parts together.

His father smiled. 'Well, it's Christmas, so there's no risk
of eating alone at Brentham. In fact, we shall have a full table
starting tomorrow night.' He divulged the information with a

twinkle in his eye that had Julien on edge. These were plans and guests that he'd not been apprised of.

'For business or pleasure?' Julien enquired, splitting his gaze between his parents. He'd heard nothing of guests visiting at Brentham for Christmas, neither in his mother's letters to London nor in his father's weekly business missives. Perhaps he'd missed it? He had been busy these past weeks in London, what with the Duchess of Cowden's Christmas charity ball and other festivities ramping up in town while he tried to ramp business down long enough to depart for a month in the country. November had passed in a whirlwind of parties and calls as he wrapped up the year.

'A bit of both, I suppose,' his father said jovially. Truth be told, Julien didn't share that joviality. He was disappointed to hear it. He'd been hoping for some quiet and for some privacy in which to plan for his new home. Hemsford was a special place during Christmas. He'd wanted to enjoy it with his family.

His mother rose with a soft smile for his father. 'I'll leave you two to discuss the business of our visitors. I have a long overdue letter to my sister to write.' Julien watched his mother depart with growing trepidation. She'd used the word 'business' and that was the last thing he wanted to do over Christmas. He'd worked all month to avoid it.

His father poured himself a glass of port and passed the decanter to him. 'First order of business is a toast. Cheers to my son. Welcome home.' Their eyes met over their glasses as they drank the toast, his father's gaze punctuated by the lateral canthal lines fanning out from the corners of his eyes, and grey dominated his temples these days rather than teased at them, all reminders that his father had turned sixty-three this year—something Julien did not spare much thought for until he was forced to, as he was in this moment when reality was staring back at him. His father was getting older. Time was passing.

His father set down his tumbler. 'Now, to discuss our visitors. The Earl of Holme and his family are coming.'

The Earl of Holme, his sworn enemy, was coming *here*? Julien's usually organised thoughts were a riot of disarray as he tried to make sense of this illogical association. His father held up the decanter, the gesture silently asking the question, *More?* Julien shook his head. He didn't think there was enough brandy in the world to handle his father's news. Of all the people in the world he would have chosen to spend Christmas with, Holme would have been last. Dead last. And he rather thought the Earl of Holme would think the same. On that one item at least they would both be agreed.

'I'm counting on your new title to smooth the way for both parties, given that you're a viscount now.'

'Have you forgotten he refused my suit for his daughter's hand?' Julien asked with all the sangfroid he could muster.

'No, I have not,' his father answered, but did not elaborate. It made Julien wonder what he was playing at, what sort of plan he was hatching.

'Why are they coming?' His father didn't know them except through him, and the impressions he'd passed on had hardly been favourable. There was no reason for the Earl to spend the intimate season of a family Christmas with them—the family of the man who'd been turned away, deemed not worthy enough for Holme's esteemed daughter.

His father gave a wry smile wrapped in smug humility. 'The same reason anyone comes to the Lennox Consolidated Trust. He is in need of funds.' Desperately so if he was willing to come to the father of the son he'd refused. Cynicism crept in. Or was it that Holme thought the Lennoxes would *beg* for his business? That they'd be so glad for the chance to loan money to a 'real' aristocrat that they'd give him more favourable terms than what he'd receive elsewhere? And there was an 'elsewhere', which prompted the question of why he'd chosen them if it wasn't because he thought they'd beg.

'There *are* banks for gentlemen with financial needs,' Julien posited his hypothesis. 'Holme does not need to come to us. We're business people.' An important point indeed. Bad blood or not, it seemed odd that the Earl *would* come to them.

Coutts was the bank of the peerage and there were others as well that had long histories of discreetly handling the financial concerns of Britain's aristocracy. Lennox Consolidated Trust was a business investment firm before it was anything else. It wasn't even in truth a bank. The money they lent was primarily for business investments and joint ventures.

His father leaned in. 'I think that's where the Earl's story gets interesting. His coffers are empty to the degree that the usual avenues are closed to him. Coutts will not advance him any further funds and his lands are mortgaged to the hilt. Between the mortgages and the entailment, he has nothing the banks perceive as collateral.' His father gave a shrug of one shoulder. 'Not even a son to secure an heiress and the promise of future wealth.' No, but the old man had a daughter. Lady Aurelia Ripley, as exquisitely beautiful as she was cold-hearted. Julien had experienced both up close and personal seven years ago.

Julien gave a harsh chuckle. 'The Earl of Holme does not sound like a good investment. No funds, no collateral. Why ever would we loan him money? He'll just sink it into the never-ending pit of failing estates and mounting debt.' It was an unfortunate pattern card for the aristocracy these days. If one did what one always did, the results did not vary, no matter how much money was thrown at the problem.

'On the contrary, I do think he is an investment in the future. He might not have money to offer us, but I think he offers us inroads into the next level of society. You've made progress there with your title. I suspect your new title is the reason he's sought us out. He feels comfortable doing business with a peer, someone like him.'

'We are *not* like him,' Julien cut in sharply. 'The man embodies the height of snobbery. He is not a kind man.' Especially when rejecting a young man's sincere suit. Julien had believed he loved Aurelia and that she'd loved him, too. Worse, he'd honestly and perhaps naively believed love would be enough to overcome any opposition to their union. After seven years, he still felt the sting of those moments.

His father waited patiently before continuing. 'He is a desperate man, Julien. Desperate enough to ask for a loan from us and we can name our terms. There's more than one way to claim interest on an investment. We can ask him to open doors for us. If others see the business association, they will come to us with their needs as well. We may not currently be a bank to the aristocracy, but we could become one.'

Julien grimaced. 'Why would we want that? They're broke and, within a few generations, they'll be obsolete, defeated by their own avarice.' It was no less than what the man deserved for his arrogance.

His father arched a brow. 'Who is the snob now?' he said pointedly. 'I thought I'd taught you better than that. It can't hurt to have an earl or a duke in one's pocket. One can never have too many friends.'

Julien chuckled, sensing the true direction of his father's thoughts. 'That's the moral of "The Quackling", the French folk tale about the duck who undoes a king. I remember it. So that's the game, is it? You want to be financiers to the Queen.' Not just the aristocracy. He should have known his father wouldn't stop at earls and dukes. His father hadn't simply been rusticating in the country, building his image as a country gentleman. He'd been thinking and plotting.

His father gave a nonchalant shrug. 'Well, why not, Julien? You're a viscount now. You've found favour with her. Why shouldn't we aim for the throne? With the rate the empire is expanding, we're the sort of money the Queen needs.' There was no arguing that. Julien knew his father's reasoning was sound, as always. The empire didn't need just money, but the expertise of men like himself and his father who knew how to invest and spend that money wisely.

But first, one had to prove their worth, cut their teeth on other aristocrats before being allowed access to the throne. That's where his father obviously saw Holme come into it. Doing business with Holme was a chance for the Lennoxes to pay their dues, put in their time and prove their worth. He understood the reasons, but that didn't make him like the idea any better.

Julien pressed the bridge of his nose with his thumb and forefinger. 'If Holme thinks we'll beg for his poor business, he'll be disappointed.' Holme was not a friend Julien needed or wanted in his arsenal of social contacts. It was the larger concept of what Holme represented. In that, Holme was merely a placeholder. 'I may not do your cause any good,' he cautioned his father. 'Holme did not approve of me once upon a time.' The history between them shadowed and shaped the present. It could not be ignored.

'You weren't a viscount then and he wasn't desperate. Seven years is a long time. Things have changed.' His father smiled. 'We have the upper hand now. If you're willing to humour me, my son, and allow me to extend on the fowl metaphors, I might say his situation is such that he is willing to eat a little crow.'

Julien laughed at his father's humour in spite of his need for caution. 'Well, if so, it sounds to me as though *he* ought to be the one currying favour, not us. Yet, *we* are hosting *him.' And* the man's family. Which meant Lady Aurelia Ripley, Julien's very own ghost of Christmases past—a reminder of the one time he'd given his heart, only to have it thrown back at him.

Seven years on and his gut still twisted with the memory. An upwardly mobile financier had not been good enough for the daughter of the Earl of Holme to consider as more than a dance partner. And now she was coming here, invading his home during Christmas, the season he loved. Julien didn't like it one bit.

Chapter Two

Aurelia didn't like it one bit. She wanted to be home for Christmas at Moorfields, amid the familiar, surrounded by the traditions she loved: the yule log crackling in the fire, the bells at midnight pealing from the village church, greenery draping the mantels and lintels of the hall, the rooms bursting with good cheer and villagers even if those rooms were bursting a little less these days with other things like art and paintings.

She peered out the train window at the grey landscape speeding past, each mile carrying her further from Moorfields and closer to facing a spectre of her past. The prospect of seeing Julien Lennox again raised reminders from a complicated time and concerns about what her future might hold if her father were given free rein to decide.

'You should be thankful the journey is just a long day by train from York to Sussex instead of nearly a week on insufferable winter roads by carriage.' Her father looked up from his newspapers with a quelling stare.

'I didn't say a thing,' Aurelia countered, but the knot in her stomach tightened. Despite the first-class luxury of their surroundings, the train seemed more like a tumbril to her, the infamous conveyance that had brought thousands to the guillotine. If needed, she was to be bartered in order to secure the loan, her own preferences of no consequence. She might not see Moor-fields, her beloved horse, her little reading school or the people she cared about again for a very long time.

Her father wagged an irate finger in her direction. He was always angry. She couldn't recall a time when he wasn't. 'No, but you were thinking it, gel. This is not a season for ungrate-fulness, especially when one is packing a trunk full of new clothes bought at great personal expense to your mother and me.' That was a lie, in Aurelia's opinion. They'd been bought at her mother's expense, not his.

Her mother set aside her book, ready to act the peacemaker as always. 'I hear Hemsford has a reputation for its Christmas festivities. You might enjoy it if you give it a chance, my dear.' She smiled apologetically. Aurelia had seen her make that smile countless times. Her father was angry, her mother was sorry and it was all Aurelia's fault. Everything had been her fault since the day she was born—the twin that lived. That she'd been a girl and the other a boy had only added salt to the wound of her father's disappointment.

'I'm sure I will enjoy it since I don't have a choice.' Aurelia ignored her mother's silent plea for peace and fixed her father with a stoic stare. She wouldn't pretend to know what he'd done. He'd contrived an invitation from the Lennoxes to spend Christ-mas in Sussex to discuss a loan that could have been discussed in a matter of a few hours in London. The moment he had the invitation, he'd rented out Moorfields for cash to an American businessman eager to embrace British Christmas. What her father had done bordered on sacrilege. Medieval witches had been burnt for less. Christmas was for hearth and home, not for travelling and living among strangers.

Only the Lennoxes weren't strangers, not quite. At least not Julien Lennox. Viscount Lavenham, now. That made her fa-ther's posturing all the worse. He was giving himself airs when everyone, Julien Lennox included, knew the Earl was the beg-gar at this particular feast. Her father had no shame, asking for money from a man he'd shunned seven years prior when for-tunes were a bit reversed, when it was impossible to believe the Earl of Holme would fall so far or that a common financier would rise so high that now they met somewhere in the middle.

Her father had misjudged Julien Lennox all those years ago, dismissing him as a fortune hunter looking to buy his way into the peerage, but Aurelia was not surprised by Julien's continued success. From a distance, she'd watched his star rise. It was hard not to. His name was etched on every orphanage and hospital in the city. He was a determined man who knew how to get what he wanted. Except for her.

Did he want her still? Once, he'd wanted her desperately. Now, did he even think on her? The last time they'd been together, she'd not been kind. She'd refused his proposal. She'd hurt him and it had hurt her to do it, although she doubted he would believe that.

What would it be like to see him again? Would there be anything left of the old thrill she used to feel? Would her skin tingle where he touched her? Or was all that entirely buried beneath the well-deserved hatred he must feel for her? Did she *want* there to be anything? Perhaps it would be best if there wasn't anything. Feelings could be…well, expensive, as she'd once learned. She'd been careful with her feelings since then, keeping them under wraps and closely guarded. She was not interested in paying such a price again.

The real question was whether or not he would make her and her family suffer for that past set down. Had that been the motive for the invitation? Revenge? Did he mean to lead them on, make them grovel for the loan her father desperately needed? Would he make her beg on her father's behalf? Determined men were often vengeful men.

If so, she could not blame him. It would be no less than what she and her family deserved. Was he laughing at her already, knowing that she'd once been the toast of the *ton* and now she was twenty-five and unwed? Her father's misfortunes had become hers when it came to the marriage mart. People were not interested in marrying an impoverished earl's daughter.

Too many gentlemen of rank needed an heiress with money, not bloodlines, if they had to choose and her father had been too proud to let her go to a cit with funds. Then, by the time her father might have relented on his standards, her dowry was gone, sacrificed to the never-ending money pit of keeping up appearances. The cits were gone, too. It turned out that even they expected a dowry.

Her father leaned forward and glanced out the window. 'We're nearly there.' A hundred nightmares played through her mind. Would Julien meet them at the station or would she have a little longer to gather herself before seeing him? Her father's gaze gave her a quick perusal. 'Look smart. Pinch your cheeks or some trick you women do. You look pale. I didn't pawn your mother's tiara to not have you do justice to those new clothes.'

Her mother's jaw clenched. The Rose of York tiara was a sore subject between them. It had been in her family for centuries and had joined Aurelia's dowry in service to the Holme debt. 'You look lovely, my darling, just as you are. The blue brings out your eyes.' She reached over and made a little show of adjusting the gold pin Aurelia wore. 'There, now it's perfect. You are more beautiful than ever.'

'She'd better be. She's all the collateral we've got left,' her father muttered, 'if it comes to that.'

Aurelia stiffened. Her father couldn't possibly think Julien Lennox would offer for her after how he'd been treated. Julien had too much pride for that. As a matter of fact, so did she. Too much pride between them to go back and address old wrongs. 'I won't be bartered like chattel.'

If her parents' marriage was an example of what constituted the inner workings of marital bliss, she wanted none of it. Every year she remained single, the more the state recommended itself to her, although it came with a cost—there'd be no family, no loving husband like she'd dreamed of in the days of Julien's courtship. Still, she would not give that freedom up idly. She had new dreams now: the little school she was building, ways to serve the village at Moorfields.

'You will do your duty to this family. You will do your part to see we are not sunk in poverty.'

'What is that part, may I ask?' She was being impertinent on purpose, wanting him to say the words out loud.

'To ensure we are not turned down.' He gave her a dark, gimlet stare full of implicit meaning. 'The young Viscount liked you well enough once. Enchant him again.'

'That was before you and I threw him over because he didn't have a title,' Aurelia reminded him, her gaze going to the window as the train slowed. They were pulling into the station. Her eyes scanned the little crowd on the platform, nervously looking for him, a knot tying itself tight in her stomach. Would he be there? Would she have to face him immediately? Despite her father's edict, she did not think Julien Lennox would charm so easily a second a time.

Luck was with her—a little. Julien Lennox had not come to the station. No one had—only a carriage and a driver were waiting with a separate wagon for their trunks. It was all handled efficiently and expertly. The Lennoxes were used to entertaining. Of course, it upset her father, who wasted no time expressing his disapproval to her and her mother the moment the carriage door shut behind them.

'It's a damn slap in the face not to meet us. Certainly Lennox or the Viscount could have come. It suggests they're embarrassed to be seen with us, that they didn't want to acknowledge us as their guests. And it's a plain carriage. There's no coat of arms. What sort of viscount has a carriage without his arms on it?'

A viscount who valued frugality and discretion, Aurelia thought. Not just his own discretion, but that of his guests. She did not need a coat of arms on a coach trumpeting to everyone where she was going. But she also had to admit that it might be a subtle reminder of who held the upper hand now.

'It was quite thoughtful of the Lennoxes to think of our privacy,' her mother tried to reframe the scenario in a positive light. 'This allows us a few moments to get our bearings between travelling and arriving.' In other words, it saved them from the public awkwardness of meeting people they didn't know well and needing to make small talk all the way back to the house as if they were old friends come for Christmas instead of strangers.

Aurelia was less kind. 'It's nonsense to think they're embarrassed to be seen with us. They're hosting a Christmas ball in a few weeks and we'll be sitting with them at church.' Mrs Lennox had sent a rather detailed itinerary of activities, none of which indicated any desire to see them hidden away. 'Perhaps you're overthinking it too much. Maybe they were simply too busy to come themselves, or too polite.'

In the time she'd known Julien, she'd never seen him idle. He believed every minute of the day should be accounted for. There was always so much to do, so much life to live in both work and pleasure. Julien Lennox worked hard but he also knew how to have a good time, a man who was disciplined but not necessarily strait-laced. She'd liked that balance about him.

So many of the young men she'd met were driftless idlers with no more purpose to their days than waiting to inherit. Then and only then would their lives start. Given that many of them wouldn't inherit until their middle years, she thought their attitude of waiting a waste of prime decades. Julien Lennox and his ambition had been a breath of fresh air.

Too fresh, it turned out, for her father: *'This is how the aristocracy dies, infiltrated, and polluted by commoners with money.'*

When Julien had been made a viscount at the Queen's annual announcement of New Year's honours last January, her father had said, *'Lennox will never really be one of us. His family will always be new.'* As in, the Lennoxes hadn't held a title that could be traced back to the Conqueror, or even to the Glorious Revolution. It had been positively galling for her father to have to revisit those opinions now that the Lennoxes were the only ones willing to lend him money.

The station was not far from the estate and Aurelia couldn't decide if she was grateful for the short journey so that she was no longer confined to the close quarters of a carriage with her irascible father, or if this was a case of out of the frying pan and into the fire. If Julien hadn't been at the station, the likelihood increased that he'd be here. Meeting him again was becoming inevitable.

'Well, at least Brentham Woods isn't entirely disappointing,' her father offered by way of begrudging compliment as the carriage came to a halt and the coach step was set.

'No.' Her mother smiled, letting a footman hand her down. 'It's quite charming, grand and yet comfortable.'

Aurelia might have appreciated her mother's assessment more if she hadn't been so nervous, so on edge, prepared to fight, to protect. Brentham was pleasing with its redbrick façade and white trim around the windows—and, oh, there were a lot of windows.

Aurelia could imagine how it might look all lit up night, a lamp in every window. It would be beautiful and serene, a welcome brought to life, a refuge at dusk for the weary traveller. But not for her. This was not a place of welcome or refuge for her. This was a battleground, a place where she might be ambushed at any moment and revenge extracted. She must be on her guard here. How much easier it would be if this were a cold Gothic castle or draughty medieval manse.

Easy and obvious was not going to be the order of the day. Aurelia saw that immediately. Inside, Brentham Woods was an homage to elegant comfort. The dark hardwood floors were polished to a sheen, the sage-and-cream wallpaper in the wide entrance hall was fresh, unmarred by signs of wear where art had once been hung and then later moved or, in the Ripleys' case, *re*moved. The rug beneath the round pedestal table in the centre of the hall was Thomas Whitty and it was *not* frayed at the edges. The vase on top of the table was filled with deep pink cyclamen and wintergreens. New. Fresh. When had such adjectives described anything at Moorfields with its antiques and worn carpets?

'Welcome, I'm so pleased you've arrived.' A striking dark-haired woman in her late fifties, dressed in a deep-maroon afternoon gown with a bodice done in the latest open jacket style, stepped forward from one of the rooms off the hall, a smile on her face, her hands outstretched in greeting as if she were genuinely glad to see them, as if they'd not all but invited themselves to be interlopers in her home and come to beg her husband for money.

'I hope the journey wasn't too arduous. I'm Mrs Lennox, but please call me Caroline, or Caro, even. Everyone does.' Such warmth was far too familiar for greeting an earl. On purpose?

Aurelia wondered, to set the tone, or because it was simply this woman's way—this woman who might have been her mother-in-law if the world had been a different place.

Aurelia hazarded a quick glance at her father. This was not the fashion in which her father was used to being greeted. There was no curtsy, no deference. What would he make of that? She saw his jaw tighten and, for a moment, she was unsure whose side to be on. She liked seeing him thwarted. Yet the Lennoxes were not her friends and were no doubt out for a little revenge of their own. She rooted for them at her peril.

Her father took one of Mrs Lennox's hands and made a small bow over it. 'How good of you to invite us. We are looking forward to sharing Christmas with you. Allow me to introduce my wife, Lady Holme, and my daughter, Lady Aurelia Ripley.'

Caroline Lennox turned her smile on them, a twinkle of mischief in her warm brown gaze—a gaze that was joltingly familiar even after seven years. Those were Julien's eyes, dark and warm like hot chocolate from the pot on a cold morning. 'And does Lady Holme have a name?'

A set down didn't get any subtler than that. Women would not be objectified in Caroline Lennox's home even if they were the mother of the daughter who'd rejected her son.

Aurelia saw her mother hesitate, perhaps as torn as she was about whose side to be on. Then, she took Caroline Lennox's hands and smiled her courage. 'You may call me Elizabeth if you like.'

'Winter travel can be tiresome even with the trains.' Caroline Lennox gestured towards the room she'd come from. 'I've asked for tea to be set up in my private parlour. My husband will join us shortly. He's been delayed at the stables. He's the master of the local hunt and in charge of the hunt club string. There's always something to take care of with the horses.'

She led the way into a cheery room done in pink-and-cherry chintz overstuffed furniture that had a decidedly comfortable and feminine quality to it. Aurelia divined at once that this was *her* room, Mrs Lennox's private domain: part-sitting room, part-writing room and lady's office and, best of all, part-library.

The woodwork was all painted white to brighten the space and bookcases lined the wall opposite the fireplace.

'Are you a reader as well?' Caroline Lennox asked, catching her drifting eye as they took seats by the fire. 'We have a larger library, of course, but this is my personal collection. I keep my novels here and my gardening books for quick reference. Please feel free to borrow anything that takes your fancy while you're here.' Julien was a reader, too. So, he'd got his eyes *and* his love of books from his mother.

There were bootsteps in the hall and Aurelia tensed. Would this be the moment she saw him? But in the next moment, the worry was eased. It was only Cameron Lennox, returned from the stables, followed by the arrival of tea, both of which led to a bit of upheaval as introductions were made and the tea was laid out.

'Will the Viscount be joining us?' her mother asked in deceptively casual tones once everyone was settled again.

'I do not know.' Caroline Lennox looked up from pouring the tea. 'We'll see him at dinner, of course. But when he's out on a ramble it's hard to say when he'll be back. Do you prefer sugar, Elizabeth?'

Caroline Lennox could not know how much her words put Aurelia at ease. There was peace in knowing when she would have to face Julien. She could set her guard aside. For now, she was safe. She could afford to take comfort in the tea and the warm atmosphere of the room. Her mother could benefit greatly from such a space, a place where her mother could have her own things and interests on display. She ought to encourage her mother to replicate this room at Moorfields.

Aurelia was already decorating the room in her mind when she realised her mistakes—both of them. She should never have set aside her guard. And she should never have allowed herself to be lulled by this room or by Caroline Lennox's kind smile and hospitality. Otherwise, she would have heard the front door open, the low tones of the footman greeting the new arrival, the quick tread of boots on the polished hardwoods. She would have had valuable seconds in which to steel herself for the encounter. As it was, she looked up from her tea, her gaze randomly drifting to the doorway, and there *he* was: all tight breeches, boots, and windblown hair. The man she'd almost married.

Her breath caught. For the briefest of moments, she had him all to herself—hers to look upon in frank enquiry. In those moments his gaze was unguarded, his smile open and inviting. Here was a man who was content, happy. Had she'd ever seen *this* man? It was as if she was looking upon Julien Lennox unmasked. Then he saw her and the moment was gone. The mask slid into place. The smile faded, the light in his dark eyes dimmed.

'I beg your pardon for barging in, Mother. I was unaware our guests had arrived.' Julien was all proper decorum, perhaps conscious of the mud on his boots and the informality of his attire. His dark gaze swept the room, his eyes colder, more calculating than they had been seconds ago. Those eyes rested on her only briefly, perhaps to show her his indifference. She was no more than a guest of his parents, someone he need not be bothered with beyond the merest of civilities.

'Please, sit, have some tea with us,' his mother invited, and her mother nodded encouragingly in support of the idea.

'No, thank you. I am not fit company.' His gaze lingered on hers long enough for the innuendo of his words to strike home. 'I've been setting out duck boxes for the winter and tramping through all nature of mud and dirt.' He gave the room a bow. 'Excuse me, I must get cleaned up.'

At least the room seemed a few degrees warmer when he left, or perhaps that was just her blood. Aurelia took a contemplative sip of her tea. She'd expected such a cool reception. He had not disappointed in that regard. Well, so be it. The battle was officially joined.

Chapter Three

〜〜〜〜〜〜

It was to be full armour tonight for supper. That meant evening wear fit for London. It meant the dark, formal suit from Henry Poole, tailor to England's finest and Europe's as well. It meant the gold-and-topaz cufflinks at his wrists, the topaz discreetly winking, the matching stickpin fastened in the folds of his pristine white cravat while the bronze-and-maroon paisley-patterned silk waistcoat sported a thin chain tethering the elegant watch from Phillips on Bond Street in his pocket. It meant the cologne and aftershave from Harris's, uniquely mixed for him—a scent no one else was allowed to purchase.

Julien flexed his hand, stretching his fingers as his valet opened the ring case. Most all, it meant adorning the little finger of his left hand with the solid gold signet ring sporting its lion's head, the symbol of the Lavenham viscountcy. It would be a subtle reminder to their guests that he was in possession of a title now. To Aurelia, the ring was a rebuke. She should have trusted him seven years ago. She should have believed in him, in them.

Kymm slid the ring on, the gold cool against Julien's skin. Julien curled his hand into a fist and flexed. 'Thank you, Kymm.' His brother made a habit of teasing him over having a valet, but it was for occasions like this when he absolutely had to look his best that a valet was essential. Tristan might have been a soldier, but Julien's battlefields were ballrooms and billiards tables. He closed deals over drinks, acquired information on new clients during quadrilles. To make those things possible, one had to look the part, *be* the part. London society could scent an impostor at a hundred yards, like Benjamin hunting a rabbit. No one had thought him an impostor for six years.

'Remember, sir...' Kymm smoothed the shoulders of his evening jacket '...they have come to you. You are the feast. They are the beggars and they are not fit to wipe your boots. They never were.' Kymm had been with him a while, privy to the tragedy of his failed pursuit of Lady Aurelia Ripley.

Julien gave a wry smile as he headed for the door. 'Thank you, Kymm, for your validation.' He checked the expensive but simple gold pocket watch on his way downstairs. Half past six. Everyone would be gathered in the drawing room. Waiting for dinner. Waiting for him.

The drawing-room doors were open and voices in the throes of conversational small talk drifted up to him. From the direction of the sounds, he could tell his father was with the Earl, perhaps standing by the fireplace. The women were together, likely on the other side of the room. He could hear the rise and fall of their gentle tones. The light, airy laugh that sounded like bells on a crisp, snowy evening belonged to Aurelia. He'd been led on by that laugh once, had thought it meant...something. He would not be led on by it again. Only a fool allowed the same knife to cut him twice.

Julien gave a final tug at the hem of his waistcoat and shot his cuffs, fully armed in his Bond Street best, every item designed to display his authority. He was in control here. This was his territory, his money, his decision. He stepped into the room, his arrival drawing all eyes in his direction, but his gaze went immediately to her. To Aurelia. One should always know the position of one's enemy at all times. And because there simply seemed nowhere else to look.

He was not the only one who'd come dressed for battle. She wore a gown of deep, lush midnight blue, made from the new camayeux silk that had the ladies scouring the Bond Street drapers for its exquisite expensive lengths. The neckline, trimmed in a fall of cream-coloured Brussels lace, was scooped and off the shoulder, exposing the delicate elegance of her collarbones and the queenly slenderness of her neck. The skirt was plain, falling unadorned without tiers and flounces over the crinoline cage beneath, allowing an unobstructed view of her trim waist and the hint of curving hips.

Simple. Elegant. Expensive. Too expensive given the state of the Earl's finances. Julien had seen the files, read them this morning before going out. To say the Earl's pockets were to let was an understatement and a gown like that would cost two hundred pounds. That fabric was of the highest quality. He'd invested in enough silk shipments over the years to know.

Julien approached the women and made a bow to the group. 'Good evening, ladies.' He let his gaze drift to Lady Holme. Hmm. *She* was dressed neatly, but not in camayeux silk, or even in the first stare of fashion. These were gowns from a few years ago. Then again, Lady Holme could not catch a viscount. The thought put Julien on the defensive. Was Holme here for more than a loan? Did he think to secure himself a permanent route to funds? It bore thinking about.

Due to his past failures in that department, it had not crossed Julien's mind that Holme might be rethinking that option as well. He glanced at Aurelia, with her midnight-blue gown and golden curls, her good looks on obvious display, prompting the question—how was it that such a beauty was still unwed after seven Seasons? Not that *he* was tempted. He saw behind that beauty to the coldness, to the calculation in her gaze when she looked his way. Another man might see a coy invitation, might be taken in by those blue eyes. Julien knew better. Her gaze wasn't an invitation as much as it was an interrogation. In her own way, Lady Aurelia Ripley was a skilled huntress.

'Tell me about your duck boxes, Lord Lavenham.' Lady Holme fixed him with a polite smile designed to draw him into the conversation. 'I've never heard of them.'

He offered her a polite recitation. 'They're places where ducks can nest. Wood ducks particularly prefer to nest in holes in the ground or in trees. They don't make their own nests, so they rely on whatever cavities or depressions currently exist. Sometimes, there are no places to nest within a mile or more of water. In those cases, the boxes can be a necessary substitute for the absence of natural habitats.'

'So, they become sitting ducks, quite literally.' The razor-edged reply came from Aurelia, emphasised by the snap of her ivory fan. 'How convenient. Easy prey.' Her gaze was sapphire-sharp with accusation.

Julien answered with a cool stare of his own. 'On the contrary, Lady Aurelia. The boxes actually offer protection from predators and the purpose of the boxes is to help grow the duck population in areas where there aren't enough natural cavities for the population to grow on its own.'

'So, you're not a hunter?' she queried, looking to trap him.

'Only when population control requires it.' He gave a cold, polite smile, his gaze tracking her response, taking in the little tic in her jaw at having been foiled in her attempt to bait him into an argument.

That tic still jumped. How funny to notice such a little thing after all this time.

The butler announced dinner and Julien's mother wasted no time in seeing everyone paired up, not that it took a genius to figure out how it was all going to work. His mother went in with the Earl, his father with Lady Holme, leaving him to bring up the rear the Aurelia on his arm. Once, the merest touch from her would heat his blood, once he'd resented the layers of cloth and silk that had kept them from one another. Tonight, he was glad for them as she laid her white gloved hand on his sleeve.

'You're looking well, Julien,' she murmured. 'Still patronising Harry Poole and Co., I see.'

'And you're still keeping Madame Devy's in the black.' Madame Devy was one of the most sought-after modistes on Bond Street and one of the most expensive.

She gave a cool laugh. 'I had forgotten how you could dress a woman down to the very pence.' It was meant to be unkind, a reminder of how gauche it was in her circles to admit to the existence of money, even if it was the very thing that made her world possible.

'Occupational hazard, I suppose,' Julien replied frostily with an emphasis on *occupational*. Occupations were nearly as taboo a subject as money. 'Although I do find myself surprised Madame Devy deigns to dress you, given your father's current circumstances. She'll expect to be paid.' It did make him wonder what sort of promises Holme had traded on to get such a gown. It certainly added credence to the nascent thought that Holme was hunting a husband for his daughter along with a handout for himself.

'My dress bill is hardly any of your business,' she snapped at the offence, her chin tipping upwards in her trademark show of defiance—yet another of her motifs. Another little thing he'd apparently not forgotten despite the years.

'I must disagree. Everything where your father is concerned is my business. That's why you're here, after all, for *my* business.' He ushered her into the dining room, pleased to see the table was laid to discreetly reinforce that lesson. His mother might be a warm hostess, but she did not miss any opportunity to assist her husband and son in their endeavours.

She understood the merits of a well-set table: the Bloor Derby plates with Thomas Steel fruit paintings at their centres done in muted golds, greens and plum shades to highlight the winter season, the Baccarat Parme crystal, the polished English silver all laid out in honour of the season and in homage to the extent of the Lennox wealth—an extent that said quietly: *This is how we can afford to set the table for a quiet night in among the six of us*. It also implied: *Just think what we can do if it were a formal occasion for twenty*. And that was before his father rolled out the wine, which would no doubt feature the Duke of Cowden's favourite red from France, which only a few could afford.

Julien held Aurelia's chair for her, taking the opportunity to lean near and whisper in low tones as she arranged her skirts, 'That's twice you've been wrong tonight, Lady Aurelia. It's very unlike you.' It may also have been a mistake to get that close. The scent of her, all rose and amber with an undernote of vanilla, ambushed him with memories. How many evenings had he held her chair like this? Sat beside her? Danced with her, breathing in that sultry sweet scent?

Those were better times, to be sure. Happy times. No, not better times, he was quick to correct, taking the seat beside her. Not better or happier times, just *other* times when he was not as well educated about the dangers of her charms. But he had her measure now. He knew empirically she wasn't the girl he'd fallen for seven years ago. She never had been. That girl was a fantasy. He would not charm so easily a second time.

Charm him, her father mouthed over his wine glass from across the table, a scold in his eyes.

They were halfway through supper and Julien hadn't offered a single comment in her direction. That was probably her fault. She ought not have baited him about the ducks. She'd been out of her depth. She'd thought to make him admit to using the boxes to trap the ducks and increase his own pleasure of simply sport hunting, something she did not agree with. One could not live in Yorkshire without being attuned to the dynamics of grouse hunting, but those rules had not readily applied to the situation Julien described and he'd put her in her place. Not once, but twice.

Aurelia sipped her wine, a delicious red that paired brilliantly with the jugged hare. She'd deserved the first set-down, but not the second. It had been bad form of him to mention the dressmaker's bill and the obvious reason for their visit. No one liked to be reminded of their unfortunate circumstances even if those circumstances were an open secret. But Julien wasn't pulling his punches tonight. Well, she'd expected as much, hadn't she? He despised her. Time had not softened his heart as much as it had hardened it. Against her. Her father could not expect her to overcome Julien's resistance in the space of a night. Except that he would. Her father was not a man for patience and she'd already tried his for years now.

'Tell me about the wine.' She set her glass down and turned to Julien, making it clear this was a question for him alone. 'It must be French, but from where?'

'Cumières, which is usually Champagne country.' Julien offered a short answer.

She tried again, this time with a smile. He'd always liked her smile, had always indulged it. 'Which doubly intrigues me. How does a fine red wine come from such a region? One would expect the quality from Bordeaux or Burgundy, but not Cumières.'

'It's a *couteau champenois* from a small, private winery. The gentleman who runs it tells me it's the soil that makes all the difference.'

'Do you believe him?' She took another sip and tried a little light flirtation. 'Perhaps it makes a good story.'

'Yes, absolutely. I make it my practice to only do business with those whose word I can rely on. Loyalty is a precious commodity. Once it is lost with me, it is difficult to regain.'

The lesson was not even subtle. Aurelia felt the twin stabs of anger and guilt prick at her. She'd not been loyal to him, although she might argue, if given the chance, that she'd not had a choice, that it hadn't entirely been up to her. To be a woman alone was a frightening prospect. The wealthier the woman the more frightening the prospect, the further she fell if her judgement should fail her. To put all of her faith in him had been too daunting for an eighteen-year-old girl. None the less, he had condemned her as much as he condemned her father for what had happened.

'Do you mean to say inviting us here is all folly, then? That you've already made up your mind?' she parried, dropping all attempts at warmth. She couldn't resist needling him a bit. She desperately wanted to win at least one argument with him tonight. 'Perhaps there's room to win back your loyalty after all? Or at least to buy it.'

His dark eyes hardened to obsidian. 'My loyalty is not for sale. It cannot be purchased. It must be earned.'

She offered a tiny smile. 'Then one can hope they'll be given the chance to earn it.' She picked up her wine glass and tapped it gently against his. 'Here's to loyalty, Julien, and here's to earning yours.' Across the table, her father gave the merest of nods, pleased with the little show she'd worked hard to put on for him. If her father thought it was going to be easy to win over Julien with a few smiles and pretty dresses, he'd sorely underestimated the man Julien Lennox was. Indeed, her father hardly understood him.

Chapter Four

'You don't seem to understand the gravity of our situation, Daughter.' Her father lounged uninvited in the chair set in the corner of her large, prettily appointed guest chamber, where a fire warmed the entire space, an absolute luxury compared to her room at Moorfields where coal was meticulously meted out and monitored daily. 'You squandered your opportunity at dinner tonight, hardly saying a word to him until the end.'

'He wasn't talkative.' Aurelia snapped from the dressing vanity where she took down her hair and began to brush it. They'd not brought a maid. She'd have to call for one to help her undress once her parents left the room.

'*Make* him talkative. That's your job. What's a pretty girl worth if she won't use her charms to entice a man?'

She didn't need to glance in his direction to know how livid her father was. Her mother stirred from the window seat. 'It's just the first night. They need time to reacquaint themselves with each other,' she placated.

'Our time is limited,' her father reminded.

'We have five weeks,' she soothed, flashing a smile in Aurelia's direction. 'I have every confidence in our daughter.' Aurelia wished she shared that confidence. But her mother hadn't sat beside Julien at supper and felt the chill of him, hadn't had him whisper her mistakes in her ear before he'd even sat down, or turn each conversational offering into a verbal fencing match that ended with him imparting reminders of her betrayal. He was prepared for a siege and well fortified behind the high walls of his pride.

'Five weeks,' her father scoffed. 'I want this settled before Christmas. Compromise him if you need to. I'll play the righteous, wronged father to the hilt and see him marched to the altar in penance.'

'Absolutely not!' Aurelia's head whipped in her father's direction, temper flaring. 'I am to charm him, not wed him, not compromise him. That was the deal.' She was to charm the money out of him, nothing more. And in return, she'd have Elspeth and her freedom.

'If charming proves impossible, we may need to up the stakes.' Her father feigned benign idleness. 'You said yourself he's proving difficult. Charming may be too subtle, too indirect to get the results we want.'

'The results *you* want,' Aurelia replied sharply.

Her father smiled coldly. 'You rise and fall on the merits of my success. What do you think happens to you if we fail here? Do you relish going back to Moorfields to cull the house for silver and art, expendable furniture like your pianoforte and luxuries like your horses? Like Elspeth?'

Not Elspeth. Not her mare. Real fear thrilled through her. Jewels and artwork were one thing. Her mare was quite another. She'd grown up with Elspeth, learned every path and trail of Moorfields on the mare's back. Elspeth was a best friend. 'You would not dare,' Aurelia countered.

He held up empty hands. 'I won't have a choice. The jewels are gone. Your mother's heirloom tiara is gone. Most of the silver is gone. We're down to last things. If we lose the Lennox money, we're rolled up.'

'Charles, stop. You're frightening her.' Her mother crossed the room and put a hand on her father's shoulder.

'The girl should be frightened.' Her father glared in her direction. 'Perhaps if my daughter can't sleep tonight, she'll go down to the library and find a book to read or a viscount to charm.' His face was turning red as he worked up a full head of steam. 'My son would not have allowed it to come to this.' His son who'd only existed in this world for a handful of minutes, but for whom her father had designed a whole history, a whole life of might-have-beens.

Her mother intervened swiftly. 'Come now, there's no need to be worked up. We are not desperate yet. Come to bed, it's been a long day and we're none of us ourselves.' Her mother took her father's hand as he stood and Aurelia envied her father in that moment. She'd have liked her mother's comfort, too, to feel someone's arms about her, to hear soothing words and promises that all would come out right. But her mother couldn't be in two places at once. It was enough, perhaps, that her mother was getting him out of the room.

Still, the damage was done. Aurelia's hands were shaking. She couldn't hold the hairbrush. The threat of selling Elspeth had real teeth. She closed her eyes and drew a deep breath. She couldn't call for a maid in this state. She would not let it happen. She would not lose Elspeth. She would run away with the mare if it came to that, join the Gypsies, or a circus show like Astley's. A couple of years ago, she'd seen Pablo Fanque, the black equestrian, perform there. Perhaps she could do the same, not in London of course, it would be too easy to find her... It wouldn't come to that, to running away. She wouldn't let it. She opened her eyes and slowly let out her breath. If she must, she would throw herself on Julien's mercy.

Surely she would find a way past his dislike. Surely his hate did not run so deeply it could not be overcome? Yet he'd never looked at her the way he had looked at her tonight, with guarded gaze and eyes dark with wariness.

Tonight, he'd been in full control of himself and his surroundings. Everything about him had been calculated for best effect. The windblown woodsman was safely tucked away but, oh, what she wouldn't give for another look at *him*, free and relaxed, unencumbered. In truth, she'd not been immune either to the calculated banker-cum-Viscount in his immaculate, tailored dark evening clothes and carefully combed hair.

All that manly perfection only tempted her to want to mess

him up, to run her fingers through that thick hair, to keep him talking late into the night so that she might see dark stubble take root along that strong jaw. She wanted his chocolate gaze to melt with laughter, to twinkle with the secrets of a private joke, his mouth to curve in a smile of pure joy. She'd had those things once before. Once, he'd shown himself to her and in his authenticity, he'd been like no other. It had been the reward of her loyalty and losing those things had been the price, a very high price for her betrayal.

'My loyalty needs to be earned.'

However would she earn it? How could she reclaim the trust she'd thrown away? She had to find a way. Day by day, slowly and steadily she had to prove herself to him. She had to show him that she was worthy. Not just because her family needed the money, but because she wanted to prove that he was wrong about her. It might be too late to undo the past, but she had her pride, as well as he, and she wasn't exactly the villain he made her out to be.

'She's as much the villain as her father.' Julien sat down heavily in one of the matching leather chesterfield chairs beside the library fire.

'How do you rationalise that?' His father took the other, a tumbler of 'thinking brandy' in his hand. The house was still, everyone having retired an hour ago. He and his father had shot a few rounds of billiards to take the edge off the evening. They'd invited the Earl, but Holme had refused. That was fine with Julien. He'd had quite enough of the Ripleys for the night. His own emotions were high. Despite his coolness at dinner, his anger was running hot, not all of that anger was for the Ripleys.

Julien gave his brandy a swirl. 'It wasn't just Holme who refused my suit. *She* refused me, too.' He had never discussed that unsavoury detail with his father. At the time it had hurt too badly and after that, it only mattered that he'd been refused. He'd had no interest in resurrecting such hurt, such shame, so he'd buried it deep. If it had just been Holme's refusal, he might have come to grips with it the way one comes to grips with a balance sheet. But her refusal had not been about pounds and pence. She simply hadn't loved him, hadn't shared the feelings he'd thought were there.

'I see now why you're angry at me for inviting them,' his father surmised after a swallow.

Julien looked into the depths of his own glass. 'Yes. I am angry with you, too. It feels like a betrayal to have you invite them into our home when I was so looking forward to a moment's peace during Christmas.' He glanced up, studying his father. 'Which leads me to think there's more at play here than becoming the favourite financier of the aristocracy and the Crown. What's the game?' He and his father were close, close enough to speak hard truths and ask hard questions. He'd always valued that about their relationship.

His father shook his head. 'There's no game. I must apologise to you. I misread the situation. I didn't know, Julien, about the other... It's true I thought there was an opportunity for us to gain entry into higher circles. I still think that. But it wasn't my entire motive. I thought perhaps there might be opportunity for a second chance for you, that the Earl might reconsider your suit. You have the title now. It softens the reality that you have a fortune you've worked for. You have overcome his initial opposition to you.' His father sighed. 'I see now that isn't the only opposition. I had hoped to kill two birds with one stone.' He gave a self-deprecatingly wry smile.

'What two birds would that be?'

'Taking the next step into society, building on the foundations you've so well laid with your work in London, and to see my son settled with a wife and eventually the children I know he desires.' His father's eyes shimmered with emotion as they held his. 'She's the one you wanted all those years ago and I thought it was a stroke of luck that she'd not married, that you had a title and her father needed our money. I thought perhaps she had waited all these years for you. There were too many coincidences to be overlooked.'

'Coincidences? Luck?' Julien chuckled. He would not have taken his father for a matchmaker. 'My father, the most efficient, practical man I know, is a hopeless romantic at heart. Do you really believe in such things?'

His father gave a cryptic smile. 'I believe in love and the power it wields.' He paused. 'But I didn't know, Son. I didn't know.'

Julien's anger vanished in the wake of his father's confession. 'Well, I must bear some of the blame. I didn't tell you. I didn't want you worrying over me.' But his father had worried anyway just for different reasons.

'Tristan was always the wild one, the one who spent the summers running and riding pell-mell with Teddy Grisham, the one who had the wanderlust,' his father mused. 'I worried about him, but it turns out he's the one who is settled now with Elanora at Heartsease, two children trailing in his wake.' His father's eyes turned soft. 'And my practical son, the one who has stayed with me and seen the family business exceed expectations, seen us take our place in Hemsford society and got us a foothold among the peerage, counting the Dukes of Cowden and Creighton among his friends, is still alone. You deserve a family, Julien.'

'I deserve a woman who loves me. I do not think love is something Lady Aurelia Ripley is capable of. She is capable of many things, but not that.' And no wonder, given the family she came from. There was no love there. How did one learn love if they didn't see it at home? He'd come to understand that even if he wasn't ready to forgive the consequences. It did not excuse how she'd treated him at the end.

His father nodded thoughtfully. 'I appreciate the need for wariness. One must learn from mistakes, not repeat them. But one should not let anger cloud their judgement.'

'I'm not,' Julien assured his father. 'I saw the Earl's files this morning. I see him clear. What he wants, what he needs. And again, I would counsel you against the investment. I'll find another way to further our presence in the peerage. You should refuse him.'

His father was pensive for a long moment. 'Have you thought about what happens to Lady Aurelia and her mother if we refuse the Earl?'

'No, not particularly,' Julien confessed honestly. 'I try hard not to think about Lady Aurelia at all.' He tried not to think about her being in his house in the present, tried not to think about her in his arms in the past and he certainly didn't spend time thinking about her in the future—his or hers.

'Perhaps you should,' his father prompted.

Julien finished his drink. He could say no to the Earl of Holme as Holme had said no to him all those years ago. There would be vengeful satisfaction in that: to shatter a desperate man's hopes the way Holme had shattered his own dreams. Julien's would be the larger victory, though. Holme's rejection had affected one man. His rejection would affect an entire family. There was no brother. When Holme died, his heir, a distant cousin, would take possession of the estates. The women, should Aurelia not marry, would lose their home. They would have little income to live on. Aurelia would go from living a life of luxury in expensive silk gowns to living in mean circumstances. She would no longer be an earl's pampered daughter. She would be a nobody with seven Seasons and nothing to show for them.

'Is that what you want?' his father asked quietly. 'Vengeance? You can choose to ruin her life or you can toss her a lifeline. She may not deserve it, but are you sure she deserves the other?' When his father put it like that, his conscience began to prick. Ruining people was Holme's method. Did he want to put himself in that same category? He was a man who built orphanages and hospitals. He did not ruin women.

His father rose and put a hand on his shoulder as he passed. 'I'm not asking you to give her a second chance. But I am asking you to consider that this is the season of love and forgiveness and new beginnings. Perhaps if you can forgive her, you can heal yourself and move on.'

'Thank you, Father. You always know how to frame things in a new light.' He clasped his father's hand briefly in gratitude.

Julien stayed in the library long after his father left. Perhaps he could find it in his heart to forgive Aurelia for her betrayal, but that didn't mean he had to spend time with her. This evening at dinner had raised complicated emotions and reactions there was no purpose in exploring.

He would make himself scarce. He would ride out early in the mornings, check his duck boxes, visit his new property, spend afternoons at Heartsease with Tristan and the children. His actions would make it clear that he was entirely neutral and that his consideration of the Earl's application for a loan was completely objective. He was above being influenced by a blonde beauty in an expensive gown with a laugh like Christmas bells.

Chapter Five

Aurelia gave Julien three days in which to indulge his disappearing act. His absence was not subtle, nor did she think it was intended to be. Instead, it was intended to be a very overt reminder as to what he thought of her and what he thought of her family being in his home over Christmas. Which was not much.

They were to be invisible to him, just as he made himself invisible to them, joining them only for dinner and then retiring at the first opportunity decency allowed with a never-ending supply of excuses: he had duck boxes to ride out and check at dawn, he had a string of horses to exercise for the hunt club, he had business in town, business at Heartsease with his brother—the list went on. She thought he'd ride to London in the frigid cold if it meant avoiding her family, most particularly her. And she simply couldn't have that.

Aurelia dressed quickly in the dreary grey half-light of an early morning winter, donning a warm, holly-berry-red riding habit of finest Italian wool with black frogging on the jacket. She smoothed her skirts and took a glance in the mirror. It was a rather dashing ensemble and a rather daring one, too. But red could be excused on the grounds of the Christmas season and her age.

At twenty-five, with a record seven Seasons to her tally,

she couldn't be expected to limit her wardrobe to pastels. This morning, she needed a bit of daring along with a bit of luck. She let the maid pin on her hat, a jaunty red cap with a black feather, and she was off, hoping she was early enough to catch him. Julien's avoidance had to end today.

Her father had been unrelenting last night in what had become his nightly visit to her rooms for an update on her progress with the Viscount. She hated the intrusion, knowing it for what it was—a jailer checking in on his charge, a reminder that she was his hostage, that for her, life was going to change regardless of the outcome of this visit. There was no going back. The life she'd known at Moorfields was over. All she could do was protect Elspeth and attempt to manoeuvre the outcome of this visit to benefit her favourably. So, she was on her way to the stables for herself even though her father would no doubt benefit from it.

Aurelia pulled on her riding gloves and rubbed her hands against the chill. The cold in Sussex was a different kind of cold than the cold at Moorfields. It was damper, wetter, on account of being closer to the sea. Its fingers reached through one's clothes. In the stable, a big Cleveland Bay stood patiently in the cross ties as a groom tacked him up. Aurelia let out a frosty breath of relief. She was in time. Julien hadn't arrived yet. The groom acknowledged her with a nod.

'I'm riding out with Lord Lavenham. I'll need a horse readied,' Aurelia ordered with friendly assertiveness. If one was confident but polite, one was less likely to be gainsaid.

'Yes, right away, milady.' The groom hurried off to the give the order and Aurelia took the opportunity to step up to the Cleveland Bay. She stroked the horse's velvety nose and fed him a bit of apple, talking in low tones.

'Are you trying to steal my horse?' Low gruff tones announced Julien's arrival. He was dressed for winter riding in tall boots and a dark greatcoat that looked quite sombre next to her red riding habit. She wondered for a moment if she'd overdone it. Then, his gaze swept her and something moved in the depths of his eyes—an appreciation, perhaps, that he'd never admit to. It was a start, something to build on.

'No, I'm just waiting for the groom to bring my horse,' she offered with a smile. 'We haven't had much time together and I thought this would be a good opportunity to speak away from the families. Just us.' Another smile. 'Besides, I admit to some curiosity over the duck boxes. I thought you might show me.'

Julien lifted the saddle flap to check the buckles on the girth. Ignoring her. 'Do we *need* time together?' His tone was as cool as the morning. 'I was under the impression the first night that we would be happiest if we kept our distance. I've been trying to ensure that. I was not aware there was a "just us."'

She stroked the horse's nose, giving the horse all of her attention. She would not allow herself to be distracted by the broad shoulders beneath the capes of the greatcoat, or the enigmatic flicker in his eyes that might denote myriad emotions. That was not a guessing game she wanted to play. 'That first night you also spoke of proving loyalty. I'd like to earn a bit of that. There are things we should speak of, but not here.' A groom brought out her horse, the clop of hooves on the stone floor of the stable interrupting their conversation.

Julien glanced between her and the saddled mare. 'All right, but I am taking a chaperon. Joseph, saddle up, you'll come with us.' He gave her a strong stare as Joseph left to saddle another horse. 'I will not be compromised into marriage, if you had plans in that direction.'

'Isn't it usually the other way around? It's the woman who needs the chaperon.' Aurelia laughed—it was rather comical to think of the gentleman standing before her being in any sort of danger he couldn't handle. She dropped her voice to a con- spiratorial whisper. 'Marriage is the last thing on my mind, that's what I wanted to tell you. But we'll need a better plan than mere avoidance if either of us want to get out of this snare alive, as it were.'

'The enemy of my enemy, my friend?' Julien was all cool wariness as Joseph returned with a hardy country cob.

'Something like that.' Aurelia replied with equal coolness, leading her mare to the mounting block before Julien felt com- pelled to offer to help her mount. She might need a reason to see him, but she did not need a reason to touch him, or vice versa. It would only encourage more wariness on his part. He would think she was taking advantage and she hated the idea of him thinking she was the sort of woman who would manipulate a man. No matter what he thought, and no matter how badly they'd ended, she'd never once deceived him.

They rode out of the stable, Joseph maintaining an appropriately private distance behind them. She waited until they were on a bridle path, the stable far behind them, before she began, bringing the mare up beside him so that they rode two abreast.

'My father brought me to act as bait,' she offered without preamble, the shocking statement earning only the briefest of nods from Julien. His eyes remained fixed on the path. 'But perhaps you've already surmised that for yourself,' she continued undeterred. 'I am to charm you to ensure he is granted the loan and, if possible, I am to coax you into a proposal by any means possible. He's decided that a more permanent access to your funds would suit him better than a one-time loan.'

She gave a shake of her head. 'I do not wish for the latter and I don't think you do either. But it may not be up to us. If my father suspects I am not doing my part to charm you, he may manufacture something on his own, something beyond my control. I'd prefer things stay in my control as much as possible. And for that, I need you to...'

'You need me to soften.' Julien interrupted with a chuckle that bordered on a disbelieving snort. 'So, I am to grant the loan in order to spare you from marriage. I see how this works. Your father gets the money, which he's wanted all along, and you and I don't have to worry about spirited matchmaking efforts.'

'To spare *you* from a marriage you don't want. I think you're missing that part.' Aurelia furrowed her brow. 'You're missing the part where I am trying to save you. I am trying to *earn* your loyalty.'

'And yet your father gets what he wants. You say you're warning me, but in reality you're advocating for him, ensuring that he gets what he wants.' Julien did turn to look at her then, his dark eyes sharp. 'And you get what you want by extension.'

'What do you know about what I want?'

'I don't need to know anything to know that your fate is tied to his as long you remain under his care. You made that very clear several years ago, I believe.'

She felt her cheeks burn at the reminder. She could see that moment, hear those words as if they'd happened yesterday.

'It's just down to us now. Come away with me.'

'I couldn't possibly leave my family, leave my life. You don't know what you're asking me to walk away from, from all I've ever known.'

'Yes, I do. I am asking you to trust me.'

And she had not. She'd had her reasons, her defence. What did a well-bred eighteen-year-old girl fresh from the school-room know of taking chances?

'Perhaps there is someone else waiting to marry you back home in Yorkshire?' He reached a hand up to push a low-hanging branch out of the way as they passed.

'I do not wish marry *anyone*. In another year or two, I'll officially be a spinster. I'll be twenty-seven. I can access a modest trust a great-aunt left for me. I'll be completely free.' Free of her father. Free of his threats which had kept her bound to him when she was eighteen. The trust had not come her way until she was twenty-one. Since then, it had been her one hope, the light at the end of a very long tunnel.

'Do not wish to marry or cannot marry?' Julien probed mercilessly. 'I have seen your father's financial files. They are devastating. It is no wonder you are unwed after seven Seasons. These days, you would be a liability to any man who took you on. Many titled gentlemen whom your father would deem appropriate don't have the funds. They need an heiress, not a pauper. Perhaps now your father is more open to approaching a commoner with wealth in order to trade his title for money.'

'Then you know I speak the truth when I say you are at risk.' And perhaps she was at more risk than she thought. Simply charming him might not be enough to stop her father.

'I perceived the depth of my danger the moment I saw you in that midnight-blue gown of camayeux silk and every gown since affirms my assessment. You are hunting me—'

'Not me. My father,' Aurelia interrupted. 'That's why we need a plan. I want my freedom. I have to survive two more years and I can't do that if I am married to you or if my father goes under financially.' Her voice cracked.

Hearing the words out loud from her own lips made it all too real—what her father was asking her to do, what would happen if she failed and, despite her private promises to herself that she wouldn't allow those consequences come to pass, she didn't honestly know how she'd prevent them. She had no power to stop her father. Nothing belonged to her. Everything belonged to him, including her. He could do with her things and with her as he wished, and the law would not stop him. It would, in fact, support him and she was overwhelmed.

At the tremble in her voice, Julien drew his horse to a halt and reached for Aurelia's reins. He should not. He should leave this alone. He didn't want to ask the question, didn't want to know the answer. Would the answer even be true? But she was in distress and he could not ignore it on the off chance that the distress was real. It was not what a gentleman did. Everything she'd shared this morning had been real so far. 'You seem very concerned about what could happen to me, but what happens to you if I don't give your father the money?' Julien asked in the quiet of morning. Somewhere in the bushes the winter wren warbled.

He detected the slight set of her shoulders beneath her red jacket. She was gathering herself, putting back together the bravado that had been on display in the stables. 'He will go home and continue to sell what assets and objects we have left, which is not many. Everything non-essential has been sold already.'

Julien nodded. He'd seen those reports as well. The art was gone, the jewels gone except for those entailed by the estate. The rare book collection was gone. The rest of the library would follow. Aurelia would hate that. She loved to read, play the pianoforte and ride. His gaze narrowed. 'The books, the horses,' he said softly. Holme had an expensive stable, full of horses too good for a man who didn't ride seriously although his daughter did.

'Yes,' she replied tightly. 'The books, the horses. The pianoforte, too.' All the things she cared for. Anger began to burn, a slow licking flame in his stomach for how the Earl treated his family with callous disregard. A man was supposed to protect his family.

A thought came to him. 'Elspeth, your mare.' To say she loved that mare did not do her feelings justice. And rightly so. Elspeth had come to London with her that first Season. He'd seen them gallop on the Lady's Mile in the park, and he had been at a house party with her. She'd brought Elspeth for the ride the party was famed for. Together, they were unstoppable—hedges, hurdles, or just plain speed on the flat.

She flashed him a blue-fire stare full of fear-driven determination. 'I won't let him take her.' Ah, so that was what the Earl was holding over her. This was what had driven her out into the morning to beg him to stop playing his avoidance game. She was being made to pay for his absence. That had not been his intention. He'd meant only to foil her pursuit, seeing her in league with the Earl. Instead, she was fighting her own battle. *If she could be believed.*

'What can you do to stop him?' Perhaps it was a cruel reminder.

'I'll run away if I have to. Ride off in the night,' she said with the staunchness of one who'd given such a plan much thought.

'And have him bring you up on charges of horse theft?' Julien cautioned. Holme would do it, too, to ensure that he had one more piece of leverage over his daughter. She said nothing and he felt guilty for puncturing whatever bit of hope she'd managed to cobble together. 'What do you propose, then?' If he knew Aurelia, she'd not asked him out here to simply inform him of a risk he already perceived. She had a plan.

'I must look like I'm trying with you and that I am gaining ground. It would be in your best interest to offer the loan sooner rather than later. He wants the deal set before Christmas. If you are quick to agree, perhaps he'll give up the notion of marriage if terms are amenable. My father has a tendency to see what is right in front of him instead of what lies down the road. With money in his hand, he'll be less likely to push for other things.'

'If I grant the loan tonight, you could all leave tomorrow.' How pleasant that would be. He could have his Christmas back.

'No, that's too fast. He'll just be back for more. That speed will see you blackmailed into another loan. If he thinks you'll pay him to get rid of him, he'll play that card again and again.' Aurelia looked horrified at the notion. 'Besides, we can't go home. He's rented Moorfields out to an American for Christmas. You're stuck with us.'

Too bad. But it did give Julien an idea about terms. He did not want this happening again and there was something he could do about that although he'd need time. He could show the Earl how to actually run his estate. He could show the Earl how to safely invest his funds so that there would always be passive income. The aristocracy didn't know a thing about money, they truly thought it grew on trees to be picked at any time they desired. But money was only a renewable resource if one knew how to use it.

He urged his horse into a walk and they continued on the path. The duck boxes were just up ahead and he wanted this settled before they reached them. 'So, you're suggesting that we pretend to get along, to act as if interest in each other has kindled anew?' Her idea was as daring as that red habit.

'Yes.'

He thought for a long moment. She had broken his heart, shown no regard for his feelings. He would not, could not let her do it a second time. Her ploy was just begging to slip past his guard, to let her get under his skin and into his heart again. Perhaps this was a game within the game? Where she pretended to not want a marriage in order to get close to him, to convince him they were on the same side, both of them allied against her father, that she was protecting him, trying to earn a bit of the loyalty she'd squandered years ago, and then trap him into a proposal she'd wanted all along.

This was the devious depths to which his mind had sunk in the years since she'd denied him, the level of wariness he carried within himself as a result. 'Even if I agree to this, I am not your friend, Aurelia.' He couldn't be her friend. He would not willingly walk that path again.

'But you were once. Please believe me when I say I am trying to protect you as much as I'm trying to protect myself. Perhaps in some small way I can make up for what passed between us all those years ago.' His father's conversation rang clearly in his conscience. Could he not forgive her? Perhaps he needed to forgive in order to heal his own wounds? Now, here was his chance and yet he baulked at the leap of faith she was asking him to take. Just as she'd once baulked at the leap he'd asked of her. The irony was not lost on him.

'All right then, we shall flirt and play at courtship in public, but in private the game ends. The moment your father has his money, the game ends. When Christmas is over, the game ends.' She would be on her own then.

'Agreed.' She stuck out her gloved hand in businesslike fashion and he shook it, a moment of connection passing between them as she gave him a small, satisfied smile. There'd been moments like this before, moments when being in accord with her had been intoxicating, when he had felt as if he could conquer the world if she was beside him.

'*If we are together, nothing can stop us,*' she'd whispered once in the dark of a summer night.

He'd believed her, but she hadn't meant it. Did she mean it now? He would have to walk this path with care so that old feelings and old emotions didn't rise to overwhelm what he knew was real—that Aurelia Ripley did what was best for her first and foremost, no matter what she said.

He was doing this now because the Earl was a complete bastard to his daughter, not because his heart might not be as hard as he thought when it came to Aurelia Ripley. He was too smart for that.

They reached the edge of a meadow and he turned to her. 'This a good place for a gallop. The duck boxes are across the field.'

She tossed him a smile that seemed genuine, her face lighting as she gathered her reins. 'Race you to the other side.'

The other side of what? he wondered. Whatever it was, instinctively he knew he couldn't get to the other side fast enough. Normalcy lay on the other side, life as he knew it, life without

Aurelia lay on the other side. The faster he got there the better. Red was the colour of danger. He kicked his horse and chased after Aurelia's red habit.

Chapter Six

Sunday, December 1st,
the first Sunday in Advent

The ruse began in earnest the next day, which was both apt and ironic, Julien thought as he handed Aurelia down from the carriage in the churchyard for Sunday services. It was, quite fittingly, the season for mummers plays with their heavily disguised players. And ironically it was also Hope Sunday, a time when expectation was celebrated, not only the expectation of a child, but as Reverend Thompson liked to remind his congregation, an expectation of the second coming which required watchfulness so that no one be caught unaware.

Julien felt such watchfulness was required of him now, concerning this second coming of Aurelia Ripley into his life. He needed all his wits to ensure the ruse was maintained in its fullness, that he didn't forget the true purpose of the feigned closeness between them: to protect himself from falling victim to a far more nefarious plot designed to trap him in a marriage neither of them wanted. By helping each other in the short-term, they were helping themselves in the long-term.

All he had to do was get through December and remember that none of this was real: not the easy way she slipped her arm through his as he led her up the church steps, not the way she glanced up at him with a smile from beneath the brim of her green-velvet winter bonnet. None of it was real even though it once had been. That was his biggest concern over the ruse. They were not pretending about something that had never been, but re-enacting something that once was. That had all the potential in the world to make the line between pretence and reality far too blurry if one was not vigilant, if one took his or her part too seriously. That was what Julien must be on guard against.

He smiled down at her in answer to her own smile because it was the expected response of a gentleman when escorting a beautiful woman and, ruse or not, Aurelia *was* a beautiful woman. Beautiful in looks, in carriage, and even in demeanour now that things were settled between them. There was a more relaxed quality to her that took the coldness, the edge from her good looks, that warmed her now that their pact was made, requiring a necessary setting aside of past hurts to mutually join together for the prevention of future hurts. Between them, they had their own rules for interacting, for playing this game within the game. They had grounds on which to understand each other and it had eased things for both of them.

Eased, not erased. There was a difference. Which was another reason the situation required his vigilance. As Seneca had noted, those who ignored history were doomed to repeat it at their own peril. Julien guided Aurelia down the centre aisle of the church to the Lennox pew, or pews as it were. The Lennox and Grisham family pews had become a combined effort since Tristan had married Elanora four years ago.

He was aware as they walked, of the not-so-circumspect glances thrown their way. The presence of a large party of ten was enough to garner curiosity under any circumstance in a small village, but when that large party included an earl plus a viscount who was considered the area's most *eligible parti* and who had arrived with an unknown beauty on his arm, such curiosity was ratcheted to its highest level.

At the pews there was a moment of greeting to introduce Tristan's family to the Earl's family and then the subsequent shuffling chaos of arranging seating. The Earl and Lady Holme ended up across the aisle with Julien's parents while he and Aurelia were seated with Tristan and family. Tristan sat on the aisle, Elanora beside him with their infant daughter in her arms, then Aurelia and, squeezed between Aurelia and him, his nephew, Alex. Julien slid a quick glance in Aurelia's direction to see what she made of the arrangements. Did she mind being flanked on one side by a baby and on the other by a squirrelly three-year-old? She'd once professed to wanting a family of her own. Had that been the truth?

Aurelia gave him a smile that seemed to stem from something more than play-acting, a smile that said she didn't mind the arrangement. Well, perhaps that was true at the moment. Maybe she didn't mind so much now with the baby asleep and Alex not fidgeting. He'd see how she took it later when the baby was awake and Alex was kicking his heels against the pew in boredom. She leaned towards him, over Alex's head. 'The church is lovely with all the greenery and the bows to match the cyclamen. Elanora was telling me how she grows the cyclamen for all the Advent arrangements in her green house.'

Elanora. Not Mrs Lennox. Julien noticed the discrepancy immediately. Aurelia was making friends fast, or perhaps the familiarity was Elanora's doing. Nevertheless, there was nothing Julien could do about it. He could hardly tell Elanora or anyone else not to befriend Aurelia and he couldn't tell anyone about the ruse. But surely Elanora didn't think Aurelia was a permanent fixture? She was here with her parents for business over Christmas, nothing more. Then again, he had to consider how the ruse was designed to look. He knew very well what Elanora would think, what she would hope for, loyal sister-in-law that she was.

Julien shifted in the pew, his thoughts suddenly uncomfortable as he recalled last Christmas and Elanora's declaration that this would be the year they found him a bride. If so, Elanora was running out of time, the year was nearly spent. Which made Aurelia's presence all that more dangerous to him, especially if Elanora didn't know all the details and she wouldn't know. Tristan didn't know. He'd been in the military when Julien had gone courting. Because of the ruse, Aurelia would look like low-hanging fruit to his eager sister-in-law. He would have to guard himself on that front, too. Perhaps even warn Aurelia.

Reverend Thompson took the pulpit and the church quieted. He welcomed their guests out of politeness and out of a need for self-preservation. If his congregation was too distracted by the newcomers, they wouldn't pay attention to the sermon. Then he got down to the business of worship with the prayer of Julien's adolescence.

'Today we light the candle of hope and we pray. Almighty God, give us grace that we may cast away the works of darkness and put upon us the armour of light...'

Thus it began, the comfort of Advent, the comfort of travelling this road again, this was what he'd come home for. Julien let the old words wash over him. This was what he wanted, what he needed, to be in this place with its swags of greenery and rosy bows, the cyclamen in their vases as they had been for so many years, Elanora carrying on her mother's tradition for the village. It was the perfect balm to a soul who spent the year amid the commotion and chaos of London just as it had been to come down the lane that first night greeted by the lights of Brentham Woods and Benjamin's bark.

Halfway through the service, baby Violet awoke and fussed. At the other end of the pew, Tristan took turns with Elanora settling the infant, and the sight of them working together in tandem was a quiet skewer of envy in Julien's side. How he hungered for that partnership. Beside him, Alex tugged at his sleeve, whispering loudly, 'Uncle Julie, are we done yet?'

'Nearly so,' Julien consoled, digging in his pocket for his stash of peppermints. He fobbed one to Alex with a conspiratorial grin, the little boy beaming back. 'Suck on this. We should be done by the time you've finished.' He felt Aurelia's gaze on him and he didn't dare look up to meet it. It's not real, he told himself. None of this is real. Although it might have been, once upon a time, if things had been different—if she'd been different. But she wasn't and he'd do well to remember it.

Such remembrance sustained him as the service ended and the horde of Lennoxes and guests filed out of the church through many stops and starts. Everyone wanted to greet the new guests, especially Aurelia, Julien noted. The Earl was too lofty for most to approach and his dour demeanour did not invite anyone to risk it. But Aurelia was all smiles, and smiles worked wonders for bringing people together, as did Elanora's patronage. Aurelia was surrounded on all sides with invitations to join the Christmas committees. Mrs Phelps wanted her to help with the pantomime at Heartsease and someone else wanted her to help with Christmas baskets. She said yes to both with what appeared to be genuine enthusiasm. Was it? Or was it just very good acting because she knew such things would please him? That it would add to the ruse?

How telling it was that he didn't know the difference, that he couldn't distinguish between the real Aurelia and the fake. It was a commentary on himself as much as it was on her. Seven years ago he'd thought he'd loved her enough to spend his life with her and yet he'd hardly known her at all. It was enough to make a man wonder if that ought to worry him.

This could have been her life. The thought rolled through Aurelia with the force of a mental tsunami as they sat to table at Heartsease: Sunday dinner with the Lennoxes. All of them, even the children, filled the long, polished table. Julien's mother, the elegant Caro Lennox, had been transformed into a comfortable grandmother, at ease with the infant on her lap while her daughter-in-law saw to the last details of the meal. Cameron Lennox, the obscenely wealthy patriarch, was more importantly installed as grandpa, entertaining Alex with a sliding thumb-and-finger trick while Tristan and Julien were engaged in a lively conversation about one of Tristan's new horses. There was no doubt of the affection the Lennoxes held for each other. The room was full of it.

All of this could have been hers if she'd said yes seven years ago. *This* was what she'd thrown away when she'd refused Julien: a warm family, a vibrant family life, an active community life, not unlike the one she tried so hard to cultivate at Moorfields. Inclusion. Affection. All of it had been waiting here for her and she'd turned it down. She'd been too afraid to take the leap, to leave all she knew. She'd not known this was where she could have landed. To be fair, she'd also not known her family would be facing bankruptcy either. Now, all she could have of it was through this ruse. She could have a facsimile only of what had once truly been on offer for her.

Julien took the seat beside her and gave her a smile, to which she smiled back, knowing that her father was watching her every move and would be quick to criticise if she wasn't warm enough to the Viscount. Julien had played his part beautifully so far. There was little for her father to complain about, there. Julien had been attentive at church, sharing the prayerbook with her and making introductions, his hand never leaving her arm or the small of her back as he guided her through the sea of eager strangers.

Despite knowing that his touch was all part of his role, part of their game, she'd felt more confident with him beside her. The townsfolk liked him. She knew it was for Julien's sake today that she'd been invited into the committees. The liking ran both ways. He liked them, too. Well, maybe not the banker, Mr Atwater, who seemed aloof as if there might be bad blood there—but the others.

He knew their wives, their children, their special projects, which was impressive for a man who spent most of his year in London running with a much more elevated crowd. He was Viscount Lavenham now. He called the Duke of Cowden his friend. His own consolidated trust competed with Cowden's in investment circles. He didn't need to entertain the notions of small townsfolk, but he did.

It was something her own father had never deigned to do. In the twenty years he'd been the Earl of Holme, a title he'd inherited from a son-less cousin and would pass on to another distant cousin, he'd never once mingled with the villagers. Perhaps that was why she tried so hard to make up for his coldness with all of her efforts at Moorfields—the baskets for the poor and the grammar school she hoped to establish. Or perhaps making up gaps just came second nature to her. She'd spent her whole life making up for things between her parents. It seemed a natural act to extend that behaviour to the village at Moorfields.

'Are you well?' Julien asked in low tones full of solicitous concern—all part of the role, she had to remind herself, although those tones had once been genuine, his concern real.

'Yes, I'm quite fine.' She gathered her thoughts, suddenly aware of having let those thoughts carry her from being present in this room. 'I was just thinking how different things are here.' That was putting it mildly.

Julien favoured her with a smile and nudge. 'Well, while you're contemplating those differences, maybe you could pass the potatoes.' He gave a nod in the direction of the dish in front of her. 'At Heartsease, we serve ourselves, all the dishes are on the table and we send them around,' he explained, a twinkle in his dark eyes, as if he expected that to be a surprise to her and he was watching her for a reaction.

Did he think the notion would displease her? If so, *she* would surprise *him*. Aurelia reached for the potatoes. 'Here you go. What a lovely idea this is.'

And it was. Aurelia couldn't recall enjoying a meal more. The absence of footmen and the subsequent interruption between courses had enormous social benefits. Conversation flowed in a chaotic, animated stream up and down the table. No one was limited to talking only with their partners on their right or left depending on the course.

Caro Lennox drew Aurelia's mother into the ongoing conversation, the two of them sharing an interest in plants with Elanora. The men tried to draw her father in with talk of the horses, but with less success. She could see her father's beady eyes assessing the whole scene with dislike. He might be the one in need of funds at this table, but he still thought he was above everyone here.

Aurelia wasn't the only one who noticed. Julien noticed, too. She saw it in the tightening of his jaw. That particular gesture hadn't changed in the intervening years. Julien would not take kindly to a man who snubbed his family.

A trickle of fear came to her. What if her father failed to get the loan through of no fault of her own? If *he* didn't improve *his* behaviour, Julien would deny him on principle, ruse or not. Her father would blame her. Elspeth would still be at risk. Even as the conversation swirled in her direction and bore her away in its current with talk of the committees and the Christmas panto, Aurelia knew she would have to try harder, do more, be more, to close the gap her father was creating.

Aurelia cut into the succulent pheasant and Caro Lennox beamed at her from across the table, asking questions about her own work at Moorfields, the irony coming to her again that all of this—the thing that she now needed—could have been hers years ago.

That irony followed her the rest of the day. It was there with her in the greenhouse where she and Elanora went after the meal to see the cyclamen. It was there when she relieved Elanora of fussy baby Violet so that Elanora could show her a new grafting process with both hands. How delightful it was to hold the infant, to feel the sweet baby weight of the child in her arms and to see the little face light with that special smile only an infant can make. She was used to holding the babies in Moorfields village and it had been a while since there'd been a little one. She gave Violet a finger to play with, feeling the baby's little hand wrap around hers.

The irony was still there when Julien found them two hours later.

'Are you still playing in the dirt, Elanora?' Julien stepped into the greenhouse, teasing his sister-in-law good naturedly, his dark eyes dancing, his hair mussed from being out of doors. He was the unguarded countryman once more. Once more, it did not last. His gaze and his teasing stopped when his eyes landed on her, jigging baby Violet on her hip. She lifted her free hand to her hair. Admittedly, she and Elanora were a little less tidy than when they'd come out here. Her hair had come loose in places, mostly from Violet's explorations, and at one point she'd unbuttoned the collar of her dress to remove her pin so that Violet didn't get at it.

Elanora's gaze travelled between the two of them. 'She's amazing with Violet. I got to work with both my hands today. What a treat.' Elanora wiped her hands on her apron. 'I can take her now.'

'No, you finish up. I've got her.' Julien came forward to take the baby, hefting her easily and lifting her high over his head to baby Violet's delight. 'I haven't had a chance to hold her all day yet and I miss my best girl.' He laughed up at the giggling infant.

Those moments transformed him. Here again was the countryman she'd seen that first day at Brentham Woods when he'd been caught by surprise—the man who was at ease, who was free and open. The irony that plagued her at the table was on her once more.

This might have been us. This might have been our daughter, your daughter, if you'd not refused him. If you had trusted him.

If anyone should have children, it was Julien. She thought of all the orphanages he'd sponsored in London, the philanthropic committees he was part of, all dedicated in some way to child welfare. And today had illustrated to her that his efforts weren't all for show, simply to make an impression and meet the right people. She'd seen him slip a peppermint to Alex at church instead of scolding him for fidgeting. This afternoon, he'd spent time with his nephew while they'd been in the greenhouse. Julien and Tristan had taken Alex out for a riding lesson in the paddock. Children were important to Julien. Time spent with family was important.

'I did come on a mission to fetch you, Aurelia,' Julien said, settling Violet in the crook of his arm. 'It is time to go. Your father is eager to be off.' He smiled, but there was a meaningful look in his eyes that indicated a need for haste.

The great Earl of Holme was done rusticating for the day. He'd suffered to present himself at a village church to be fawned over, he'd dined at a table where he was required to serve himself, he'd been surrounded by children and noise and laughter, perhaps even undergone the indignities of talking with commoners while he stood in the mud of a paddock watching one of those children post around the ring on a leading line. What had been a beautiful day to Aurelia had been a beastly day to her father, a day so far beneath him he hadn't any word for it.

Julien handed baby Violet to Elanora and offered Aurelia his arm. She leaned close enough to whisper as they walked in the falling darkness, 'He's going to be ghastly on the ride back.'

To which Julien merely offered the dry reply, 'I know', as they exchanged a conspiratorial glance that made them both laugh and in that moment Aurelia thought the ruse might be suspended, that perhaps he might not hate her entirely, that there might be some kind of friendship at least wrung from this mess. But that was a dangerous thing to hope for. Hope had a habit of breeding more hope. What would she do with Julien Lennox's friendship even if he should offer it?

They made their farewells and climbed into the Lennox coach for the short ride to Brentham Woods, Julien electing to ride up next to the coachman to make more room inside, but he made sure, before he climbed on top, to hand her in and flash her a smile and she demurely accepted it, both of them playing their parts to perfection for all to see. Goodness, this was just act one and already turmoil was bubbling beneath her surface.

Today had been a glimpse into what could have been. She felt very much like poor Scrooge in the story that had come out a few years ago who was visited by the ghost of Christmas future. This could have been her future with the man who was riding up top now because the coach was cramped for six adults and he wouldn't hear of his father being out in the night air, the man who'd slipped his nephew a peppermint in church, the man who'd tossed his niece in the air to make her laugh, who thought the best way to spend a Sunday was church and dinner with his family—not at the gaming halls or the other vices offered to gentlemen of high society. And she'd thrown it all away. If only she could turn back time.

Chapter Seven

The clock had just chimed midnight when she invaded his peace in the library, slipping in like a ghost, swathed in white cotton flannel from head to toe. In the dark, he had the advantage. From the fireside, he could see her, but she could not see him. He set aside his book and made his own presence known from his chair in quiet tones not meant to startle. 'Can I help you find something?' No doubt, she'd not thought to encounter anyone at this hour. He certainly hadn't. He'd wanted to think. He'd come here with high hopes of being alone. Perhaps she'd come with the same.

Or perhaps not, the cynical businessman in him whispered. *Perhaps she wanted to find you here, alone. All the better to compromise you into a marriage you don't want, despite her protestations she doesn't want it either. You know women, always saying the opposite of what they mean.*

A game within the game within the game. Now, even the ruse was beginning to look like a bad idea and not just because of this moment. The day had been potent, rife with echoes of old memories, of old hopes of a time when he'd once dreamed of just such Sundays with her beside him. His world had stopped when he'd come upon her in the greenhouse with Violet on her hip, a thousand images of what might have been rioting through his mind.

'I did not mean to disturb.' Her white-swathed form halted a few steps from the door.

Too late for that, Julien thought. The day had been an accumulation of disturbances. Out loud, he said, coolly, 'Not at all. I was just finishing up. I'll be on my way.' He could not stay here with her. It wasn't safe on any level.

She stepped forward, becoming more visible, becoming more than a gleam of white flannel. Her hair was down, braided in a long plait and hanging over one shoulder. She looked girlish and innocent. She ought not be allowed such a deception. Aurelia Ripley was not innocent. She was a flirt, a temptress, who led men on in London. Be fair, a small voice inside him cried. She was none of those things today. Violet adored her, she'd not minded the crowded pew, the ladies of the community had flocked to her.

'Don't leave on my account,' she offered. 'I hadn't expected company, but I will admit to not minding some. If it's you,' she added hesitantly, guilelessly.

'I do leave on your account,' Julien countered. 'It would not do for me, at least, to be caught here with you.' He arched a brow. 'Although perhaps it serves you and that's why you invite me to stay?'

Something in her body tensed, he could see it in the straightening of her shoulders, the tilting of her chin. There was a rigidness now to her posture that hadn't been there before. 'You don't believe me. You think there's a ruse within the ruse, that I've contrived a chance to draw near so that your guard is down and I can swoop right in.'

She gave a toss of her head. 'You didn't use to be so cynical, Julien. Now, you fear every woman is dying to marry you.' She cocked her head in mock contemplation. '*Is* that fear, I wonder, or just sheer arrogance?'

Ah, there was the woman he knew. Sharp tongued as she had been in the drawing room the first night. What had he expected? There was no need for the ruse to be in play at the moment. They were alone, with no one to see them. They might be as honest as they like with each other.

'If I am on guard, it is because I was once misled when my guard was dropped.' He matched her stare. This was not what he wanted, but perhaps it was the reminder he needed. The girl he'd courted and loved in London, the woman he'd seen today in the greenhouse, weren't real. The woman who'd refused him, the woman who sparred with him, was. That woman was heartless and self-serving. She was calculating and cool.

Aurelia broke first. 'I didn't mean to quarrel. I only wanted to get a book and, since you were here, I wanted to tell you what a good time I had today. Your family is warm and welcoming even to us, who don't deserve it. I wanted to apologise for my father. You missed out riding up on top, but he was awful on the way home. Your father was masterful and patient with him. This whole situation is hard on him.'

'Don't. Don't make his excuses when he should make apologies,' Julien cut in, his words sharp. 'And most definitely don't feel you have to play the part when there's no one to see.' His words wounded her, he could see hurt flash in her eyes. He tried to ignore the twinge in him that answered on her behalf. He was not in the habit of hurting people.

'I am not playing, Julien, not right now. Can you not countenance niceness from someone else? Are you the only one allowed to be kind?' It was not sharply said. If he'd wanted to bait her to another quarrel, he'd failed. This was said with softness, perhaps even with pity at his rampant cynicism.

'Since I stepped inside this room, you've accused me of wanting to compromise you, of reneging on our agreement and of lying. It's not a very flattering profile you have of me if you think I would do all those things.' She waved a hand. 'I understand, there is the issue of the past between us, but, Julien, I gave you my word that my intentions here and now are in our best interest. I *am* trying to save you from my father's machinations. If you can't trust in that, then you may be dooming yourself to the very thing we both wish to avoid.'

'It is hard to trust someone that I do not know.' Julien's gaze followed her warily as she took the spare chair by the fire. Clearly, she had no intentions of leaving now.

'I could say the same.' She gave him a smile and he found himself sitting back down. 'You are different here in the country. So different, I almost didn't recognise you at first. You're more relaxed. Happy, even. In London, you were always so careful, so correct, as if you expected someone to be watching you, looking for any mistake.'

She leaned forward. 'Country Julien intrigues me, I admit. He is still you, but there are depths to explore and there's access to those depths. City Julien was always so perfect, always so walled off. One would glimpse the existence of those depths, but not be allowed to explore them.'

Julien gave a cough. 'I'm not sure I like being so brutally assessed. I had no idea.' This was almost more intimate than being undressed in one's bedchamber. He wasn't sure he liked the intensity of that scrutiny.

'Does it truly surprise you?' She sat back in her chair, her hands folded across the flatness of her stomach beneath the folds of white flannel. 'I know it is something of a risk to bring the past up, Julien, but we were going to be married. At least at one point, I thought so. I spent a lot of that spring thinking about what it would be like to be married to you.'

She gave a shrug of her shoulder. 'I thought marriage would be akin to getting the keys to the kingdom. I thought if we were married, I would understand you, that I would be privy to who you were. Marriage would unlock you.' She gave a little smile. 'I never got to find out and now there are even more hidden rooms inside you.'

Rooms she would never see, Julien promised himself. He could not afford to let this minx hurt him again. Maybe she was playing with him tonight, maybe not. He did not doubt her words, only their purpose and what she sought to gain from this disclosure. 'I am glad you enjoyed today,' was all he said and then issued a warning of his own. 'My family is very important to me. I would not take any hurt done to them lightly. Elanora loves with all her heart. She will miss you when you're gone.'

Aurelia bowed her head. 'You think I was feigning friendship with her. That was not the case. I like her. I will look forward to spending time with her over the next few weeks.'

'But you know what she'll think, what she'll hope for—that you will become her sister-in-law,' Julien cautioned.

'That is the ruse's fault, not mine, if people draw such conclusions. I cannot be responsible for that. I can only be responsible for saving our skins, Julien. And, yes, it might come at the expense of others' disappointment. But they don't have to live our lives.'

Julien offered a faint smile. 'I'm just asking that you be gentle with us.' To take care with the villagers he called his friends, with his family, and perhaps even with his own treacherous heart which even now was engaged in its own confused reaction to Aurelia Ripley, whom he'd sworn to despise to his dying day because she'd once betrayed him. He should not let himself be drawn in by any aspect of her, yet he feared that possibility existed.

She rose, smoothing the folds of her voluminous nightgown. 'You and I might be play-acting but not everything today was a ruse, Julien,' she said softly as she prepared to return to her room, where she would probably fall fast asleep, drat her.

He wouldn't. He doubted he'd sleep at all after that last remark. Instead, he'd spend the night sorting through which was which. Which things in the day had been real for her and which had been ruse? And why did it matter so much to him that he decide? What did he think that changed?

Julien was still sorting the next morning when he drove her in the gig to the ladies' meeting at the church. He mentally sorted and re-sorted as he met the architect at the station who would be drafting the remodelling plans for his estate. He lost track of how many times his thoughts strayed from the architect's report and had to be redirected. He spent more time thinking about Aurelia—what she had said last night. What was she doing right now?

What did she think of the society of Hemsford Village? Was she secretly thumbing her nose at them like her father? Or was she genuinely engaged in their work? And then there was the

self-reflection that followed: why did he care? He only had to
survive the month and she would disappear back to Yorkshire
on the train, her freedom intact, her horse safe from her father's avarice.

*Until next time…*came the insidious reminder. Who would
protect her the next time? Of course, he could ensure Holme
had enough money to protect her for two more years, that was
her magic deadline, wasn't it? Then she could ride off into the
sunset on Elspeth, both of them safe. Why the hell did he care
so much?

'Lord Lavenham, did you have a preference on the sliding
doors between the drawing room and the dining room?' The
question was asked with a certain hesitation that suggested the
young architect, a Mr Floyd, whom Julien thought showed immense promise, had asked the question at least twice.

'Ah, yes, I think yes on the sliding doors connecting the two
rooms,' Julien said with a confidence he didn't feel. These were
questions a wife, a hostess, was better suited to answer. But he
had neither and Elanora and his mother were busy at present
with Christmas preparations: Elanora was chairing the panto
committee and his mother had the annual Lennox Christmas
ball to plan, both of which were anchors of the Hemsford Christmas celebrations. They were too busy to help with designs and
young Mr Floyd could not dawdle in Hemsford endlessly. He
had his own projects and family to get back to.

Julien checked his pocket watch. The ladies' meeting would
be finishing shortly and he'd promised to be on hand to pick
up Aurelia. He sighed. Thanks to his distractions, he and Mr
Floyd were not done yet. 'Would you excuse me for a short
while?'Julien solicited. 'I have an errand that I am afraid needs
my immediate attention. Perhaps we could meet at the Red
Rose Inn and continue our discussion there?' Hopefully, Aurelia wouldn't mind the delay.

At the church, he found himself playing the patient, doting
suitor as he leaned against the door and waited for her to finish.
The meeting was technically complete, but Aurelia was amid
an avid conversation with the ladies over a feminine topic he

didn't pretend to understand. She caught sight of him and tossed him a smile of acknowledgement that didn't go unnoticed by the others. Susannah Manning, the baker's daughter, leaned close and whispered something in her ear that made her laugh as the two of them shot him a considering look. He tipped his hat and smiled back.

Aurelia joined him shortly after that. 'Thank you for waiting, there was just so much to discuss.' Her eyes were lively like dancing jewels and her smile was easy as she let him help her into the green wool mantle that matched the green-and-gold tartan of her gown, a very smart, very fetching ensemble for winter and warmth. She tucked her arm through his and buried her fingers in the depths of a rabbit fur muff, still chattering about the meeting.

'I thought we might have lunch at the Red Rose Inn.' He was slowly working up to his confession. 'Although I do confess to an ulterior motive. I have unfinished business to conduct with my architect.'

'I don't mind at all. Perhaps, afterwards, we might stroll the High Street. I have a few purchases to make and you could advise me on where best to do that.'

He nodded with a chuckle. 'I see, it's a negotiation then. My business meeting for your shopping trip. It's a fair trade.'

Julien called for a private parlour for lunch and made the introductions, ordering the venison stew and a loaf of the bread baked down the street at Manning's for all of them along with a bottle of red wine and dried apple pie for dessert. If Aurelia was going to be bored, she might as well be fed. But by the time lunch arrived, it was clear Aurelia was anything but bored. She'd made a quick friend of Mr Floyd, who was telling her about all of his projects back in London and how he was working on a new plan to expand the docks. When it came time to roll out the plans for Julien's home, she chose to engage in the conversation instead of idly strolling the parlour, studying its mediocre landscapes.

'Julien, I cannot allow you in good conscience to put a window there instead of French doors,' she interjected at one point, tapping a finger on the plans. 'You will regret not having full access to the gardens from your office. Think how nice it will be for you to be able to get up from your desk after a long session of adding columns, and be able to step outside for a walk without needing to go through the house. A man like you who loves the country and the fresh air, will want the outdoor access.'

Floyd looked from him to Aurelia who favoured him, Julien noted, with a smile. 'I dare say Lady Aurelia is right, my lord.'

Julien sat back in his hardwood chair. 'A man like me, eh?' The thought warmed him ridiculously when he should not have allowed it to. But he couldn't help being caught up in the sense of play. He tipped the chair back on two legs. 'What else does Lady Aurelia feel I should have, in good conscience?'

'Well, if you insist, I do have some other suggestions,' she said with coy hesitancy, not wanting to appear too bold, no doubt, but being bold anyway.

Julien waved a hand. 'No, please, go on. I was just thinking to myself this morning that I hadn't the head for such things.' It was a reckless indulgence he was allowing himself, permitting her to make suggestions about his home, his refuge. These would be reminders of her that would be left behind. It was also a reckless indulgence of the ruse, of letting himself pretend that he could live in the moment without thinking about or being affected by all that had come before. Yet his usually calculated self was indulging heavily today.

They finished the meeting and Floyd rolled up his plans in a leather cannister. 'I'll be leaving on the three-thirty train, but I'll return next week with the decorator, Lord Lavenham.' He made a small bow. 'Perhaps Lady Aurelia will be of some use in that area as well. I do think a woman's touch is helpful, my lord.'

'Lord Lavenham.' Aurelia shot him a look after Floyd departed. 'Have you got used to it yet? The title?'

'Somewhat, but not here at home. Here, I am Julien Lennox for ever and that is fine. The title means very little. There's no land that goes with it, so it's entirely a courtesy from the Queen in recognition of my family's philanthropy.' He watched her carefully for a reaction. Had she been trying to suss out what had come with the title?

'I disagree—a title with land or without opens doors for you, allows you to broaden the scope of your work. It is no small thing, Julien.' She moved about the room, stacking their dirty lunch plates.

'I didn't think Lady Aurelia Ripley touched dirty dishes,' he commented, half-teasing, and moved to help her.

She tossed him a saucy smile. 'Or jigged wiggly infants on her hip? Or liked eating family-style at Sunday supper? Or volunteering for charity work of her own? You might be surprised at what Lady Aurelia Ripley does.'

She paused thoughtfully. 'Just like there is country Julien and city Julien, did you ever stop to think there might be country Aurelia?' She laughed and he knew his face had given him away—that, no, he hadn't. She brushed his arm lightly, a feather touch that sent a jolt of warmth up its length. 'A woman can be more than one thing, Julien, just like a man,' she lectured gently.

But Aurelia Ripley would never be anything 'just like a man'. She was femininity personified, her green-and-gold tartan skirts swaying gracefully as she piled the dishes on to a tray and shook out their napkins. Julien cleared his throat. 'The innkeeper can finish with this. We'll need to hurry if you want to shop.' He took her mantle from the peg and held it for her. He needed to get out of this room where everything had suddenly become so intimate. His reserves were slipping. The fresh air of High Street was much required.

'Don't worry about the shopping. I was going to suggest that we come tomorrow. I would like to dawdle over the stores, if you don't mind?' She turned her head, blue eyes looking up at him. Julien let his hands linger at her shoulders, settling the mantle longer than necessary. Yes, he definitely needed to get out of the room where they were alone. Outside, there would be other people and other distractions.

'I am sorry the meeting took so long,' he apologised.

She shook her head, her fingers working the frogs of her mantle. 'I'm not. It was great fun. A house, Julien, that is exciting. I hope that I was helpful as opposed to bossy.' She looked up at him, asking for an honest opinion with those blue eyes of hers.

'You were very helpful. I was in over my head on such decisions,' he assured her, then he sobered. 'But you needn't have played the ruse with Mr Floyd.'

'I wasn't playing this afternoon. Were you?' She slipped her arm through his as they exited the private parlour and smiled politely at the innkeeper while Julien treated the response as a rhetorical question—one that didn't require an answer because both of them *knew* the answer. They hadn't been playing. But it bothered him deeply. They *hadn't* been playing this afternoon. They had, instead, fallen into the old ease they'd once known together and not even realised it, not even questioned it. Five days into her visit and she was barrelling past his defences whether she meant to or not.

That was the hard part, Julien thought, handing her up on to the bench seat of the gig. Did she understand what she was doing? Was this intentional or did she not realise the kind of havoc she could and was wreaking in him? They were supposed to pretend to like each other, nothing more. But this afternoon had gone far beyond that, laying a dangerous precedence for what could follow. He did not want to be taken in by her again, did not want to fall for her again only to learn it was its own ruse.

She tucked her hand into the pocket of his greatcoat as they drove home to Brentham Woods in the cold of the winter afternoon, her head turned up surveying the sky. 'Do you think it will snow?'

'Maybe. It's hard to say. We're close enough to the sea that snow is unusual.'

'What about ice skating? Is there a pond that freezes? I love to ice skate.'

'There's a likely pond out on the estate I purchased.' His traitorous mind was already considering the possibility of a winter picnic, although the ruse wouldn't require it. There'd be no one out there to see, to care.

She snuggled closer, tugging the lap robe about her legs. 'Then we should go. I want to see the place before Floyd comes back with the decorator.'

Great, Julien thought wryly. They would go to his estate and skate on thin ice and, if he wasn't careful, his heart would crack. Just like that the sorting started again—what was real? What was ruse? And the questions nagged persistently—who really was Aurelia Ripley and could he trust her?

Chapter Eight

She didn't trust herself with him. It was too easy to slip into old patterns, old familiarities from better times. Yesterday had been proof of it and today she'd have to do much better. Aurelia grabbed her reticule and gloves from the bed and gave herself a last look in the mirror before heading downstairs for a day of shopping in Hemsford. She ran a hand over the winter-sky-blue skirts of her ensemble. Her armour—such as it was—served as a reminder of her mission. She must be charming without being charmed herself. Otherwise she'd be setting herself up for disappointment and heartache.

She had hurt him in the past. He wanted nothing to do with her and she wanted her freedom. She needed to survive the next two years in order to claim it. Surviving didn't include falling for the impossible. Whatever chances she'd had of claiming Julien's love had been ruined seven years ago. Julien was not a man who forgot or forgave a betrayal. A successful businessman didn't get ahead by turning a blind eye to the wrongs done to him.

Aurelia settled a cream bonnet trimmed in matching blue ribbon on her head and tied the bow with a sense of preparedness. Perhaps yesterday had shown her exactly what she was up against. She would be more on guard against her own reactions now that she knew them: her tendency to smile at Julien, to laugh with him, to reach for his hand, to crave the warmth of his hand at her back even when the ruse didn't require it. Yesterday had been intoxicating. Not just the touches, but the conversation, the talk of his house.

The mention of it had done queer things to her stomach, not all of them good. He was making a home for himself and for the wife he'd share it with, the children who would eventually fill it. She'd not liked the thought of it, intuitively knowing that the wife would not be her, the children not theirs. It shouldn't matter. She'd given up those dreams and him a long time ago. She'd treated him shabbily.

Helping him now was part-atonement, part-penance. That was all it could be. In the long run, they'd both be happier that way. She tugged at her jacket. Good. Now that was settled, she would go shopping. With her father's money. That made her smile. It was about time her father's money went to do some good.

Julien was waiting for her at the bottom of the stairs, leaning against the newel post and looking dashing in his grey wool greatcoat. 'Are you ready for a morning of shopping?' He crooked his arm as she approached.

'A morning?' She laughed. 'A *day*. Have you forgotten how I shop?' She teased because, no doubt, there was someone nearby who would expect such repartee: his mother, her father, her mother. She teased to put on a show, she told herself, not because it came so easily between them.

Hemsford Village did not disappoint. For being a rural town, it boasted an array of shops and high-quality goods. The High Street was bustling with midweek shoppers and people who wanted to look at the shop windows which were decked out in Christmas themes to show off their wares.

'I do admit to being impressed with the village,' she commented as they stopped before the dressmaker's window to admire this year's Christmas creation—a long, warm cloak of winter white trimmed in rabbit fur with a wide, deep hood that paid tribute to styles of days of yore. 'A woman would feel like a medieval princess in such a cloak,' she said dreamily. 'I am surprised, though; it seems like a rather frivolous item for these parts.'

Julien cocked his head, giving it some thought. 'Perhaps, but isn't that part of the Christmas magic? Some whimsy? Some fantasy? I don't think people want to walk past windows sporting farming implements and workman's gloves or sensible aprons. It's the dream people want to see looking back at them.' With a light press of his hand at her back, he ushered her next door to the window at Manning's bakery. 'This window is a fantasy for children. A winter wonderland of white-iced cakes and dancing gingerbread people.'

Aurelia studied the happy, dancing gingerbread, but her thoughts were on Julien. 'Are you a dreamer, Julien?' She would have thought no. In his line of work the numbers never lied. They left little room for dreams to intrude, yet the Julien she'd known in London, who'd brought her little presents, had a hidden fanciful streak if one could get him to break out of his carefully constructed mould—and she had been successful on that account. It had been her personal mission back then to tempt him. She ought not tempt him now, but he'd tipped his hand at the dressmaker's window and she could not resist taking another peek.

'I have dreams of a world where children have homes, where they don't go hungry. Then I build those dreams.' His answer was less than she had hoped for, perhaps he knew that. Perhaps he'd realised his earlier error and was retrenching, careful not to make yesterday's mistakes.

'I meant dreams for yourself,' she clarified, cocking her head to take in his profile with the strong length of nose and the dark lashes.

He gave her a polite, cool smile and held the door for her. 'What I am dreaming of at present is a fresh-baked batch of gingerbread biscuits to sustain me through your shopping. Let me take you inside and show you their Twelfth Night Cakes. Manning's has some of the most stunning cakes I've seen. I dare say they rival those in London. You'll have to tell me what you think.'

What she thought was that Julien was better at playing the game than she was. They'd gone off course a little at the dressmaker's, but he'd quickly righted the ship, not allowing her to probe too deeply into anything that resembled overly personal conversation. Neither did he attempt to do any probing of his own. He kept their shopping conversation pleasant but impersonal. What did she think of the cakes? Did she like the gingerbread biscuits? Where would she like to go next? Could he take that box for her? Could he carry her basket? And in between polite questions, he gave her an interesting, informative overview of Hemsford.

'The railroad branch is changing things for us,' he told her as they passed the newly built station where the early afternoon train was disgorging its passengers. 'It's only an hour and a half from London by rail. It's become much more efficient since the London–Brighton railroad joined with a couple of other lines a few years back. Now, it's the London, Brighton and South Coast Railway and the train is direct to Hemsford. People can make a day trip of it if they wish. I've encouraged the Red Rose Inn to expand the amount of parlours they have available so that day trippers have a place to rest that affords them some privacy.'

'One of the ladies at the meeting yesterday mentioned you were on the Hemsford improvement committee. What other ideas do you have?' she asked, careful to make it sound like casual, polite, non-intrusive conversation instead of a look inside his brilliant mind as they strolled.

'I've encouraged folks to think about what Hemsford has to offer the outside world. We do Christmas like nowhere else I've been.' He was warming to the subject and his guard was coming down. They paused long enough for him to greet an acquaintance and make introductions, then he continued.

'We had advertisements printed in the London papers this year about visiting Hemsford for Christmas shopping, to come and see the quaint shops decorated for Christmas, to take a special Christmas tea at the Red Rose after shopping. A tea, by the way, which features Manning's baked goods.' His dark eyes were starting to dance as he talked. 'Next week will be busier than this week.' He steered her towards the village green.

'We're setting up the Christmas fair which will start Saturday and run until Christmas Eve. We have vendors that come from all over the Continent: German craftsmen, Italian glassblowers, Swiss music box makers, French soap-makers, candymakers. There are carollers in the evening and the whole place is lit up like Vauxhall perhaps in its heyday.'

'It sounds delightful. You must bring me,' she insisted with a smile. 'My mother would love it. She adores that kind of thing.'

'And you? Do *you* adore "that sort of thing"? Or would you tolerate it for the sake of the ruse?' They'd stopped walking to watch the carpenters building the market stalls and she was aware of his gaze on her, aware, too, that for a moment they'd stepped into a limbo between ruse and reality.

She met his gaze with a soft stare of her own. 'I would absolutely love an evening at a Christmas market, strolling beneath the fairy lights, looking at goods from faraway lands. There's something magical about it, I think. At least I guess. In my mind that's how I see it. I can't say that I've ever been allowed the opportunity to experience something like it. We seldom have such fairs up in our part of isolated Yorkshire. When we do, my father won't hear of me attending with the rabble.'

She sighed into the silence that followed. 'You must think me the worst sort of snob.' In London, during the Season, she attended only the best of events. 'I wouldn't blame you if you did. I've not given you leave to believe any differently.'

'I'll be sure to bring you. This year, we've expanded to include games,' Julien promised. But she noted that he had not answered her question. *Did* he think her a snob? It galled her that he might—no—that he probably did. The girl he'd known had been the pampered, protected daughter of the Earl of Holme. It was the only face she'd been allowed to show anyone in London. And he'd loved her even so, as she'd been back then, a young girl who had known so little of the world.

For a moment, she was tempted to set aside the ruse entirely, grab him by the lapels and make him look at her while she spoke the truth: that she wasn't a snob, that she was working hard to found a school for children at home, that in Yorkshire she far preferred riding her horse and hiking the hills than sitting prettily in silks and doing needlepoint, that when she played the piano, she preferred the loud, moody depths of Beethoven to the lightness of Mozart.

She was not a porcelain figurine who would break. Although, once, she had believed the latter. She'd not thought she'd survive if she was dropped from the life she knew. She knew better now when it was too late.

Julien pointed to one of the booths. 'There will be puppet shows for the children at that one. A man who makes the most exquisite marionettes comes from Italy and puts on shows he writes himself. But perhaps it will steal some of the magic if we see everything being constructed and know it's all just simple board and nails in the end.'

'The whole world's a stage, is that it?' she quoted with a laugh and then wished she hadn't. The line struck too close to home. They were performing their ruse on a stage of their making. He'd brought her shopping because the ruse demanded it. He'd made polite conversation with her because that too was demanded. But he'd been careful today not to let that conversation veer into the personal. Today's conversation had been entertaining, but neutral. It wouldn't do for someone to accidentally overhear them being testy with one another and have word get back to her father. They'd left no margin for complaint today. Anyone who had seen them would only remark that he'd been as solicitous today as he'd been yesterday, showing her about town.

His town. He loved Hemsford Village. His pride was evident in his words and in his efforts. He felt about Hemsford as she felt about the village attached to her father's estate. Something they had in common that would surprise him if he knew. He might build orphanages on a grand scale, but she had a servant's heart, too.

'Do you have more shopping?' Julien hefted the basket on his arm, filled to the rim with brown-paper-wrapped packages from her efforts.

'If we could make one more stop?' she asked. 'I wanted to get peppermints for the Christmas baskets. Where do you get yours for Alex?' She flashed a saucy smile.

'I get them at Wilson's Emporium, but if you'd be advised by me, I would wait.' He leaned close and she breathed in the scent of his soap and cologne, all winter spice—cloves, she thought—and the sharpness of citrus, that rare thing—a Christmas orange. 'There's a vendor from Germany that brings the most delicious peppermint sticks. I'm not sure what makes them different, but they are very good.' He gave the basket another hefting lift. 'Is everything in here for the Christmas baskets?'

'Yes, you didn't think all of this was just for me?' She laughed, but she didn't miss the considering look in his gaze as if he might be seeing her anew. 'I sit on a committee at home, too, for Christmas baskets,' she added. 'Don't be so surprised…' Then dared to say with a smile to soften the intention '…who knows what you might learn about me if you looked a little closer.'

'Is that wise, Aurelia?' he cautioned sternly, steering them towards the livery where the gig waited for them. 'This is not about looking closer. This about self-preservation for both of us.' She'd deserved that. She'd stepped too far over the lines and rules of their ruse.

'Of course, I do apologise. I just thought…' She didn't finish the sentence. What *had* she thought? That they might be friends? That he could get past her refusal? Perhaps it was easier for her to slip up because she'd not been the one refused. That didn't mean, of course, that she hadn't been hurt, too. But her wound had been self-inflicted. She frowned as the livery neared. 'Do we have to go back just yet? Perhaps we could stop in for tea at the Red Rose Inn. We could try out the Christmas tea you were telling me about.'

Julien shook his head. 'I have a meeting with your father this afternoon. I need to get back.' And she had work to do for the Christmas baskets. Handkerchiefs for the women weren't going to embroider themselves. The committee had decided to include something simple but pretty for the mothers in this year's baskets. Julien put her basket in the back of the gig and paused. 'Why don't you want to go back to Brentham Woods? Is something wrong there? Has anyone caused you trouble?'

She shook her head and helped herself up to the seat. 'No, everyone has been kind, even though I am sure we're an enormous imposition this time of year. I just like being...' She almost said *with you*. But she'd already been scolded for such familiarity and such honesty. She opted for the other truth. 'Away from him. Away from my father.'

Julien gave her a sharp look as he sat down beside her. 'Has something happened I should be aware of?' She had to be careful here.

'No. The sooner you give him the loan, the sooner you and I are in the clear.' She sighed and kept her gaze fixed on the road ahead. The sooner December was behind her, the sooner she could return to Moorfields and Elspeth and the safety of her life there, one step closer to her freedom. And the sooner she could put Julien behind her again. Which would be for the best. He was part of the past and he did not figure in the future she'd envisioned for herself.

Chapter Nine

Julien had not envisaged just how odious it was to deal with the Earl of Holme. Even without their contentious past, he would have despised the man. He'd never met a person more resistant to helping himself and yet more desirous of a handout.

Julien exchanged a look with his father that said covertly, *Are you sure you want to do this?*

To which his father replied with a barely perceptible shrug that said, *I think we must, for the ladies' sake.*

His father was not wrong. The more time Julien spent with the Earl of Holme, the more he disliked the idea of Lady Holme and Aurelia being at the man's financial mercy. He wouldn't want any woman reliant on this man who moved through the world with an elevated sense of his own consequence and not a practical thought in his head for how to care for those around him: not his tenants, not his daughter, not his wife.

Julien leaned forward, his hands folded on the surface of the large desk that separated him from the Earl of Holme and his father on the other side. He did his best business thinking in this room. 'We'll want to start by looking at the estates and restructuring how they're run in order to make them self-supporting, perhaps even profitable in the future. Right now, they are a drain on your resources, but that can all be fixed with management.' Something that had been in short supply from the looks of things. 'When was the last time you visited your other estates?'

'What does that have to do with anything?' Holme growled, his sagging jowls grimacing.

Julien fixed him with a hard stare. 'It has everything to do with it. We are here to help you mend your finances so that you do not find yourself in such straits again. We must repair what is broken about your management.' He paused for emphasis. 'We will not throw money into a bottomless pit of losses, Lord Holme. We must have assurances our investment is worth something. The assurance we would like is that this insolvency won't occur again. Without such an assurance...' Julien didn't need to finish the sentence. Holme knew what was implied. Without the assurance, theoretically there'd be no loan.

Holme huffed and gave in. Julien gave a crisp nod. 'Good, we are in accord. Let's start with your family seat.'

It took the rest of the afternoon to explain how to restructure the economy of the estate, how the crops would need to be rotated and how to manage the village. He did not think Holme would remember half of it, but it didn't matter. He had Holme's signature which gave him the power to enact the changes as a condition of the loan. In addition, he had a man in mind who would act as land steward for Moorfields and who would understand the plans Julien had spent hours drawing up. Plans that would help the estate recover. Plans that would protect Aurelia's home well past the two years she required.

The voice in his head nudged: *Careful. You're getting invested, too invested, and not just financially.*

His father showed Holme out of the office, making the appropriate affirmations about how much they'd accomplished this afternoon, and shut the door firmly behind the man. 'Well? What do you think?' his father asked, returning to his chair.

'He is ungrateful. He thinks help is his due, that he is owed success by dint of who he is.' Julien tossed his pen on the desk. 'We are securing his future and he has no idea how important that is.' Julien could not begin to fathom such a concept. The future was all he thought about. Investment banking was inherently future focused, his charity efforts were future focused. How did a man *not* think about the future?

'It's not that Holme doesn't think, it's that he only thinks about himself.' His father smiled and sighed. 'Other than Holme's reticence, I think the rest of the visit is going well. You and Aurelia seem to have sorted your differences. It was kind of you to take her into the village this morning.'

Kind was all Julien wished it had been. But it had been motivated by more than that. He'd wanted an excuse to spend time with her even after yesterday or especially because of yesterday. He could tell himself he'd taken her into the village because the ruse required it. But he'd taken her because he'd wanted to. When she'd come downstairs this morning in her winter-sky-blue ensemble, a cream, fur-trimmed mantle swinging from her shoulders, bright eyes shining, he'd nearly been lost, nearly forgotten every admonition he'd given himself.

'Do you still have feelings for her?' his father asked casually.

Julien looked at him sharply. 'No, why would you ask?' Dear Lord, what had his face inadvertently betrayed? If his father guessed at such a thing, who else might also guess? That was not tolerable, particularly when it wasn't true. He was not falling for Aurelia Ripley again.

His father shrugged and gestured to the papers on the desk. 'You've gone to a lot of work for someone you do not feel an out-of-the-ordinary attachment to. Perhaps one could say she's the reason you've worked so tirelessly on ensuring long-term security for the estate.'

'Wasn't it you who said we should think about the women?' Julien pointed out. 'I am merely doing for her what I would do for any other woman who has the misfortune to be a tied to a man who has mismanaged his finances.'

'Would it be so bad if it wasn't?' his father pressed. 'If you did have feelings for her? I do wonder if she still has feelings for you. To me, it seems as if she might. When I saw the two of you together at church, or when I watch you in the evenings playing cards, I can't help but think that this time things might be different? An eighteen-year-old girl doesn't know her mind the way a twenty-five-year-old woman does.'

Julien shook his head. 'Aurelia Ripley has always known her mind and she's always known her own power when it comes to men. She's good at curating an image and cultivating feelings. I do not think it would be wise, Father, to put too much stock in appearances.' If only such advice were as easy to take as it was to dispense.

Julien rose. 'I think I'll take Benjamin for a ramble before it gets dark.' Perhaps some time out of doors with his dog would help clear his head of the traitorous thoughts that were roaming around loose in there: that this time it *could* be different, that Aurelia had changed, that what he saw of her now was the real her. Most traitorous of all was the thought that *he* wanted those things to be true. He knew better. Loyalty and love didn't work like that. They were steadfast and true, unchanging, immovable against the tides of fate. Who knew that better than a dog? He whistled for Ben and Ben came. Benjamin wasn't man's best friend for nothing.

'Oho! You're not a pretty girl for nothing—the Viscount has made his offer of a loan. We started the paperwork this afternoon. Whatever you told him in the village has borne fruit.' Her father entered her room without knocking, his face florid with excitement, her mother close behind him. 'Things are going well. We're going to be solvent,' he crowed, turning to her mother. 'More than that, we might even be able to buy back your tiara, my dear, and some of the artwork.'

Aurelia saw her mother's face relax with real relief even as her father was already planning how to spend his newfound riches. What would Julien think of that? Surely that wasn't what Julien had planned for those funds. Guilt pinched her. This was what she'd talked Julien into. Tiaras and artwork were likely low on Julien's list of financial priorities.

'Of course, we must keep kowtowing to them for a while longer, pretend we're grateful and all that.' He waved a hand her direction. 'You must keep the Viscount dangling, keep him hopeful and charmed. We're not out of the woods yet.'

'We *are* grateful,' Aurelia cut in, feeling defensive on Julien's behalf. 'No one else was willing to lend you any money. Not even the moneylenders with exorbitant interest rates.' She gave her father a hard stare. 'What do they want in exchange for such a magnanimous loan? You do understand the loan must be paid back.'

'The terms are better than I hoped for. They want to restructure the estates so that the land is self-supporting and the estates pay for themselves without excessive taxation on renters. Fine, I say. If they want to play petty landlords from a distance, I am happy to let them muck about, especially if it doesn't cost me anything.'

That was not nothing, Aurelia thought. The import of the Lennoxes' terms was not lost on her as it was lost on her selfish father, but she kept the realisation quietly to herself. Julien was securing the estates into the future so that as long as her father lived, she and her mother would be financially safe. It was the most he could do—all he could do. He could not control that her father had no male heir of his own, only a distant cousin who would dispossess her and her mother of their home upon her father's death. But until then, they would be taken care of.

'I would like to push for a match between you and the Viscount, my dear, now that things are going so well. It seems to me I could secure his backing more permanently if there was a wedding between us.'

That brought Aurelia to sharp attention. She ignored the rapid, worried beat of her heart. Julien would not thank her for that. Their ruse was supposed to preclude such an effort. 'There is no need. The estates are safe and I have done my part in charming him.'

That had not come without a cost to her. It had stirred old memories, old hurts and old guilt. Everything between them now was a lie, a show for others when once there'd been truth. That was her fault. She would rather have had truth with him instead of this ruse of politeness. He'd been strategic today in the village, a reminder that he did not trust her, that he was holding her to the rules of this particular engagement, that yesterday had been a step too far.

She'd promised him she wouldn't trap him, that she would protect him from her father's plan. Now she had to make good on that. She'd got her father the loan and now she needed to protect Julien from a marriage he didn't want. Besides, she didn't want a marriage either. She wanted her freedom to do as she pleased, to live knowing that the things and people she loved could not be used against her. Heavens, but she was weary of playing all sides. When would anyone be on her side?

'Don't push,' her mother counselled her father, helping him up. 'We have enough for now. There's no need and weren't you hoping that, once the finances cleared up, Aurelia might make a match in town this spring? Weren't you saying the other night that the Marquess of Penumberton's son was home from the Continent and looking to wed?'

Placation. No real solution, just kicking the stone down the road, this was her mother's management strategy. It was a compromise: peace for now. She would deal with Penumberton's son and the Season in a few months. Her mother smiled over her shoulder as her parents left her room. 'Maybe nature will just take its course where the Viscount is concerned, my girl.'

Her first thought once they'd left was that she had to warn Julien. She sank down on the window seat and stared out at the parkland. Where would Julien be this time of day? Would he be in his office? Somewhere in the house? Or would he be out? She'd rather talk to him now than take the risk of talking to him before dinner when privacy would be minimal.

Movement drew her eye to the tree-line where the woods met Brentham. She sat up straighter as a man and a dog came into view. Julien and Benjamin. Julien's head was bare, his dark hair tousled, his boots muddy, and he looked entirely relaxed. Julien shouted a command to the dog and threw a stick. The dog bounded after it, ears flapping, and brought it back, earning a scratch and another throw.

Had he walked out to the meadow and checked the duck boxes? She wished he'd asked her to go, too. But why would he? He'd already done his duty this morning and the ruse did not require an invitation to go walking where no one could see. Yet the temptation to go to him whispered too loud to ignore.

She grabbed her cloak, raced down the stairs and across the lawn before anyone could stop her.

Benjamin saw her first and sounded the alarm with a bark, but no menace. He came to her, licking her hand and begging for pats. 'Ben, come here,' Julien called in commanding tones and Benjamin reluctantly obeyed. 'He'll get mud on you if you're not careful.' Julien strode up and ruffled Benjamin's fur.

'I'm not worried, it's a durable cloak.' It was long and dark, not the fancy fur-lined mantle she'd worn into Hemsford. 'I saw you from the window,' she offered in explanation. Now that she was here with him, she was second-guessing her decision. She was invading his peace. Had she really come out for him or for her own selfish desire to be in his company again?

He glanced towards the house, perhaps wondering if anyone was watching. 'Did you need something?' He seemed mildly annoyed by the intrusion. Perhaps people only came to him when they needed something from him. People came to him to lay down their burdens, burdens which he would inevitably pick up. Now she was one of them.

'I don't think anyone is watching.' More was the pity. She had no reason to reach for his hand. 'But, yes, I do need something.' She stepped close to him, close enough to see his dark eyes harden with wariness. 'I need to thank you for what you're doing with my father, for what you've done for me. He told me how you've reworked the estate.'

She paused and said slowly, 'I know what it will mean for my mother, for me.' She brushed a hand down the sleeve of his greatcoat. 'You bought me my two years.' With his ingenuity and his money he'd built a wall that would protect her until she reached her majority.

'I would have done it for anyone in your situation. As for the estate, it's just good investing. I don't want my money going into a bottomless pit. I want the expenditure to mean something.'

Of course he'd deny it had anything to do with her. Of course his gaze would be impenetrable. Those were the rules. He needn't play at liking her when no one was around. 'It does mean a great deal not just to me, but to the village at Moorfields and all those who count on the estates for their livelihood.' She could see he liked that reference better, caring for the masses as opposed to one specific person.

'Is that all you needed? It could have waited until supper.' Julien was distant now, more distant than he'd been since her arrival a week ago. Even then, his anger had heat to it, but there was no heat to him now, just polite, neutral coolness. He removed her hand from his sleeve. 'Best not get careless, Aurelia. I wouldn't want anyone to get the wrong idea.' Particularly her. Or perhaps him. She heard the unspoken message quite clearly.

She tucked her hand back beneath her cloak, sorely missing her gloves in the cold. 'There is one more thing. My father feels that my charms have been met with good result. I have charmed you into the loan, in other words, and into generous terms where paying back the money isn't so literal. I thought that would be enough to keep you and me safe from any further contretemps on his part, but this afternoon...' She drew a breath long enough to study Julien's features. How angry would he be? 'He mentioned he thought a match between us would be beneficial and he suggested I ought to...' What was the right word? 'Manage it.'

Julien's face darkened to a thunderous hue. 'I am sorry, Julien,' she put in rapidly, reflexively reaching a hand out for his arm. 'I did not think he would look further than the money. I thought once he had the money it would be enough.'

His expression arrested. 'Do you think that's why I am angry? No, I am angry because the man would use his daughter to whore for him, to be bartered in marriage as if it were not the modern era.'

A trill of warm comfort swam through her at his defence. Never mind he would be the champion of any woman in such circumstances. For the moment, someone was on her side and that it should be Julien, touched her even as she knew it meant nothing. 'I thought you should know, Julien, so that you could take precautions.' For himself, for both of them. She had not meant to add to the burdens he carried, but she had.

He gave a curt nod. 'I will make sure he knows that I will pull the loan if he makes marriage a condition. He is in no position to bargain or dictate terms.'

She licked her lips and looked away for a moment. 'I don't think he will do it that way. I think he expects me to manage it entirely, so that it appears to be a natural evolution of our association.'

Julien turned from her and kicked at a pile of dead leaves. When he turned back, his eyes were like hard, dark-chocolate nougat. 'Does he do this often, Aurelia? Send you to beg? Is this why you're unwed at twenty-five? It's not just the money, is it, that keeps you by his side. He can't imagine what to do if he played his ace for good?'

'If that were true, he'd not be pushing to see us wed.' She felt herself flush.

'But with my money permanently secured through marriage, he'd not need to send you out again. And your mother, what does she say to any of this? Does she do anything to stop it?'

She drew her cloak about her, suddenly cold. 'My mother does what she can. You've seen firsthand that my father is not an easy man to live with for either of us.'

He was silent for a while, his gaze unwavering as it bored into her, seeing too much, seeing the dysfunction of her life that lay behind the silks and satins and pretty smiles. It was embarrassing to admit to against the backdrop of his perfection: the home filled with the love, the family that adored one another, the life spent in service to others and not himself. She felt supremely dirty.

'Say something. I know it's awful,' she said quietly.

'What is awful is that it keeps happening. Will you permit me to put a stop to it? I can make it a condition of the loan.'

She shook her head vociferously. 'No, then he'll know I told you.' And that would be one more thing she'd spend the next two years paying for, one more thing that would put Elspeth and the things she loved at risk.

He nodded. 'Then I won't,' he said with firm assurance. 'I will think of something else, something more circumspect.'

'You must discuss it with me first,' she insisted. 'I do not want you entangled any more than necessary.'

He nodded. 'I'll walk you back to the house, and then starting tomorrow we'll give the ruse a brief rest. I have projects that can take me away from the house during the days. That will give avaricious minds some time to cool and reassess how grasping they need to be. I think it will have to do for now,' Julien said gently, offering his arm and calling to Benjamin who was interested in something at the base of a tree.

There was comfort in the strong arm beneath her hand. What a mess this had become. The ruse had invited her father's speculation instead of repelling it. More than that, the ruse had awakened her own remembrances of a time before things had gone sour, making the situation and her own role in it all the more painful.

Chapter Ten

⟳◆◈◇⟳

She didn't see him again until Saturday, the day of the fair, unless one counted his appearance at the dinner table and in the drawing room after brandies to play cards or games or to read while the ladies sewed. One evening, she played the pianoforte, thinking to entice him to join her on the bench to turn pages, but he stayed firmly rooted at the backgammon board with his father.

In other words, there was no more time alone with him. No rides out to the duck boxes, no more drives in the gig to Hemsford where they had the privacy of the road between them and an undefined space of time where they were both in and out of the ruse. No more walks down the High Street, peering in shop windows and pretending he was escorting her for real and not because the ruse demanded it.

It made quite a long week even though she had plenty to keep her busy with handkerchiefs to embroider for the Christmas baskets and committee work to keep her occupied. When she wasn't sewing, she was organising baking for the baskets in the Lennox kitchen, which Caro Lennox had cheerfully turned over to her for the occasion. She even kneaded bread and rolled out sheets of dough for Christmas sugar biscuits that would be cut into enticing Christmas shapes like bells and stars. But while her body was busy with work, her mind found time to wander afield.

What was Julien doing? Where was he? Her ears found themselves craning for the sound of his boots in the hall. She imagined him coming to seek her in the kitchens, catching her with a smudge of flour on her cheek and wiping it away, his thumb lingering a little too long at the corner of her mouth…but those were fancies only, none of which came true. He did not seek her out once.

She went the rest of the week without seeing him. But she'd see him today for the Christmas fair. Aurelia rummaged through her wardrobe, looking for the long red-wool cloak she wanted to wear, trying to ignore the excitement that coursed through her at the prospect of seeing Julien today. Of course, she knew why he hadn't come to the kitchens. The ruse didn't demand it. Coming down to the kitchen where no one required a demonstration of their affections did not serve their masquerade. But also, they didn't want the ruse to be too convincing and start to work against them.

A little distance served them. If Julien appeared too eager, her father would take advantage. It would be better if Julien appeared to be charmed, but not besotted. Independent, not following her around like a puppy dog. Not that she could ever imagine Julien acting in such a manner. Not even when he'd been truly courting her had he played a lovesick swain. Julien was always level-headed, never unduly swept away. It was part of his charm and his mystique.

She remembered how the girls in the retiring rooms had chattered about him, about how wondrous it would be to wrap such a man around their fingers, to see that control completely undone. At the time, she'd felt very smug, thinking to herself that he was hers, that she alone had seen him set aside his gentlemanly façade and that she would be the one to see him undone once they wed. And she had seen him undone, just not in the way she'd wanted or expected.

There it was! She reached for the red-wool cloak just as her mother peeked into the room. 'Are you ready? I think everyone is downstairs.' Her mother studied her with approval. 'You're wearing the red over your grey ensemble today, that's perfect. Red brings out your hair and we want the Viscount to have his attentions fixed on you.'

Her mother came to her with a smile and straightened the narrow black belt at the waist of her grey walking costume with its black-velvet trim at the wrists and hem. 'The red will look nice and bright.' Her mother rummaged through the dressing table. 'Maybe some rouge today to go with it. Just a little on your lips. The cold will put the colour in your cheeks.' She dabbed a bit on her fingertip and patted the colour on to Aurelia's lips. 'There, perfect, my darling.' She stepped back with a smile. 'You are so lovely, my angel. When I look at you, I see so much of myself in younger days.'

But maybe not *too* much of herself, Aurelia thought, hiding her angst over the comment beneath a soft smile. She liked to believe she was different than her mother, perhaps stronger than her mother. Her mother was a peacekeeper, but her mother's idea of peace required subjugation. Aurelia did not think she was willing to bend quite that much.

'You are in fine looks. Your father will be pleased. He's been worried the Viscount's attentions have been slipping after such a fast start.'

'The Viscount is a busy man. Many things vie for his attentions. I cannot expect to dominate all of them, all the time. I don't think he'd find such clinginess attractive.' She swung the cloak about her shoulders. 'Father should let me handle the Viscount and spend his time worrying about the estates.'

Her mother clucked her tongue. 'You have a saucy mouth, Aurelia. You should respect your father; it's been hard for him.'

'Hard? For him?' Aurelia scoffed as they left the room. 'He does as he pleases and no one says boo to him. When was the last time *you* disagreed with him? Stood up to him?'

'It's not a wife's place, Aurelia,' her mother whispered sternly. Nor was it a daughter's. A father should protect his child, not use her to advance his own needy causes, not wish that she'd died in place of his heir. Aurelia let the subject go as they descended the staircase. Today, she was going to the Christmas fair with Julien and, ruse or no ruse, she was going to have a good time.

The village fair did not disappoint. The festive excitement seemed to start on the outskirts of the village, with the signs driven into the ground on wooden stakes painted to look like peppermint sticks, assuring visitors they were on the right road to Hemsford. The closer their little cavalcade—she and Julien in the gig, Tristan's family in a coach and her parents and the Lennoxes in another coach—got to the village, the more crowded the road became. Neighbours called out to one another and there was laughter on the air mixed with jingle bell harnesses. Aurelia thought it was one of the best sounds she'd ever heard, second only to the peal of Moorfield's Christmas Eve bells.

'I bet Tristan can hardly keep Alex in his seat,' she said to Julien as he parked the gig outside the church. A few young boys had been pressed into service at the church to mind those who wish to park their gigs there for a few coins instead of making their way through the crowded streets to the livery.

Julien laughed, caught up in the good cheer of the day. 'If so, it serves him right. My brother was a handful at Christmas when he was younger. He loves Christmas, always has.' He leaned close as if to impart a secret. 'He loves it even more now that his favourite time of year is also his wedding anniversary. He proposed to Elanora on Christmas Eve and married her Christmas Day.'

'Oh.' She sighed, letting her gaze slide towards Tristan's coach, where Julien's brother had climbed out and was organising his brood. 'That's quite romantic.' She watched as Elanora stepped out of the coach last and kissed Tristan on the cheek, an unmistakable look of love and contentment in her eyes before she took her son's hand and gently steered him out of the way of a newly arrived carriage. Baby Violet was in her papa's arms, her curious eyes bright and looking all about her. What a picture they made, the four of them together.

The sight tugged on heartstrings she did not think could be tugged.

Did she still want that? How could she? After all, it was the antithesis of freedom, of what she was fighting for.

The ten of them formed into natural subgroups as they strolled the village green, now fully converted into a Christmas fair: Julien's parents walking with hers, she and Julien walking with Tristan's family. She enjoyed the chance to spend time with Elanora, to take her turn holding baby Violet, to see the fair through Alex's excited eyes which lit up at every curiosity. Most of all, she enjoyed the chance to be with Julien, to have his hand at her back, to have his attentions, to feel his gaze on her and the ruse be hanged. She knew he had a part to play today as did she, but she conveniently let herself forget it, let herself pretend that today was real.

'It hardly looks like the same place,' she told Julien as they strolled the aisles. 'It's so much more than plywood and nails.' Durable, dark-green canvas and festive red-and-green bunting held up with gold bows decorated the booths. Wreaths sporting holly berries and red gingham ribbons were hung at each stall. From there, vendors had contributed their own touches and decorations to their booths, adding to the festivity. Overhead, lanterns were strung across the aisles from booth to booth, waiting to be lit later at dusk.

The aroma of fried breads and baked biscuits filled the air, tempting fair goers to a mid-morning tea or an early lunch. There were pasties, too, filled with hot, spicy meat that dripped when you bit into them, and paper cones of finger foods like roasted chestnuts a person could eat while they shopped. There was spun-sugar sweets, liquorice drops, peppermint sticks and chocolates of all varieties. There was a dancing space and a place for a band to play later. 'I feel like Alex,' she said, leaning against Julien's arm. 'I can scarce take it all in.'

Julien laughed. 'One would think you had never been to London and seen wonders far grander than a country fair.'

She smiled up at him. 'Nothing in London can match this. There's no marriage mart here, no posturing, just good clean fun.' For emphasis, she tugged him towards the booth selling milled soap of French lavender. She picked up a bar, closed her eyes and took a deep inhale. 'See, just good clean fun.' She reached for her reticule and signalled to the vendor. 'I'll take four bars of this, please.'

'Four?' Julien teased.

'Christmas gifts for our mothers and for Elanora, and one for me.' She fished for coins, but Julien's gentle hand stilled hers.

'Allow me, Aurelia,' he said quietly, but apparently not quietly enough. Beside them, Elanora and Tristan exchanged smiles full of knowing. 'Today is my treat. I want you to have a good time.'

'Julien, you don't need to,' she protested, suddenly confused. Was this part of the ruse because a gentleman *would* offer and he was playing a part for his brother and their families? Or was this...*real*...because it truly was his treat?

'I want to,' he said firmly, passing the vendor the coins and handing her the wrapped bars of soap to put in her basket. She might have enjoyed the moment more if she wasn't acutely aware of her parents looking on, her father's shrewd eyes assessing what every nuance meant...to him and how best to use it. A little of her joy went out of the day.

Perhaps Julien sensed it. His hand tightened at her waist and his smile widened, trying a little too hard for levity. 'I think your basket needs filling. We must shop some more. Elanora? Tristan? Would you care to join us?' It was a manoeuvre designed to separate them from her parents and Aurelia was glad for it.

What a delight it was to see the market though a child's eyes. They stopped at every toymaker's booth, while Alex gave serious consideration to a wooden ship with real linen sails and a colourful kite. There was a wooden Noah's Ark set complete with pairs of animals, hand-painted porcelain dolls from Venice and wooden marionettes in elaborate gay costumes.

They stopped to buy a cone of roasted chestnuts to share among them all and Julien teased her. 'I think you might be as mesmerised as Alex.' He eyed her now much fuller basket. 'And you've got the basket to prove it. Can you carry it for a while?' He passed it off to her and reached down for his nephew, swinging him up on to his shoulders. 'Are you ready for some games, Alex?' He winked at Aurelia while Alex cheered. 'You ladies have had your shopping, now the gentlemen must have their games.'

There were games for all ages: a ring-toss and a ball-in-the-basket toss for the children, darts, archery, knife throwing and a more aggressive knock-'em-down wooden bottle ball-throw for the adults. They clapped when Alex won a prize at the ring toss. They laughed when Julien and Tristan had a high-spirited match of dart throwing against Reverend Thompson and Mr Scofield from the bank which ended in a tie.

Aurelia found herself with a teary eye she had to turn around to wipe away when Julien presented baby Violet with the rag doll he won at the archery butts, the little girl gurgling with happiness as her uncle tucked the dolly into her arms. It was only because she'd never had a day like this, Aurelia told herself.

Reverend Thompson and Mr Scofield stayed with their group after darts and they drifted towards the game booth sponsored by the church's ladies auxiliary. Mrs Phelps was thrilled to see them as she waved them over to where three or four couples lingered in front of the mistletoe arch, laughing.

'It's a bit scandalous,' the Reverend said with a grin, 'but my wife assures me it's for a good cause. All of our takings today will go to the parish welfare fund. There's more and more folks on the rolls every year.' He exchanged a commiserating look with Julien, whom Aurelia was certain knew to a penny just how much was needed to support those who couldn't fully support themselves.

'What is it?' Aurelia tried to guess the scandalous undertaking. This had not been in her committee's purvey.

'We call it mistletoe madness,' Mrs Phelps boasted proudly. 'Gentlemen *or* ladies can pay to kiss whomever they want,' she ended with a giggle.

'I've got sixpence to kiss Miss Addy Brightman!' a young man slapped his money down at the booth, hoots and cries going up as the girl in question blushed coyly. This was followed by other couples committing their pennies for a kiss, but Mrs Phelps and Mrs Thompson, the Reverend's wife, kept glancing in her direction, clearly expecting something.

Tristan fished in his pocket and pulled out a coin. 'A guinea to kiss my lovely wife.' He made a grand show of it, sweeping Elanora into his arms beneath the mistletoe arch and kissing her full on the mouth. Then, to the crowd's delight, she kissed him back, murmuring, 'That's two kisses, Tristan. You owe the ladies auxiliary another guinea.'

Mrs Phelps crowed at their good fortune. Guineas went further than sixpence in the collection box. Caught up in the euphoria of the moment, Mrs Phelps boldly turned to Julien. 'Are you to be outdone by your brother?'

For a moment Julien seemed to hesitate, casting about for a suitable excuse. Mortification pulsed through Aurelia. What would people think if he didn't want to kiss her? It was only a ruse, but her pride couldn't handle the trampling. 'I'll match Captain Lennox's guinea,' she spoke up loudly. 'One guinea to kiss his brother.' The ladies in the crowd laughed and clapped their delight. Why not, Aurelia thought, extracting the coin from her funds. She was going to spend the money on Christmas baskets anyway. It was all going to the same cause.

Her eyes clashed with Julien's, sharp blue sapphires colliding against the hard onyx of his dark gaze. Then she was wrapping her arms about his neck, drawing him to her, her mouth taking his, all the while praying that he would help her put on a show, that he would kiss her back, even if it wasn't real.

Come on, Julien, dammit all, kiss me.

Then she felt it, the press of his hand in her hair, the opening of his mouth against hers, coaxing and sweet. She melted into him with relief. He might be angry with her later, but he was not going to leave her in this alone. She had acted rashly, but all that mattered was that Julien had come to her rescue. His rescue, though, had left her a bit breathless and maybe even him, too, although she didn't think he'd admit it.

Chapter Eleven

'Whatever possessed you to do that?' Julien's lips were still burning from the kiss, his body still humming with the echoes of it, his mind buzzing with all the things he'd say to her once he could get her alone and now, at last he had done that, although it had taken a Herculean effort. There'd been Tristan's family to see off after the mistletoe arch. The children were tired after a day at the fair. There'd been her parents and his to see off as well, her father claiming sore feet. Now, finally, he had Aurelia alone beneath the bare branches of the oak in the churchyard.

'Don't be angry about the kiss, Julien,' she cajoled, flashing him a little smile as Tristan's coach disappeared into the gathering dusk. He knew that smile from days past. It was a dangerous smile, for all its sweetness. 'It was nothing, just a sop to my pride.' It might have started that way, although it hadn't ended quite like that. Sops to pride didn't leave one breathless and wanting another. He'd seen the look in her eyes, and he'd felt the rise of his own hunger.

She gave a toss of her head, playing it light, trying to convince him and perhaps herself that the kiss meant nothing, that they hadn't unlocked Pandora's box. 'How would I ever face the Christmas basket committee again if they thought you didn't want to kiss me?'

'It was impetuous,' he countered, a scold in his voice. Someone had to take this breach of etiquette seriously. And yet he knew why she'd done it. *He* had hesitated and that would draw questions and speculations. It had embarrassed her, made her feel unwanted, something she was, perhaps, too used to feeling given what he'd seen of her parents. He was coming to learn that being wanted was the chink in her armour, the thing she craved and been denied—*seven Seasons with nothing to show*, the refrain came again.

'It was the only thing to do.' She gave a delicate shrug.

'It was illogical, using a kiss to cover up not kissing. It was backward, ironic logic at best.' Because she couldn't have anyone thinking he didn't want her, not even himself. But wanting her led to all sorts of problems, problems he couldn't solve by throwing money at them. *That* was the chink in *his* armour.

'Well, no more impetuous kisses, Aurelia. It's not what we agreed on.' He didn't think he'd survive any more. That one kiss had tempted him to remember too much, feel too much, want too much. The best he could do was secure her financial future until she could claim her inheritance and he'd done that for her by giving her father the ill-advised loan.

Her blue eyes glinted with mischief. 'What about planned kisses? Are those off limits, too?' She was teasing him now, making him laugh at himself and his strictness.

'We would never plan kisses, we know better. Kisses are private, hence, not part of what the ruse requires.' It was a reminder they both needed to hear. 'Now, we have the fair to ourselves.' Julien offered his arm, wanting to be away from the tree and conversations of kisses. 'What would you like to do?'

The mischief in her blue eyes remained undaunted. *As usual*, came the thought, but he quickly squelched it. He could not start thinking of her in terms where the past ran into the present. She was not his, perhaps had never been his. She had betrayed his love once. It had all been a game to her. 'I want to try the knock-'em-down ball-throw.'

'Really? I think it might be more challenging than you anticipate.' He tried to dissuade her as they walked. 'The wooden bottles are weighted with sand to make them harder to tip over.'

'Like you, Julien?' She smiled up at him, bold and careless. 'Sometimes I think *you* are weighted with sand and harder to tip over, too, although not impossible. I think I will try anyway.'

To tip him over or the bottles? Julien wondered, wishing his blood didn't heat at the prospect of her trying to win him over, which was not likely to happen because he couldn't allow it. 'I think the difference is that *I* am not a game,' he offered the warning in gruff tones. Neither was love itself a game.

They reached the bottle throw and she put down her coins, refusing to let him pay. 'You think it's folly,' she scolded. 'Julien Lennox doesn't make poor investments.' She hefted the first ball and eyed the pyramid of five bottles. 'I may have to play a couple of times to figure out the best strategy.'

She shot him a glance. 'Do I knock out the middle, take the top of the pyramid with it, and then gradually work away at the base one by one, or do I gamble it all on sweeping the base away and all else will follow?' she mused out loud, absently running her tongue across her teeth, and Julien had the unbidden thought that this might be how she strategised about men—eroding away their resistance to her charms as she was doing to him now whether it was purposeful or not. Did she come at a gentleman full force, or cut his legs out from under them? He'd experienced both and knew that few men could stand against either.

The bottles were proving more resilient than men, though. She managed to get two of the five bottles knocked off, but the other three remained steadfastly in place, perhaps giving a man hope, Julien thought. 'Stack them again,' she told the vendor, putting down a coin. She varied her throw, trying to work the pyramid from the bottom, but to no avail. She tried again, and again, this time throwing harder, the next time throwing at a single bottle. The fifth time, Julien intervened.

'Perhaps we should try another game,' he suggested delicately, only to be met with a burning blue stare.

'No, I want to win at this one. I want that prize,' she said stubbornly. She nodded towards a pile of cheap rag dolls garbed in colourful, eye-catching dresses with white aprons and braided yarn hair, much like the doll Julien had won earlier for Violet.

Julien leaned close to whisper privately, 'The doll isn't worth as much as you're going to end up spending. I'll buy you one at the emporium, probably even a better quality one.' It was absolutely the wrong thing to say.

She gave a vehement shake of her head. 'I want to *win* it. I want to do it myself.' She put down another coin and Julien thought she was like her father in that regard, blindly stubborn to reality. She would not thank him for the insight, though, so he wisely kept the thought to himself.

He let her try again and fail again. By now, even the vendor was starting to feel sorry for her. The vendor flashed him a manly look that said, *Why won't you do something?* But what was he to do? The vendor thought he should step in and win for her. But they were too far gone for that bit of chivalry now. Stubbornness had set in and it would only make things worse if he managed to do in one attempt what she'd spent several trying to make happen. *That* would make her mad.

Julien stepped to her side once more. 'Will you allow me to give some advice?' he said quietly. 'See the three on the bottom? Aim for the one in the middle. Throw as hard as you can with everything you've got. If you throw hard enough, all of them will fall.'

'Are you sure?' She eyed him grimly like a general discussing battle plans. The simple game had taken on grand proportions.

Julien put down his coins with an emphatic slap on the counter. 'I am *that* sure.' It was also a neat strategy for being able to pay for the game. She had to be running out of coins along with her pride. He would save her both if he could and worry about his motives for caring later.

She tossed him a smile. 'Bottom centre, right.' And then she threw and missed, the ball bouncing short and rolling harmlessly away. She took a deep breath and concentrated, throwing her second ball which reached the target, but not with enough force to do damage. It took all of Julien's willpower not to offer more coaching advice full of the obvious: throw harder next time. She threw her third ball, hard and true, and the wood bottles clattered to the floor.

'I did it!' She threw up her hands in victory and gave a most decidedly unladylike whoop. 'I did it, Julien! Did you see it? I threw at the bottom centre, just like you said, and it worked.' Then she was in his arms, her arms about his neck, hugging him and laughing, and he was acutely aware of hugging her back, his arms about her waist, perhaps even lifting her toes from the ground and swinging her around, her laughter infectious as he gave a laugh of his own. They might have just won Waterloo for all the excitement coursing through them in the moment.

Later, perhaps, he'd think how ridiculous, how excessive the celebration was, but right now, it felt right to hold her, it felt good to laugh with her as if he hadn't a care in the world, as if he could trust how it felt to be with her. And for a moment he didn't question it.

'Which doll would you like, Miss?' the vendor asked after a while, breaking into their celebration.

'The one in red and green, the Christmas doll,' Aurelia chose, breathless in her excitement. She hugged the prize close, her eyes sparkling like gems in a crown. 'I've never won anything before,' she confided to Julien. 'I'll call her Christina, Chrissy for short.'

'And she'll live in the pocket of my greatcoat tonight.' Julien chuckled. 'I see where this is going.' Her basket had gone home with the carriages. She had no way to carry the doll.

'Yes, perhaps she'll need your pocket later,' she admitted. 'When we're dancing. I have nowhere to put her.'

'We're dancing, are we?' The euphoria of the gaming booth was still running strong in his blood. Suddenly, anything felt possible tonight. Julien would like to say that was the magic of fairs, but he knew better: it was the magic of her. He'd always felt that way with her. When they were together, anything was possible, until it hadn't been. Like the fair with its pasteboard and lights, it was an illusion only. But tonight, he was enjoying living in the illusion.

'Come stand right here.' Julien positioned them in a spot on the green where one could view the whole fair, she standing in front of him, her head barely reaching his chin. People were starting to gather on the perimeter, coming out of the shops on the High Street. 'It's dark now, the fair will turn on its lights,' he explained at her ear, breathing in the rose and amber scent of her—part-winter, part-spring, all parts comfort and woman. 'There will be carollers after the lights come on.'

She leaned against his chest, inviting his arms to wrap around her as many other couples were doing near them. It was an invitation he took as Squire Elliott, a bluff, heavyset country man, took the stage and made a folksy speech about the fair and about Hemsford Village's Christmas spirit. 'Next week,' Squire Elliott went on, 'Hemsford will have its first tree lighting. We'll be erecting a tall fir right here…' he gestured to a space on the square '…and lighting it in honour of Her Majesty's own Christmas Tree tradition, for all to see. There will be complementary cider and gingerbread provided by Manning's Bakery and the Red Rose Inn, for which we can thank, Viscount Lavenham.'

There was applause and Julien gave a brief wave of acknowledgement, but he wished the Squire had asked him before revealing that last piece of information. He didn't need everyone to know he'd funded the event. Recognition wasn't why he'd done it.

'Oh, we must come next week, too. I can hardly wait to see that.' Aurelia tilted her head to look up at him, her eyes shining. 'How good of you, Julien, to do something for the whole community.' Oh, God, that look was intoxicating. A man could drown in that adulation if he wasn't careful and Julien was not being careful, not with the memory of the mistletoe arch on his lips, the feel of her in his arms, the exhilaration of her joy coursing through his veins. 'Tell me we'll come,' she insisted.

We'll come.

What a dangerous elixir those words were. As if they were a real couple. 'Of course I'll bring you,' he promised recklessly, already imagining himself on the dais with her beside him in her red cloak looking like Christmas itself, her gold hair gleaming, her smile beaming at him. He laughed at himself. He'd not known he was so vain. Or that he was so hungry for companionship, for something that was real.

This is not real, do not make that mistake.

But the warning of his mind was soft. The scold hardly registered against the joy of the moment, of watching the fair light up, of hearing Aurelia's gasp of delight at the coloured lights, of listening to the carollers singing familiar songs from the little stage. This was what he'd come home for, for Christmas, for hope, for renewal. One could not throw money at joy.

It was hard to say who felt joy the most in the evening that followed. Him or her? After the carollers, the music began and she took him by the hand, dragging him to the dance floor for country dance after country dance until they were exhausted. They shared a tankard of cider, her cloak and his greatcoat long since discarded with Chrissy safely tucked inside, their bodies warm from the dancing despite the December cold.

People came by and shook his hand as they drank, telling him how much they loved the new additions to the fair this year and how much they were looking forward to the tree lighting next week. 'We won't have a tree of our own, of course, our place is too small,' Manning, the baker, said, his arm about his wife. 'But we can all share in the town tree. That will be something.'

'That's the point.' Julien shook Manning's hand with a smile. 'The Queen's tradition can be for all of us, not just a select few.'

Manning smiled. 'And good for business, no doubt. More people will come to Hemsford to see the tree. I've laid in extra flour for baking. We can't keep the gingerbread biscuits on the shelves.'

'I am glad to hear it,' Julien said honestly. 'Sell enough gingerbread, Manning, and you might be able to expand to a shop in London soon. I'd love to get your cakes and biscuits into the right hands.' He clapped the man on the shoulder. 'Let me know if you want to talk business after Christmas before I go back to town. I'd like to help you get started.'

This was the sort of the investment he preferred to make, helping a man realise his dream, instead of propping up greedy men like Holme. But Holme would have his uses, too. Manning had to have access to men like Holme to sell his product, or more specifically, people like Holme's wife. He would be the bridge to that connection.

They finished the tankard and Julien looked about. The crowd was thinning. 'What else would you like to do tonight?'

he asked Aurelia. There might be time for another game or another dance, although the music had slowed and the couples were dancing close. He wasn't sure his nerves could handle it.

She gave him a slow smile. 'I want to go home. Before they turn off the lights. I don't want to be here when it goes dark.'

His thoughts exactly. He helped her into her cloak and they walked back through the street to the church and the gig, arm and arm, her head resting against his shoulder. They were in no hurry. He helped the boy on duty hitch the horse, who'd been allowed to graze and wander about in a roped-off area during the day, and they set out into the starry night, Aurelia's Christmas doll sitting on her lap.

Chapter Twelve

'Why does that doll mean so much?' Julien chuckled. He asked in part from curiosity, in part to distract himself from the nearness of her and the heightened vulnerability of his senses which seemed to be attuned to everything from the jingle of the horse harness to the rose-amber scent of her soap, to the warmth of her body tucked beside him on the bench. A body he'd spent too much of the day thinking about, too much of the day resisting after that kiss at the mistletoe arch had left him alive and aching in a way he'd not felt for years and not with any other. Only her.

'Because I won her. She's mine. I *did* this,' Aurelia declared with a winsome smile that did nothing to soothe the ache she raised in him. She looped her arm through his and leaned against him with an easiness that was oblivious to his own discomfort. 'I've never had a day like today, Julien. Not just the fair—I know I told you before that I'd never been allowed to go to one. It was more than that. I got to be part of a group, part of a family. I loved seeing everything through Alex's eyes.'

He had, too, and a part of himself he'd prefer to ignore warmed to the realisation that this was something they shared. It had made all of his hard work putting the fair together, all the meetings, everything the fair board had endured for months, worth it to see the smile on Alex's face, to see the smiles on all the childrens' faces as they'd walked the aisles.

'I'd not realised you liked children so much.' It was one of the discoveries he'd made during this visit, something he'd not fully understood when he'd known her in London. In those days, she'd been at charity events, it was how he'd met her, but it had seemed then that her interest was more in the event itself than who the event benefited.

Perhaps he'd misjudged her, although it would be easier if he hadn't. It didn't necessarily suit him to discover similarities, to reassess who he thought Aurelia Ripley was.

Remember, once you thought you would marry her, knowing less about her than you do now.

Yes, but that was before he'd seen her true colours, felt the sting of her betrayal. He didn't want to reconsider now.

She sighed. He could feel the rise and fall of her body against his arm. 'Children are precious. I don't know why the world seems to treat them as nuisances instead of luxuries.' She played with the doll in her lap.

'At home, at Moorfields, I've been trying to establish a school. Right now we just meet wherever there's space. We have no dedicated place, just a few slates and benches. In the summer, we meet beneath trees and, in the winter, we meet sometimes in the church.' She gave a shrug perhaps to minimise her efforts. 'It's nothing grand, not like your projects. The children come when they can.'

She'd started a school. How amazing. Yet it was one more thing he'd not known or guessed about her. For the sake of his own sanity, he ought to ignore the remark and let it pass. He didn't need one more thing to draw him to her, force him to reconsider his previous assessments. But in good conscience, he could not dismiss the disclosure.

What she was doing was important and she was doing it on her own. He didn't think for a moment her father supported the work. She needed, *deserved*, encouragement. It was becoming clear her family provided her very little of that. 'You're wrong, Aurelia. It's a start. That's the most important thing of all, to simply begin. It was how I started. I didn't begin by building a whole orphanage.'

She cocked her head, looking up at him with those blue eyes a man would willingly drown in. 'How did you start, Julien? I confess to never having wondered. I suppose I thought of you as having sprung full grown into the world like Athena from Zeus's head.'

That gave him pause as she reached for his gloved hand and held it, her touch sending a jolt of awareness through him despite the leather between them.

'I think that's a mistake we can all make,' Julien said quietly. Hadn't he made the same mistake about her? When he'd first known her, before the betrayal, she'd been a debutante, lovely, perfect, a polished diamond. In those early days he'd been overwhelmed by her. He'd not thought about the obvious—that diamonds are formed over time.

It had taken this visit to start to see that. Aurelia Ripley had layers that he was just beginning to peel back. Although that peeling came at his own risk. Between the halcyon days of what he'd once thought of as their courtship and now, there was the not insignificant issue of her betrayal. When the question had been put to her, she'd not wanted him as much as he'd wanted her.

'Tell me, Julien. What was the first thing you did in regard to your philanthropy?' she murmured, and it struck him that here, beneath the Sussex stars, with seven years of hurt between them and no hope of a future, this might be the first truly personal conversation they'd ever had.

'I got on to boards. I applied the same principle I applied to my investing. A man never invests alone, the risk is too great. It should always be a joint venture so that the risk is shared, distributed across many. I could not build an orphanage on my own, but I could align myself with men whom, together, we could build an orphanage,' he explained. He talked for a while about those early projects before looking down at her. 'Are you a good listener or have I put you to sleep?'

She brought her head up. 'I'm a good listener, thank you very much.' She laughed before adding, 'You could never put me to sleep. You're interesting. But I suppose that's not what I was really asking. What I want to know is why did you take an interest in children in the first place? Not every man does. There are lots of charities you could have chosen if it was simply to make a name for yourself.'

Julien gave a self-deprecating laugh. 'I got myself into some trouble. I was out late one night in town, walking between Mayfair and Piccadilly and I was pickpocketed. It was a novice mistake of mine to be out alone but I thought I didn't have far to go and I'd wanted to walk. Tristan was away in the army, so I was on my own. A girl approached me, she was maybe nine and she was crying, or so I thought. While I was busy helping her, her accomplice picked my pocket. I ran them down once I realised what happened and I did catch them. But I hadn't the heart to turn them in. That wasn't going to fix anything. It was only going to be revenge and that didn't sit well with me.

'Why should nine-year-olds be on the streets? Why should they already be committed to a life of crime with no hope for escape? These questions meant more to me. I bought them a meal at a tavern and I took them back to the town house. I gave them jobs in the kitchen and running errands. They're still with me. John is a footman now. Ellie is a cook's assistant and makes the best bread in Mayfair. But that didn't solve the problem. I couldn't hire every pickpocket in London. The system had to change.'

'And so you've begun to change it.' She gave a contented sigh at the happy ending.

'One step at a time, like your school in Moorfields. Keep at it, Aurelia. It will make a difference.' He would see to it. Perhaps there was a way he could induce her father to offer support as part of the estate restructuring.

They'd reached the drive at Brentham Woods and she squeezed his hand. 'Stop the gig,' she instructed softly. 'I'm not ready for the night to be over.' She shifted on the bench seat and turned to face him. Julien felt his pulse quicken in anticipation, excitement. What did the minx have planned now? Such a reaction alarmed him. He knew too well how intoxicating she was, how her mere presence could work on a man without even trying.

Did she mean to do it, to charm him? Or was this part of the ruse? Or perhaps she was simply being herself? After all, there was no one to see, no need to play the game at the moment. 'I had an extraordinary day with an extraordinary man and it had very little to do with the agreement we made. It may have started that way...'

But it had not ended that way. His heart knew what she might have said had she continued. Had it all been about the ruse, they might have come home earlier with the others. Nothing in the ruse had required him to remain with her, to dance with her, to stand by while she threw balls to win a cheap rag doll that meant the earth to her, to swing her about and celebrate that victory with her. None of it had been required, but all of it had been desired.

Her gloved hand stroked his jaw and he caught her wrist, caution exerting its last defence. 'Aurelia, we said no more kisses.'

'We said no more *impetuous* kisses. We decided nothing about planned kisses and I've been planning this one for quite some time today.' She leaned in and feathered his lips with hers. His body rocketed to attention as she whispered against his mouth, 'Truth be told, Julien, I think you have been, too.'
And damn it if she wasn't right.

He let her be right, let his choice be ruled by his body, let his mouth take the kiss from her, deepening it as his hand sank into the thick coil of hair at her nape where the winter bonnet exposed it. He tasted the sweet cider and the spice of ginger on her tongue, a lovely, apt metaphor for the woman in his arms, who tempted him to taste and to take, and to travel a path his common sense forbade him.

'Aurelia, this is madness.' The hoarseness of his voice surprised him, undermined him. Who would believe him if his body didn't believe him? If it betrayed him at every turn?

She sat back, her eyes filled with disappointment. 'Is a little wildness not allowed? Not even for old time's sake? You kissed me once in the Graftons' garden in the rose bower. We rather more than kissed there, actually. Do you remember?'

It was a dangerous memory. He'd been sure of her then or he would not have allowed them to pursue the heat between them, just as he was *not* sure of her now. On the grounds of that unsurety, he needed to resist this heat for both of them. This interlude did not suit their ruse. Memory of the Graftons' garden was no less dangerous now, his body craving her touch as she'd touched him then, his hands aching to stroke her as he had then. 'You are burning me alive, Aurelia.' The admission was a scold, a warning.

She was not put off. 'The universe burns, Julien. The sun burns, the stars burn, why shouldn't we burn?'

'Perhaps it's best then that we burn alone,' he said gruffly, abruptly picking up the reins. He clucked to the horse and just like that, the magic of the evening was behind them, the perfect day over.

She was playing with fire and it was she who was going to get burned. Aurelia settled on the window seat of her chamber, her white nightgown billowing about her, and looked out into the night, out on to the drive, stretching down the road she and Julien had driven just an hour ago. Her doll sat waiting for her on the bed with its turned-down covers inviting her to sleep, but Aurelia thought sleep would elude her for a while.

She ought to have been exhausted from a long day spent out of doors full of activity. She ought to go to sleep with a head full of happy remembrances: mind pictures of little Alex's laughter, the thrill of the fair games, the delicious foods, the fun of strolling the booths and purchasing gifts. Instead, what dominated her thoughts were not those mental pictures, but other pictures: images of Julien, tall and commanding in his greatcoat, striding through the fairgrounds, stopping to talk with the townsfolk, to shake hands and listen; Julien's dark eyes lighting up as he talked about expanding the bakery with Jonas Manning; Julien helping his nephew win a prize at the ring toss.

Those images stoked sensations, too, like how it *felt* to stroll booths beside this man who'd organised the fair, who'd found a way to combine Hemsford's love of Christmas with the new railroad branch line to bring economic opportunity to his village.

But he'd not been a slave to his own importance, as a lesser man might. Instead, he had made her experience his concern, shopping with her, handing out coins for her purchases without complaint—very unlike her father who begrudged her every penny. Even after the families had departed for home, Julien had made sure she enjoyed the fair, even after she'd set him up at the mistletoe arch.

She sighed and fingered her braid, watching a star. The night had been magical, almost as if they'd been able to step out of time, able to step away from the past and its mistakes when darkness had fallen. These were the remembrances she treasured most from the day. When the ruse hadn't mattered, she'd leaned against the strength of his chest, and his arms had wrapped about her as the lights came on and the carollers sang.

Then they'd danced. She wrapped her arms about herself in a hug. That had been the most magical by far, his hand in hers, his hand at her waist, his smile, his eyes unguarded as they laughed, enjoying the music, the night and each other, their bodies remembering the ease with which they used to dance together, used to touch.

'It made me reckless.' She looked across the room to the doll. 'It made me want more.' She stifled a yawn and made her way to the bed—perhaps sleep would come after all now that she'd let her mind relive the day. She flopped back on the pillows. 'I shouldn't have pushed him. It's just that he's so handsome and so kind, always thinking of others,' she told the doll. 'I've never known a man like him before.'

In truth, she'd not known him half as well seven years ago as she felt she knew him now. That story he'd told her on the way home about the pickpockets had moved her, but it had also informed her. Here was a man who turned difficulties into opportunities. He offered a hand up instead of a hand out. He inspired her.

'I've done it now, Chrissy.' Aurelia pulled up the covers and turned down the light. 'Just when I'm on the brink of winning my freedom, I've gone and fallen for the one man I can't have, the one man who doesn't want me.'

Except that he had wanted her. He burned for her—his own

words. Both kisses had supported that. She'd heard the ragged desire in his voice tonight even as he'd warned her, denied her. She knew when Julien Lennox was on the verge of breaking. He'd been there tonight and so had she. The only difference was that he had been able to resist the pull between them and, in the last moments of clarity before sleep claimed her, she knew the heartbreaking answer as to why.

Chapter Thirteen

That night she dreamed of him. Of them in the Graftons' rose arbour, of her memory where hands and mouths and feelings need not be constrained, where he whispered his desire at her ear, laughing at his own romantic nonsense while she clung to his broad shoulders, urging him on...

'You are driving me wild, Aurelia.'

There was an edgy rasp to his voice that exhilarated her, that made her want to push the boundaries of their control.

'No, I think it's you *who are driving* me *senseless.'*

She laughed up at him, leaning back on the bench hidden in the bower and drawing him down with her, the pastel-pink skirts of her gown falling back in invitation.

Julien gave a growl, pressing a kiss against the column of her throat as he followed her down, his body coming over her on the bench, covering her with the delicious breadth of his shoulders, surrounding her with the heat and strength of him, the hard proof of his desire pressing against her through the layers of skirts and petticoats. She reached for him, tracing that long length through his evening trousers.

'Did you doubt me?' Julien laughed. 'The proof is in your hand.'

She looked up at him, locking gazes as she gave an exploratory stroke. 'It's amazing.'

She'd never touched a man like this, never seen a man without so much as his jacket off. But with Julien, she wanted so much more than what protocol and manners allowed.

'Am I too bold?' she whispered up at him, half question, half coy flirtation, watching his chocolate eyes go onyx-dark.

'Never too bold. Only honest. You admit your passion, not like these other girls who simper and feign shock.'

He kissed her, long and lingering, his mouth moving down her body to her neck, to the bare expanse of skin shown off by the delicate pink of her decolletage, his hands pushing her skirts further up until she could feel the cool evening air on her thighs, his mouth moving to the silk-stockinged length of her calves, kissing one and then the other, working his way upwards, her breath catching as she realised his destination.

He kissed her inner thigh and paused, hot, dark eyes looking up at her from his intimate crouch, his hair tousled from their efforts. She would hold that image of him in her mind for ever.

'You must tell me if now I am the one who is too bold.'

Even in the throes of desire, his concern was for her.

She gave a wicked smile. 'Be as bold as you like. After all, you're speaking to my father tomorrow.' She gave her hips an upward undulation to encourage him. 'Don't you dare stop now.'

And he didn't, bringing his tongue to bear at her damp seam, at her wet core, his hands gripping hard at her thighs, her own hands tangled in his hair, desperate for an anchor against the sea of sensations he roused in her until those sensations collided in one resounding cataclysm of euphoria that, for a few seconds, splintered through her like lightning through a tree, shocking, electric and powerful.

He was panting, too, as if the giving of such pleasure had its own satisfaction for him as well. For a long while they laid against each other, draped on the bench, her skirts askew and trailing, and there was a peace such as she'd never known, a peace so serene, she didn't want to leave the bower.

She wanted to lie here for ever with the weight of her lover's

head against her body, her hands in his hair. If he wasn't her
lover in truth, he soon would be. As soon as she could man-
age it. She would argue for a short engagement and a special
licence.

'I wonder why some women fear the marriage bed,' she mur-
mured, stroking his hair into order. 'I can hardly wait.'

Julien looked up at her, eyes dreamy with contentment, and
in those eyes she saw her future. She was the luckiest woman
alive to claim this man as her husband.

'Because they are not in love...not like we are.'

It was the last time he would ever looked at her like that...

Aurelia woke slowly, hot and aching as if the dream had
been a fantasy come to life. Her body felt the echoes of it, as
did her mind, perhaps both wanting to cling to the images, the
sensations. To wake meant to give those images and sensations
up, to face the reality she'd fallen asleep to last night—that she
wanted him like that still, but he would never want her enough,
not like that again, and it was her fault.

It wasn't until the maid came in that she noticed how bright
out it was. 'My lady, you're awake, that's good. We'll have to
hurry. You slept a bit late and there's church to get to.' The maid
set down the ewer with warm water for washing and briskly set
about gathering what she'd need for dressing. 'Do you have a
dress in mind, Milady?'

Church. The second Sunday in advent. Peace Sunday. Was
that apropos or simply just ironic given her current circumstance?

'The pink wool will do with the short white mantle of fox
fur and Great-Aunt's pearls.' The same great-aunt who'd left
her the small trust. Pearls and independence. Perhaps today she
needed a reminder of that.

If the pearls were a tangible reminder to herself of what her
real goal was—to live independent of a man's support, to make
her own choices, to no longer have to work in tandem with her
father, to be used by him for his own gains, then perhaps the
soft pink wool would serve as a reminder to Julien of another
pink gown, of another time when he'd felt differently about her.

If she couldn't have peace, he couldn't either. The ghost between them wasn't hers alone. They would have to find a way to exorcise it together.

'This Sunday we light the second candle, the candle of peace,' Reverend Thompson intoned solemnly as an altar boy lit the first and then the second of the four advent candles. 'I urge everyone to consider the promise of Christ's peace for themselves, and for their community against the tumult of the world.' If only it were that easy. She slid an unobtrusive glance at Julien sitting beside her. Was he thinking of peace as well? His face was inscrutable.

There were no secret glances, none of yesterday's warmth. His eyes had lingered on her when she'd come downstairs—perhaps her pink dress had evoked old memories for him as well. He'd not looked her way since, although he'd gallantly seen the ruse through, escorting her to the carriage and to the pew. But there'd been no words. All of his words and smiles had been for others at church, people who congratulated Julien on the first successful days of the fair, people who were excited for the tree lighting next Saturday.

There were women who'd talked to her as well. What a difference a week had made. She'd come to church last week as a stranger, but this week she felt a part of the group, as if this was the beginning of warm friendships. It was irrational, of course, she'd be leaving at the end of the month. When Christmas was over, this would be over. But still, she'd not had such easy friendships before, thanks to Caro Lennox's and Elanora's efforts.

Most women at Moorfields were intimidated by her being a lady. That had been one of her biggest obstacles in starting her school and recruiting students. But here, it had been surprisingly different. Her father's influence had been mitigated, replaced instead by the warm friendliness of the Lennoxes. For a place she'd been dreading, she was now not nearly so eager to leave. *And the man you'd been dreading seeing?* Well, that was complicated and it took the rest of Reverend Thompson's sermon to figure that out.

He raised old feelings, old passions, old wants that threatened to supersede new wants, and the constant reminder that she managed to numb at Moorfields that such fantasies were out of reach. Unless...unless she tossed caution aside and threw herself on Julien's mercy. It was why she'd worn the dress, after all. She was dressed for a reckoning.

That dress was killing him. She was so damned beautiful in pink, especially that shade, like a rosebud, full of innocence and promise. It was easy to forget such things were a lie when she turned that golden head and those blue eyes his way. A winter fairy she'd been in her short white cape in the frost this morning. His heart, traitor that it was, had constricted with unfortunate longing at the sight of her.

Had she worn it on purpose, remembering how much he liked that shade on her? Or because of the memories it might evoke? She'd mentioned the Grafton arbour last night. Was this her idea of torture? Or revenge for him having stopped their kiss? What did she think such a reminder proved for either of them except that he still roused to her?

It had taken a cold ride up top with the coachman to get his senses back in order. He'd barely managed to recover himself from last night's episode before this new assault had been launched. Tristan had not helped matters, sending him knowing glances and smiles all through church that said he knew exactly what was up. Worst of all, that he approved. But Tristan had been away, he didn't know all that lay between him and Aurelia. Perhaps his brother would think differently.

He'd survived church, now he just had to survive the ride home. Family supper would be at Brentham Woods today, but it would be supper—not dinner. Tristan and family would drive over later in the evening. It meant he could escape this afternoon. He would take Benjamin and ride out to check his duck boxes. It would give him time alone to get his thoughts in order, to remember what was real and what was play. The two had become mixed in recent days.

He was nearly free. He'd made short work of changing into breeches and boots when he got home and he had his foot in the stirrup, about to swing up on his big bay, when she cut off his escape.

'Trying the old avoidance tactic again, are we?' Aurelia's dark silhouette stood in the stable doorway, dressed for riding in a dark-blue habit, a crop in her hand.

'I need to check the duck boxes,' he answered coolly, nudging his horse forward, making it clear that she was not invited and she was expected to get out of the way.

'And I need to talk to you. We'll ride out together. I'll be tacked up in no time.' She gestured for a groom.

'I mean to go alone, Aurelia,' he said firmly.

'I mean to go with you. If you leave now, I'll simply follow and run you down.' She gave the crop a whack against her skirts for emphasis. She would do it, too—hound him to the ends of the earth. She was already hounding him in his sleep.

The groom returned with her mare, a saddle over one arm. No, not *her* mare, Julien berated himself. He couldn't think like that, it gave her permanence, a sense of place. Her place was far away in Yorkshire where she couldn't trouble him.

'Thank you, Joseph.' She favoured the head groom with a smile that Julien envied and helped speed the tacking up by slipping on the bridle. She managed the buckles with deft fingers, flashing him a cooler smile than the one she'd given Joseph. 'We don't want to keep the Viscount waiting.' Julien rolled his eyes. Somehow he'd ended up giving her permission to tag along which defeated the entire purpose. Well, he didn't have to happy about it.

Once she was saddled up, Julien kicked his horse into a light trot, making her work for the chance to come alongside him on the trail. He slanted her a look when they were away from the stables. 'What is it that you so desperately need to talk with me about?'

She shot him a look that equalled his in coolness and he felt that they were back where they were a week ago before they'd made their pact: rivals. There was no reason why that should disappoint him. But it did. 'I know why you stopped our kiss last night,' she said with a haughty air as if she were in possession of an important piece of knowledge, some grand secret of the universe.

'What might that be?' He raised a brow to indicate he held only a mild interest in what she thought, although that was hardly the truth. He cared too much for his own peace of mind to ignore what she thought.

'You are carrying a grudge. Which compels me to ask the only question that matters. Will you ever forgive me for London, Julien?'

He huffed, his breath coming out in puffs. She did not know what she asked. 'You say it as if I should forgive you for reneging on an invitation to the theatre or a forgotten dance on a dance card.' He slid her a sideways look. What was she playing at? What new game was afoot? To forgive her was to lay down his last and best piece of armour against her.

'You were the one who refused me. You threw me away for rather superficial reasons given what we'd shared.' Intimacies he would not have initiated with an innocent he didn't intend to marry for one, their hearts—at least his—for another. 'Perhaps there's another question to be asked. *You* rejected *me*. Why do you care if I forgive you or not?'

She slowed her horse. 'Because you're the only man I've ever loved and I can't stand being in a world where you despise me.'

Julien scoffed. He would not be taken in by such twaddle. Those were easy words to say now when there was apparently something she wanted—something more than what he'd already managed to give her. 'You call that love? You had a funny way of showing it.'

'Well, maybe you would, too, if you were raised in my house. We can't all be Lennoxes living the perfect life. Some of us have to fight and scrape for everything we have.'

'You expect me to believe that Lady Aurelia Ripley lives a deprived life?' Julien gave her a stern look that said he didn't find her charge humorous in the least.

'Yes, I do. You've seen my family. Would you have wanted to be raised in that home? What sort of lessons do you think a child would learn there?' Her chin lifted with determination. 'Perhaps if you knew the whole story you would believe it.'

Julien halted his horse at the edge of the meadow where the duck boxes were. He swung down and picketed the horse. They would go the rest of the way on foot. 'All right, you win. We have time as I conduct my observations. Make me believe it.' And with that, he surrendered to the inevitable. Aurelia Ripley was going to have her say.

Chapter Fourteen

To her credit, she delayed until they were seated on a log some distance from the duck boxes and he'd had a chance to pull out his field glasses. Or maybe not. Perhaps she wasn't waiting. Perhaps something else held her tongue: he'd called her bluff and now she had nothing to say. Julien surveyed the field, noting a few brown heads of wood ducks poking up from the boxes. He reached for his field book and jotted a few notes about the numbers. Still, she remained silent and stoic beside him on the log.

He raised the field glasses again and said drily, 'For a woman who insisted on talking, you've suddenly become quiet.'

She slid him one of her smug looks. 'I am waiting for you to recognise your error.'

'*My* error?' He chuckled at her audacity. 'You manoeuvred into coming with me and then begged for a chance to talk.'

'*Begged* might be too strong of a word,' she countered. 'I asked you a question—why won't you forgive me? I came because we should talk about what really happened seven years ago and why. You see, it's not that I need to talk, but that we need to talk and listen.' She reached for his hand, forcing him to put down the field glasses and face her. 'Don't you think we deserve a second chance?'

He said nothing. This was exactly the conversation he'd

hoped to avoid, the very reason why he'd given her a wide berth in London these past years. If they spent enough time together, they'd have to talk about it, eventually. Talking about it meant reliving it. Apparently ten days of enforced proximity was the required amount of time that would cause the rather toxic topic to surface. 'Don't freeze me, Julien,' she admonished at his silence.

'I'm not freezing you, Aurelia. It's just that I don't see how talking about it does any good.' He set her hand aside and raised his field glasses again. It had been a bad idea to let her come. He should have anticipated *this* was what she wanted to discuss. 'The past is finished and gone.' He borrowed from one of Reverend Thompson's favourite lines, ironically for prayers of atonement.

'Everything has become fresh and new?' she concluded for him. She'd heard the line, too. 'But it hasn't, has it? You carry the past, our past, around with you all the time.'

'*Finished* doesn't require it being forgotten.' He set aside the field glasses and jotted another note, pressing too hard on the page. His pencil broke. He nearly swore beneath his breath, but caught himself just in time.

'It's all right, Julien.' She laughed at his restraint. 'You can curse in my presence.' She reached for the field glasses. 'Where did you get these?' She held them up, experimenting with them. 'They're like opera glasses, only bigger and sturdier.' She wrinkled her nose. 'Everything's blurry.'

'I had them sent from Vienna.' He watched her fumble with them for a moment before giving in to the urge to help. 'Here, hold them to your eyes like this.' He rose and knelt behind her as he offered instruction, his hands guiding hers into position. That was a mistake. Even with the barriers of gloves and outerwear, he loved touching her. 'Then, adjust them like this. The bridge is flexible.' He made the motion. 'Is that better?'

'Yes, much better. I can see the ducks and their heads peeping up from the boxes.' There was a natural enthusiasm to her voice, the thrill of success, perhaps. 'Oh, what wonderful things these field glasses are.' She stretched out a hand and laughed.

'It feels like I could touch the ducks and yet we must be several hundred feet away.'

'Any closer and we'd scare them. But the glasses make it possible to do elaborate observations.' He guided her hands to move the field glasses around the meadow, his voice low and quiet at her ear out of necessity for their surroundings, but also because he liked the intimacy, the privacy of it, too much. 'Do you see it, at the other end of the meadow, the deer?'

He heard her breath catch as she breathed, 'Yes, he's magnificent.' Then in the next moment, she turned into him, her face alive with worry, one hand clutching his coat. 'Julien, you won't hunt him will you? You won't kill him? You said you didn't hunt ducks for sport.' There was hope in her eyes that that moratorium extended to deer.

Her worry startled him, so intent and genuine it was. Out of a reflex to comfort, he covered her hand with his. 'No, of course not, not unless the deer population has run amok in Brentham Woods.' He gave a chuckle. Part of good land stewardship was living in harmony with all who shared the land: farmers, gentlemen and the animals. 'I do ride out occasionally and take tallies of the animals so we can keep track of the herds. But to be honest, when there is a surplus of deer, hunting does fill the village larders with a needed meat source and ensure that people eat through the winter.'

'It's just that he's so majestic.' She smiled and blushed, perhaps belatedly embarrassed by her outburst. He should have released her, should have gone back to sitting on his section of the log. He should not have said the first thing that came to his mind. But he did.

'Of course. You have a good heart, Aurelia, a soft heart.' It was a truth that had always been on display. In London, she'd accompanied her mother to charity meetings although he'd not understood the motives for that as he did now. It was certainly a truth that had been in evidence during her visit here—her efforts in joining the ladies' committees to ensure everyone had a Christmas and in the kindness she showed young Alex and Violet. But it was also a truth that made him vulnerable, that suggested he noticed, that he thought about such things.

Something shifted in her eyes before she cast them downwards, modest at his praise. 'I do, Julien, which is why your forgiveness matters to me.' She lifted her gaze again. 'I hate that I hurt you. I hate that you have avoided me ever since. I hate that when you look at me all the love you once professed for me has entirely disappeared. For someone who doesn't like to hate, that's a lot of hate. I do despise what I became when I hurt you.'

Her earnestness was reflected in her blue eyes, in the tightness of her grip where she held his hand. It was a potent combination that challenged the logic of his mind and the armour, with which he'd protected himself for years. He would not, could not, let those protections be washed away by the sea of her blue eyes in a matter of minutes.

Yet a large part of him wouldn't mind if that happened. Things would be so much easier if the little realities that had seeped through the boundaries of the ruse could be pursued, could be allowed to take root, could be believed. The most important one of all being that he could trust his feelings for her and that he could trust her feelings for him. Once it had been beautiful between them. Did the possibility exist that it could be beautiful again? Did he dare test it?

She gripped his hand more tightly. For his attention or for her courage? Confession was never easy. 'I was scared, Julien. Too scared to do what loving you required. I was weak while you were strong. I could not stand up for myself or stand up *to* my father.' Her eyes darkened with sadness and regret. 'So, I chose hurting you instead. I chose failing you, failing us. I was the lowest of cowards.'

He was silent for a long while. What did he say to that? He supposed it depended on what he thought of it. Did he think it was true? She was looking for absolution. She'd made that plain from the start. She wanted him to forgive her. But she also wanted something more. 'You are seeking empathy. Understanding,' he warned. Forgiveness *and* acceptance. It was a tall ask and yet he might want or need the same.

'Can you give me that? Do I need to beg, Julien? To ask you to put yourself in the position of an eighteen-year-old girl who'd never been beyond Moorfields until that year? A girl who'd been groomed by her parents to make an advantageous match upon pain of familial disappointment? Everything had been so carefully calculated—the early arrival that November in London to "practise" upon society at Christmas fairs and charity balls.'

He'd met her at the Duchess of Cowden's November charity ball. She'd been fresh and exuberant, laughing, full of life. Uncomplicated. Or so he'd thought. 'Then, to take the winter among the full-time politicians who never leave the city so that I'd make no mistake come spring.' She furrowed her brow, pleading with him for understanding. 'The pressure was immense. I was to be one of the Season's Diamonds, to make an extraordinary match.'

Bankers' sons with aspirations were not extraordinary matches for daughters of earls. 'I had known you only seven months when you proposed.'

Julien gave a dismissive snort. 'People marry after having known one another for less time. The Season itself is only twelve weeks. Seven months is a lifetime by comparison. You say you want understanding, but I want some, too. I laid my heart at your feet. We had an understanding based on what I thought were real, deep and enduring feelings. You loved me when it was easy but not when it was hard, not when it required sacrifice. That showed your true colours.'

Flames fired in her eyes. 'You were asking me to choose between a man I'd known seven months and my family.' She let go of his hand and stepped back from him. 'Listen to how that sounds, Julien. Would you have given up your family for me?' She made a wild, wide gesture with her arm. 'Of course, you'd never have to make such a decision. Your family is perfect. But I did have to make that decision. I had nothing but my family. I'd not received my great-aunt's trust, nothing to support me if I lost them.'

'You had me,' Julien interrupted, his own old anger heating him.

'I didn't know about all of this, about Brentham Woods, about your family, about Hemsford.'

'That's why it's called a leap of faith, Aurelia,' he snapped with equal intensity. 'When two people love each other they step into the unknown together with trust that they will see each other through.' He paused before adding, 'Of course, I didn't have the title then. That seemed to matter a great deal, although you didn't bother to mention it in seven months of courting.'

'It mattered to my father, not to me,' she corrected. 'He said no daughter of his would marry a commoner.'

'Yes, I know. He told me that as well,' Julien said acerbically. 'I told him it wasn't his decision to make, that it was yours. I was that sure of you. I've never been so wrong in my life.'

'Is that what hurts? That I refused you or that you were wrong? The great Julien Lennox, who never made a financial misstep, who never guessed wrong on the Exchange, was wrong about a woman.'

Good heavens, the woman didn't fight fair. 'Yes, I felt like a fool. But what hurt the most was that you didn't trust me,' Julien said quietly. 'It's what still hurts when I look at you, when I think about our ruse and how it makes me feel. I can't trust those feelings because now *I* can't trust *you*.'

He stuffed the field glasses into their leather case. It was time to head back. Tristan and family would be arriving shortly. 'We've aired our feelings. I hope you got what you came for,' he said shortly, turning his back to her as he headed to the horses picketed in the little copse.

'I damn well didn't get what I wanted!' she called after him, her voice loud with anger and rife with frustration. She was beside him in five strides, running to catch up to him, grabbing his arm and yanking him to a standstill. 'I came for you, Julien. I came out here for *you*, to fight for *you*!' Her arms were about his neck, and her mouth pressed to his, forceful, full of hunger and his own hunger answered, roughly, completely.

This, *this* was what she craved, to be devoured by him, to break him out of his defences and protections, to feel him against her, alive and throbbing with real and overwhelming emotion: hunger, anger, want and need, and the truth that despite what he thought he knew of her, despite the hurt in the past, he still hoped. For what he still hoped didn't matter in the moment. It mattered only that hope flickered there. That she still had a chance to right the wrongs.

A sob caught in her throat, tears wet her cheeks, chilly in the late-afternoon cold. His thumbs were at her cheeks, stroking away the wetness and she let the words spill out, searching his dark eyes. 'My father demanded I refuse you. I told him I wouldn't, that I wanted to marry you.' She'd mounted a rebellion, but it hadn't lasted long. 'But I had nothing to defend my position with, no leverage, no threat that would cause him to waver, and he had everything. He said I'd never see my mother again. He wouldn't allow his wife to associate with commoners.'

She felt her lip tremble as the horror of the threats came back to her. 'He said he'd disown me, that I'd be dead to him, that he'd shoot Elspeth since she might as well be dead, too, if her rider was dead. Julien, I was afraid to stand up to him because others would suffer. I had to choose who suffered.'

Julien's eyes went impossibly dark. 'It wasn't really a choice. To choose between two impossible situations?' His voice was a low growl, the anger coursing through him was alive and pulsing, but it was not anger directed at her. 'And the bastard wields those cards often and still.' Julien let out a harsh breath and she felt a type of comfort in the shield of his anger. For once, someone was on her side, for once, she had a champion.

'Tell me you at least understand why I did it? No one was going to die for me. I could not have lived with that. I could not have loved you, or committed to a marriage without being burdened by inescapable guilt knowing what the cost of that love had been.' This had been the rock of logic upon which she'd made her decision. She could not have lived with herself knowing others had suffered for her happiness. The dead could not be brought back to life.

Julien lifted her hand to his lips, kissing her gloved knuckles with slow tenderness between careful words. 'Sacrifice. Selflessness. These are not the acts of a coward. You were wrong about that earlier.' His dark brows furrowed. 'All these years, I've been hurting, but you have been hurting as well. I blamed you for my hurt. I condemned your motives for refusing me. I was committed to seeing you in the worst possible light because you stood in your father's shadow and everyone knows apples don't fall far from the tree. Now I am the one seeking forgiveness.'

She shook her head. 'You mustn't be hard on yourself. How could you have known? There was evidence a-plenty to support your position.'

'You were brave.'

'My bravery hurt you.'

'I let my hurt be more important than your need. All this time I have left you to fight that monster alone.'

This was more than she'd expected. She'd not come out here seeking his penitence, only his understanding. For once, she was overwhelmed, out of words. What was there to say and yet there was so much perhaps *to* say. Perhaps he was overwhelmed, too. It was a long while before they moved, before they spoke, impervious to all else around them except each other.

'Julien,' she whispered at last, a flake fluttering from the darkening sky. 'It's snowing.' He turned his dark eyes skywards, a smile curving on his lips. 'Quick, Julien, make a snowflake wish.' She closed her eyes and sent a wish heavenwards. 'What did you wish for?' she asked when she opened them.

Julien tucked her arm through his as they sought the horses, his voice full of regret. 'I wished that years ago you'd come to me and we could have solved the problem together instead of letting someone else's threats throw it all away for us.' He gave a rueful smile. 'What did you wish for?'

'I wished things could be different between us now, that we might have a second chance.'

They reached the horses and he helped her mount, fussing overlong with the stirrup of her side-saddle. 'Do you think wishes come true, Aurelia?'

She cocked her head and looked down at him with a smile. ''Tis the season for it.'

As they rode the trail home to Brentham Woods, side by side, sneaking careful glances at each other, she thought that perhaps today the candle of peace did burn a little brighter within her, after all, right alongside the candle of hope. Never mind that having peace was not the same as having a solution or knowing what came next. For the moment, peace and hope were enough. All else could follow.

Chapter Fifteen

'I do not know what comes next. I can solve the man's money problems, but I can't solve *him*. Short of duelling, at least. The man's an evil bastard.' Anger hummed in Julien anew as he recounted his afternoon to Tristan.

They were alone at last, after a long Sunday supper that seemed to go on for ages, after playing with Alex and after hours of watching Aurelia with his family. He had minded none of these, begrudged his family not one minute of his time, but each moment with her, each glance in her direction had indeed added to the complexity of his problem—his *new* problem— Aurelia's wish: a second chance. He wanted desperately to sort through his thoughts with his brother, his best friend.

'I can't say I am surprised. You've been distracted all night.' Tristan swirled the brandy in the snifter, a little smile teasing at his mouth. 'I would say my brother has fallen in love at last, but I don't think that's quite the truth, despite what you led me to believe when I was courting Elanora and seeking your advice. You told me you'd never been in love. But I think that's not true. You've fallen before and for her.'

For a moment the revelation stunned Julien. How had Tristan known? Then he rolled his eyes and laughed. 'Father told you? That man is a gossip.'

Tristan sat back in his chair, stretching his legs out and resting his heels before the fire. 'Why didn't you tell me yourself?'

'It was in the past, it was embarrassing. She refused me outright, made me believe everything we'd shared was a game, a sham to her while I'd been wearing my heart on my sleeve. It's nothing a man brags about. At the time, I didn't think it was love in retrospect, just infatuated, misguided feelings, considering how it ended. But now I know differently and it's more confusing than ever.'

'Do you, though? Know differently? You believe her?' Tristan asked, the query catching Julien by surprise.

'Why, yes,' Julien said slowly, not understanding the import of that until the words were required of him that he had indeed decided to believe her, that he had accepted what she'd shared at the duck boxes as truth. He shifted in his seat to watch Tristan's face. 'Don't you? I thought you liked her.' All those nudging glances Tristan had been throwing at him at church today certainly suggested as much.

'I do like her, at least I like the person I met here. She's delightful with the children, she gets on with Elanora splendidly. She's fit right in with the town ladies and joined their committees, thrown herself into Christmas work whole-heartedly. She's pretty.' Tristan paused his litany of Aurelia's traits long enough to take a swallow. 'There wasn't a young man in church today who could take his eyes off that pink dress and golden curls. Does it bother you how seamlessly she fits in? How easy it is to imagine her as a future sister-in-law or permanent member of the Sunday supper table?' Tristan sighed. 'I do like her, but I like you more. I don't want you hurt again. When we're in the throes of love we can't think. When that was me, you thought for me. You helped clear the way. Now, I will do the same for you.'

Tristan's scepticism surprised him. Tristan was always positive, always looked for the best in everyone and in every situation. He shot his brother a long look, his brother's questions taking the sharp, euphoric edge off his own elation. 'Why do you think she'd lie this time? What would she gain?' In his mind there was no reason for it. In fact, it was an about-face on the freedom she'd contracted the ruse with him to protect.

Tristan gave a shrug. 'She's here because she is her father's tool, as she has always been.' Julien's fist clenched at his brother's choice of words. Tristan gave a friendly laugh. 'I can see you don't like my framing, but that's my job. To help you see beyond what you want to see.'

'What do I want to see, Tristan?' Julien sighed, feeling suddenly weary from the mental gymnastics he'd been doing all day, his mind turning endless cartwheels as he tried to sort through the revelations and realities.

'You want her love to be real. You want to trust her. You want to claim the life you once imagined you'd have with her. It's not so very hard to know.' Tristan set his glass aside and leaned forward.

'You want a family, a home of your own. You're hungry for it. I see it in your eyes when you play with Alex, when you hold Violet. They are wonderful things to want, Brother. They have changed my life, cured my wanderlust. But only because of the woman I have beside me. The happiness you want will not follow if you cannot trust her or if she insists on remaining tied to her family. If she's to be believed, they're the root of her problems. Marriage won't solve that. But it may intensify it.'

Julien nodded. He'd thought of that. Before, he'd not known the depths of the Earl's treachery, or his avarice, only that he was a man with a certain conceit as many aristocrats were. But now, Holme was even less appealing as a father-in-law.

He could imagine scenarios where Aurelia was caught between the two of them just as she had been before. As before, there would be no good choice for her, or even *a* choice at all. As his wife, she would be obliged to choose him. 'No, marriage exacerbates certain problems, not solves them.' He gave a brief smile. 'But I am not sure we're there yet. Marriage seems a bit of a jump from merely exploring the possibilities of a second chance.'

Tristan gave him a sharp look. 'What else is there but marriage? What is the point of a second chance if not to get back to where you once left things, which was on the way to the altar?'

'I'm just saying we don't have to run there. We can walk. Perhaps last time we were too quick.' Indeed, he felt he'd learned more about her in the last ten days than he had in the months he courted her in London.

Assuming the face she'd showed him here at Brentham Woods was real.

Tristan finished his drink and rose. 'I promised Father I'd check the foot on that new gelding he's brought in before we left and it's getting late. The children will be tired.' He grinned. 'Nothing like a cranky toddler in an enclosed coach.' But Julien knew his brother wouldn't trade it for the world and he envied him, even the crying child.

Julien raised his glass in salute. 'Thank you for the advice and the caution, I do appreciate it. Would you mind if I said goodbye here? I want to sit a while longer with my thoughts.'

'I'll make your excuses, Brother.' Tristan smiled and clapped him on the shoulder in understanding. 'Enjoy your reprieve.'

Her father had been pleased with yesterday's outing, understanding it in a far different light than how Aurelia had intended it. But since it had resulted in a reprieve from his nightly visits and harangues as to why the Viscount had not proposed, she'd not bothered to argue his assumptions. She'd enjoyed the quiet of her room, the time for reflection and the time to savour the day, the dinner.

She smiled to herself as she dressed for going into town for the Monday committee meeting. She was coming to enjoy those Sunday dinners. She'd held Violet on her lap, giving Elanora a chance to eat with both hands, and she'd not missed the subtle looks that had passed between her mother and Julien's, the stories in those glances, those hopes. Perhaps both mothers' hopes were honest and heartfelt, matching the hopes she carried in her own heart. She was certain Caro Lennox's were. It was harder to tell with her own mother, who walked such a thin line between her daughter and her husband that her own wants had long since been lost.

Hopes was a generous word for it. Daydreams more like it. Aurelia chided herself for such foolishness as she rifled through her wardrobe, looking for her green winter bonnet. It would be better to focus her thoughts on today's committee meeting. They were going to finalise the Christmas baskets. She had her stack of embroidered handkerchiefs packed and ready to go. Elanora was discussing the pantomime today as well. It was going to be a busy meeting. She was looking forward to it.

Perhaps she'd coax a lunch at the Red Rose Inn from Julien afterwards if he wasn't too busy with arrangements for the tree lighting at the end of the week. She was already planning what she'd wear: the green-velvet ensemble. She'd thought to save it for Christmas Eve, but she'd just have to wear it twice. It seemed perfect for the upcoming occasion.

More daydreams. She couldn't think any further than the moment because she had no answers. What did happen after Christmas? What did a second chance look like? Lead to? Kisses and another farewell? More than kisses? Perhaps that was for her to decide, to show Julien she trusted him, that she was ready for this relationship this time, that she would choose him. For what? For now? For ever? Those considerations came with complications.

Would he want her for ever? Did she dare claim him for ever, knowing that her family was her greatest liability? Did she dare to claim his love should it be offered and shackle him not just to her, but by association to her father? But surely the loan arrangement already associated him with her father. However, that was a legal agreement which could be completed or terminated. Marriage not so much.

She settled her green bonnet on her head as her mother entered without knocking and in her usual state of half-excitement and half-anxiety, always on the brink of anticipating something going wrong. 'Are you ready? The Viscount has just pulled up with the gig.' Her mother adjusted the bow of her bonnet. 'There, I think it's more fetching off to the side. You look like a picture of the season in your green and gold.' She was wearing the Christmas tartan again.

'The Viscount is taken with you,' she said softly. 'He couldn't keep his eyes off you at supper last night. His thoughts were clear watching you with his niece.' She leaned near. 'Your father thought it a stroke of genius to offer to take the babe. For me, I thought it was kind. And I am sure, for the Viscount, it was a peek into the future. He has a title now, he must be thinking about the succession, an heir. He's thirty-eight. It's high time he settled down.'

Never mind, Aurelia thought, he could have settled down at thirty-one if she could have managed it. That particular idea was tinged with sadness. What a waste of time. Seven years suddenly seemed an eternity.

'Do you think we might have a Christmas Eve proposal?' her mother asked softly, but Aurelia knew she wasn't asking for herself.

'Father has sent you to spy,' she scolded. 'He knows I won't give him an answer, although my answer would be the same as it was before. I did not come here to snare a proposal from Julien Lennox. I said only that I would charm him to help Father get the loan.'

Her mother fussed with the folds of her mantle, although it didn't need adjusting. 'But this seems quite apart from that, as if you and the Viscount have found your footing with each other again. You once held him in high esteem and he once wanted to marry you. Is it so hard to believe he might entertain those thoughts again?'

'We've changed. We're different people now. Perhaps we no longer suit as we once might have.' Or suit even better, came the errant, rather unhelpful thought. Knowing Julien had changed her, empowered her to take on her own work in the years that had passed. As a result, they had far more in common now than they'd had in the beginning. There was something more to build their marriage on than passion.

'Still, should things evolve and he proposes, his suit would not go amiss this time.' Her mother smiled and stepped back, having delivered what Aurelia had no doubt was her father's latest dictate, not her mother's own thoughts on the matter.

She stared at her mother, looking deep into her eyes, searching for some sign that *she* was still in there somewhere, that she wasn't entirely lost. She loved her mother and pitied her, that this was what her life had come to: a messenger between her headstrong, self-centred husband and her stubborn daughter. If her mother was lost, perhaps that was Aurelia's fault, too.

Aurelia took her mother's hand. 'If I were to marry, Mother, would you come live with us?' Perhaps if she could get her away. Not a divorce, of course, her father would never allow it and the legalities were too time consuming and costly. But she could fabricate excuses to need her mother, especially if she lived far from Moorfields. She'd need help setting up house. With luck, she'd need help navigating a first pregnancy and then help with the new baby. Her mother would like being an active, involved grandmother. Out here in the country there would be no one to see or judge like in London. Her father might even discover he liked the arrangement.

The offer seemed to shock her mother. 'Well, I don't know. Newlyweds need time on their own,' she prevaricated.

Aurelia squeezed her mother's hand. 'Just think about it. I don't even have a proposal yet.' Perhaps there was no sense in getting any hopes up over hypotheticals. Did she want to marry? It would mean the end of the freedom she'd spent the last five years imagining for herself. That was not a dream set idly aside, yet it paled in comparison to the dream of Julien, of life in Hemsford Village.

Downstairs, Julien was waiting patiently. When they tooled the gig down the drive and out on to the road leading to the village, she gave him a swift peck on the cheek.

'What was that for?' he asked, startled.

'That's because we don't have to pretend any more.' She gave a smug smile as the enormity of that settled on her. They didn't have to pretend to like each other, because they did. Perhaps they'd never stopped the liking. Perhaps it had just been buried beneath the weight of the roles the world made them play. 'And because I want to persuade you to take me to lunch at the Red Rose after the ladies' meeting.' She'd not realised how light she felt, the weight that had been lifted after yesterday. Did he feel the same? Or had their conversation added to his heaviness?

He made an exaggerated show of considering it and she thought perhaps the former was true. 'Here's my counter. Yes, to lunch. No to the Red Rose Inn. I have a better idea. I'll ask Peter at the Red Rose to pack a picnic hamper and we'll eat out at my estate, the one the architect discussed last week. He'll be here tomorrow and I haven't made one single decision that he asked for.'

She offered her own mock consideration. 'And ice skating?' It had snowed last night. Although the snow hadn't stuck to the ground, it was still cold. Cold enough to sustain a frozen pond.

'We can ice skate, if the ice is thick enough,' he acceded.

'Then I accept.' She paused. 'But I think it best we keep it to ourselves. I haven't told my father about the estate. If he were to know you were setting up house, or that you were consulting me... Well, you know how it would look to him.'

'Just between us, then.' Julien gave a thin smile she couldn't quite decipher, although she could guess. She answered him by snuggling close on the bench seat. For real. A Rubicon of sorts had been crossed. The ruse was over. Reality had begun. She'd got her wish. The rest was up to them to make the most of it however they could for as long as they could.

Chapter Sixteen

Julien's new home was beautiful, or at least it would be once the work was done. There was ivy to clear from the walls and the outer façade could use a good wash to do away with the moss and weather. But even in the grey light of winter, the potential of the house was evident to Aurelia. 'It's enormous and so stately. Whatever will you do with a house this size?' Aurelia looked about, trying to take it all in from the drive. As she dismounted, a young groom ran up to take the horses. She tossed Julien a smile. 'You already have staff on hand? I'm impressed.'

'I think it's necessary given the amount of workers that will be out here shortly. I will be spending more time here as that work progresses, and I imagine Mr Floyd will need a few overnight stays to oversee his work as well on occasion.'

Aurelia nodded. That was likely all true, but she saw beyond that. He simply failed to mention it also gave a few more people work before Christmas, which was also true *and* kindhearted of him.

'One of the things I liked about this house was that it was built using local resources, not just local labour.' Julien gestured to the Georgian façade and the rounded vestibule that stood over the front entrance. 'The sandstone was all quarried at West Hoathly and inside you'll see that the wood is local timber as well. The house itself isn't terribly old as houses go,' he explained, ushering her under the roof of the vestibule as the drops of hard rain began to fall, part-rain, part-sleet. That would put paid to the idea of ice-skating later.

'It was built after the wars by one of Robert Adam's protégés. The owner was an eccentric who wanted to embrace the Sussex lifestyle, which is a nice way of saying he wanted to observe smuggling, race thoroughbreds and hobnob with the Duke of Richmond at Goodwood. When it turned out the smuggling trade died out after the war and the Duke of Richmond wasn't interested in his horses, the man moved back to London, deciding town life was more his style.

"That was ten years ago. Since then, the previous owner has let the property at varying times, enjoying the rental income it provides. But I finally convinced him to sell this autumn.' The last was said with undisguised pride. As well it should be. Homes like this were rare finds outside of family inheritances.

Julien held the carved oak door for her to step inside to the marbled hall with its soaring ceiling and sweeping staircase off to the right side. 'Sussex marble?' she queried, more to tease him than anything else. The marble at Moorfields had been imported from Italy as had the marble at Holme House in London.

'Yes, Sussex marble from Petworth.' Julien's answer surprised her. 'And English oak for the banister.' Which his new housekeeper apparently kept polished and glistening religiously.

'It's beautiful, Julien,' she said, her words picking up an echo.

'And empty. That's where you come in. I have rooms that need filling. The place did come with some furnishings,' he told her, leading the way to the public drawing room on the ground floor. 'Although the owner took much of it back to London with him. Mother has kindly loaned me spare dish sets and things like that until I have the place settled to my satisfaction.' He opened the drawing room's double doors and Aurelia could only stare at what was inside, well aware that Julien's gaze was on her, watching for a response. What did one say to *this*?

Julien spoke first, perhaps to give her permission to say the obvious. 'As you might be surmising, the things left behind are useful but not to my taste.' That was a gracious way of putting it.

'Not to *anyone's* taste that I know of,' Aurelia responded without thinking and then covered her mouth. 'That was mean. I should not have said that out loud.'

'It's truthful. It's hideous, isn't it?' Julien sighed,

'Well, thank goodness the owner didn't leave too much behind then,' she said, and they laughed together. It felt good to laugh with him, *not* because it reminded her of old times, but because it was the beginning of new times. This was who they were now, in the present: two people enjoying each other's company.

They walked the perimeter of the room, Julien taking notes as she dictated. 'I think the problem with the room is that every piece is talking at once; the turquoise-tangerine sofa, the bright orange tall-backed chairs, the patterned vases on the mantel, the multi-coloured stripe and floral wallpaper—all of them want to be noticed when all we really need is one bright item to build the room around if you wanted to keep a few pieces.'

Julien shook his head. 'I don't want to keep any of it, at least not for this room. I am not sure bright, exciting colours are an accurate extension of me. You said earlier that you thought the exterior of the home was stately. That's the message I would like to send with the interior public rooms as well.'

'Warm creams then, or cool blues and greys,' she suggested, studying him anew. 'Creams might be more versatile in that they can be both masculine and feminine in tone and I think they're more economical because they can adapt. Should you wish to change the furniture or carpets, many things complement cream wallpaper.' She was already imagining the walls covered in cream on cream, with peach-and-cream or blue-and-cream Thomas Whitty rugs on the floor, the spacious room accommodating three different clusters of seating, a pianoforte on one wall for musical evenings, Sussex landscapes on the walls evoking scenes of the seasons and Julien's love of the region.

'You've a good eye,' Julien complimented, listening intently to her ideas. 'When you talk, I can see the room come alive. Here's where Floyd wants to put the sliding doors between the drawing room and the dining room.'

They went from room to room, Aurelia designing with her

words, Julien writing furiously as the house came to life between them. She saw the office where Floyd had suggested the French doors. 'The doors are a good choice.' She smiled over her shoulder at Julien.

'There isn't much to do to this room.' She looked around, taking in an oak desk of a suitable size for a businessman like Julien who would want to work from home and the empty built-in oak bookcases. 'You'll have to fill those, of course,' she teased. 'Perhaps I would add a new carpet, something in deep greens to complement the outdoors beyond.'

She trailed her fingertips over the surface of the desk. 'I can see you here, Julien, working. Planning.' She gave a sigh. Perhaps this would be the space she'd imagine him in when all this was over and she was gone. 'You can look out over your gardens. You'll have a lovely view. I envy you a room like this. How wonderful it must be to have a private place that is yours alone.'

'Surely you must have a similar place at Moorfields.' Julien came to her, slipping his fingers between hers. Did he know how much she loved it when he was the initiating contact? Did he guess she took it as a sign of togetherness, of the walls between them coming down? Did he mean it that way?

She shook her head. 'I have my chamber, but my parents make a habit of disturbing me regularly there without warning if there's something they need. In a big house like Moorfields there's always a servant nearby. Being unobtrusive, of course. But between unobtrusive servants and intrusive parents one is seldom alone.' She smiled. 'It was one of the first things I noticed at Brentham Woods. Your mother has her own space where she keeps her own books, apart from the library. She has a space for her own things, a place where she conducts her own work. It gives her a voice. I like the idea so much I think I might try to set a space up similar to it for my mother.' Perhaps having her own space would translate into having her own thoughts, to rediscovering herself.

Julien gave a little smile, his dark eyes soft. 'You care for your mother very much.'

'She is all I have, really, but that doesn't mean it's not complicated. She is always standing between my father and I, trying to make peace, which means I can't always count on her to take my side.' In fact, almost never. She was always begging for a compromise on Aurelia's part. 'It's not like your family, Julien. When I see you and your brother together, I wonder what it would have been like to have a sibling, to have a best friend like you have in Tristan.'

'It must have been hard growing up alone.' Julien raised her hand to his lips, kissing her finger tips. Perhaps it was the nearness of him, the heat of his body, the softness of his eyes, the hope that they might have a second chance, that encouraged her. She whispered her secret without thought.

'I had a brother once.' She had shared space with him for nine months in the womb—nine months with their little souls suspended together between heaven and earth. Julien's gaze fixed on her and she knew she'd surprised him.

Of all the things she could have told him here in the quiet of the office, he'd not expected that. He'd done his research thoroughly on Holme as part of the loan process and that had never featured in his paperwork. 'I'd never heard, I never knew,' he offered solemnly, his mind rife with questions, but his heart was attuned to the sadness, the thoughtfulness in her eyes.

'No one knows outside of Moorfields,' she said quietly. 'We were twins. He died shortly after birth. He was born second. He was smaller, not as strong. He couldn't get enough air.' It was a factual recitation of events she'd no doubt been told over the years by her parents, perhaps in answer to a young girl's question about her own origin story, or perhaps in answer to the question 'when am I getting a baby brother or sister?' Alex had asked Tristan and Elanora that question not long before Violet had come into being. Julien remembered laughing about it when Tristan told him Alex had given him his 'marching orders,' he'd best get busy on a sibling. But this was not a funny story. Who would tell a child such a tragic tale?

The answer came too swift. Someone who wanted leverage, pitiful as it was, over a child. Julien would not put it past the Earl. Of course, the story could be told delicately, but he did not think that would have been case with Holme. 'I am torn about the wisdom of telling a child such a thing,' Julien confessed.

Anger mixed with the sadness in her eyes and she looked down, focused on her hand where it worried the carved edge of the desk. 'My father felt I should know it was my fault. My fault his heir died. My fault that my mother could not have more children. One must understand their place, one must understand all that has been sacrificed for them so that one can give obedience in equal measure to that sacrifice.' Despite the anger, her voice trembled. 'I have tried, I really have, to pay that debt, to close that gap, to make up for it.'

He had never seen her so vulnerable. Julien's own anger surged in response, his desire to protect, to care for those who were in need erupting. He wrapped her in his arms and held her close as if his body could be a shield against years of hurt and guilt, against the emotion he knew she was feeling.

'It's not your fault. It could never have been your fault, not your debt to pay,' he whispered against the softness of her hair. Surely her mother had told her that at the least. But if she had, it had carried no weight, overridden by a father who felt the universe had played a cruel trick on him, giving him a son and then taking the son away.

She was crying softly against his coat, her head buried in his shoulder, arms wrapped about him, her hands clutching his back. He saw much now that he hadn't seen before, understood more. Dear Lord, what it must have been like growing up in Holme's home, carrying the knowledge that you had lived while your sibling had died and knowing that your father blamed you personally for something that had been a matter of luck and fate.

What it must be like still to know that the debt for the sin could never be erased and having payment constantly exacted often and arbitrarily. Julien could imagine how those conversations went. He could hear in his head Holme's loud, angry voice threatening his daughter all those years ago.

Refuse Lennox or I will forbid you your mother and I will kill your horse as you killed my son, so that you will know what it is like to go on without the thing you want most.

Of course she'd turned down his proposal under those conditions. Of course she'd dared not run away, although she might have wanted to. Marriage to him would be a physical escape, but with a price too high and a mental anguish she'd never outrun. Such a marriage would have been doomed before it ever began. Her father had known that. He'd known from the beginning he'd win either way. His real victories were about exerting control, about manipulating people, starting with his wife and his daughter and rippling out from there. The man was a bastard of the highest order.

'Your father must be stopped,' Julien whispered. 'He can't go around terrorising people, intimidating them like that.' With something as simple as words. Julien might control the man's money for now, but he couldn't control what came out of the man's mouth, at least not directly.

She lifted her head and laughed up at him, her tears drying on her cheeks. 'Oh, Julien, you're always looking to save the world.'

'Right now, I'd settle for just saving you.' He meant it. The sight of her tears and the reason for them undid him, it did things to his heart, to his head, that made it hard to think, hard to breathe. He wanted to fix this for her. Nothing else mattered.

She gave a tiny shake of her head. 'I don't want to be pitied, Julien.'

He kissed the top of her head. 'I wouldn't call it pity, Aurelia,' he said quietly, although he dare not name what he would call it out loud. 'I *can* feed you though,' he cajoled, trying to change the tenor of the moment. 'We've done good work, redecorating the rooms. I think we deserve some sustenance.' With that, he took her hand in his and led her out of the room to the kitchen where the groom had left the hamper on the worktable. 'Do you mind eating here?' he asked, unpacking the luncheon.

'Not at all.' To prove it, she moved about the space, pulling out dishes and utensils, setting places for them at one end of the worktable. 'I've been down baking in your mother's kitchen. Did you know? Nothing to rival Manning's, of course, but breads and biscuits that will keep for the Christmas baskets.'

Julien chuckled. 'I'd heard a rumour. Smelled a rumour, more like it.' He sat and watched her finish. The sight of her puttering around the kitchen pleased him, settled him, not that a viscount's wife would spend much time working in a kitchen. Maybe his would. He allowed himself the luxury of that thought. He'd allowed himself the luxury of several similar thoughts today.

Walking through the rooms of his house, listening to her bring them to life, had been a potent elixir to swallow and one he hadn't choked on. It was easy to picture her here, hosting evenings in the cream-on-cream papered drawing room, entertaining from the piano she'd place against the inner wall. She fit effortlessly into the spaces she'd brought to life today and effortlessly into the pictures in his mind as if she was meant to be there, as if perhaps she'd never left, but had simply lingered on the edges.

'Doesn't that worry you, that she fits in so well with your life? As if she's curated herself to be exactly what you need, what you want?' Tristan's concern nudged itself into the peace of his thoughts.

No. It didn't worry him, not after today. She could absolutely not be in league with her father after what she'd revealed to him in the office. For the first time, he fully understood what she'd been up against, even after yesterday's disclosures at the duck boxes. For the first time, he understood the dark, driving depths of her life. And yet, her own innate kindness and concern for others had miraculously survived the emotional brutality of life with the Earl of Holme.

'There, I think we're ready.' She set down two mugs to complete their place settings and favoured him with a smile. 'Why don't you slice the bread and tell me what in the world are you going to do with all of this space? We haven't even gone upstairs yet.' There was a reason for that, Julien thought. If it had been easy to see Aurelia as his hostess downstairs, it would be all too easy to see her as another type of partner upstairs: his lover, his wife, the mother of their children, the person with whom his dream of family came true. But it was too much too soon for him to fully embrace the possibility of that. Did they dare run ahead that fast for fear they might trip? Again. He did not think he could bear it if that was the case.

Julien cut into the loaf of dark country bread, putting thick slices on their plates, and then carved into the quarter of ham sent by the Red Rose Inn for sandwiches. 'I want this home to be a gathering place for the best minds of Sussex and London, perhaps later for all of Britain. We're living in an extraordinary time with extraordinary technology: mills, factories, railroads. Life and its tempo is changing and opportunities abound to make that life better for so many if we're willing to be innovative and open.'

He poured cider for them from a stone jug. 'I'd love to have the Duke of Cowden's Prometheus Club join efforts with the Lennox Consolidated Trust on a few investments that could create jobs here at home. I'd like to invite them out, to spend a week riding, hiking, fishing, eating good food, drinking good wine and talking business in congenial, relaxed circumstances.'

They ate and he talked about his idea of creating a retreat, spurred on by the intent in her eyes and the interest in her questions as if she were already a partner in this vision. He talked until the stone jar was empty and there were only crumbs on their plates.

'Shall we go upstairs and see the other rooms?' Aurelia asked as they cleaned up the dishes and wrapped the ham. She made to put the ham in the hamper, but Julien shook his head. He didn't quite trust himself to go upstairs, nor did he trust his feelings. Today had been...overwhelming and he had something to take care of back at Brentham Woods after he consulted Tristan and his father. The Earl of Holme must be dealt with.

'The rain has let up.' Julien nodded to the window. 'We better make haste while the weather permits.' She was notably disappointed. 'But let's leave the ham and the rest of the bread so it will be here for us tomorrow.'

'Tomorrow?' She brightened at that.

'Yes, we'll do the upstairs rooms and then we'll be back with Mr Floyd the day after.' Julien smiled at her eager response. 'And, of course, we'll need to look at the stables, too, so perhaps the day after that as well. If you have time.'

She laughed and came to him, wrapping her arms about his neck, his body revelling in the easy intimacy even as it put his mind on alert, warning him to be careful, to acknowledge that his own feelings were running high. 'I might be able to squeeze you in between helping with pantomime costumes and Christmas baskets, and helping Elanora with the flowers for Sunday,' she teased.

'I am glad you like it here.' Here being Hemsford, Brentham Woods, his new house. All of it.

'I do like it here, Julien.' She gave a coy whisper, her lashes downcast, sweeping against her cheek before her gaze looked up at him. 'Because you're here. Because these are the spaces you've made, the spaces you've marked with your visions.' She wet her lips. 'Do you think you might kiss me before we go?'

'You would tempt a saint.' Julien gave a wry grin at her suggestion. 'I would like nothing more than to kiss you…' His mind was rife with images of what a future could be if…there were so many ifs. *If* Tristan was wrong, *if* her father could be silenced, *if* all she'd told him was true. 'But I think that if I did, I would not want to stop, Aurelia.' It was a confession and a warning. But it had to be acknowledged. He wanted her and he wanted to believe that she wanted him, too, the way they'd once wanted each other—honestly and completely, with no holds barred.

She nodded solemnly, fixing him with a blue-eyed stare that seemed to him more intimate in that moment than any kiss. 'And I would not want you to.'

Chapter Seventeen

'If I started kissing you, I would not want to stop.'

The words were an aphrodisiac, an absolution to Aurelia in the days that followed. Surely it meant that he'd forgiven her, that he understood what she'd been up against. Surely, it also meant that they were free to move ahead as they saw fit with this second chance they'd carved out for themselves.

He'd not said the words, but Julien Lennox loved her still, wanted her still and she wanted him. For the first time since coming south on her father's ill-conceived venture, she could allow herself some hope that perhaps the future she'd once imagined might honestly be within reach.

'I wouldn't want you to stop.'

She'd meant it with every fibre of her being. She wanted to be with Julien. Perhaps she'd always wanted it. Perhaps her dreams of freedom and independence were simply replacements for what she thought she could no longer have. But now the real temptation lay in thinking she could have both Julien and her freedom. There would be freedom with him, freedom to continue her work and even be encouraged to do it.

With Julien there would be that rare combination of freedom within partnership. What she felt with him, she'd felt with no other and there'd been plenty of others. There'd been seven Seasons of dancing and courting and no one had raised in her the level of emotion that Julien had. She'd burned for no one, had not craved another's kisses, although there'd been a few stolen pecks in lantern-lit gardens as an experiment. She had not hungered for another's touch.

There'd been gentlemen who had made her laugh, who had danced divinely, who had showered her with gifts and attention commensurate to her fortune until that fortune had ceased. Perhaps it was for the best she'd not been emotionally invested in those gentlemen. They'd dwindled exponentially with her family's financial situation.

Marriages were financial and dynastic alliances. Once, she might have settled for such a match, having been raised to expect not much more. But meeting Julien had shown her the possibility of more, that marriage might be based on love as well as practicalities. In short, he'd ruined her for other men, for other marriages. In that ruination, he'd unwittingly sowed the seeds of a new dream—one of freedom and aloneness. If she could not have love, could not have Julien, she would have no one. Now that she knew what was possible, she would not settle. But now, Julien was back, their past resolved, their future uncertain but possible.

Was it, though? Reality nudged, horning in on her joy. There would be a cost if she meant to keep Julien for ever. Could she truly do that to him? Tie him to her family? Or was it best to think of her happiness in the short term. To have Julien for a wondrous Christmas and find the courage to let him go again, to keep him safe as he'd tried so very hard to keep her safe. Perhaps it was best to focus on claiming happiness for the moment.

If this was to be a pursuit of short-term happiness, she was determined to make the best of it. Aurelia rose in the mornings full of energy and purpose. There was so much to do. The Christmas preparations were coming together as the calendar days sped by, Christmas rapidly nearing. And there was so much to look forward to: the tree lighting at the end of this week, the Christmas cantata at the church, the Lennox Christmas ball, the Grisham–Lennox panto at Heartsease, then Christmas Eve and Christmas Day, St Stephen's or Boxing Day, all the twelve days' fun, and Twelfth Night with cakes from Manning's.

She didn't let herself think beyond that. That was weeks away. Who could say what happened then? It was hard to imagine leaving this place that had become like home to her in such a short time. That was the power of relationships, of caring and love. People made the place, people were what caused one to feel they belonged.

Even her beloved Moorfields seemed far away as if it belonged to a different life, despite her efforts to make a difference there, despite her school and the relationships she was so painstakingly cultivating one day at a time. These days she didn't mind being in Hemsford for Christmas. She was looking forward to it actually. Because of Julien. Because she would not let him stop the next time he kissed her.

It had become an implicit understanding between them, underlying their interactions. He had confessed his want and she had thrown down the gauntlet with a confession of her own, daring him to act on that want. His desire would be welcome. She would not turn it away, she would instead feed it with her own.

That tension quivered between them aspic-like when they were together, silently asking the question of 'when?'. It was there when he drove her into Hemsford to work on Christmas preparations, when he picked her up after the ladies' meetings and took her out to the estate where they found reasons to spend every afternoon, walking the halls, mentally decorating and rearranging the rooms, or sitting in the kitchen and eating long lunches, skating on the pond, and always the big four-poster bed of English oak in the master's suite, tempting and taunting them with the question, *When?* And always the answer was: *Not yet.*

Days passed, marked with activity. The tree lighting came and went in all its brilliance, she standing beside Julien on the dais in the town centre dressed in her green velvet. Gaudete Sunday passed, the third Sunday, the Sunday of joy and anticipation which was rather too apropos for her. *She* was full of joy and anticipation and it seemed he was, too, but still, Julien resisted acting, which meant she had to settle for his touches, but none of his kisses.

He went a frustrating step further, announcing that Monday when he dropped her at the ladies' meeting—the last one before the pantomime at Heartsease—that he'd be taking the morning train to London to handle some business, business that he would not specify other than to say there was a chance he might be away overnight.

'If he can't get in to see the archbishop.' Mrs Phelps gave a sly smile while the other ladies nodded.

'Or if Rundell's is out of rings,' Mrs Manning added coyly. Aurelia smiled and laughed with her new friends. She knew they meant well. To them it was clear: she and Julien would marry. To them it was a whirlwind Christmas romance between two well-suited people. They couldn't possibly know the angst behind the scenes, the uncertainty that still simmered beneath the surface of her happiness, the hope that lingered there, too, and the obstacles that remained.

Silent questions plagued her as the ladies sewed the final sequins on the costumes for the pantomime. Was Mrs Phelps right? *Did* Julien mean to propose? Is that why he'd gone to London? To get a special licence and a ring? Was that why he'd resisted the urge to act on their private contract? Was he waiting until he proposed or until they were wed, traditionalist and stickler for propriety that he was? That one night in the Graftons' garden had occurred only because he believed they would wed. Perhaps he believed that again. As did she. But did she dare say yes, knowing what she'd saddle him with—a father who would not hesitate to use him for money. But perhaps Julien had a plan for that?

'*Your father must be handled*,' he'd said the day she'd told him the horrible story about her brother and she had cried against his shoulder. Still, her conscience pricked. Hadn't he done enough for her? He'd given the loan in large part because it protected her dream of freedom and this was how she was going to repay him: by taking away his.

She stabbed her finger with a needle and drew blood in her distraction. She quickly stuck her finger in her mouth and sucked on it. 'Here, let me wrap it or you'll be staining the costumes.' Elanora was beside her with a bit of gauze, winding the bandage about her finger, her voice quiet and soothing. 'Don't let the ladies get to you.' She smiled reassuringly.

'How did you know?' Aurelia glanced at her new friend.

'You just had that look about you.' Elanora gave a knowing shrug. 'I remember the angst that comes with the lead up to a proposal once you sense it might be on the wind. I both wanted and feared Tristan's proposal. Come outside and get some fresh air?'

The outdoor air was welcome and, to her credit, Elanora didn't press her with questions, just sat next to her in the little courtyard at the side of the church. From there, they could watch the Christmas fair in progress, full of week-day visitors.

'I remember growing up, the fair was only three or four booths. It's expanded gradually over the years, but the last four years, it's become extraordinary, thanks to Julien,' Elanora said quietly. 'He's a man with vision. He can take something that is nothing and see its potential. When Tristan was in the military, Julien was just starting out with his investments and Tristan would send whatever funds he could spare home to help Julien build his stake. When Tristan sold his commission and came home for good, Julien had amassed a portfolio worth slightly over ten thousand pounds for him out of Tristan's pocket change, essentially.'

She gave a little laugh. 'It made me wish my family had taken his offer when he'd volunteered to do the same for us. But it was too risky and we couldn't afford to lose any more. We had some other investments turn out poorly. We should have trusted Julien to see us to the other side. I nearly lost Heartsease because we didn't. I would have lost it, in fact, if Tristan hadn't come home when he did.' Aurelia wondered if that disclosure was meant as a parable for her, that she ought to trust Julien's instinct?

Elanora was quiet for a moment, suddenly unsure of what she should say. 'Forgive me for me prying, but I know there is history between you and Julien.' She gave a little laugh. 'Perhaps it's Tristan you should forgive. He's the one who told me and it may be bad form for me to bring it up, but Julien is my brother-in-law, the best of men. I want to see him happy. When my father passed away and then when my brother passed away, Julien and his family were there to help me. I was stubborn.

I wanted to do things on my own. I was embarrassed by my family's situation. I'd been left in horrible financial straits. I should have swallowed my pride. Julien would have handled everything. I don't know many men who would have done it for someone they were not obliged to help.'

'I know,' Aurelia said softly. 'That's what worries me. My family hurt him once. I don't want to set him up for that again.'

Elanora looked confused. 'You would refuse him?'

Aurelia shook her head. She knew what she wanted to say to him should he ask again. But did she dare? 'I would spare him the hurt of me saying yes. I do not want to tie him to my family through me. He would come to regret it and me.' She sighed—even disliking her father as she did, she was reluctant to speak poorly of him to Elanora, to shame him and the family with exposition of their finances.

Instead she said, 'You've met my family. My father can be a difficult, prideful man. When people marry, they don't just marry each other. They marry each other's families. I would definitely be getting the better end of that bargain.'

Elanora studied her with thoughtful eyes. 'Julien is very capable. All the Lennox men are. My advice would be to let him make that decision. No doubt he's already decided if he can live with your father or not.' Elanora squeezed her hand. 'As for me, I would be very glad to have you as a sister-in-law and I would miss you very much if that's not how Christmas ends. Don't be hasty. Let Julien and love handle whatever obstacles you imagine.'

It was good advice even if Aurelia felt that leaving things to luck and love hadn't necessarily served her well in the past. It was time to take matters into her own hands, although she'd have to wait until the next day to do it.

Aurelia was waiting for him at the station when the late morning train pulled into Hemsford, loaded with festive day-trippers eager for the fair. She was on the platform, dressed in her green velvet, her green winter bonnet on her head. Aside from the pink dress, this was definitely his favourite outfit. She was beautiful in it, quite possibly because she represented Christmas and all it stood for when she wore it.

He would remember always the way she'd looked the night of the tree lighting, standing to the side of the dais, looking up at him, her eyes aglow with undisguised affection, dressed in her green velvet, like Christmas come to life, the embodiment of peace, joy and love. She looked like that today, her gaze searching the windows of the train cars for a glimpse of him. Did he imagine that? Did he fancy she sought him because *he'd* missed her so desperately while he was gone?

Everything he'd seen in London had reminded him of her. He'd found himself turning to tell her something, to say, *Did you see that?* or to laugh with her, only to discover she wasn't there and to realise over and over again that he wanted her to be there. For everything. For the little things like shopping along Bond Street or the Hemsford High Street, and the big things like turning his new house into the retreat he imagined and the family home he craved.

If the trip up to London had shown him one thing, it was that there was no use denying it. For better or for worse, he was in love with her. He patted his coat pocket in reassurance. He was determined this time that would go differently. She waved, giving an excited hop as she spied him through the window. He smiled and waved back, finding that he could hardly wait to get off the train.

She met him with a smile, her arms flung about his neck, holding him close. He breathed in the sweet scent of her. 'This is the best surprise. I didn't think you'd be here.' He held her too long for propriety's sake.

'We need to go out to the house and I thought it would be quicker if we went straight from here. If you don't mind?' Her eyes sparkled. 'Mr Floyd and the decorator have sent swatches. They arrived yesterday after you left. But we have to make decisions as soon as possible. I have a hamper packed so we can spend the day before anyone knows that you're back. You can tell me about London on the way.'

Something was definitely up. Julien was convinced of it as they drove past the turn to Brentham Woods and on out to the house. Her eyes were bright, her colour high and he'd never found her more alluring. At the house, he was sure of it. He stepped inside the hall to discover the place decorated for Christmas. 'What is this?' He turned about, taking it in: the boughs draping the oak banister, the swag of greenery over the drawing room door.

'I thought we should see how the house looked for Christmas, since it's your favourite time of year. I did it myself yesterday after the ladies' meeting. Elanora helped.' She tugged his hand, dragging him to the drawing-room door. 'Do you like it?'

'I love it.' His voice was husky, betraying the emotion the scene evoked for him, a ghost of Christmas future if he could have his way. The only thing missing was three or four children pelting down the green-boughed staircase on Christmas morning.

Her arms were about his neck again, her face tilted up to his. 'You owe me something,' she flirted, her eyes flicking upwards to the green boughs. 'Mistletoe. I think that means you need to kiss me, Julien.'

He smiled, willing to play along. He loved this about her, her sense of fun, her spontaneity. 'I've been wanting to do that since I stepped off the train,' he murmured taking her lips in a lingering kiss that said, 'I'm home.' He gave her a lazy grin, confused when she became stern.

'You stopped. You promised you wouldn't,' she scolded, her eyes turning a desire-darkened sapphire-blue. 'I expect a gentleman to keep his word.'

His body, already roused, hardened at the implication of her words. 'Aurelia,' he warned, 'this is not play.' His want, his need was very real.

'I'm not playing, Julien. I've had enough of games between us.' She took his hand. 'Come upstairs. I've decorated up there, too.'

'Aurelia Ripley, are you seducing me?'

'Actually, I'm inviting *you* to seduce *me*. Is it working?'

In answer, he swung her up into his arms and carried her upstairs. If it worked any better, they wouldn't even make it that far.

Chapter Eighteen

Her heart was pounding as he carried her to the bed festooned with greenery wrapped around the four posters, a mistletoe ball hanging from the frame. This was what she wanted, this moment with Julien, when it could be just the two of them, all obstacles and interferences set aside. But now that the moment was here, her stomach was a flurry of butterflies.

He set her down, his hands at her waist, his mouth at her lips, his kisses confident and soothing even as they heated her blood, his words reassuring. 'May I play the lady's maid?' He gave her a smile, his fingers working the taffeta bow of her green bonnet and tossing it gently aside.

'You'll have to tell me what you want, Julien.' She was suddenly nervous.

He kissed her softly. 'You know what I want, you have touched me, our bodies are not entirely strangers to one another. Trust your instincts, but, yes, I will be there with you every step of the way.' He cupped her jaw, his palm warm against her cheek. 'Are you sure you want this?'

'Yes.' She moved into him then, kissing him full on the mouth in demonstration of her want. It must be now *before* they talked about the future that couldn't be, especially if he'd gone to London for a special licence, especially if her father chose to make trouble and tried to leverage their marriage to his benefit. And if none of those things were to happen, if Mrs Phelps's intuition was wrong, then she most definitely wanted this with Julien before she had to leave, before she went back to pursuing her dream of personal, lonely freedom. In either case, she would be losing him. 'You have played my maid, now I shall play your valet.'

The kiss had warmed her, stirred her to more action and less thought. The idea of undressing Julien, of revealing him to her eyes, was a heady one that outweighed the nerves of being undressed herself. Her hands worked the knot of his cravat, unwinding the length of cloth from his neck and setting it aside before undoing the polished tortoiseshell buttons of his waistcoat, the buttons of his shirt... 'Goodness...' She gave a breathy, teasing sigh 'You're like an onion with all these layers.'

Julien gave a husky laugh. 'I hope I smell better than an onion, though.'

She reached up on tiptoes to the pulse at his neck and took a deep breath in. 'Most definitely. You smell like citrus and sandalwood, like oranges on Christmas morning.' She smiled, pleased to see his eyes darken with desire at the description. 'Perhaps I am unwrapping you like a Christmas present, instead.'

He drew her close for a kiss. 'I like being a present far better than being an onion,' he murmured against her mouth, sending his shirt to join the pile of clothes accumulating on the floor. 'Now, perhaps it's time I did some unwrapping of my own.' His dark eyes glinted with mischief and want.

'But I'm not done with you,' she protested, a hand sliding between them, the hardness of him against the flat of her hand, a heady reminder of just how she affected him. She was not in this alone. Beneath his gentlemanly exterior, Julien was all hot male.

'You need to catch up,' he whispered against her throat, his hands working the frogs of her fitted green jacket. 'And I don't want to hear about how many layers a man has when I have to contend with all of this female frippery,' he growled playfully. He made delicious but short work of her jacket, of the bodice beneath and the tapes of her skirts, petticoats and all, leaving her in quite 'reduced circumstances' by comparison, his gaze hot on her as he took in his work.

He shook his head. 'No, not done yet. The chemise absolutely must go—shall I do it or shall you?' His tone was low, seductively wicked. This one last piece and she'd be entirely nude and yet she didn't feel exposed in the least. She felt powerful.

'I'll do it.' She matched his tone, her eyes never leaving his, her gaze enrapt by what it saw in his—desire, want, hunger, all for her, all because of her, and it was empowering. She *wanted* to stand before this man naked, wanted the sight of her to please him, wanted his gaze on her and her alone.

She reached for the hem of her chemise and drew it over her head, acutely aware as she'd never been before, of how the movement affected her body, how her breasts were pushed forward by the motion, how she could hear the sharp inhalation of his breath. She tossed the garment aside. 'Do I please you, Julien?' she whispered, surprised by the throaty huskiness of her own voice.

'You know you do.' There was a primal rumble to the words and it emboldened her.

She reached a hand to her hair and began to remove the pins from it, one by slow one, letting each tress tumble down, a silken, wavy length of golden curl. 'And this? Does this please you?'

'I think *please* is too tame a word.' He growled appreciatively as she shook down the last of her tresses. 'Minx. I can't decide if you're Rapunzel from the fairy tales, or Venus rising from the sea.'

'Venus.' She gave a wanton smile. 'I've seen that painting, too. The one by Botticelli.' She licked her lips, her hand dropping to the juncture of her thighs. She was going to be very wicked. 'I used to think she covered herself here out of modesty.'

'But now?' Julien's dark eyes glittered, following her hand down, his voice a dangerous rasp.

'Now, I think she feels the birth of her own arousal, the birth of love, the awakening of her desire.' She stepped towards him, her hand against the smooth plane of his chest, her voice sultry. 'When Venus touches herself she feels the dampness of want between her legs as I feel it now, as I have felt before with you.' She cast her gaze upwards to his face, finding his eyes aglow, his jaw set hard against the onslaught of her touch.

Her hand drifted downwards to take him in her palm, to wrap her fingers about his trousered length as she whispered against his mouth, 'Venus doesn't acknowledge her desire only to herself, she *proclaims* it to the world. Venus says, "No matter that men tell me I should rise above passion, that I should forgo it because passion is sin and nudity is sin, I am woman. I am not afraid of what I feel, of what I think, or of claiming what I want from a man in bed or out."'

She breathed the seductive revolution, the very thoughts spoken out loud exciting her as much as the man before her. 'Thus, I claim you, Julien Lennox. It is time for those trousers to go.' And she set to work on the fastenings of his trousers, because neither of them was free until they were both free.

His member sprang free and pulsing into her hand the moment his trousers fell away. Julien could not recall a time in his life when words had nearly made him spend on the spot. But he was definitely in danger of doing that now. Aurelia was not just a seductress, but a revolutionary, a woman who had awakened to her own power, her own want, and it was a whole new level of intoxication to be with her. The time for gentleness was gone, replaced by a hungry desire that drove them both.

They fell to the bed together, his member grasped tightly, decadently, in her hand, their mouths seeking each other in a chaotic hunt for satisfaction that only spurred them to further want.

She was perfection in his arms, her hand stroking his phallus as his mouth sought her breast, laving it with the same attentions she lavished on him, his body trembling with pleasure, with anticipation of the completion to come, the joining. But trembling, too, with the responsibility of that joining. He wanted her, he wanted the pleasure of the joining, but he also wanted pleasure *for* her, he wanted her initiation into passion's ranks to be a source of joy and selfishly he wanted the prideful knowledge of knowing he had done this for her.

She gasped and moved against him, her body urging them forward in their passion. He needed no further encouragement; he was more than ready. Then, he was over her, her beautiful face laughing up at him, her eyes dark, her hips pressed to his, her legs open, instinctually inviting. And he accepted, his phallus nosing at her entrance, adding its own slickness to hers, sliding inwards and forward, his body attuned to hers, to each gasp, each arch of her hips as she shifted to accommodate him, to take him and the very thought of it filled him with a primal thrill. He gave a strong, final push, feeling the triumph of arrival, and her eyes went wide, her breath catching with the realisation that he was fully sheathed, fully within.

Her arms were about his neck, pulling him down, her voice a whisper at his ear. 'Oh, Julien, we are one now,' she breathed and Julien chuckled.

'This is not it, there is more.' And he began to move, slowly at first to accustom her, to teach her the rhythm, although she needed little instruction, picking up his tempo with wide-eyed delight in the intimate dance. She wrapped her legs about him, her hands clutching him, nails digging into his back as their pace increased and intensity soared, their bodies caught up in the pleasure together.

He felt sweat bead on his brow as he struggled to keep himself in check, his body wanting to run rampant in the surf of pleasure cresting towards him. His body was gathering, tightening, racing to meet the waves, his thrusts became faster in repetition, closer together as his need surged. Her hips rose up and pressed hard into his, signalling the rising of her own need, the nearing of her own completion. His hair fell forward into his face, wet with his sweat, his exertions.

His gaze locked on hers, the sight of her exhilarating to him, her hair spilling across his pillow, her entire being swept away in the moment, caught up in the discovery of pleasure. She gave a gasp of disbelief, of wonder, and then they were there together, letting the final wave of pleasure wash over them as they held each other tight.

Good Lord, lovemaking had never rivalled this intensity for him. It had both completed him and left him undone. It was a long while before he let her go, let her shift to lying beside him, her head tucked into the hollow of his shoulder, her body aligned against his side, her fingertip drawing a lazy masterpiece on his torso, her breathing gentle, her own words a soft aphrodisiac even spent as he was. 'Dear God, Julien, that was the best thing I've ever done.' Immediately he felt his body stir beneath the approbation of her praise. His arm tightened about her, possessive. Please God that she never do it again with anyone else.

It was both an unnerving and yet realistic place to have arrived at after the tumultuous pleasure of their love making. Of course she would do this with no other. Of course no other man would behold the naked splendour of her. She was his and he was hers. Yet, that held an enormity of its own. She ran her thumb over the tiny peak of his nipple. 'Am I not supposed to say such things? Is it not ladylike?'

He bent his head to look down at her. 'You may say whatever you like to me, about whatever you like. I am glad it pleased you. First times are not always as pleasant as subsequent times.'

She raised her head with a saucy smile. 'First times. I like that. It implies more times to follow.' She sat up. 'Are you hungry? I am ravenous.'

He groaned, wishing he'd had the foresight to bring food upstairs, but how? He'd been too busy carrying her, too swamped with desire, as he recalled, to have thought much about lunch hampers. He was going to pay for that now. 'Are you going to make me go downstairs and fetch lunch?' He'd never felt less like leaving bed.

She grinned. 'No, the hamper is under the bed. I thought it might come in handy.' She leaned over the side and pulled out the basket.

'I adore you.' He laughed as she hauled the basket to the bed. He shot her a wicked look as she wrapped herself in a sheet and laid out the food on the bed. 'You were pretty sure of yourself, Minx, if you were stashing food beneath the bed.'

She made him a ham sandwich and passed it to him. Their bed picnic was underway. 'I've heard of breakfast in bed, but never lunch.' He took a bite, thinking how delectable she looked, her hair falling loose over her shoulder. 'I like you this way, better than your white nightgown. Voluminous is hardly an apt description of that particular garment,' he teased.

She cocked her head, studying him, her bold gaze making him quite aware that he sat there with only a sheet across his lap for modesty, his torso on full display, and that the sheet didn't quite disguise the rising fascination his member had with lunch. 'I like you this way, too, Julien. Naked and relaxed. Country living agrees with you.' She reached into the basket again and pulled out a bottle. 'There's champagne, if you would open it. And glasses.'

He took the bottle from her and popped the cork, laughing when the foam spilled on to the sheets. 'It's easy to like the country when it comes with bed picnics in the middle of the afternoon.' If he had his way, such picnics might become a regular fixture of his days. He poured them each a glass. 'Cheers.' He clinked his glass against hers, privately toasting to a future of lunches in bed, feeling that his life had finally come full circle. They would need to have that discussion before they left this place, but not yet.

They polished off the ham and bread, and made love again, she laughingly compared his phallus to the bottle of champagne and its foamy eruption and he revelled in it, in her. Their lovemaking took on a playful quality that delighted him. She was bold and coy by turn, leading him a merry chase, one moment the temptress with her daring, the next moment the innocent eager for his instruction.

'Can I be on top some time?' she asked drowsily as the long shadows of afternoon reminded them of the shortness of winter days. He didn't want to get out of bed, didn't want to go back to Brentham Woods. He'd not meant to have this discussion in bed, but rather downstairs, or on a walk through the woods, but he was running out of time for that unless he wanted to delay it and he did not. His honour demanded it.

'You can be on top next time.' He closed his eyes with a sigh, already imagining next time and enjoying the assurance of knowing there *would* be a next time.

'Tomorrow, then?' she said playfully, levering up on one arm to face him.

'If you're not too sore.' He opened one eye, counselling caution. 'Lovemaking can be hard exercise. It uses muscles we don't always engage.' In her case, muscles that had never been used. He reluctantly tossed back the covers and got out of bed in a fluid movement, padding naked to the wash basin, feeling her eyes on him, his body celebrating the attention and the knowledge that the woman he loved was pleased by him. 'See anything you like?' he drawled, wetting a rag for her.

'Why don't you turn around and I'll tell you,' she teased. 'I didn't get to look at you when you undressed. We were in too much of a hurry and you're my first naked man, artwork aside.'

He turned, aware that his member was eager to please her scrutiny, rallying its recently exhausted self to half-mast for the sake of her approval. Her eyes settled on the core of him as he padded back to the bed. 'It's amazing to think something that size fits, well, where it fits,' she said at last. 'You seem rather large, rather thick, Julien. Are all men designed like you?' she asked boldly, taking the rag from him, her eyes coy and innocent while her enquiry was anything but.

'What sort of question is that?' He laughed, gathering his clothes from the floor and turning his back to give her some privacy.

'An honest one, a curious one. Did I embarrass you?' He could hear the sheets rustling behind him.

'I don't go around looking at other men's parts, so I'm not sure I have an honest answer for you. Perhaps I am a bit larger than the usual.' He turned in partial dress, his shirt open and loose, his trousers undone. She'd given him an opening and there was no time like the present—he was, in fact, running out of time. 'You will have to take my word for it though, Aurelia. I don't intend for you to have a chance to compare.'

She stilled, her gaze serious, looking like an angel, her golden hair over her shoulder, the sheet drawn up over her breasts. Julien sat on the edge of the bed. 'You cannot be surprised, Aurelia. I am hardly the sort to take a virgin to bed without the expectation of marriage between us.' He'd made assumptions today; the most important one was that he'd not withdrawn from her body. He'd assumed there was no need. In his world, marriage followed lovemaking *and* he'd assumed they both understood that, agreed to that.

As if to prove his intention, he reached for his greatcoat and withdrew a folded paper from its pocket. He took her hand and simply pressed the paper into it. He did not list the arguments for accepting him, he did not lay out his wealth and worldly goods to be tallied in his favour. Just his affections. This was to be a love match, not an alliance.

It wasn't about money, about position or a title, although he had all three. It was just about them, about two hearts who had found one another amid the chaos and distractions of living. 'Will you marry me, Aurelia?' It was the simplest of proposals and he hoped it would be followed by the simplest and most immediate of answers: yes.

That was not the case.

She lifted her gaze from the paper in her hand, but her gaze gave nothing away, at least not the joy he thought he'd see in them. Julien felt his heart in his throat, the old fear coming to him again that somehow he'd misjudged the situation, that he would be refused. But he was certain there was no rationale for such fear, just the nerves of an anxious bridegroom. 'Julien, what is this?' She held up the paper and he breathed a little easier. He'd only managed to stun her.

'Unfold it and see,' he urged. Most men proposed with jewellery, but in his opinion jewellery did not carry the power of a binding contract. After all they'd been through, he wanted her to know in a very palpable way that he meant to marry her. And he'd wanted an honest answer from her, one that was not influenced by a dazzling diamond ring, although he had that, too, in his pocket for later.

She undid the paper and spread it on her lap, staring at the words as if they didn't make any sense. 'Read it out loud,' he said quietly. His own nerves were straining at their tether. Patience was taking all he had. He'd rather hoped patience wouldn't be necessary, that she'd simply answer the question.

'"The Archbishop of Canterbury has granted exceptional

permission for Lady Aurelia May Ripley..."' She looked up, 'You remembered my second name.'

'Of course I did. Keep reading,' he prompted.

"'And Lord Julien Ebenezer Lennox, Viscount Lavenham, to wed at a time and location of their choosing."' Her voice trembled at the last. When she looked up at him, her eyes were glassy. 'Julien, this isn't just a licence to wed, it's a special licence.'

The first tear fell and Julien reached out a thumb to wipe it away, concerned by her reaction. 'Yes, I went all the way to the Doctors' Commons in London yesterday for it. Aurelia, why are you crying? This was not meant to make you sad.'

She smiled through her tears. 'I'm crying because my heart is full. I'm crying because you love me.'

'Of course I love you.' He pulled her to him, relief pulsing through him. She hadn't said yes yet, but she would.

Chapter Nineteen

He *loved* her. Her heart wanted to explode with the knowledge of it. Her eyes wept with the joy of it. 'No one has ever loved me before,' she breathed the awful truth against the comfort of his chest, the safety of his arms. Her parents did not love her. Her mother perhaps had affection for her, but affection didn't also attain the status of love. She'd known the absence of love for years, but not love itself. Now, here was Julien offering her that rare and precious thing.

Julien *loved* her. It was evident in his forgiveness, in his willingness to extend her a second chance at the happiness they'd once thought to have together. Perhaps it hadn't been freedom she'd been seeking all along but *this*. Love. The way it made her feel was extraordinary. He wanted to marry her! She wanted to revel in that, celebrate it with him. Perhaps she could allow it for the moment. But she couldn't claim it, not for ever. It was never meant to be for ever, only for now, and she wanted to hold on to this perfect moment as long as she could.

'You can decide the date.' Julien was rocking her gently. 'We can wed as soon as you like or as late if you'd rather plan something. If it were up to me, it would be sooner rather than later. Will you let me announce our engagement tonight at supper?'

For an instant she let her mind imagine the scene. His family would be present. He would send word to Heartsease and invite Tristan's family for the occasion. She would be beside him, his hand in hers. She would wear the pink dress and her great-aunt's pearls. He would kiss her in front of his family. There would be candles and champagne. Hugs and tears and joy. But she was not destined to travel that path. Her father had ruined it.

She lifted her head—fear, dread, even anger warred in the pit of her stomach, turning the glorious moment dark. He was not allowing her to put off the inevitable. Instead, he was pushing her towards it, forcing her hand. The anger she felt was for him. Why had he asked her today? Why couldn't he have waited so that they could have enjoyed more stolen afternoons like this one without having to make a decision? Without having to talk about the future? The dread was for Julien, too, and for herself. Dread over what she'd have to do to make things right, to protect him. But the fear was for her father.

'Julien,' she said slowly, 'have you spoken to my father?' Dear Lord, she hoped not. But Julien was a stickler for traditions. He'd asked her father's permission the first time. She didn't want her father to know Julien had proposed. Of course, this time, her father would say yes without hesitation. He'd already be trying to use his new son-in-law's money to his advantage. Perhaps he'd even attached financial strings to the granting of his permission.

'No, this is between us.'

Julien's dark eyes held hers and she was reminded of his words years ago. *'There is just us now.'*

'Marriage is between two people, Aurelia. That is all. This is our decision alone.'

She still disagreed with him, even more now than she had the first time he'd made the argument seven years ago. 'A marriage does not exist in isolation, Julien. You know your family will be part of our lives. It stands to reason that my family will be, too, like it or not. Our decision to marry will have consequences.' She scooted away from him. She'd be stronger if he wasn't touching her. She would need all of her courage once he realised where this was going.

'What are you afraid of, Aurelia?' Julien was studying her intently, the special licence lying forgotten on the bed. 'Is this about your father? He has no sway here, not any more. The past is finished and gone, my love. No one will hurt you again as long as I have any ability to prevent it.'

It would be easy to believe that in Julien's love she would be safe. It was what she *wanted* to believe. She allowed herself to bask in that belief for one last moment before she steeled herself for the task before her: protecting Julien by letting him go. And for that, she'd have to convince him she didn't love him enough to marry him. It would break her heart and it would break his. But it was better to break those hearts now than to watch them break gradually, worn away over the years as her father came between them and turned Julien against her with his constant demands.

Julien was silent for a long while. He wetted his lips. 'You haven't said yes yet, Aurelia. Is your father the reason you withhold your consent from me?' There was a terseness to his tone that boded ill.

'You know it is. He'll be there, always, in the background, managing, manipulating, threatening.' The irony was not lost on her that once she'd refused Julien because her father had asked her to. Now, her father would be elated if she said yes. Once, she'd lacked the courage to say yes and now she needed the courage to say no.

'I can manage your father, Aurelia. I am managing him now,' he reminded her sternly and for a moment her argumentation faltered.

What had Elanora said? *'Let Julien handle things.'*

'But despite my assurances, you hesitate. I have to say I did not expect hesitation after this afternoon. I expected you to readily accept, if I'm being entirely honest. I was sure of you, Aurelia.' She'd upset him, taken a beautiful moment and turned it into a defensive one.

'I want to say yes,' she told him solemnly, wanting to mitigate the hurt while still ensuring that she could protect him. 'Inside, I feel all those things—joy, elation, wonder that this man beside me wants to spend his life with me. I am overwhelmed with what that life might be, here in this house. You are everything I ever dreamed of, Julien, and more.' She looked down at her hands. 'When I think of wanting to marry you seven years ago,

I can hardly imagine my audacity. I barely knew you. I wonder if that is a tribute to love or the naivety of youth?'

She dared a look up at him, at his handsome face with his dark eyes. 'Now, I feel I know you better than I ever did, seeing you here in your home, with your family, in your community. What I am wondering, Julien, is not if I *want* to say yes, but if I *can* say yes.' Oh, how she wanted to say yes, with him sitting beside her, his shirt open, showing off the smooth, sculpture of his torso, his muscular thighs shown off in tight fitting breeches that had yet to be fastened. There was something erotic about a man in half-dress which hinted at the possibilities of his body, of the pleasure he might be capable offering. There was no 'might' about it. In this case, she was very clear on the pleasure Julien could offer. Her body echoed with it even as she was on the brink of losing him.

'If you *can*? I've told you, your father is being handled.' There was a growl to his voice, his anger was surfacing. Good. Let it come. She would need all their anger to get through this.

'I don't think you understand what life with my father is like. I've tried to tell you. I've shared my story with you,' she said. 'It's one thing to control him on paper. A loan is a legal document. But real life isn't like that. Everything has to be negotiated with him. One is always walking around on tiptoe for fear of springing a trap or being ambushed or having some misstep held against them.'

Julien nodded. 'Aurelia, I love you and I will handle your father, that is all that matters. Will you marry me or not?'

He was going to make her say the words. She could feel her heart break as she summoned the courage. 'I will not drag you into the dysfunction that is my family, Julien. He wants you to marry me, Julien. I've told you as much. I've warned you. That he wants to see us wed ought to scare the living daylights out of you.' Her voice rose with her anger. Why did *she* always have to do the hard things?

Dear God, she was refusing him. Again. Julien rose from the bed, shocked to his core by her response and the reason for it. Anger began to surge. He let it. It was better than the alternative. He wasn't ready to hurt. He was ready to fight. He crossed his arms over his chest. 'You're being stubborn, Aurelia. You are saying no because he wants you to say yes.'

'I *am* being realistic. How can we ever think to find happiness with him looming over our shoulders? Or us looking over our shoulders, waiting for the next crisis?'

'*Will* you be looking? I won't be. Because first, the loan ties his hands. I have appointed stewards to do his job for him and to do it well. Any misstep on his part, any threat towards you, and I will leverage the loan against him and call for immediate repayment. Secondly, I will not be manipulated. He will find out very quickly that he cannot outmanoeuvre me.'

'If anyone is being stubborn it's you. And naive, if I might add.' She rose from the bed and began to dress. 'You refuse to see reality. I will always be your weakest link. He will get to you through me if we're married. I have lived in his shadow long enough to know better than you.'

Julien levelled a glare her direction, his mind whirring, his insides churning. This wasn't only about her father. 'You don't trust me. That's what this is about. You didn't trust me back then and you don't trust me now. You simply won't leap.' And, oh, God, did the knowledge of that hurt him. Once more, when it came to doing the hard thing, she simply wouldn't do it, wouldn't commit to him. She might love him—*might. C*ome to think of it, had she ever *said* the words? Even so, a man had to wonder if her love was not equal to his.

He swallowed. Hard. It occurred to him that perhaps her father was a shield for a bigger question. 'Do you *want* me to convince you? Is there anything at all that I can say to change your mind? Any proof you will choose to accept?' Because he could not change a mind that didn't want to be changed and the conclusion that led to was positively damning. She didn't want to fight for them, for him.

He began to button his shirt. She had only her shoes to put on and he felt the sand running out of his hourglass. 'You don't trust me. You don't or won't put confidence in me to manage your father. You pretended towards feelings.'

'My feelings are not pretence, Julien. I have told you that

on multiple occasions. Should I name them for you?' Her blue eyes flashed.

'Did you ever mean to act on those feelings? What was your end game?' He was feeling used. She'd invited him to play a game with her, a ruse to mitigate her father, but all along for her there'd been a game within a game. She'd been playing with him.

She gave a snort and gestured towards the bed, one shoe dangling from her hand. 'I did act on those feelings, this very afternoon, in fact.'

'To what purpose? Was I just a conquest? An affair?' In his anger he slammed his hand against the oak poster. 'Were you using me for sex? You condemn your father for manipulation, but you are better at it than he was. A man never sees you coming. You had me believing you cared for me then and you cared for me now. Right up until that pretty speech just a few minutes ago about wanting to say yes, but knowing you couldn't. Perhaps you missed your calling. You should have trod the boards.'

'You're being mean, Julien.' Her eyes were hard, so unlike the misty, glassy gaze she'd turned on him such a short time ago when he'd shown her that special licence. How did such extremes happen to them? One moment on the brink of celebrating and the next on the brink of despair? 'You're hurting and I am sorry for it, sorrier than you'll know.'

She brushed past him and he reached for her arm. He couldn't let her go without knowing. 'Did you ever intend to marry me, this time?'

Their eyes locked. He searched hers for a truth that made sense to him, a truth that he could understand. She shook her head. 'If you're asking if my feelings for you are real, the answer is yes, but, no, I never intended to marry you, although what you offer is potent. I'm sorry, Julien. It's better this way. You want me to trust you, but now I am asking you to trust me.'

His grip on her arm loosened and she gave a dry laugh. 'Trust is so much easier to ask for than to give, isn't it?'

'This isn't trust, Aurelia. This is an impasse. You want it your way and I want it mine.' And they were both too stubborn to relent. 'I am asking you to take a leap of faith into marriage with me and you are asking me to walk away from…' From what? Real love? *Was* this real love? It didn't feel like it at the moment.

'From trouble, Julien. I can only make you unhappy. Thank you for these past weeks and for everything you've done. This must be the end between us. I think it would be best if my father never knew about this.'

Best for her, Julien thought as he let her go. She would not benefit at all if her father knew what she'd turned down. But he nodded anyway. He would do this one last thing for her. He waited until he heard the front door shut before letting loose his rage in a howl that shook the windows and the depths of his soul. Why hadn't he seen it sooner? That the bridge between them was unmendable? What could ever be possible between two people who couldn't trust one another? Aside from love, trust was an essential foundation of any long-term relationship.

She'd broken his trust not once, but twice. Once because she'd been coerced to it, and once because she chose to. That latter hurt the most, not because it was the most recent, but because she had control over it and had chosen to do it anyway. She could have chosen him and she hadn't. How would he ever find his way back from this?

Chapter Twenty

'**I** thought I might find you here.' Tristan's voice roused him a few hours later from his chair by the fire in the office. 'Your new space is cosy. Were you planning on spending the night?' Tristan moved about the office, turning up the lamps and setting down a hamper of food. 'Mother was worried when you didn't make it for supper.'

'I wasn't hungry.' Julien tracked his brother's movements with a narrowed gaze, resentful of the intrusion. 'If I wanted company, I would have come back.' He let his tone make it clear that he wanted to be left alone. He was in no mood for companionship. His world had fallen apart and he was entitled to at least a few hours of wallowing in the despair and the anger that swamped him. 'If I promise to eat something, will you leave?'

Tristan responded by sitting down in the chair across from him and getting comfortable. 'No, I will not be leaving without you. Whether you eat or not is up to you. Do you want to tell me what happened, or should I guess?'

Julien glared at him.

'All right then, I'll start.' Tristan crossed one leg over a knee, ignoring the stare. 'You and Aurelia came out here for an afternoon, perhaps for a tryst and it turned into a lovers' quarrel. Now, it's your turn. *You* tell *me* the details of that quarrel and we'll solve the problem together.' His brother was trying to cajole him into reason.

'Tristan, really, I don't need this.' Julien pushed a hand through his hair. 'I don't need you to help solve *my* problem. Besides, it can't *be* solved. I love her and she does *not* love me, not enough.' Not enough to make a life together. Saying the words aloud opened the wounds afresh. The hurt began again.

'It's not only an issue of love, Tristan. It's also an issue of trust. She doesn't trust me enough to take a leap of faith.' The anger of the afternoon began to stir again—anger at her for not trusting him to make things right, to ensure her father was controlled, and anger at his own inability to make her see reason, to see that he was right.

Tristan nodded, silent and encouraging as the words, the hurt and the anger spilled from him. Now that he'd started to talk, he couldn't seem to stop. 'I was so sure of her. This time was going to be different.' Julien let the feelings come. He talked of the night at the Christmas fair, of how it felt to sit beside her at church, to have her beside him at the tree lighting.

'I was so sure of her, of *us*, I went to London for a special licence and a ring. I was so sure that I made love to her upstairs here in my home, the place where I want to raise my family, and then I proposed.' His fist clenched, anger and hurt rocketing through him. 'I never dreamed she'd turn me down. I thought we'd already implicitly agreed.' The recriminations came again. What had he missed? How had he allowed himself to be duped one more time?

'I can't go back to Brentham Woods, Tristan. She'll be there.' Heaven knew what it would do to him to see her right now and know that he'd lost her.

'Then we won't go back,' Tristan said quietly. 'We'll stay the night here.'

'She's here, too.' Julien could hear his voice shake with emotion, with *every* emotion. His body was a riot of them: anger, rage, disappointment, failure, stupidity. He could deal with those, eventually over time. They could be rationalised, dissected and understood. Anger would sustain him as it had before. The hurt was harder to cope with, its pain more immediate.

'I brought her here. We planned every inch of it,' he told Tristan as he grappled with his self-control, something he had little experience with. He was always in control, always knew what to do. This was new and unpleasant territory and she had brought him to it. 'She touched every room here. When I walk into them, I hear her voice in my head talking about cream-on-cream wallpaper and Thomas Whitty rugs.' More than that, he saw the future he'd imagined. A future that was possible because he'd chosen to believe in her.

Julien paused. 'I forgave her, Tristan, for not accepting me the first time because she was too young, too alone to stand on her own, too threatened with the loss of those dearest to her to rebel. I forgave her because that was the only way we could go forward. I forgave her because that was the way to change things. But it wasn't enough.'

Tristan pressed a roasted beef sandwich into his hand. 'I am sorry, Brother, so very sorry.'

Julien held Tristan's gaze. 'So am I. In the end, she still didn't choose me. She was never going to choose me, not for the long run. I didn't see the truth because I wanted the truth to be different. Maybe she can't love. It would be understandable after being raised in that home.' Even now, when hurt and anger were riding him hard, some part of him was willing to make excuses for her or at least try to explain away her actions in her defence or to mitigate his own hurt.

Julien scrubbed a hand over his face, feeling the night's growth of stubble on his chin. 'I hope there's no child,' he said quietly. Damn, why hadn't he been more careful? But he knew why. Because he'd been imagining three or four children on the staircase Christmas morning, a life where his wife could be trusted, where she loved him and they were a team, unencumbered by outside agendas. It would serve him right, though, if she was pregnant, if he spent his life shackled to his folly, like Prometheus, having his liver eaten out every day only to grow back every night. Only for him, it would be his heart.

Tristan tendered an opinion at last, carefully wading into the fray of his feelings. 'Leaps of faith can be tricky things, though, no matter how cautious we are.'

'It was just so good with her, all of it—the laughing, the loving. What I wonder is how could all that have been a lie?' This was the one question that had plagued him, the one thing that didn't ring true about her arguments. How did one feign those things so thoroughly? So consistently without meaning them?

'Are you sure you're reading the situation correctly?' Tristan spoke the other question. 'Her father is strategic and manipulative. You know that's true. Do you think she still fears his power more than she trusts your love? Fearing him is a habit and habits are hard to break. Love, real love, is new to her, a foreign thing.'

Julien nodded, remembering. 'She cried today when I showed her the special licence. She said it was the first time anyone had loved her.' He glanced at Tristan. 'She was reluctant to accept the proposal, she worried about her father using the marriage to his advantage.' That had been her first level of rejection. There'd been other levels, too.

By the end they'd said harsh things to one another in the heat of the moment. But fire often revealed hidden truths. Those words had been harsh perhaps, but that didn't make them lies. Maybe it was best those things had been aired before things had gone further. Maybe it was simply impossible for them to be together. But that didn't make losing her hurt any less.

'I simply don't know how I'll move on without her,' he told Tristan. 'I don't know that I can do it again. But I must if I am to have a family.' He shook his head. It was like his world truly had stopped and would never start again. 'I can't imagine any of that without her.'

'Then don't imagine it.' Tristan stretched out his legs and yawned, settling deep into his chair. 'You've never given up on anything in your life. Don't start now. It's late, you need to rest.'

'You're a good brother, Tristan, to sit up with me. I'm costing you time away from Elanora and the children,' Julien said, only to be answered with a snore. Well, maybe Tristan had the right idea. At least if he slept, he wouldn't hurt so much, wouldn't think so much. He slouched down in his chair, letting the fire warm him. How was it that a man who successfully invested pounds by the thousands had managed to lose the woman he loved not once, but twice?

* * *

A pounding on his door woke him and Tristan rather joltingly the following morning. Their father strode in, brisk and efficient, his greatcoat and boots spattered with December mud. His demeanour suggested he'd ridden hard for good reason. 'Good, you're both here, I thought you might be.' He looked from one grown son to another. 'You need to get up and help us search. Lady Aurelia is gone. She wasn't in her room when her mother looked in on her this morning.'

Julien's first reaction was fear—for Aurelia. She was in a strange place where she didn't know the land, she could get easily be lost. He was out of his chair, ignoring the crick in his neck and the stiffness in his shoulder for having slept sitting in a slouch. Then he remembered. She'd betrayed him. Again.

That wouldn't do.

That same part of him which had made it possible for her to keep her freedom by securing her father's estate regardless of their past spoke in his mind.

She's out there alone, somewhere, maybe lost, maybe hurt in the heart of winter.

Tristan was asking questions. 'Did she take a horse? Did she take anything from her room?'

'No horse. Nothing from her room. Only whatever she was wearing. Her mother says her green carriage ensemble is gone and her winter cloak.' The green-velvet ensemble she'd worn to the tree lighting, Julien thought, the ensemble which made her look like Christmas. Julien's heart began to ache.

'And whatever fits into her pockets. Jewellery?' Julien asked, tamping down on the pain that followed thoughts of her.

'I don't know, I don't think anyone looked for smaller items. Lady Holme is beside herself,' their father said with a meaningful look.

'Well, it's about time. She didn't seem too concerned about her daughter when everything fell apart last night,' Julien growled. He had little sympathy there.

'Julien, we can't ever really know what goes on in someone else's home,' his father chided. 'I know you don't care for the Earl.'

'He's a bastard.' Julien didn't mince words. 'No one cares for him.'

'All that aside, we should also consider why would she run?' Tristan interrupted with a queer look that made Julien stop and think. Tristan put a stalling hand to his shoulder. 'Do you think her father found out about the proposal and her refusal? The proposal would have elated him, but her refusal would not have.'

No, it wouldn't have. Her father would be furious. 'She would not have told him. He couldn't have known,' Julien said.

'If she was as half as upset as you were yesterday, I doubt she could have hidden it. Or perhaps she told her mother and her mother told her father,' Tristan postulated.

If her father knew, Julien could imagine how that would have played out: threats. Threats against Elspeth, against her mother. His gut twisted. There was more than one history repeating itself.

'What if her father *didn't* know? We should consider that as well.' Tristan voiced the question quietly. 'Perhaps she ran pre-emptively *before* he could learn of it.'

Julien held Tristan's gaze, a long look passing between the brothers. Hope warred with despair, tying an uncomfortable knot in his stomach as Tristan said the words he could not. 'If she ran pre-emptively, she ran in order to protect someone. To protect you.'

'Dear God.' The realisation left Julien struggling to breathe. She'd intimated as much yesterday that she was refusing him on the grounds that she wanted to save him. He'd not listened then, not with the right ears. He'd heard only refusal, only excuses from a woman who didn't trust him enough to make things right, a woman who didn't love him as much as he loved her. But this morning, it looked different. She'd run to protect him.

And people protect the ones they love.

He recalled the afternoon they'd ridden out to the duck boxes the first time and she'd put the ruse to him. She'd told him then, the first time her father had threatened Elspeth she'd vowed to take the horse and run, disappear, where no one could find her.

Three things ripped through Julien at once. First, he knew where she'd gone. Second, he knew where she'd be. Third, he knew he'd been wrong yesterday. She'd left for him, his brave, selfless girl, always seeking to protect those she loved instead of fighting for herself. Julien groped in a pocket for his watch. Damn. It was later than he thought. 'I have to go after her. I know where she went.' He was already striding through the hall, grabbing his greatcoat from a peg. He patted the pockets to make sure his purse was on him.

'I'll come with you,' Tristan offered.

'No, you stay here. You have a family and it's Christmas, Tristan. You've done enough. If I don't make it back in time, make sure Mother's ball is a success.' He was fairly sure he wouldn't make the Christmas ball.

'You're going that far, are you?' Tristan queried in low tones.

Julien nodded. 'I'll go as far as I have to. I owe her an apology.' And the protection of his name if she was still willing to take it. It seemed like the only thing they were good at was betrayal. This time it was he who had betrayed her.

Julien saddled his horse with instructions to have him picked up at the livery later and set off as fast as he dared for town on roads that were icy. He tried not to think of Aurelia covering those three miles on foot in the early morning cold. He tried only to think of the next step, which was catching the eleven o'clock train to London and from there, the next train that would get him to Yorkshire, or at least close. Aurelia had gone home, although she wouldn't stay there. She'd gone to get her horse and then she'd be off again. He'd lose her if he didn't get to Moorfields before she left.

The village was bustling with Christmas celebrants, mainly those who'd come to town on the early train to join Reverend Thompson's advent service before shopping. With just two days before Christmas Eve, people were in the holiday spirit and eager to see the fair and prettily decorated windows of the High Street, eager to spend coins on sweets and small gifts. Ordinarily, Julien would have been happy to see the crowds, but today, the crowds meant he had to struggle to get a space on the Christmas train, which ran an abbreviated schedule due to it being Sunday.

He had to settle for standing room only on the train. Aurelia would have been on the first train back to London. She had a two-hour head start on him. He wouldn't know how much that meant until he saw the train schedules to the north. If she had to wait a while for a northbound train, he might be lucky enough to catch her in London.

He had no such luck in London. London was, in fact, down-right unlucky for him. He could not tell which option Aurelia might have taken to get north. Had she waited for a train that took a more direct route with fewer stops or had she taken the first train north that took a more circuitous route out of fear that someone might catch up with her before the direct train could leave? By someone, Julien meant her father. She knew her mother wouldn't come and she would not think he'd come.

Julien opted for the last direct train north instead of an ear-lier train that made more stops. His train left at three o'clock and would arrive in York a little after six, barring any difficulties. Then, he'd have to make a decision: try to find a post chaise that would take him to Moorfields in the dark or take a room at an inn and head to Moorfields in the morning, hoping she would still be there.

The weather made the decision for him. York was freezing and there was no post chaise to be had for love or money will-ing to brave the Dales in the dark and the ice until morning. He found a quality inn, ate a hearty meal and fell asleep in his clothes, hoping he wouldn't be too late.

It was shortly past six when Aurelia arrived at Moorfields. The big Gothic-style manor looked dark and deserted. There was no life to it, which came as a surprise. She paid the driver and lifted the heavy lion-headed door knocker, waiting for a servant to answer. She was fully prepared to throw herself on the mercy of the Americans who'd rented the place for Christ-mas for the space of a night, just long enough to pack some things, get Elspeth and go. She looked over her shoulder, as she had been doing all day, for fear her father would divine where she'd gone and come after her. But if no one was behind her now, she'd be safe until morning. No one would get from York to Moorfields this time of night in this freezing weather.

She knocked again and stamped her feet against the cold. Still no answer. She trudged to the stable block, where a light flickered in the upstairs garret, home to the grooms. 'Hello!' she called out, stepping into the warmth of the stable. In the depths, a horse nickered at the disturbance. Boots sounded on the stairs.

'Milady! What are you doing home?' Whit Tyler, the head groom, came into view, pulling on a jacket. She'd caught him at supper, no doubt, and the end of his day.

'Where is everyone at the house? The Americans? No one answered when I knocked.' She strode the aisles, going directly to Elspeth's stall, the horse looking up as she approached, recognising her voice.

'That's a bad business, Milady,' Whit said. 'The Americans got bored so far from a city. The village was too rustic for them. They decamped last week to a town house in York to celebrate Christmas with some new friends they made on the trip over.'

'Where are the servants?'

'A bit of a mutiny, if you must know. They felt no reason to stay on until the Earl returned. Felt they were entitled to a bit of a holiday themselves since there was no one to look after and no one to know better as long as everyone was back in their places a few days before January the seventh.'

'I see.' Aurelia stroked Elspeth's nose and breathed in the horsey scent of her. After a day on the run, a sleepless night filled with tears and emotions, there was peace here with her horse, in the stable. She did see. The staff felt no particular loyalty to her father. Salaries had not been paid on time and there'd be no Christmas bonuses this year, ostensibly on account of the family being gone for so long over Christmas. But everyone knew the real reason. The Earl of Holme was rolled up.

'I am sorry it's not much of a homecoming, Milady.' Whit scratched his balding head. 'Did you travel all this way alone? Do your parents know you're here?'

'Yes, to the first, no to the second. I don't mean to stay, Whit. It's a long story. I suppose, like the servants, I've simply had enough. I've come for a few belongings and Elspeth. If I tell you any more, you'll be obliged to share that information.' She smiled. 'Thank you for staying. The horses would have starved.' A thought occurred to her. 'Are you the only one at the stables?'

'Ollie stayed, too. The two of us can look after the horses fine.'

She nodded. 'Things will get better here, Whit. My father did secure a loan and there will be a new estate manager to ensure things stay right.' She paused, dreading the idea of going up to the dark, big house, and sleeping there alone in the cold. 'Do you think I could sleep here tonight in one of the grooms' beds?' Based on Whit's calculations, there wouldn't have been a fire lit in the hall for over a week. The place would be freezing.

Whit left her to go fix up a bed and she pressed her head to Elspeth's. 'It's been a day, girl. But I am here now and we're both going to be safe.' Julien was going to be safe, too. She would be as far from him as she could be. She wouldn't be a tool to be used against him any more.

It was the first time today she'd allowed herself to think of him. One of the boons of being on the run was that it consumed her thoughts and demanded her attention. She had no energy or time to spare for reliving the pain of last night, the horrible words they'd said, tearing apart their hard-won happiness. But it had to be done. She could not allow Julien to marry her, to tie himself to the dysfunction that was her family, her father. It would be a bottomless pit that would suck him down like it had sucked her mother, like it was sucking her, costing her everything, including the man she loved and the life she truly wanted.

He had hated her yesterday for refusing him. Would he come to understand that her actions hadn't been motivated by hate or a desire to hurt him? She'd left before dawn *for* him. To protect him. It had felt wondrous to know the depths of his love, to be loved. She'd not lied when she'd told him that being with him was the first time she'd ever felt truly loved for herself, not her title, or what fortune she might have possessed once upon a time.

She didn't want to see that love ruined and eroded after dealing with her family over a lifetime. He deserved better than that. She had to trust that he would come to see that, to understand that eventually he would thank her for it even though she knew it would hurt for a while, because she hurt.

'I love him, Elspeth,' she whispered to the horse whom she'd told a lifetime of secrets. 'And he loved me. It was the most wondrous feeling in the world. Now it's over.' For good this time. A tear trickled against her horse's face. Not even the magic of Christmas could change that. She'd had her second chance and she'd lost him.

Chapter Twenty-One

The luck of the season was with him. Julien found her in the Moorfields stables the next morning, after rousing a post chaise driver at the earliest possible moment and making the rather long trip out into the countryside, hoping each mile of the way that he wouldn't be too late, that she'd still be there. The weather was clear today, which worked both for him and against him. If he could travel, so could she.

Now that he'd found her, he took a moment to savour the sight of her, dressed in boy's breeches that showed off the curve of her hip, the firm, round derrière that usually hid beneath her skirts, an oversized shirt and boots, a golden braid hanging down her back as she tacked up a beautiful chestnut. Elspeth. He was in time, but only just barely. Another hour's sleep would have seen his cause lost.

'Aurelia,' he called her name softly to announce his presence without startling her or the horse and to let his tone suggest that he did not come in anger.

He watched her hand freeze on the bridle strap and she turned slowly. 'Julien.' The wariness suggested she thought he'd come to harangue her further. He never wanted the woman he loved to have reason to look at him like that again. 'What are you doing here?'

'I've not come to scold or to drag you back under duress. I have come to apologise.' Julien cut straight to the matter in the hopes of giving her assurance. 'But what I really want to do is hold you, to prove to myself that you're safe and well.' He realised it was true. There were words that required saying, but they paled next to the need to hold her, to feel her in his arms and know she was not lost to him.

'Perhaps talk first.' She gestured to a groom working in the stalls. 'Ollie, can you take Elspeth to her stall. I need to speak with this gentleman.' Then she looked around, unsure.

'Perhaps we could go upstairs, a hay loft will do,' Julien suggested. 'I rode past the house and saw that it was empty.' And dark and cold. He could not imagine a more foreboding place. He certainly couldn't imagine growing up there.

'That's a long story, but I do have a hayloft available, although I don't have anything to offer you to drink or eat.'

He shook his head to indicate food and drink were of no import. 'I only want to see you, Aurelia.' He let her lead the way up to the loft, warm and redolent with the bales of winter hay. They settled, each on their own bale. She was being very careful to keep her distance, he noted. Perhaps that was a sign of how thin the thread of her control was. Perhaps it, like his own control, would snap upon contact, sweeping reason away with it just when it was needed most.

'How did you know I'd be here?' She twisted strands of hay together to give her hands something to do, another sign, he thought, of her upset. Aurelia was usually so lively, so confident.

'I listened to you. If one listens, everything becomes obvious. The breadcrumbs were all there, all I had to do was put them together. You told me your father regularly holds Elspeth against you, and you told me how you would go away the first chance you got, to live free with your horse.

'I should have listened to you better yesterday, but I didn't. You weren't refusing me. You were trying to protect me the only way you knew how. Tristan helped me see that. Now, I need to help *you* see that you don't have to do this alone. You don't have to live life alone and you don't have to manage your family alone.

She nodded slowly, thinking over his words while he waited impatiently for a response. He'd come all this way and now he just wanted it to be over and for her to be with him again. They would sort the rest out. As long as they were together, nothing was insurmountable. But she'd not had the advantage of the hours he'd spent on the crowded trains to think through the possibility that he'd come for her, that he'd *want* to find a way through this.

'What happens next, then, Julien?' she said at last in quiet, subdued tones that spoke of weariness, but gave no hint to her emotional reaction. Julien's heart sank. He'd hoped for better.

'In a perfect world, you tell me I'm forgiven, you throw yourself in my arms and we take advantage of the hayloft,' he said, only half-joking.

'This isn't a perfect world. I can forgive you, Julien. I owe you one on that account at least. Our ledgers will be balanced. You'd like that. Settled accounts.' She smiled, to make it clear she didn't mean it cruelly, but that she understood how his mind worked. 'But what does it change?'

'You're talking about your father.'

'Yes, he will wreck our happiness. I can't bear to watch that, to watch you come to hate me.'

'Because you love me.' The acknowledgement that came with hearing himself speak the words out loud moved through him with ferocity, intensity. *She loved him.* He wasn't in this alone.

Her eyes were shining dangerously bright. 'Yes, because I love you, because I've always loved you.'

'You've never said the words.' But she hadn't needed to. He knew, hadn't he? It was there in her kisses, in her smile, in the gifts of her body, in her laughter, even in this misguided attempt to protect him.

'Saying the words makes it real, Julien.' And real things had leverage, real things were always used against her. Real things could be lost.

'You won't lose me, Aurelia, not again. I thought foolishly and behaved foolishly the other night.'

'Yes, you did.'

Was that a bit of humour with the scold? Julien wondered.

Was the icy reserve thawing a bit at last? 'Marry me. Like we planned. Let us have the life we have imagined for ourselves. I can have that life with no one else—I want it with no one else. I've come all the way to Yorkshire to tell you that. And to remind you that your father doesn't get to steal your happiness.'

'You want to try?' There was disbelief in her voice as if she couldn't fathom being wanted after this latest debacle.

Julien chuckled. 'I don't think marriage is something we just "try." I think it's something we *do* and we don't stop doing it, we don't stop loving or trusting each other because things get hard.'

'Those are difficult things to accept when one has never had them,' she said shyly.

'You have them now, with me. Always. I will not make the mistake of doubting you again.' His heart burned as he looked at her, in hope for the future he saw in her eyes and in anger for all she'd been denied and the damage it had done. But he would change that, day by day, until she knew without reservation that she was safe in his love.

She came to him then, wiping away her tears, letting him take her in his arms, but the kiss was all hers, long and sweet and full of promise. 'I'm sorry you had to come all this way,' she murmured.

'I'm not.' He laughed as they tumbled into the hay.

'You will be, though.' She looked up at him with solemn blue eyes. 'You missed your mother's Christmas ball. The pantomime is tonight and you'll miss that, too. The costumes were going to be fabulous.'

He picked a piece of straw from her hair and levered himself up on one arm. 'Will you be sorry to miss it? They were your costumes, after all.'

'Not nearly as sorry as I am to take you away from all that you worked so hard to provide. You love Christmas with your family and I ruined that for you. You're here and…well, just look at this place. It's empty. The renters didn't even want to stay.'

Julien thought for a moment. 'But you like it here. Didn't you tell me you wanted to be home for Christmas? That you'd dreaded being away?' As an outsider it was hard to understand her attachment to a place that looked so full of foreboding and he told her so.

She laughed. 'I dreaded leaving Moorfields because I feared seeing you. Most of all, I worried if I wasn't here, there wouldn't be any traditions. My father doesn't lift a finger to put on the Christmas rituals—that falls to me. But I relish the opportunity to care for those whom my father neglects all year. There are no servants at the house because they know my father can't pay their wages and there will be no bonuses.' She sighed. 'Moorfields has no soul, not like Brentham Woods.' He could tell the admission hurt her, that she'd wanted more.

'I think you're wrong. I think you're its soul and it just needs to be awakened.'

She reached for his hand. 'You say the sweetest things, Julien. Maybe some day. What we ought to do now is get you back to York, get you on a train and get you home at least for Christmas Eve.'

'I don't think that's the plan at all. I intend to spend Christmas in Yorkshire with my wife before returning home to celebrate with my family.'

His wife. The words warmed her, touched her deeply, overwhelmed her. 'You mean to marry me here? Now?' What a wondrous thought, something she'd not dared dream of yesterday. 'Surely you want a big wedding with your family there. We need time to plan something appropriate to your station. You're a viscount now.'

'No, we don't need any of that,' he argued. 'Besides, *you* are my family as well and we've seen how transient plans really are. We spent the month planning the perfect Christmas in Hemsford and we won't be there to see it. Maybe that's because Christmas needs us here at Moorfields.'

'Christmas at Moorfields? Julien, that's not possible,' she sputtered. 'There's no time.' It had taken weeks of careful planning to arrange the Christmas festivities in Hemsford. He couldn't expect to pull something like that off here with just a day and a wedding on top of it.

'I say differently. We have all we need. I have a special licence in my coat pocket. There's a church in the village and you very likely have a wardrobe full of beautiful gowns that will suffice for the occasion. We'll open up Moorfields tomorrow afternoon for Yule festivities and we'll wed that night on Christmas Eve, catch the Christmas mail train on the twenty-fifth and be at Brentham Woods for supper. We live in a marvellous modern age. We might as well take advantage of it.' He was smiling broadly, but his words were in deadly earnest. He meant to do this, she realised. *For her.* Because he understood how desperately she needed it.

Still, there were practicalities that could not be overlooked. 'What about food, Julien? What will we serve our guests? I can't possibly bake enough in the time we have.' But this obstacle, too, was nothing to him.

'We'll take a leaf out of the London hostesses' book and bring the food in. I am sure the village baker would like to make some extra money and the village butcher, and even a few who wouldn't mind acting as footmen for an evening. Perhaps we might even find a fiddler or two. But we have to get started. It's already the twenty-third and there's a lot to do, including you changing clothes.' He helped her to her feet and she brushed the hay dust from her breeches, his body vibrating with a contagious energy that set her pulse racing with excitement.

'Are you sure we can do it?' she asked before they climbed down from the loft. What Julien proposed was exhilarating, but also likely impossible when one thought about it.

Yet, she could hear Elanora's words once more. *'Let Julien handle it. He can turn nothing into something.'*

'Doubter,' he scolded with a tease. 'I mean to show you, Aurelia Ripley, that Christmas is where you are, who you're with and it is absolutely what *you* make it.'

One person could make so much difference. When that one person was Julien Lennox, the impact was magnified tenfold. She'd not realised the extent of his power, how he wielded that power subtly through the simple act of listening to people, encouraging them and always looking for the possibility. 'There are no obstacles,' he told her as they exited the butcher's shop in Moorfields village. 'Only opportunities.'

She laughed up at him, enjoying herself thoroughly. 'You're certainly making plenty of those today.' Their shopping expedition had taken on a life and routine of its own as she accompanied him from store to store in the little High Street of the Moorfields village. She would introduce him as Julien Lennox, Viscount Lavenham, and he would take the visit from there, discussing the shop and business with the shopkeeper, offering an idea here and there. There'd been the discussion of gingerbread with the baker, who'd not thought of selling Twelfth Night Cakes with a prize hidden inside.

Such discussions were followed by an order for foodstuffs to be brought to the hall tomorrow for the Yule celebration and, Julien would add proudly, a celebration of their wedding. Hearing Julien say it sent a thrill through her every time she heard the words.

She was going to be his wife.

Not just the new Viscountess Lavenham. In truth, she hardly spared a thought for the title. Her thoughts were all for the man she watched in the shops.

The shopkeepers offered their congratulations, their eyes lighting up as Julien paid in advance for the goods and pulled out additional pound notes to clear the Earl's accounts. 'I believe everyone should start the year with a clean slate.' He'd wink at the shopkeepers, who agreed wholeheartedly. Julien had asked her to make a list of the debts before they'd set out and put it to memory. Business and bills concluded, Julien would then place a separate amount on the counter and say quietly, privately, 'This is from the both of us, from our family to yours, for your own Christmas celebrations or whatever you might need so you can start your own year in the clear.'

The chandler, from whom they'd purchased candles for the table and the fireplace mantel, had actually wiped away a tear and Aurelia had found the need to wipe her own tears when the chandler had confessed he would use it for medicine for his sick child. At which point, Julien had put another note on the counter.

'When we started this venture,' she said solemnly as they

stepped outside the store, 'I thought it was for me, but that is only a very small part. This Christmas celebration is for them.' She let out a shaky breath. 'It makes me grateful and ashamed. Grateful, because you are doing what I could not and these people deserve it. But ashamed because I've been able to do more over the years and that my father did less.'

'*We* are doing this,' Julien insisted. 'I need your introductions and it is clear that they adore you, that they understand you've done your best. I may be giving them funds, but I am still asking for a large task from them. They wouldn't bother to do it for a stranger. But they'll do it for you. It is their wedding gift to you.' He raised her hand to his lips. 'Our gift to them is the promise of better times and the restoration of the Christmas spirit. This is a new era for Moorfields.'

They made two more stops, one at the confectioner's and the other at a toymaker's whose face beamed when Julien bought nearly every toy he had: wooden whistles, balls and hoops, dolls and drums to be delivered by wagon up to the big house early tomorrow morning. 'Thank you, Milord. Toys need children and children need toys at Christmas. This year, the harvests were poor and with the economy the way it is no one has had much extra to spend on a toy.' And the man had suffered as a result, collateral damage to her father's erratic land management.

'We have a new land steward,' Julien told the fellow. 'Good times are coming.' And Aurelia's heart swelled with pride at this man who would soon be her husband.

'You're so sure and you pass that on to them, you give them hope. Don't you ever doubt?' she asked as they drove back to the house, a few of their purchases piled in the little wagon bed. Most would be arriving tomorrow morning. 'When was the last time you were ever nervous over something?'

Julien chuckled and she thought she detected colour in his cheek. 'Just a week ago when I made love to you for the first time. I wanted it to be good for you.'

Now, she was the one blushing. 'It was. But perhaps you were nervous because you need more practice,' she suggested coyly. 'Maybe when we get home, you'd like to practise a bit more?'

'Do you think we have time? We have a party tomorrow and

a wedding,' he joked, but there *was* a lot to do and just the two of them and Whit and Ollie to do it—sweeping the hall, moving furniture so that the hall was ready to receive its guests.

'Whose idea was it to have a party and a wedding all on the same day?' she scolded, cuddling close against the cold.

'Well, on second thought, practice *does* make perfect,' he relented playfully. 'We'd best practise this afternoon. We might be too tired tonight.'

And so they did.

A good idea it was, too. Aurelia yawned, falling into bed slightly before midnight beside Julien who was just awake enough to wrap his arm about her waist and pull her close. The hall had been decorated for the American guests, but there'd still been plenty to do and they had done it. Moorfields was ready for Christmas and she was ready for her new life. She'd had a glimpse of it today and it was good.

Chapter Twenty-Two

Life was good. Better than good. It was grand. This would be a Christmas neither he nor Moorfields would forget. Julien stood at the front of the candlelit church as people shifted from the Christmas service into the wedding service. It was late, nearing midnight. When the Christmas bells rang out, he would be a married man, a happy man.

It had been a day of joy, the perfect celebration to lead up to this celebration on the year's holiest night of love. He and Aurelia had been busy from the moment they'd risen until the moment they'd been driven to church in a festively decorated gig, the partygoers following them down, carols on the air.

What a whirlwind it had been, with food arriving mid-morning and being laid out along with Moorfield's best plate. Aurelia had outdone herself, overseeing that laying out: gingerbread on silver platters, candies in cut-crystal jars, long tables set with white cloths and china. 'What's the use of having such nice things if no one sees them? If they're just gathering dust?' she'd told Julien, sailing past him as he supervised the unloading of more wagons.

When he'd returned inside, the great hall had been transformed as it might have looked in more medieval times, offering guests a night of food and fun out of the cold. The guests had arrived in the early afternoon, the men to trek out with him and cut the Yule log, the children to play the games Aurelia organised for them—snapdragon, apple-bobbing, blind man's bluff—the women to sit and talk, enjoying being the hosted ones instead of the hostesses. When the men returned, log in tow, there'd been the grand ceremony of presenting it to the master of the house, in this case, the lady of the house, and it had been lit to great applause.

Dinner foods were brought out to replenish the already groaning tables, the fiddlers struck up dancing tunes and the hall was filled with merriment, the men clapping him on the back and giving him marital advice as if he were already one of them. Then it was time and, for Julien, the evening took on the cast of a more sober joy as he discreetly went upstairs to change his clothes. He'd bought a dark suit in town and, if it lacked the finesse of a Bond Street tailor, it was certainly cleaner than the clothes he'd left Brentham Woods in two days earlier.

Now he was here, awaiting Aurelia's 'arrival.' She and the ladies had stepped out at the end of the Christmas service, mostly so she could come back in and walk down the aisle. A newly made friend winked at Julien from the front row and Julien smiled. This was not the wedding he'd imagined. The one he'd imagined had been in Hemsford with Reverend Thompson presiding and Tristan at his side, his parents in the front row instead of a friend he'd just met hours ago.

But he was coming to discover his imagination might have been limited. He never could have planned a wedding like this. He supposed that was the whole point. He could not have planned a Christmas like this if he had a year to do it and it was better than anything he could have conceived.

The church door opened and there was whispered exclamations as Aurelia stepped inside, wearing her green velvet, a bouquet of evergreen and holly in her gloved hands. Her hair had been taken down and brushed. He smiled—now he knew what they'd been doing. On her head she wore a wreath of mistletoe. Perhaps in honour of their first kiss. He felt his smile tremble with an unlooked-for burst of emotion. Despite all the fun and busyness of today, she'd thought to wear meaningful symbols of their love, private messages of the promises they'd make each other.

At the altar, he took her hand and leaned close. 'My mistletoe bride,' he whispered at her ear. 'You look stunning, Aurelia.' No Bond Street gown or French silk could have looked finer. She looked like Christmas and love.

The ceremony was short. Julien preferred that it was. He wanted to kiss his bride and when he did the Christmas bells in the belfry rang out and the congregation cheered. His bride's cheeks were wet with her joy as he led her out into the Christmas night where they were surrounded by well-wishers who'd spent the day with them and the most important night of their life.

'Happy?' He squeezed Aurelia's hand as he helped her into the gig. 'Do you mind? I think they might follow us home,' he whispered, glancing at the villagers gathering around the gig.

'Throw them some silver pennies.' She laughed. 'They might leave us alone. It's an old tradition.'

Julien laughed and stood tall on the gig. 'Christmas pennies, for all!' he called out and tossed a handful or two or three in the air. They did the trick. He was allowed to go home and make love to his wife on the best night of the year and the first night of their life together.

'They're here! Uncle Julien is here!' Alex's loud cheers preceded them into the hall of Brentham Woods, at dusk on Christmas Day.

'So much for the element of surprise,' Julien said wryly as he and Aurelia stepped inside. He had a moment to take it all in before the family swarmed them in the hall. It had felt different this time, coming up the drive to Brentham, seeing the calming lights in the lace-curtained windows. This was truly his father's house now. He had his own house, his own family with his bride beside him. The circle was full. He had the closure he'd come home to seek. Or nearly so.

The family had just sat down to supper and now they spilled out from the dining room with exclamations of excitement. 'Julien!' His mother hugged him and turned triumphantly to his father. 'I told you he'd be here for supper.' Then, noticing that

Aurelia's parents hadn't moved forward to hug her, his mother embraced her with all her characteristic warmth. 'It's good to see you as well, my dear.'

Julien took Aurelia's hand. 'We would have come sooner, but we had a bit of business to take care of. We were married last night, at Moorfields in the stone church in the village after the service. Everyone, may I present to my family, for the first time, my bride, Viscountess Lavenham, Aurelia Lennox.'

This was met with unbridled celebration. His mother was hugging Aurelia again. His father was clapping him on the shoulder, Tristan was holding him tight in a brotherly hug of bear-like proportions and Elanora sighed with misty eyes. 'A Christmas Eve wedding, Julien. It's perfect.'

He smiled at Elanora and his brother. He'd nearly forgotten. 'It's your anniversary today, what is it? Four years now?'

At his side, Aurelia laughed. 'It's fitting, then, that two men who love Christmas as much as you two do have Christmas brides.'

Elanora looped her arm through her new sister-in-law's. 'We will be able to celebrate together every year.'

Julien caught a glance from Tristan and the brothers exchanged a look. How wondrous that their wives would be friends, that the two women held each other in genuine affection, what a grand promise life held. In time their children would grow up together, play together, run the fields together, ride their first ponies together, fish in the same rivers their fathers had fished in.

Tristan wrapped an arm about his shoulders. 'I know what you're thinking, Brother,' he said in low tones and Julien smiled.

'I'm thinking here's to Christmas futures.' His eyes might have been wet with a little sentiment but it wasn't quite time to give in to that yet. There was one more item to settle.

He turned to where the Earl and Lady Holme stood apart from the group. Their distance was a bittersweet sign. Aurelia was a Lennox now. She had a family that loved her, that would embrace her as she was. She did not need them and whatever they passed off as love and affection. 'Do you not wish to greet your daughter and congratulate her on her marriage?'

His own father had the discretion to usher everyone else back into the dining room. Julien gave him a nod, which promised they would join them shortly. His business with Holme wouldn't take long. He'd already made his terms. He merely needed to remind Holme of that.

Her mother came forward and hugged her tight. Perhaps the Earl had not allowed her to come forward earlier. The sight tugged at Julien's heart as did her words. 'You must have been a beautiful bride, I wish I could have seen you. I've dreamed of your wedding day for so long.'

'It would have done your dreams proud, Milady,' Julien swiftly intervened lest the woman make Aurelia feel guilty about the speed of the wedding and its rather non-traditional aspect. 'When Aurelia looks back on her wedding day, it will be with joy. She was surrounded by the spirit of the season, the villagers she's known her whole life and we opened Moorfields' doors for a Yule celebration the likes of which I don't believe they've ever seen.'

That pointed comment was meant for the Earl.

'It's not your place,' Holme huffed. 'You may have given me a loan, but Moorfields is not yours, nor will it ever be.'

'No,' Julien said coolly. 'But it is Aurelia's home as long as you're alive. It is her obligation and her pleasure to make everyone feel welcome there. Or perhaps you've forgotten the symbiotic relationship that should exist between tenant and landowner, each having a duty to the other?

'Out of honor for that symbiotic relationship, as a wedding gift to your daughter, Holme, I paid the merchants what was owed them. I do not expect to see that level of debt accrued again. It's not good for the local economy nor for your reputation among them. If there is debt, it will negatively impact the conditions of our loan. Likewise, I know you and Lady Holme will want to offer Aurelia a wedding gift as well. That gift will be the safe and immediate delivery of Elspeth to my new stables. If anything happens to that horse before her delivery, I will foreclose on the loan. Send Ollie with her.'

'Ollie?' Holme looked baffled, or perhaps overwhelmed.

'He's one of your grooms. I will add that to the list of tasks

I've assigned you at Moorfields. Learn your servants' names.' Julien gave a polite smile. 'Tomorrow, after the Boxing Day gifts are delivered, my wife and I will depart for my home. Lady Holme, you are always welcome there. I am sure my bride would delight in your support as she sets up our house. You could always accompany Ollie. The choice is yours.'

'Now see here, Lavenham,' Holme sputtered. 'You go too far.'

'No, it is you who went too far and now that is done.' Julien offered his arm to Aurelia and led her into Christmas supper where he was surrounded by the people he loved most: Alex crawling on and off his lap, showing him his new carved horse, baby Violet dribbling on his jacket, Elanora regaling them with the success of the pantomime at Heartsease and his mother's news of the Christmas ball. This was exactly where he wanted to be, just as last night in Yorkshire had been exactly where he wanted to be. Because Aurelia was beside him. Because love changed everything.

'You're happy to be home,' Aurelia whispered as he lit their way up to bed in his old chamber hours later. 'I can see it in your smile. It was worth the mail train to be here.'

He stopped before their chamber door. 'If home is where you are, then, yes, I am happy to be here. As long as I am with you, I will always be home for Christmas.'

Epilogue

December 25th, 1854,
four years later

'Jamie, slow down, lad, before you trip over something and fall,' Julien gently chided his energetic three-year-old son who came barrelling down the stairs on Christmas morning.

'But I smell sausage! Yum!' he cried as Julien intercepted him and swung him around.

'No sausage until Mama is down,' Julien cautioned. 'But maybe this will do until then.' He slipped the boy a gingerbread biscuit and watched his son's eyes light up at the unexpected treat. 'But don't tell Mama,' he whispered. 'It will be our secret. You know how she is about sweets before breakfast.'

The little boy laughed and Julien set him down, his heart filling with love for this wondrous creature who was his son. His son! It had been three years since he'd first held Jamie in his arms and the thrill never grew old. He woke each morning thinking how blessed he was to have a child. Aurelia's child.

'What shouldn't you tell Mama?' Aurelia's not-quite-awake voice spoke from the stairs where she was carefully making her way down. 'Are my men keeping secrets?' she teased.

'Mama!' Jamie cried. 'There's sausage! I can smell it!'

Aurelia forced a smile for Jamie's sake, her gaze meeting his over Jamie's head. 'Yes, my dear, I smell it, too.'

Although not with the same enjoyment, Julien would wager.

Julien went to her and took her arm with solicitous concern. 'Steady now. Is your stomach bothering you this morning?'

She laughed. 'Always. You know how it is in the early months. But never fear, I'll be ravenous by noon, once the family gets here.'

She gave him the soft smile that never ceased to melt him.

'Shall we tell them the news today?'

Aurelia was three months into her second pregnancy and it had been the best early Christmas gift Julien could have imagined.

They reached the bottom of the stairs and Jamie wrapped his chubby toddler arms around his parents' legs in a hug that encompassed them both.

Julien picked him up. 'Do you think you'll have a brother or a sister this time next year?'

'A pony!' Jamie laughed and Julien exchanged a look with Aurelia.

One had to be careful in what one said around children, even little ones. Cousin Alex, who was six now, was getting a pony for Christmas and there'd been a lot of talk about it between the adults in the past few months.

'That is not one of the options.' Julien tickled the little boy's belly. 'Do you want a brother or a sister for a playmate?'

Jamie screwed up his face in hard thought before declaring, 'One of each!'

Julien laughed and Aurelia swatted him playfully on the arm. 'That's easy for you to laugh at. You're not the one having them.'

He leaned in and kissed her cheek in response. 'Since your stomach is queasy, why don't we do presents first and breakfast second? Cook can hold it back for a while.'

'Presents *now*? Yay!'

Jamie squealed and Julien set him down to let him run to the Christmas tree room ahead of them. There would be more presents later, when the cousins came, but Christmas morning was just for them, the three of them, soon to be four.

'How long have you been up?' Aurelia asked as they trailed behind their son. 'The pillow was cold when I woke.'

'Since six,' Julien admitted, taking her arm and looping it through his. 'You know how I like a moment's time to reflect on Christmas Day. I love the chaos of Christmas, but I also like a moment of quiet to give thanks for you, for Jamie, for what I am able to do for others, for this home you've made for me.'

That time was important to him. December was an exceedingly busy month for him. He was the head of the Hemsford Village Improvement Society. That meant he'd been in charge of the Christmas fair, which continued to expand as attendance continued to grow. The days leading up to Christmas had been hectic with the pantomime and the ball. This year had been Jamie's first pantomime. He'd played a small pixie and Julien thought his son had delivered his one line with aplomb.

Of course, December wasn't his only busy month. He'd also been busy designing a summer market programme that would bring people to Hemsford for the fresh produce and splitting his time between London and Hemsford.

Thanks to the trains, gone were the days of spending the year in London due to work. He was able to work from his home and go up to the main office every few weeks. He loved being on hand to see to his estate, his community and his son. There was nothing more rewarding than being an active father involved in his son's childhood…unless it was riding down the drive and seeing Aurelia's lamps shining in the windows of Meadowlark Hall, which was what they'd chosen to name the place, in honour of the birds that sang in the morning at the promise of each new day. Those lamps were a symbol of their love, leading him home.

Jamie was waiting for them expectantly in the Christmas tree room, eyes wide as he studied the tree draped in its colourful winterberry garland.

Aurelia tugged at Julien's arm. 'Just a moment,' she whispered, halting in the doorway. 'I just want to look at him. I want to make a mental picture of this moment, of his little face turned towards the tree, his eyes full of wonder. Before he loses it.'

He squeezed her hand, knowing that she was thinking of

other Christmases filled with less joy…the Christmases of her childhood.

'He won't lose it, Aurelia,' Julien said confidently. 'I never have.'

Julien gave her a moment and then went to his son, kneeling down beside him, a hand at his back. 'Do you see the star atop the tree?' This was a new addition. 'Do you know what it stands for?'

'For Bethlehem and the three wise men,' Jamie recited proudly.

Julien tousled his hair. 'Yes, for the three wise men,' he affirmed. 'It gave them guidance, showing them the way. It also gave them hope that they would find their way. Today, it does the same for us, my boy. The star is a reminder of hope for ourselves, and hope for the world, which it sometimes desperately needs.' He tapped his son's chest with a finger. 'Hope isn't just a Christmas thing, Jamie. Hope is for all year and it lives inside each of us.'

Jamie looked down at his chest. 'In me, too?'

'Most definitely in you. You are all your mama and I hoped for. Every time we look at you, we are reminded of hope. You are hope, just as your brother or sister will be hope to us, too.'

The boy probably didn't comprehend half of what he was saying, but Julien felt it was important to say the words anyway. He and Aurelia wanted their children to grow up knowing how deeply loved they were. Love bred confidence and security.

Aurelia settled on the sofa, rubbing her stomach and smiling at them.

Julien reached beneath the tree for a box and handed it to Jamie. 'Why don't we start with your gift for Mama?' He wanted his son to learn early that giving was the greater joy.

Jamie solemnly took the little box over to his mother and curled up beside her on the sofa while she lifted the lid. Jamie had been so excited about it, Julien had worried the little boy would blurt it out before Christmas.

'I made it myself, with Papa and Uncle Tristan's help,' he announced as she lifted up a whittled wooden heart strung on a green ribbon. 'I carved it myself, with...' He grimaced and turned to his papa. 'What's the word, Papa?'

'Supervision!' Julien chuckled, enjoying the scene on the sofa very much.

'Supervision, Mama,' Jamie said. 'Look, there's words, too. Can you read them? It says *love* on this side of the heart and *family* on the other. Do you like it? I burned the letters on to the wood myself.'

'I love it.'

She pressed a kiss to her son's blond head, her eyes shining as Julien caught her gaze. She was the bravest woman he knew. She'd chosen him, chosen their love, at the expense of leaving behind her family for a new life, a life she deserved.

'Now, it's your turn, dear boy. What shall you open first?'

Delightful chaos ensued as Jamie opened his presents, exclaiming gleefully over each one, followed by Julien's favourite part of the day—the time between the opening and exclaiming and breakfast—a golden half-hour when he could sit on the sofa with his wife and watch his son play with his new toys beneath the tree, thoroughly engrossed.

'Are you happy, my love?' He raised her hand to his lips.

'You know I am. Happier than I ever dreamed I could be.' She smiled.

'I am sorry your mother isn't here,' Julien said quietly, knowing that was on her mind, as it always was at Christmas.

Each year, Lady Holme had been invited and each year there'd always been an excuse. Julien had even offered to go up and travel down with her, in case pressure from the Earl was preventing her from leaving.

Aurelia glanced at the star atop the tree. 'Perhaps next year, when she has two grandchildren to meet. I keep hoping.'

Her parents remained one difficulty they'd not yet conquered. She'd not seen her mother since Boxing Day four years ago. But Elspeth had arrived safe and sound soon after her father's return north and Julien's conditions had kept her father in check. The Holme estates were thriving, Moorfields had become self-sustaining under Julien's appointed steward and Aurelia enjoyed the long letters from Whit about the state of the village. Julien had promised the village better times four years ago and he'd delivered on that.

'Perhaps if we have a girl we'll name her Hope.' Julien smiled at his wife. 'For all the things yet to come.'

'I'd like that.' She kissed him softly, whispering, 'Happy Christmas, Julien. I love you. Now, off you go to play with your son.' She laughed. 'I know you've been wanting to get your hands on those tin soldiers since we bought them.'

Julien gave her a mock salute and did as he was told. Because if there was anything he liked better than sitting beside his wife on Christmas Day, it was playing beneath the Christmas tree with his son.

He gave the star a quick glance as he scooted beneath the tree and made a silent wish in his heart. *Please, let it be like this. Always.*

* * * * *

One Night With The Duchess
Maggie Weston

MILLS & BOON

Maggie Weston is a Victorian-era enthusiast. Though she grew up voraciously consuming classical literature, she stumbled upon her first romance novel at age eleven and never looked back. When she's not writing or researching all the weird things our predecessors did, she can be found reading, taking on home improvement projects that she thinks she can handle (but can't) and watching period dramas. Maggie lives with her husband, two dogs and innumerable houseplants in California.

One Night with the Duchess is Maggie Weston's debut title for Harlequin Historical.

Look out for more books from Maggie Weston coming soon.

Author Note

I've always been obsessed with the Victorians, especially the aristocracy, with their strange rules and conventions, most of which applied to women and dictated how they could (or, more accurately, *could not*) behave. Rules that changed significantly with a woman's marital status. So, when it came to writing a historical romance trilogy, I wanted to explore a trio of young widows who leave convention behind, take scandalous risks and, most importantly, fall in love with men who cherish them exactly as they come.

Thus, the Widows of West End was born.

And there was so much to explore! Funerals, mourning periods, mourning garb (commonly called "widow's weeds"), legal consummation of a marriage, virginity testing... Yes, you read that right. Though virginity testing would have been considered quite outdated by the 1840s (in the United Kingdom, at least), what better way to usher in a sordid love affair than by having a newly married and widowed duchess seek out a notorious rake to rid her of her virginity so that she could retain her title?

I adored creating Matthew and Isabelle, and I sincerely hope that you enjoy reading *One Night with the Duchess* as much as I enjoyed writing it!

For my parents, who have always been
irrationally confident in my ability to succeed.

Chapter One

London, 1840

'Excuse me, my lord.'

'What is it, Taps?' Matthew Blake, Lord Ashworth, regarded his butler over the rim of his crystal whisky glass.

Taps, who had served the Blake family for nearly twenty-five years, was a contradiction in motion, a man as firm and stout in appearance as he was fidgety by nature. Even as Matthew watched him, Taps shifted from one foot to the other.

'There is a young lady here to see you, my lord.'

Matthew raised one dark eyebrow and spared a glance at the rosewood clock on the mantel. The delicate brass hands indicated that it was nearly one o'clock in the morning. 'Who?'

'She refused to give a name, my lord. However, she said it was a matter of great urgency.' Taps paused almost imperceptibly before adding, 'She seems quite distressed.'

'Is she alone?'

'She is accompanied by another woman, perhaps her lady's maid.'

Intrigued despite his fatigue, Matthew asked, 'What does she look like?' He didn't know any young woman who'd risk visiting his private residence unchaperoned at such a time.

'She is in mourning, my lord.'

He waved one large-palmed hand lazily. 'Show her in.'

Taps paused and cast a subtle look at Matthew's attire—or lack thereof. 'Would you like some time to make yourself presentable, my lord?'

'Taps,' Matthew chided without looking down at his partially unbuttoned shirt, 'it is one o'clock in the morning. Any woman coming to see *me* now doesn't give a fig about propriety.' He slouched further into his chair. 'At this time of night, she's lucky I'm clothed at all.'

While his butler would never dare to question him, Taps had long ago perfected a tone that displayed disapproval while somehow sounding nothing but polite. He used it now, issuing a crisp 'My lord' before bowing and leaving the room.

Matthew ignored his butler's subtle reprimand and pondered his unexpected visitor instead. He wasn't aware of anyone he knew having died recently, which could only mean that either he didn't know the lady in question or she was wearing mourning garb as a disguise. Considering whose house she had entered, he considered that wise. Bold, undoubtedly. But wise.

There was a gentle announcing knock on the door before Taps re-entered the room, this time with a small woman in tow. Her slight frame was hidden under a mass of black fabric, her face completely obscured by the weeping veil that fell in one smooth sheet from the brim of her hat to the exact point at her throat where her high-collared dress started, leaving not even a single inch of skin exposed.

Seeming at a loss for how to introduce the woman, Taps floundered for a second, then gave up entirely, bowed, and left the room.

Curious as to what she'd do, Matthew said nothing. He made no move to greet the stranger, essentially breaking every rule of decorum that had been drilled into him from birth. He took a sip of his peated whisky, crossed one booted ankle over the other, and waited in silence for her to say something.

The woman bowed her head in greeting. 'Lord Ashworth.'

Her voice was cultured and young—young enough that he instinctively knew nothing good could come of their meeting.

'If you're going to barge into my house in the middle of the night, I at the very least deserve the courtesy of knowing to whom I am speaking.'

Her head tipped forward, almost as if she were trying to regain her composure—or pray. 'My name is Isabelle Con—' She took a small breath and slowly straightened her spine. 'I am Isabelle St Claire,' she corrected, 'the Duchess of Everett.'

Matthew's heart constricted in his chest. Slowly, he put his drink down. 'Your Grace,' he greeted her politely, but his mind warred with this new information. He knew the name, of course. There were, after all, less than thirty dukes in all of England.

There'd been news lately... At the club, maybe... No, he remembered, *at Giovanni's School of Arms.*

'Your husband died a few days ago?'

'Yes.'

Her affirmation was all he needed to have the memory surfacing. His best friend—Leo Vickery, Lord Pemberton—had told him about the Duke of Everett, who'd had a sudden heart attack at the age of fifty-five. A sad event, to be sure—made all the more unfortunate by the fact that he'd left behind a bride of eighteen, a woman barely out in society. *This* woman, as fate would have it.

'My condolences.'

'Thank you.'

'Your Grace,' he chastised gently, 'it is hardly proper for you to be here at this hour. If anyone were to see you in my home...'

There was no need to explain further. Matthew's reputation aside, some things simply were not done, and visiting a strange man in the middle of the night was certainly one of them.

'I am well aware,' she countered immediately, her tone leaving no room for further argument on his part.

Hopelessly fascinated, Matthew leaned back in his chair. 'Your Grace...?'

'Isabelle.'

Uncomfortable with the familiarity, he simply nodded.

'I am going to be frank, Lord Ashworth.'

She sounded like an ancient matriarch, chastising an errant

toddler, but Matthew found the contrast of the stern tone and the young, birdlike woman intriguing.

'Please do,' he said, and although he did not move from his position, he fought the insane urge to go to her and tear the weeping veil off. For some unholy reason, he wanted to see her face.

The Duchess did not mince her words. 'I was married a mere two weeks before my husband died.' She anxiously clasped and unclasped her small gloved hands. 'The marriage was decided upon when I was just thirteen.' She cleared her throat daintily. 'The Duke was a trusted friend of my father's.'

The Duchess took three quick steps towards the door, spun around, and then hurried in the opposite direction like a mouse trapped in the corner of a barn.

'You see, my husband was not a...' She paused to consider her word choice before settling on, 'He was not an *unkind* man. He was older, to be sure, but rather...soft...'

She tugged at her bodice with both hands, as if she could somehow rip the heavy dress off her body.

Matthew pushed himself to a stand, getting warier by the second. 'Your Grace,' he said, interrupting her nervous chatter, 'please speak plainly.'

The Duchess spun around to face him. She inhaled a huge breath and as the black veil was suctioned inwards, plastering the dyed lace to her lips, she spluttered. Reaching up with both hands, she frantically ripped the entire hat off, scattering pins and scraps of fabric on the floor.

In any other circumstance Matthew might have been amused. His mouth even momentarily fought a smile as he watched the hairpins bounce across the carpeted floor before settling. But the moment he looked up his smile faded and any humour died.

The Duchess of Everett blinked at him from worried eyes the colour of onyx...eyes framed by impossibly long, inky lashes. Her skin was golden, stark against the cascade of black hair that had come undone and fell in thick ringlets down her narrow waist to her flared hips. Her sharp features were softened by a small, straight nose and a delicate mouth. She was a vision.

'My marriage was not consummated,' she blurted, and then

immediately slapped a hand over her mouth, clearly mortified by her admission.

Matthew watched, fascinated, as a pink blush spread from the high collar of her dress up her neck and through her cheeks. At a complete loss for the appropriate thing to say, he merely repeated, 'My condolences.'

The Duchess opened her mouth, closed it. She placed both hands on her hips and began to walk around his parlour.

'With all due respect, Your Grace. How may *I* be of service exactly?' he asked.

'Is it not obvious?'

'I'm not sure that it is.'

'My late husband's cousin is insisting upon a doctor's...*proof* that I am really the Duchess of Everett.'

Matthew scowled at that. 'Why did you not refuse? I'm sure most doctors would find such an examination archaic.'

'I should have,' she agreed. 'However, that only occurred to me after the fact, and now the risk is that my marriage will be annulled.'

Matthew began to see her dilemma. 'And you would lose your new title... *Duchess.*'

The Duchess straightened her spine and shot him a look that would have sent a lesser man running. For Matthew, her narrowed eyes and tight mouth had the complete opposite effect, and for some absurd reason he suddenly wondered what it would be like to tease those seriously set lips into sighing open for him.

'I am a virgin,' she stated, and although he'd inferred that much, hearing the actual words turned his momentary fantasy to dust. Though she tried to hide her embarrassment, she fidgeted with her gloves again. 'A new match, however humiliating for my family, could be arranged...'

Her voice was clear, but Matthew could hear the heavy dread in it still. He did not move; he barely breathed.

'My concern is for the new Duke of Everett—my husband's son by his previous wife.' She spun around again, making her stiff skirts sway back and forth like an ancient church bell. 'Luke is only seven.'

Matthew saw her logic then. 'And you fear what would happen to him should you be sent away?'

'My husband's cousin—Gareth St Claire—is an unbearable man. And he is next in line for the Dukedom after Luke.'

'Common law would prevent him from assuming guardianship of Luke if he is next in line for the title,' Matthew pointed out, even though he knew that such things rarely mattered. Without protection, a titled child alone in the world was easy prey.

'Yes, I am aware,' she replied dryly. 'But my late husband named his wife—if there should be one—as Luke's guardian in the event of his death. That is me.' Her voice rose with her panic. 'If my marriage is annulled, Luke will be placed as a ward of the Chancery. He's a *child*, my lord. It will be years before he's of age and able to assume the responsibilities of his title, and in all that time there will only be one stranger appointed to come between Luke and his uncle.'

'You think he would harm the boy?'

Although he kept his tone cool, Matthew saw her distress was genuine. He knew even if it weren't for her obvious anxiety, the facts remained. No man was as close to power and wealth than when he was separated from an inherited title by a single child—nor would he ever be that close again.

'There are many ways to damage a child irreparably, my lord. More ways to manipulate and control one. I don't know if Gareth would physically harm Luke, but I would not put anything past him. And I am the only person with the means to do something.' She took two bold steps closer. 'Many of my childhood summers were spent at the Everett country home, Moorhen House. I was always a bit…solitary. An only child. When the previous Duchess died in childbirth, Luke was completely alone. He is a little brother to me in many ways.'

'Some might even say a son?'

'Yes. Although he is only eleven years younger, some would say he's like a son to me.' Again, those thin shoulders squared, those black eyes slowly rose to meet his. 'It's my responsibility to ensure his well-being.'

'And secure yourself the title in the process?'

'I'm not denying that I would benefit, Lord Ashworth. Merely that benefit to myself is not my primary motivation. Being the Duchess of Everett is a duty I take seriously. However, Luke's safety is my only concern.'

Matthew was no idiot. He had an inkling of why she was in his house, hiding in her widow's weeds, at one o'clock in the morning. And even though he'd never touch an unspoiled daughter of the peerage, he couldn't help but push her to her point. He needed to hear her say the words.

'And you're here because…'

She exhaled a deep breath. 'I've come because…'

'Yes?' It was a single word, a simple word, but it left Matthew's lips weighted with anticipation.

'May I ask a favour?'

'You may ask,' he countered, 'but I will most probably refuse.'

'I would like you to bed me.'

Having become somewhat used to people expecting such behaviour from him, Matthew smiled grimly. But, in spite of that, when he said, 'No,' the word left his lips tasting bitter.

Isabelle was startled at the abrupt answer, issued from Lord Ashworth with no hint of doubt. 'You're not even going to *think* about it?'

The giant man standing in front of her grinned, his white teeth flashing wolfishly. He ran one large hand through his unstylishly shaggy hair.

'There's no need. I don't *bed* virgins. I don't ruin reputations—'

'That is not what I heard.'

Matthew ignored her comment. 'And I certainly will not be led by the nose into a situation where you could hold any sort of power over me. I'm not the man you're looking for, *Duchess*.'

Isabelle couldn't help the slightly hysterical giggle that worked its way up her throat. 'You… You think that I would trick you into *marriage*?' she asked, somewhat stunned by the notion. 'Have you not been listening to anything I've said?' She waved both hands down towards her heavy black dress. 'I'm in *mourning.* I will be for *years*!' she practically shouted. 'And even if I wasn't, marriage to you is the *last* thing I'd want!'

Because she felt hot and flustered by his looming presence and the entirely inappropriate conversation they were having, she started to pace.

She lowered her voice. 'I'm a *duchess.* I don't need your title. And marrying again before my mourning period is over would cause a scandal that would be completely antagonistic to my main goal—helping Luke.' When he only raised his eyebrows, she continued, 'Moreover, I have no *desire* to get married again.'

'But you're not a duchess—technically. And am I just supposed to trust whatever you say?'

Isabelle turned abruptly to find that he'd closed the space between them, and that instead of looking at his face she was staring at a patch of tanned skin where his collar lay open. She slowly craned her neck back, shifting her eyes away from his chest to his steel gaze.

'Do you honestly believe that I'd be here with any other motive? That I'd want to lose my—' she lowered her voice '—my *maidenhead* to a stranger whose name I picked off a list?'

Lord Ashworth did not try to fight his grin. 'You have a list?'

Isabelle ignored the unsteady fluttering in her stomach, and even though it had not really been a question she felt compelled to clarify. 'A list of ne'er-do-wells that I got from my very well-informed companion.'

'Ne'er-do-wells?'

She waved her hand flippantly in his general direction. 'You know…' And when he just shook his head, she leaned closer and whispered, 'Rakes.'

Lord Ashworth threw his head back and laughed. It was a lovely sound, deep and rusty, as if he wasn't in the habit of using it often. But instead of appreciating the way it rolled over her skin, Isabelle felt the first true panic stick in her throat. It had been easier to get her feet moving once she'd had a plan and made up her mind, but now… Now her plan seemed as ridiculous as Lord Ashworth clearly found it.

Hot tears prickled her eyes.

Panic clawed through her chest.

Her breathing grew tight, each whoosh of air grating up her throat as if it were being forced.

If she couldn't convince one of the five men whose names she and her cousin Mary had carefully selected to help her, she'd lose Luke mere weeks after she'd been put in a position to help him.

Luke was the entire reason she'd agreed to marry the Duke in the first place. Every time she'd thought of running away, of leaving to go and stay with her aunt Angela in Italy, she'd thought of Luke, alone and neglected at Moorhen House. And so she had stayed.

She'd stayed because it wasn't Luke's fault that his birth had killed his mother and practically estranged him from his grieving father. She'd stayed because on her worst days, including the day she'd been told she was to marry the Duke of Everett, she'd had only one person whom she knew loved her regardless, who looked at her as if she could solve any problem in the world, protect him from anything...*slay his dragons*. She'd stayed because she remembered what it was to be alone in a nursery with only speechless dolls and an uninterested nursemaid for company, and she could never abandon Luke to the same fate.

Remembering now had her taking a deep, calming breath. She removed the list of names from the inside of her glove and opened it with fumbling hands and blurred vision.

Leo Vickery, Lord Pemberton, was next.

Isabelle had met Leo before at a birthday celebration held for her dear friend, Wilhelmina Russell, which made things a little less awkward... Or at least one might hope it made things less awkward. Unlike the brooding Lord Ashworth, whose illicit affair with the Marchioness of Dunn had marked him a reprehensible rogue, Lord Pemberton was the quintessential peer—for, while he kept an expensive mistress, he did so fairly discreetly, and did not ruin any marriages in his pursuit of his own pleasure.

Isabelle took a harried step towards the door. Paused. When she turned back, Lord Ashworth was no longer laughing. Those cold, grey eyes were studying her with a quiet dread that she felt in the depths of her soul.

'If it's all the same to you, I would appreciate your discretion in this matter,' she said.

She didn't wait for a reply.

She got all the way to turning the brass knob before that deep, gravelly voice called, 'Wait.'

She swallowed nervously and turned back to face Lord Ashworth.

He held her hat in his hand.

'Oh. Yes. My hat.'

Isabelle strode across the room and attempted to pluck the hat from him, but instead of releasing it, his strong fingers closed tighter around the brim. She yanked—*hard*—but he didn't move a single inch.

'Is there a problem, my lord?'

'Who else is on your list?'

Shame suffused her, heating her blood and crawling unpleasantly over her skin. 'I'd prefer not to—'

Before she could finish the sentence, he'd plucked the crumpled paper from her hand and held it up to read.

With an indignant gasp, Isabelle tried to snatch the list back; however, Lord Ashworth merely placed one heavy hand on her shoulder and held her in place, stopping any further attempt. Humiliated beyond reason, she stood still and stared at a loose gold thread in the plush rug beneath her feet.

His big palm on her shoulder was heavy, almost comforting despite the restraint. His clothes carried the familiar scent of cigar smoke, but it was faint—as if he'd been standing in proximity to someone who'd been smoking. And instead of making her ill, as it had when she'd been a girl, curled up with a book in her father's study while he'd smoked, the bitter tang soothed her now.

Her father, who was not an affectionate man by nature, had never minded Isabelle's company, so long as she had remained quiet and not interrupted his business. And, Isabelle, who had never had much opportunity to interact with him otherwise, had spent many an hour sitting in silence in her father's office, making herself ill on tobacco smoke in the hope of a casual word or a glance of affection that never came.

Lord Ashworth finished reading the list and released her, leaving Isabelle oddly unsteady. It was as if he had been grounding her, keeping her panic at bay, so that the moment he let go, it all came flooding back.

'You can't do this, Duchess.'

'I *have* to,' she insisted. 'I *lied*. I told everyone my marriage was consummated. The physician is coming in *two days* to put Gareth St Claire's mind at rest.'

'No. I'm telling you now, Leo—Lord Pemberton—won't touch you. He likes to have fun, but he'd never go through with something like this. Atkins and Williams might—but they wouldn't keep quiet about it, which would not only ruin your reputation, but risk your marriage's annulment anyway. And even if Cedric Finchley didn't say anything it'd be because he had far worse intentions. His family's fortune is in dire straits. He's more likely to spend his entire life hounding you, blackmailing you to pillage Luke's inheritance. Is that really what you want?'

A cold tendril of fear snaked through Isabelle's resolve. 'No. Of course that's not what I want!'

'There are other ways, you know... To make it seem as if you've...' Lord Ashworth sighed deeply as his eyes studied the ceiling. Her hat dangled forlornly in his hand.

The hope that rose in Isabelle's chest was so sharp, so real. 'How? Tell me.'

'It's really just a matter of...penetration. You... I mean.'

Isabelle frowned. 'I... I don't understand.'

'I apologise, Your Grace. But explaining the basics of screwing to a young woman wasn't exactly something I'd prepared myself for when I got home an hour ago.'

Isabelle ceded his point with a small nod. 'I'm not a child, Lord Ashworth. I am a widow—one who wouldn't even be having this conversation if I'd been brave enough with the Duke that first time.'

Lord Ashworth pinned her with those unsettling eyes. 'He tried...?'

'He *tried*,' she admitted tartly. 'It was horrifically awkward. Once he started removing his clothes I just lay there and cried, and he couldn't…or wouldn't… He left. He said I needed some time to "grow accustomed" to the idea.'

'I doubt time would have made it more appealing,' Lord Ashworth drawled. 'What was he? Fifty-five? And fat as a Christmas goose, if memory serves.'

Isabelle didn't argue. 'It doesn't matter. I should have been braver. I should have done my duty—for Luke.'

'It does matter,' he snapped. 'You should never have been betrothed to him—and age is the least of it.'

Seeing that he was growing increasingly frustrated with her, Isabelle calmed her tone. It didn't matter that she agreed with him, or that she still sometimes woke in the night drenched in sweat and terror before she remembered that it was all over. She had married the Duke, as her father had demanded. And she had survived it as her mother had said she would.

'If I don't do this, *nothing* will change for me. I will be marked a virgin, my marriage will be annulled, and I will be married off a second time—this time to someone whom I don't know and who very possibly isn't as understanding as the late Duke was. I have lived through it once, and by God I could survive it again.' Just the thought made her stomach roil with dread, but Isabelle pushed through it. 'But Luke will be shipped off to boarding school. He'll never be given the love and attention he needs. And that's the best-case scenario.'

'That I do understand,' Lord Ashworth surprised her by saying.

'Well, then.' She held out her hand, palm up, fully expecting him to hand her the paper and send her on her way.

Instead, he turned and threw it straight into the blazing fire.

For a long moment, all Isabelle could do was stand and stare at the rapidly disintegrating paper. It flamed and curled, turning as black as the rage that snapped through her.

Instead of storming out, she simply lifted her chin defiantly. 'It was five names; I can remember all of them.'

'You don't have to.' Lord Ashworth walked back to the large tufted chair he'd previously vacated. He collapsed into it and picked up his whisky, the picture of a man up to his neck in trouble. 'I'll help you.'

'You *will*?'

'Yes.'

'Why?' she couldn't help but ask, given his sudden change of heart.

He shook his head. 'My options are either to let you try with someone who'll undoubtedly ruin your life. Or explain to you the mechanics and then pray to God you don't impale yourself on something. My way is quicker, and less dangerous to everyone involved.'

Isabelle couldn't quite believe what she was hearing. 'You'll help me? Do...*this*?' A shiver of nerves crawled over her body.

'Yes. And just in case you get any ideas, I leave for a tour of the continent in two days' time. I won't be back in England for two years.'

Desperate to sidestep his remaining doubts, Isabelle crossed her heart on the bodice of her heavy black gown. 'I swear on my life, my lord, I won't ever contact you again.'

He nodded once and then, setting his whisky down, stalked to the door. For one mortifying second she thought he might call someone to come and remove this insane woman from his house, but instead he turned the key, locking them in together.

Chapter Two

The Duchess looked so terrified when he turned around that Matthew didn't dare go to her straight away. Instead, he wove around her—frozen in the centre of the room like some morose statue—and proceeded to where his whisky decanter sat on the sideboard.

He still wasn't sure why he'd changed his mind. But there'd been a moment when she was talking about Luke, about needing to help him, when Matthew had understood her motivation perfectly. Moreover, he'd admired her for it. He didn't know a single woman who'd be more invested in her stepchild's well-being than her own under the same circumstances.

So, her determination to help Luke had admittedly struck a chord. Then, once he had seen the names on her list, his resolve had started to crumble. All it had taken was the steely determination in her eyes and her rigid march to the door and he hadn't had a choice. Matthew was not the perfect gentleman—nobody would argue that—but he would never deliberately hurt or expose Isabelle, as Michael, Andrew or Cedric might. And Leo… Leo wouldn't harm her, or betray her confidence, but for some absurd reason that he didn't want to dwell on Matthew couldn't quite explain why the thought of the Duchess approaching his best friend unsettled him. It simply did.

Taking his time now, he poured himself another whisky, all the while achingly aware of Isabelle's eyes on him. 'If I'd had some warning, I might have been a bit more prepared.'

'I think decisions such as these are best made without time to dwell,' she countered fluidly.

'So, it was a strategy, then?'

'I think *desperation* would be a more accurate term.'

Matthew finally turned to face her. Isabelle was watching him warily, but her hesitation did nothing to detract from the long, slow slide of lust through his system.

She was a gorgeous woman, all sharp and delicate with those remarkably large witch's eyes. For one so young, she had a courageous spirit and a backbone of steel. Any man would want her, but in some uncanny twist of fate she was his—at least for tonight.

And wasn't that how he preferred it? Although his reputation as a rake had been somewhat exaggerated, due to an affair that had ended badly, the unfortunate event had served as a self-fulfilling prophecy of sorts. Because Matthew had only needed to be humiliated by a woman once to understand that it would never happen again. Now, if he accepted an invitation to a woman's bed, he did so knowing it would be a welcome distraction for one night—and only one night.

On impulse, he passed Isabelle the drink he'd poured for himself. He couldn't quite hide his grin when she snatched it out of his hand, as if she were afraid he might grab her and ravish her. 'You still have time to walk away.'

'I won't.' She swallowed the peated whisky in one go.

Matthew took a step forward, fully prepared to rescue a gagging, gasping female from the shocking burn of the expensive Scottish whisky, but Isabelle merely closed her eyes and curled the glass against her chest, exhaling deeply as if she were enjoying the hot slide of it down her throat.

He stared at her for a long moment, studying the way her dark lashes rested against her golden skin. 'You drink whisky?'

Her eyes fluttered open, revealing dark irises heavy with nerves. 'I would occasionally sneak some of my father's spirits to the head groom, Henry. On his birthday and for Christmas. He used to scold me horribly—and then tell me we had to "dispose of the evidence".'

She smiled her first sincere smile. Matthew felt its effect like a punch to the stomach.

'It became a tradition of sorts,' she said.

'Would you like another?'

'No.' She placed one slender hand across her stomach. 'I need my wits about me for this.'

'It's not a mathematics test, Isabelle.'

'But it's painful?'

He sobered immediately. 'I hadn't thought of that. I haven't…'

He rubbed at the back of his neck, unsure of how to proceed. He wasn't one to struggle with words, but for the first time ever he wasn't in a situation he could talk his way out of. He wouldn't lie to her. He wanted her to understand what she was asking of him.

Isabelle saved him from having to reply. 'I remember: you don't bed virgins.'

'I've heard that it's uncomfortable, but that it will ease after a little while.' Realising that she was growing paler with each word that came out of his mouth, Matthew changed tack suddenly. 'I'll make it pleasurable for you.'

'I don't care,' she insisted bravely. 'I just want to get it over with.'

And, so saying, she took a bold step forward, coming so close that he could smell the honey-toned whisky on her breath when she tipped her head back to look at him.

'Tell me what to do.'

Matthew reached out and gently took the glass from where she still pressed it against her heart. He tried not to think about how cold her fingers were through her netted gloves, and avoided looking at her as he turned to place the glass on the side table. He tried, rather unsuccessfully, to calm his galloping pulse. He was thirty years old and no green lad, but she was such a contrast—so brave and yet so innocent—and the contradiction of her had him trembling with a foreign anticipation.

He looked around the room. His townhouse, a stone's throw from Piccadilly, was ideally located and luxuriously furnished.

The parlour was neatly organised, with intricately carved wooden furniture and thick rugs imported from India. The fire in the grate cast a warm glow, softening a room that he'd never considered too masculine until now. His parlour was fit for a viscount—but by no means fit for a duchess.

'For what it's worth, I'm sorry for the situation you're in. If I could think of some other way to help you, I would.'

She tugged at her bodice again. 'You are helping me.'

Matthew gently grasped her, circling her thin wrists with his hands. 'May I help you with that?'

Isabelle froze. Her eyes widened. 'Do I need to take *everything* off?'

'In the interest of me not suffocating under all that fabric—'

'Crepe.'

'For what I have in mind, we're going to take the *crepe* off.'

But because he could see that she was scared, he gently turned her around so that her back was to his chest.

She stood completely still in front of him as he ran his hands up and down the stiff black fabric covering her arms. The scent of whatever soap she'd washed her mass of hair with reached him and, unable to resist, he leaned closer and nuzzled the soft skin of her neck as he breathed her in.

Isabelle tensed immediately, and Matthew drew back enough to whisper, 'Don't be afraid of me, Duchess.' He buried one hand in the mass of her silky hair and tilted her head back so that she could see the truth in his eyes when he promised, 'Any time you want to stop, you tell me. I'll stop.'

She nodded shyly, and although she didn't speak she stepped back and removed her black gloves with a few deft tugs.

There were so many ways he could make this quick and efficient—clinical, even. But even knowing *how* to, Matthew wouldn't. If he was going to be with this woman only once, he was going to show her what it could be like, so that years from now, when she eventually took a lover, she'd know not to accept anything less than complete pleasure—*her* complete pleasure.

'I'm going to take this off now.' He started on the dozen tiny buttons down her back, but when she still didn't reply, he paused. 'Isabelle? Is that all right?'

'Yes.'

His fingers kept working, undoing the tiny pearls from their clasps. Matthew, who'd always seen the layers of women's clothing as an irksome impediment at this juncture, was perfectly comfortable with the thick erection pressing against his trousers. What he couldn't quite make sense of was the new tremble in his hands.

'Are you afraid?' he asked.

'No.'

The question had been issued gently, so as not to scare her, but Matthew couldn't quite stave off his chuckle at her no-nonsense reply. Who was this strange woman? And, more importantly, where had she been hiding all these years? If he'd met *her* in a ballroom...

'I'm a little afraid,' he admitted as he unclasped the last button and spread the back of her heavy dress open, revealing the tight corset laced over a short-sleeved chemise.

'*You're* afraid?' She sounded horrified. 'Why are *you* afraid? You are supposed to be quite a Casanova.'

His stomach flipped uncomfortably as he walked around her and crouched down to help her out of her gown and petticoats, now puddled on the floor up to her knees. She steadied herself by putting her hands on his shoulders and stepped out of the heap of black fabric. There was something so new in the gesture, something so trusting and intimate, that Matthew couldn't quite help but compare this moment to every other time he'd bedded a woman. There was no rushing now—only the strange urge to keep the Duchess with him for as long as possible.

He looked up the length of her body, from the place where her drawers travelled beneath the long chemise at her shins, up the centreline of her corset to her nipped-in waist, the gentle swell of her breasts, and finally to her face.

'You're the most beautiful woman I've ever seen. You're also innocent.' He pushed to his feet. 'I'm afraid I'll hurt you. Or embarrass you.'

He was bloody terrified that he'd lose his self-control and embarrass himself too.

'You don't have to worry about me,' she told him primly.

But he didn't miss the way she crossed her arms over her chest to hide herself, and he certainly couldn't miss the wide-eyed fear unspooling in her inky irises.

'I'm only reminding you that it's normal to be afraid, given the circumstances,' he replied gently, and draped her dress and stiff petticoats over a nearby chair.

'But I'm not afraid.'

Rather than argue, Matthew stepped up to her again. He trailed his fingers up her bare arms, giving her time to become comfortable with his touch. Beneath his fingertips, despite her insistence that she wasn't afraid, he felt each tremble that passed through her. It was as if their nerves were connected by some phantom thread that compounded every touch until he was suffused with an unbearable level of awareness.

When he pressed up against her, letting her feel the weight of his hard length against her corseted stomach, she issued a small, strangled swallow, but he calmed her by cradling her face with both hands and forcing her gaze to his. He traced her high cheekbones with the pads of his thumbs even as his fingers sank into her thick, silky hair to frame her skull.

'I'm going to kiss you now.'

Her hands rose to grip his wrists tightly, but it wasn't fear in her eyes any more. It was confusion, layered with need.

'Yes,' she whispered, in reply to a question that hadn't been asked.

He lowered his mouth to hers. It didn't matter that she didn't return the kiss. The moment his lips touched hers, Matthew groaned against a fiery flood of desire. She was impossibly soft and sweet, and just this, the faintest, most innocent of kisses, was enough to have a torrent of wicked fantasies corrupting his imagination.

'Open your lips for me, Duchess.'

'I—'

He wasn't sure what she'd been about to say, only that he didn't give her the chance. The moment she opened her mouth to speak he slid into her wet warmth and tasted her, his tongue gently coaxing hers to return the kiss.

After a few long, torturous seconds, she tentatively stroked him, and her innocent offering was enough to have him throbbing against the fabric of his trousers. Matthew sank deeper into the kiss, basking in the way Isabelle grew bolder, meeting his increasing urgency with her own with each second that passed.

Although she couldn't be aware of it, she pressed her body up against his, almost as if she might angle herself to take him. Her hands released his wrists, but she didn't push him away. She roped her slender arms around his neck and held on as if her life depended on it...on *him*.

Feeling the edges of his self-control begin to fray, Matthew broke the kiss first. He exhaled deeply and, resting his forehead against hers, took a moment to pull himself back together.

'For an innocent, you pack a sinful punch, Duchess.'

When he opened his eyes she was staring up at him, her small, panting breaths escaping through her parted lips to whisper against his throat.

'It is wrong,' she said seriously—so seriously that he couldn't help but smile. 'But I... I enjoyed that. Very much so.'

Matthew had never needed words—had always counted sexual success in his partner's release, in moans and gasps—but the simple words from Isabelle tore at him. They disassembled what he knew about pleasure and rebuilt something entirely new and exhilarating in his mind.

'Did you, now?'

Instead of answering, she flushed scarlet and plonked her face against his chest, hiding her innocent embarrassment.

Overcome by an impossible urge to comfort her, to eradicate her self-consciousness, he raised one shaky hand and ran it over her hair. 'Can you hear my heart racing, Duchess?'

In a gesture that undid him, she turned her head and rested her ear against his chest. She nodded.

'That hasn't happened to me before.'

She pulled back to look at him, her dark brows dipping inwards. 'It's not always...like this?' She lowered both her hands to one of his and lifted it to the centre of her chest, pressing his palm over her heart.

Matthew, understanding what she wanted to tell him, ignored

the urge to palm her breast and focused on the excited cantering of her heart instead.

'Not always,' he said.

Never, his confused mind corrected.

Unsure how exactly she could remedy the fact that she'd placed Lord Ashworth's hand directly on her bosom, Isabelle simply let his hand go in the hope that he'd drop it.

He didn't.

Instead, he stroked his thumb over the small swell of her breast above her corset. 'How about this?' he asked, and brushed over her skin again. 'Do you like this?'

His eyes, silvered with focus, flickered to her face.

Isabelle wasn't entirely sure how much of what was happening inside her was due to pleasure and how much was due to nerves—only knew that she definitely felt both. Her skin felt alive, and every time he touched her it seemed to respond to him. A quiver here. A shiver there. Her stomach fluttered uncomfortably, and there was an odd heaviness building between her thighs.

'I do,' she admitted unsteadily.

The sound he made in the back of his throat was the closest thing to a growl she'd ever heard a human make, and in her mind, she couldn't help but think it must prove why Mary had added Lord Ashworth to the list. Isabelle rather liked it. He reminded her of a mercurial cat, one who seemed *laissez-faire*, but had eyes that tracked her as if she were easy prey and he was waiting for an opportune time to pounce.

Lord Ashworth raised his other hand to her left breast and repeated the same stroke, this time with a murmured 'So beautiful...'

Isabelle couldn't help the stuttering whoosh of air that left her lungs. Unsure of what to do with her hands while his were so skilfully employed, she raised them stiffly to his shoulders. With only his thin shirt separating her palms from his skin, she could feel the hard, muscular shape of him, so different from anyone she had touched before. There were no angles, no softness. Only sinew and brawn pulled tight beneath golden skin, and when he turned her around again, this time to unlace her corset, she felt the absence of him.

He gave a few sharp tugs to the laces at her back, but when the corset collapsed around her, and the cool air slipped over her sweat-slicked chemise, her forgotten nerves began to resurface.

As soon as he'd freed her from the confining garment, Isabelle wrapped her arms around herself. Gone was the momentary pleasure she'd felt when he'd kissed her and touched her. Now all that was left was embarrassment. And shame. Here she was, undressed and about to sleep with a stranger, mere days after her husband had died.

This is the only way to help Luke, she reminded herself. But even that didn't settle the pang of dread settling low in her stomach.

'Isabelle?'

God, if people find out, I'll be ruined. And then I definitely won't be able to help Luke—Gareth will make sure of it.

'Isabelle?'

She came to the second time he said her name. 'Yes?'

'What's wrong?'

Isabelle was mortified to feel the cool trail of tears down her cheeks, but not nearly as mortified as when she saw the look of dread in Lord Ashworth's grey eyes.

Needing to remedy the situation immediately, she cleared her throat. 'Do you remember when I told you I wasn't afraid?'

His kind smile softened the hard steel in his eyes. 'It wasn't exactly true?'

'Not exactly.'

'I can imagine.'

He didn't stop her from covering herself, or try to talk sense into her. He leaned down and lifted her, holding her close against his chest.

'What are you doing?' she whispered, painfully aware of the thin layers separating them. Even through his clothes, his body heat reached for her like an embrace.

Matthew didn't reply to her question right away. Instead, he carried her to the settee and sat down, settling her on his lap with her feet resting on the plumped red cushions next to him.

'I'm trying to help you to relax, Duchess.'

'I don't know if this is going to help.'

He tipped her chin back, forcing her eyes to his. 'Trust me.'

Isabelle squirmed, trying to get comfortable, but when Lord Ashworth groaned, and pinned her in place with his large hands, she stopped moving immediately.

He nudged her with his hips, pressing upwards into the back of her thigh. 'Do you feel me?'

'Of course,' Isabelle said pertly.

She had, after all, helped bathe Luke when he was a baby. And once she'd accidentally stumbled upon a stable boy urinating at the back of the stables. Although…neither of those experiences had given her the impression she felt so firmly beneath her now.

'I know basic anatomy, my lor—'

'Matthew,' he corrected. 'Given the circumstances, I'd say we're on a first-name basis, Duchess.' He leaned in close and blew a deliberate breath against the column of her throat. 'Wouldn't you?'

Isabelle shuddered helplessly against the sensation. 'Y-yes.'

'Isabelle… What exactly do you know about screw—?' He cleared his throat and corrected himself. 'The marital act?'

'That I should not fidget, *never* talk, and always listen to my husband's instructions.' She parroted her mother's tone. Frowned. 'Or, in this case, your instructions, I suppose.'

He sighed and, closing his eyes, pinched the bridge of his nose. 'Fantastic.'

'I guess that would depend on what you tell me to do,' she observed. 'It could be terrible.'

The deep chuckle that rumbled through his chest and into hers pulled a genuine smile to her face. When he laughed, it made what they were doing seem less consequential, somehow. More natural. If she'd been any less nervous, Isabelle would have tried to imagine that this was her wedding night—*their* wedding night.

'You mentioned your head groom earlier, so I'm assuming you have horses?'

Isabelle frowned at the odd question. Maybe he was trying

to distract her. More than willing to oblige, she replied, 'Yes. There are many at Moorhen House. But I have two of my own. Both are thoroughbreds that I brought with me when I was married. Saskia and Truant.'

'Have you ever *bred* horses?'

'Yes,' she answered seriously. 'My father's horse stock has prime bloodlines, descended from Silver Prince.' She saw his mouth twitch. 'Oh, you mean...' She leaned in and whispered, 'Have I *watched*?'

'Yes.'

She nodded happily for a moment, but when she saw the pointed look on his face, felt the hardness pressing into her again, her blood froze. 'But... Good Lord, are you certain?'

Though his eyes sparked with amusement, he explained, 'I fit inside you.' Reaching down, he cupped one big hand over her chemise and drawers. 'Here.'

She shifted under his hand as an uncomfortable tension gathered between her thighs. Matthew didn't move away; he gently rolled the heel of his hand against her, turning that sliding weight into something tight and aching.

'I suppose that makes an odd sort of sense,' she said breathlessly, trying her best to be brave. 'We are, at our most basic selves, mere animals.'

'Are you always this rational?'

Matthew's smile took any mockery out of the question.

'I try to be. My father always tells my mother that hysterics solve nothing and merely waste time for everyone.' Although she didn't say it, that exact phrase was what her father had used when she'd cried at the news that she was to marry the Duke of Everett. 'But sometimes, when I get very angry, I lock myself in my room and...' She looked over her shoulder in an instinctual habit to check that nobody was nearby.

'And?'

'I *throw* things,' she whispered.

'You... You throw things?' Matthew asked, and raised the hem of her chemise to slide his palm up the fabric of her drawers, following the line of her inner thigh.

As absurd as it was, Isabelle wished she hadn't hurried to

change and left her stockings off. Impropriety aside, it would have made her infinitely more comfortable to have an additional layer between her skin and Matthew's now.

She held very still, trying her best not to panic as that heavy hand brushed her in sensation after sensation, moving closer to her most private part.

'Yes. I—I throw things,' she managed with a shaky breath. 'Shoes at the door, pillows at the window, bonnets at the floor. Once, I even threw a vase. It—'

She inhaled sharply as he ran one finger through the slit in her drawers, touching her for the first time.

Her breath stuttered out as he gently traced her seam. Caught between the pleasant coiling sensation low in her womb and complete humiliation, Isabelle buried her face against his warm neck, inhaling linen and the lingering scent of tobacco.

'I don't know...' *Anything.* Whatever he was doing felt sinful. Wicked. But she didn't want him to stop either.

'Don't hide from me, Duchess. Look at me when I touch you.'

Mortified, but wanting to be brave, Isabelle slowly prised her face away from his neck and looked into eyes the colour of a brewing storm.

Matthew lowered his head and crushed his mouth to hers, dragging her into a kiss that stole any objection. When he would have pulled away, she placed one palm against his cheek and drew him back to her; it was easy to forget what she was doing when he kissed her.

Matthew's chest rose and fell quickly beneath her, as if he'd just finished some strenuous activity. The arm supporting her back tightened around her, holding her close, while the hand between her legs continued to tease and coax. Just when she thought she'd got used to him touching her, he parted her folds and slid his finger up and down, over her damp inner flesh.

'Can you feel how wet you are, Duchess?' His deep voice was tight, hoarse.

Incapable of voicing a reply, Isabelle simply nodded.

'That's to make it easier for you to take me. Here...' He caught her hand in his and began to lower it.

Horrified, Isabelle resisted. 'I don't want that. I *can't.*'

'Duchess, touching yourself is no sin.' Raising her hand to his lips, he gently kissed her fingers, encouraging her to relax. 'Let me show you,' he whispered, and carried her hand to her own centre when she acquiesced.

He placed his hand over hers and guided her fingers through slick warmth, showing her where he'd slot in and the bundle of nerves that he said would help bring her release. When Isabelle could take no more, and tugged her hand back, he caught her fingers and, instead of kissing them as he had done before, he suckled them.

She watched with wide-eyed horror as his warm tongue curled around her digits. She should have been shocked by the crudeness of it. She should have pulled away with scorn. But instead, the heavy tightening in her centre grew by degrees, turning almost painful—so painful that a small mewl slipped from between her lips.

'Duchess, you are the most exquisite thing I've ever tasted,' he whispered, and when he brought his lips back to hers she could taste it—*her*—on him.

Isabelle was too hot. She felt sick with excitement and nerves. And when he lowered his hand back to her centre and touched her she was helpless to stop herself from writhing against his touch. Every brush of his fingers against her pulled her nerves inwards, coiling them tighter and tighter, and when he began to gently ease a single finger inside her she roped her arms around his neck, clinging to him even as she arched against his hand.

Matthew groaned. 'Duchess, you're so tight.'

Isabelle couldn't reply. She merely closed her eyes and fought the sensations racking her body.

'Does this hurt, sweetheart?' He moved inside her, pushing deeper.

Isabelle tried to make sense of her body beneath the building pressure between her thighs. 'No,' she replied. 'It burns a little,' she whispered, pressing closer as her instincts took over.

'Hold on to me, Duchess,' he whispered. And the moment she wrapped her arms around his neck he took her mouth in a fierce kiss and, adding a second finger, pushed into her completely.

Beneath the heady kiss Isabelle was aware of discomfort as

her untried flesh stretched to accommodate him. But then Matthew was moving, sliding his fingers in and out of her rhythmically, and instead of discomfort she felt a pleasurable tightness that preceded a painful roll of pleasure.

She tore her mouth away, moaning his name. 'Matthew... I...' She didn't know what she wanted to tell him, only knew that as he curled his fingers inside her it seemed quite urgent that he either stop or hurry up.

'I know, Duchess,' he whispered, and circled his thumb against the nerves at her apex.

Isabelle's stomach tightened as the new sensation consumed her. She moaned helplessly as it crested, cried out his name when she could no longer contain it, and when it burst through her, draining her muscles of strength, she could do nothing but collapse against him as her body greedily clung to him, trying to pull him deeper, keep him closer, hold him longer.

Tremor after tremor coursed through her, trailing shivers over her skin. It was the most unusual sensation Isabelle had ever felt—as if she was somehow satisfied and exhausted and energised all at the same time.

Matthew kissed the side of her head and then gently moved his hand to grip her thigh above her knee. When he moved away they both saw the smudge of blood he'd left behind; it was stark against the white of her drawers, but also rather underwhelming compared to the virgin blood she'd expected.

'It... It is done?' she asked, confused by how simple it had been.

'Enough that they won't suspect anything, Duchess.'

'But... You didn't...'

He gently picked her up and settled her onto the settee. 'You shouldn't have to give yourself to a stranger just to help your family.' Taking her hand, he placed her fingers over the distinct ridge in his trousers. 'I can ache for you and still believe that to be true.' He gently lifted her hand away.

'Matthew...' For some inexplicable reason her eyes burned. Her body, so satiated moments before, felt empty. As if she had been deprived of something—something *integral* that was supposed to have happened but hadn't.

'Your secrets are safe with me, Your Grace.'

Isabelle hated the honorific—hated that he'd used her title moments after...*that*! She watched helplessly as he stood and walked to the fireplace, distancing himself from her.

'I trust you,' she whispered, staunching her inexplicable sadness.

Matthew leaned heavily against the arched mantel, as if he needed to support his own weight with it. He didn't look back at her, but she saw the bunched muscles in his back and shoulders and the tired lowering of his dark head.

'We need to get you dressed.'

Unsure of what was happening—unsure of herself—Isabelle merely replied, 'Yes.' But she didn't move from the settee.

She watched Matthew take a deep, steadying breath and straighten. He turned to face her again, his eyes now calm and placid. If it hadn't been for the protrusion in his trousers, she'd have thought him completely unaffected.

Isabelle's mind raced. 'Matthew...'

'Isabelle?'

'I just had a rather dreary thought.'

'Oh?'

He took a step forward. Stopped. He linked his hands behind his back, as if to physically stop himself from reaching for her, and it was that hint of subtle restraint that steeled her courage.

She folded her hands in her lap and tried to calm the nerves dancing in her stomach. 'If I don't remarry, I'll never be able to experience...' She instinctively placed her hand on her chest, over her thumping heart. '*This* again.'

'Isabelle, you're young.' He gave an exasperated shake of his head. 'Beautiful. Brave. Kind. You'll remarry.'

There was no doubt in his tone.

'But what if he's not...?' *Like you.* That was what she'd been about to say. Instead, she blurted, 'If this is going to be my only chance to feel *this*... I'd like to do it properly.' And then, because she'd rather die than verbalise any more, she finished with, 'If you know what I mean.'

'I'm afraid you're going to have to clarify, Duchess.'

'You know exactly what I'm talking about.'

Matthew took one large step in her direction and then stopped abruptly. 'I'm not sure that I do.'

'I would like you to finish what you started.'

And even though a hot blush rose to her cheeks, Isabelle didn't back down. Somehow she knew that any sign of doubt on her side would send Matthew running.

'Isabelle, there's no need. I—'

'*I* need,' she interjected.

The statement rang loudly through the room, embarrassing her. Still, somehow knowing that it felt *right*, she persisted.

'Years from now, when I'm old and childless and alone, I want to look back and remember that I chose this for myself. Not my parents. Not my husband. *Me*. And I want you to show me.'

His eyes widened with surprise, and Isabelle used it to her advantage.

'Please, Matthew. Aside from Mary and Wilhelmina, you may be the person I trust most in the world. A literal stranger. A notorious rake. How pathetically sad is that?'

Isabelle had no idea where her passionate speech had come from, but even through her naïveté she was distinctly aware of one fact: not all men were like Lord Ashworth.

'Mary and Wilhelmina?'

'Mary is my cousin and both are my dearest friends,' she explained.

Lord Ashworth nodded once before continuing, 'Isabelle, once we go there, neither of us can go back. I'd love you for one night and then leave England. I depart in two days' time.' He watched her face closely, as if searching for the truth there. 'Is that really what you want?'

'Yes.'

He visibly winced at her blunt admission, and she wondered if he was rejecting or relenting.

'You've made me no promises.'

His eyes darkened. Raising both his hands, he linked them behind his head and swore. 'And what if there's a child? I don't have any protection with me...'

'Protection?'

'Sheaths.' At her blank look, he swore. 'Condoms. Rubbers. French letters.'

'Is the risk so great?'

'It is not insignificant, Isabelle. I could try to…to prevent it, but there is no guarantee.'

After that admission, Isabelle couldn't think any more of the possibility of a child. If she did, she'd balk. So, for the first time in her life, she chose to be reckless and simply took what she wanted.

She rose off the settee and slowly crossed the room to where he stood. When he still didn't move, she placed her palm on his cheek and drew his mouth down to hers.

Matthew did not resist, and the moment their lips touched she knew she'd won. His control broke. His tongue prised her mouth open and swooped inside, daring her to keep up with his unrestrained need. His hands reached for the top of her chemise and, instead of undoing the three small buttons there, he merely ripped the garment open, sending the buttons to join her hairpins on the floor. He yanked the chemise down to her waist, exposing her bare breasts.

Matthew seemed to drink in the sight of her for a long moment, before leaning down and sucking her aching nipple into his mouth. Isabelle mewled in pleasure and surprise and he gentled immediately, replacing his greedy sucks with long, slow swirls on his tongue and gentle scrapes of his teeth.

That same building pressure started up between her legs again.

Her hands found his hair, brushing the thick locks back from his face. Then his muscular arms coiled around her and lifted, forcing her to kick off the torn chemise as it slid down past her knees. She wrapped her legs around him.

Matthew carried her back to the settee and gently laid her down. He removed her drawers and took a step back as he stripped his own clothes, his eyes on her the entire time.

Isabelle lowered her hands, trying and failing to hide herself.

'You are magnificent, Duchess,' Matthew murmured. 'Don't hide from me. I could spend my whole life just looking at you.'

Emboldened by his words, humbled by the honesty in his eyes, Isabelle let her hands fall away.

And only minutes later, when he whispered her name as he edged inside her, she felt no pain, only an impossible fullness, toe-curling pleasure, and the dizzying sense that she'd somehow traded her soul for a favour...for one perfect night with a stranger.

Chapter Three

London, 1842—two years later

'I don't quite understand why Mary and I must attend, Willa.'

Isabelle flipped through a fabric sample book at the modiste, gently separating out fabrics of different colours and textures that appealed to her.

After over two years in dreary blacks, greys and grey-purples, Isabelle was determined to choose only those colours that would momentarily startle anyone who saw her. She wanted to appear like a rare tropical bird or an exotic plant: bright, colourful, and potentially dangerous. She had already removed a velvet the deep red of port wine, and a green silk that reminded her of the fields of Moorhen House after a long rain.

For her new day dresses, among others she had chosen a lilac cotton dress with small white daisies printed whimsically over it, and a navy-blue linen gown that Madame Tremblay had trimmed in cream lace.

'It's your first ball since the Duke died—God rest his soul. Wouldn't you rather it be in a home familiar to you, surrounded by people with whom you are already acquainted?' Willa nestled back on the tufted pink settee and sipped her tea. 'The season is underway, Izzy. Before you know it, sessions will be over and you will have missed your chance.'

Alone with her friends, Isabelle felt comfortable speaking her mind. 'I wasn't actually planning on re-entering society.' She enjoyed the life she'd built over the past two years. Her widowhood afforded her a quiet existence, with little interruption, while motherhood kept her active and entertained.

'Nonsense. You're only twenty, Izzy. You've no need to hide away from the world.' Willa's brown eyes glazed over. 'The things I'd do if I were in your position... Filthy rich and widowed. Young.' She sighed wistfully. 'Why, I'd walk around my estate in breeches—'

'I should never have told you I did that!' Isabelle laughed. 'And I don't wear them all day—only to ride.'

'I'd curse in public.'

'Scandalous!' Isabelle said in mock horror, enjoying the game. 'You could take a lover?' she suggested.

Mary spluttered on her tea.

Willa raised her eyebrows. 'Oh, no. Were my husband to die, I would never let another man touch me.'

Isabelle didn't point out that not all men were like Earl Windhurst, Wilhelmina's horrible husband, and that some men could make a woman feel *everything*.

'Please, Izzy. I need you there. As a duchess, you're one of the only people Windhurst still approves of.'

Mary and Isabelle exchanged a worried glance. It was no secret that Willa's marriage to the Earl was an unhappy one. While Willa often refused to partake in society for weeks at a time, her husband had set his mistress up in an extravagant terraced home in Regent's Park and was often seen gallivanting about with her in public. The resulting humiliation had been too much for Willa, and over the eighteen months of her marriage she had been transformed from a beautiful, joyful girl into a woman well accustomed to the realities of life.

To Isabelle's surprise, it was Mary who interceded. 'I agree with Willa, Izzy. You cannot simply ignore your position in society for the remainder of your life. And Lord and Lady Russell's ball would be an opportune time for you to make an appearance.'

Isabelle, who had gone from her father's house to her husband's house and then into mourning, without coming out into society first, hadn't had a chance to practise being a duchess. Instead, she still felt very much like the odd, lonely girl she had been growing up. She wasn't accustomed to swarms of adults vying for her attention either. And, as a duchess, she'd found attention came whether she wanted it or not. She couldn't go for a walk without people greeting her as if they were old friends and not very slight acquaintances—her mother's cousin's best friend, or her father's friend's brother's son.

'I never know what to say,' she admitted finally. 'And the worst thing about not knowing what to say is that I am a duchess, and people always wait for me to speak first.'

'For heaven's sake, Isabelle. You *are* a duchess,' Willa reiterated. 'And a widow to boot. Say whatever the hell you want to say. What are they going to do? Flog you? Scorn you? Declare you scandalous?' Willa rolled her eyes. 'And even if they did, what difference would it make? You could go back to your reclusive life having proved me wrong.'

Mary, who rarely disagreed with Isabelle on anything, nodded. 'Willa is right. It's time, Izzy.' As if she could sense Isabelle's anxiety, she added, 'It may be trying at first. But it will become easier over time.'

'I dare say you might even learn to enjoy yourself,' Willa drawled. 'Besides, I'll be right there to curse or say something alarming should you flounder.'

Unlike Willa, who didn't give a damn, and Mary, who never made any mistakes, Isabelle was glaringly self-conscious over all her shortcomings. 'I can't—'

'*Please*, Izzy,' Willa urged quietly. 'You and Mary are my only true friends, and it's so hard to pretend to enjoy myself. I don't want to be a burden, but I would be happier knowing you were nearby, in case...'

'Yes?' Isabelle prompted.

Willa flashed a smile that never reached her eyes. 'In case it's a dreadful bore.'

Isabelle wasn't fooled, but she didn't press the matter either, understanding that it was Wilhelmina's private life, hers to share or keep close as she saw fit. Still, a friend in need was possibly the only thing that could sway her.

'I suppose one night won't kill me.'

Mary clasped her hands together excitedly.

Even Willa managed a small smile. 'Thank you.'

Madame Tremblay chose that moment to re-enter, with her three assistants each carrying several day dresses which Isabelle and Mary had ordered during their last visit and were now ready to undergo final fitting.

'I'd best be going.' Willa levered her slight frame off the settee. 'My mother is supposed to be visiting. I shall inform her that you both plan to attend.'

Isabelle watched Willa as she left the private fitting room, her back ramrod-straight, her head held high—and her doe-brown eyes completely empty.

On his third day back in London after nearly two and a half years away, Matthew meandered out through the stately doors of his social club, Barber's, at the side of his closest friend, Leo Vickery, Lord Pemberton. The London air in spring was still crisp, despite the time of day; however, there seemed to be a renewed vigour about the city now that winter was slowly sliding behind them.

As the two men walked together, they talked of mutual acquaintances, most of whom Matthew had not seen or heard from since he'd been gone.

'Both Heathcote and Tramley got married,' Leo said. 'Heathcote to a merchant's daughter who came with a dowry that puts the royal family to shame, and Tramley to Lady Louise Eastfield—you remember her. Her mother was always throwing you two together.'

Matthew grimaced, thinking back on his interactions with the shy, awkward girl. Louise had been so scared of him that it had made every encounter unbearably uncomfortable. 'She wasn't much of a conversationalist, if I remember correctly.

She tended to simply circumvent discussion by saying, "Yes, my lord" or "No, my lord".'

Leo sighed deeply. 'I should have made her an offer...'

Matthew, who knew his friend's taste in women rather well, raised one brow in surprise. 'You courted her?'

'No. But if I'd known she didn't talk I might have. A wife who says nothing except to agree with my opinion would suit me very well, don't you think?'

Matthew laughed. 'If you paused to listen once in a while, Pemberton, you might find that some women have interesting things to say.'

'I have yet to meet such a woman. Unless you consider embroidery, music and the latest fashions interesting.' Leo distractedly removed his hat and twirled it between his hands. 'Tell me about the women you met abroad. I've heard that Italian women are—'

'Bloody hell!'

A frustrated feminine voice cut off what was undoubtedly going to be a crude suggestion from Leo.

Matthew watched with amusement as a tall, slim woman rushed past them, her hands holding her skirts indecently high, as if they were an impediment she needed to overcome. A short lady's maid struggled to keep up with her long strides.

'Why am I always late?' the lady queried.

Clearly assuming that the question had been directed at her, her maid replied breathlessly, 'You get distracted easily, my lady.'

'My husband is undoubtedly going to have something dreadful to say about this, Peggy.'

'Yes, my lady.'

Matthew turned to Leo, but his friend was staring after the woman, his blue eyes glazed with recognition. Just as she was about to go out of earshot he cupped his hands to his mouth and called, 'Willa!'

Up ahead, the woman came to an abrupt stop. Matthew watched as she turned around slowly, her posture straight and stiff. She leaned forward slightly, eyes narrowed.

'Leo!'

Leo grinned and, without a word of explanation to Matthew, hurried forward. 'I *knew* that mouth could only belong on one woman,' he teased.

Matthew raised both brows. Leo might be a mischief-maker, but there were certain things even he didn't do, and mentioning a lady's mouth so suggestively was certainly one of them—or was supposed to be anyway.

As they approached, Matthew took stock of the stranger. She was tall, and looked as fragile as glass. Her upper arms couldn't be thicker than his wrists, yet despite her startling thinness she exuded a strange, frenetic energy, as if she couldn't quite stay still for more than a second at a time. Her mass of blond hair had been curled and swept back to reveal an enviably angular face and sad brown eyes that seemed oversized when compared to the rest of her features.

'Because I'm the only woman you know who swears in public?' Her tone was clipped with dry humour.

'Because you're the only woman I know who swears at all,' Leo countered.

Matthew didn't miss the way his friend's eyes flickered over the woman with surprise—and neither did she. She shifted uncomfortably under his gaze, passing her slight weight from foot to foot as if she were preparing to run.

Matthew bowed and, ignoring Leo's lapse, introduced himself. 'Matthew—Lord Ashworth.'

'Wilhelmina, Countess Windhurst.' She studied his face for a moment as if she were trying to piece something together. 'Have we met before, my lord? You look awfully familiar.'

'Willa was the youngest of the Russells,' Leo informed him, having regained himself. Turning back to Willa, he explained, 'Matthew went to school with me. I spent as much of my childhood with him as I did with Jameson and your other brothers. You two will have undoubtedly met somewhere over the years.'

'I believe I was a guest at a ball your parents hosted before I left for my tour of the continent,' Matthew supplied. 'Perhaps we were introduced?'

She seemed unconvinced. 'Perhaps. You'll have to forgive

my memory; my brothers have introduced me to so many acquaintances over the years.'

'Where are you running to?' Leo queried.

'Home. I'm supposed to be meeting my mother.' She waved a thin hand. 'Although heaven knows why I have to keep a social engagement with the woman. We see each other all the time.'

Leo laughed lightly. 'Allow us to escort you part of the way? We're heading in the same direction.'

The offer was in no way suggestive or improper, but Wilhelmina took a full step back. 'I would like that, Leo—it's been so long since we talked. But…' She cast a glance over her shoulder, as if searching for her maid to come and rescue her.

'We won't tell Windhurst if you don't,' Leo said, and when Wilhelmina didn't reply, only opened and closed her mouth uncertainly, he simply stepped forward and gently took her elbow. Wilhelmina hesitated for a small second, but it was long enough for Leo to use his superior weight against hers. He simply started walking, leaving her to fall into step with him or be dragged along.

Matthew remained politely quiet as they resumed their walk, but his curiosity had been piqued by this strange interaction— by Lady Windhurst's show of fear and by Leo's quiet possessiveness. Matthew had known Leo for almost twenty years, and he'd never seen his friend treat a lady with such unpractised deference. His typical approach was simply to avoid any eligible young woman as if she had the pox and flirt with every ineligible woman as if she were Aphrodite herself.

Matthew listened intently as Leo gently drew Lady Windhurst into conversation.

'We saw your brother at the club,' Leo said.

'Which one?'

'Jameson,' Leo clarified. 'He said that Grayson is engaged to be married?'

'Yes. And his fiancée, Rose Hudson, is exquisite. He's so besotted I'm almost convinced it's a love match.' She paused for a small moment. 'In fact, were she not *quite* so beautiful, I'd be sure of it.'

Matthew found himself smiling at the comment and the casual affection it was made with.

'And the rest of your brothers?'

'About the same. Gambling, whoring, and—perhaps worst of all—getting away with it.'

Leo's laugh rumbled.

'You laugh, Leo, because you will never know what it is to be born a woman in a family of men.'

'Thank God.'

Willa's mouth turned upwards in the first hint of a smile. 'I have to watch them live in freedom, with complete disregard for any social compunction. It's awfully annoying.' She turned her gaze to Matthew suddenly, as if remembering he was there. 'You will forgive my manners, Lord Ashworth. Leo and I are old friends. I sometimes forget myself when we're together.'

'There's nothing to forgive,' Matthew assured her.

He found that he liked her candid manner. There was no pretence, no feigned incompetence or missish manners.

Wilhelmina regarded him as they walked with Leo between them. 'You do seem rather unoffended,' she affirmed. 'I dare say I like you.'

'Matthew has just returned from a two-year tour of the continent,' Leo supplied. 'He was about to describe all the scandalous women he encountered when you barged past.'

'I do not *barge*, Leo—I *glide*.' When Leo merely shook his head, Wilhelmina returned her focus to Matthew. 'I am intensely interested to hear about these scandalous women, Lord Ashworth.'

'Fortunately they are a figment of Leo's imagination.'

Leo scoffed.

Willa's eyes glistened with humour. 'As much as I doubt that, I do understand your moral dilemma.' She sighed wistfully. 'My dear friend Isabelle's aunt lives in Italy. And she's always writing us scandalous accounts of the Italians.'

Though the years had done nothing to dull his memory, Matthew barely flinched at the name. After all, it was a common enough name, one he had heard spoken numerous times over the years and learned to steel himself against—until Wilhelmina added, 'You know Isabelle, Leo. The Duchess of Everett.'

'I do.'

Their voices dimmed as Matthew's mind was flooded with images of the Duchess, her golden skin and bewitching eyes. He had never forgotten her...never been able to recapture the feeling of her in his arms.

Wilhelmina and Leo kept talking, oblivious to Matthew's sudden interest in their conversation as he listened intently for snippets of the Duchess, though none came. He wanted to stop Wilhelmina from rambling and direct her back to talking of her friend. He wanted to ask this strange woman how Isabelle was and if she'd maintained guardianship of her stepson. He wanted to know everything. *Anything.*

'My parents are having a ball next Friday,' she was saying. 'I expect you'll be there.'

'I have accepted your mother's invitation already,' came Leo's firm reply.

'Lord Ashworth, may I presume to extend to you an invitation on my mother's behalf?'

Matthew had no need to think it through. 'It would be my pleasure.'

'I'll send a formal invitation to you via one of my brothers.'

Matthew bowed politely as their party stopped at the edge of the park.

Leo reached out and took Willa's hand, holding it for a moment longer than was proper. 'We'll see you next Friday, Willa.'

She bobbed her head in a quick gesture. 'Thank you for walking with me.' Her brown eyes turned to Matthew. 'Both of you.'

They murmured appropriate replies and then watched as she glided away, her lady's maid hurrying behind her once again.

'Good God,' Leo said as soon as she was out of earshot. 'I almost didn't recognise her.'

'She's changed?'

'She's so slight...' Leo's brows dipped inwards.

'Perhaps marriage doesn't agree with her,' Matthew suggested. 'Windhurst has always been a lout. I'm surprised Lord Russell agreed to the marriage.'

'Yes,' Leo replied quietly. 'Jameson objected to the match. But Grayson and her father thought Willa needed to be reined in. She's always been...'

'Unconventional?'

'Wild,' he corrected, but there was no judgement in his tone and a smile on his lips. He absently twirled his hat again, an anxious habit that he'd had even as a young boy, but his eyes never left the corner Wilhelmina had disappeared around.

Intrigued by his friend's obvious attachment to the lady, Matthew tried to offer some consolation. 'She's smart. Canny. She'll be fine.'

Remembering himself, Leo grinned suddenly. 'Well, at least you can now prove me wrong on one point.'

'Oh?'

He shot Matthew a wry glance. 'I stand corrected on my earlier observation about women. Wilhelmina Russell has always had something interesting to say—even when she shouldn't.'

Chapter Four

Matthew saw the Duchess the moment she stepped into Lord and Lady Russell's ballroom—and so did everyone else. A rippling murmur passed over the gathered guests as Lady Russell welcomed the widow who, despite her young age, had surpassed the older woman in rank when she'd married the late Duke of Everett.

Time had not altered her. Isabelle was still striking. Her black hair was piled atop her head and adorned with a single rose that complemented her burgundy dress and contrasted with the golden skin of her exposed shoulders. Though her posture was perfect, her rigid spine and neutrally set mouth somehow gave her the appearance of being extremely uncomfortable in her surroundings. In fact, she looked like a startled deer that had stopped to assess the danger and was contemplating bolting at any moment.

His stomach danced with nerves as he watched her murmur something to her companion, and when the women turned in the opposite direction to him he exhaled deeply and loosened his vice-like grip on the crystal punch glass he held.

He hadn't been sure of what his own reaction would be after all this time. But he would never have guessed that he'd be stunned senseless by her—again. He'd blamed his reaction all those years ago on her sudden appearance in his home and her outlandish request, but now... Now he realised that he hadn't been quite honest with himself all this time. The Duchess of Everett was everything that he remembered—and more.

'Would you like an introduction?' Leo asked. 'The Duchess is a friend of Wilhelmina.'

Realising that he had been staring after Isabelle, Matthew turned his back in the direction she'd gone. 'Perhaps later.'

It wouldn't do to make a fool of himself—and, considering his history with the Duchess, he thought it best to let her discover him by herself rather than have his company thrust upon her. She would be mortified if he suddenly appeared before her for an introduction, and although she was one of the more pragmatic women he'd ever met, Matthew didn't know if she'd be able to school her reaction to seeing him again adequately. Better to be seen by her first—better to give her time to come to terms with the fact that he was in attendance at the ball.

Easier said than done.

As the night progressed, and he and Leo made the social rounds and danced countless dances with the numerous girls that Lady Russell insisted on introducing them to, it became clear to Matthew that the Duchess would not be one of them. It wasn't surprising, really. Unlike the other young women at the ball, and even though she was barely older than many of them, Isabelle was a widow. And a duchess to boot. The result was that she and her companions seemed to be spared Lady Russell's attention.

Instead of dancing or talking with the other guests, they sat in a corner with Wilhelmina. They talked and laughed amongst themselves as if they were at a private tea party, not a formal ball, and the close-set layout of their chairs discouraged interruptions of any kind.

'If you keep staring at them like that, people are going to talk,' Leo commented during one of their brief respites from dancing.

'As three young, attractive women, they are decidedly uninterested in being social.'

'And why should they be? Willa is married—and a countess.'

Matthew noted Leo's odd tone when he spoke of Wilhelmina. 'And the Duchess of Everett and her companion are both widowed. If you ask me, they're damned lucky. They've done this already, and now—unlike the rest of us poor sods—they're spared the inconvenience of having to dance with every unattached person of the opposite sex.'

'I wouldn't call being married and widowed before the age of twenty *lucky*, Leo,' Matthew chastised.

'I'll wager the Duchess wouldn't agree with you,' Leo quipped, pulling a quick laugh from Matthew. 'Irrespective, it appears as if your opportunity for an introduction has come and gone.'

Matthew spun on his heel just in time to see Isabelle and her companion walking around the edges of the room towards the door. At first he thought she hadn't seen him, but then Isabelle turned and looked back directly at him. When their eyes met, her face paled.

For one long second they stared at each other.

And then she whipped around again, continuing her escape at an increased pace.

Matthew cursed. 'Leo—can I trust you?' he asked urgently.

Leo frowned at him. 'Of course.'

'Stop her.'

'What?' Leo arched back to stare at him. 'Are you quite all right—?'

'There's no time. I'll explain later.' He nudged his friend in Isabelle's direction. 'Hurry.'

Leo took off without a backward glance, cutting through the crowd easily. He didn't circumvent the dancing, as Isabelle had, merely sliced right through the quadrille, interrupting the structured dance and earning several reproachful glances.

Matthew didn't care. Leo got to the ballroom door seconds before Isabelle and her companion and, bowing at the waist, greeted them both.

Not wanting to be too obvious, Matthew turned back to where Wilhelmina now sat alone. The Countess was watching him, her head tilted ever so slightly, her brown eyes narrowed on him. He approached her warily, aware that she must have seen Leo's mad dash through her mother's ball.

'Lady Windhurst,' he greeted her with a small bow.

'Lord Ashworth. I thought it was you.'

'Apologies for not greeting you sooner. You and your friends seemed occupied.'

'Oh...' Willa waved her hand dismissively. 'Izzy, Mary and I see each other all the time. It would have been no interruption.'

Her gaze flitted behind him, and he didn't have to look to know that Leo was leading the Duchess back through the room towards them. Matthew could feel her at his back. The fine hair at his nape pulled tight, and even though he desperately wanted to turn and watch her approach, he braced himself against the urge. He needed a few more seconds to acclimatise himself to the panic spreading through his galloping heart.

'It would seem that you are acquainted with my friends,' said Wilhelmina.

It was not a question, but Matthew replied anyway. 'To my regret, I am not acquainted with either of them.'

Willa made a non-committal sound. 'I will have to introduce you, then.'

She stood and boldly linked her arm through his just as Leo approached, Isabelle and her companion on either side of him.

'Leo, what on earth were you thinking—accosting my friends like that?' the Countess chastised. 'It's a wonder you didn't cause injury to one of my mother's guests.'

'My apologies, Willa.' Leo relinquished formalities, using Wilhelmina's nickname instead of her title. 'I realised that Her Grace was leaving and remembered that I had not had the privilege of introducing her and her companion to my friend.' Leo took a small step back and sent Matthew a pointed glance. 'Your Grace, may I present Lord Ashworth? Lord Ashworth—the Duchess of Everett, Lady Isabelle St Claire. And her cousin, Mrs Mary Lambert.'

Matthew bowed even as his heart lurched in his chest. 'It is a pleasure to make your acquaintance, Your Grace... Mrs Lambert.'

The women returned the pleasantries, but Matthew was looking at Isabelle, and he noticed the red blush of embarrassment riding high on her cheekbones. Even her small mouth seemed to be struggling, her lips wobbling slightly before settling in a nervous half-grimace.

'Lord Ashworth has just returned from a tour of the continent,' Willa offered, breaking the awkward silence. 'The last time we met he was on the precipice of telling me about his scandalous Italian women.'

'Oh…' Mary said awkwardly.

Isabelle remained silent, but he saw her risk a peek at him from under her heavy lashes.

Willa and Leo grinned like a pair of feral children who'd been tossed a bone.

Unsure of anything except that he needed a moment alone with the Duchess, Matthew asked, 'Would you do me the honour of dancing with me, Your Grace?'

He braced himself for the refusal he saw in her eyes.

'I'm—'

'Oh, she would love to!' Willa exclaimed. 'Isabelle was just telling me how much she misses dancing.'

Isabelle turned to stare at her friend. If he hadn't had a vested interest in getting her alone, Matthew might have laughed at the way her eyes narrowed in Willa's direction. But instead of arguing, the Duchess deferred and gave the polite response. 'Yes. It would be an honour, Lord Ashworth.'

Matthew, seeing her discomfort, didn't offer her his arm. Instead, he bowed again, and indicated for her to lead the way to where couples were preparing to waltz.

Isabelle stopped in the centre of the ballroom, in the hope that the other dancers would shelter them as much as possible, and turned to face Lord Ashworth. He was immaculately turned out in traditional formal attire, his skin dark against the stark white of his linen shirt and silk waistcoat. His black hair, although trimmed and styled, was still too long, yet Isabelle could not deny that he made a striking image.

She opened her mouth to speak, to say something trivial about the weather or the ball, but no words came. Instead, her tongue felt thick and clumsy. A hot flush worked its way up her neck, and even though she hadn't eaten anything she had the most awful feeling that she might be ill.

The waltz started. The music gently drifted to them through the crowded room. Matthew tipped at the waist, his gaze never leaving hers, but all Isabelle could do was stare at him. His grey eyes, so familiar to her, did not calm her, though they were gentle and filled with understanding.

When she did not move, Matthew gently arranged her in the waltz position, placing his right hand lightly on her upper back. The barely perceptible touch somehow burned through all the layers of her garments more than any ham-handedness could have done. Their bodies remained politely separated, but he was still too close. The heat from his skin seeped into her hand, and when she dared to meet his eyes again he was close enough that she could see the black rings around his grey irises.

'Were you running away from me, Duchess?' he inquired, his deep voice lowered and only for her.

No etiquette existed for a situation like this—Isabelle knew that. So, unsure of how to behave, she merely nodded honestly, and in a small voice that was so pathetic, and so unlike her, replied, 'I once promised that I would never seek you out…' She straightened her spine and with more force added, 'I have kept my word.'

Together, they turned in a gliding circle, easily following the dance, though neither of them was paying any attention. Matthew was watching her face so intently that Isabelle feared he would see that she was hiding something far more scandalous than their past encounter.

But instead of ceding her point, as she'd expected, he surprised her by leaning forward, shockingly close, and whispering, 'Did you ever, even once, think about breaking your word?'

Isabelle was too shocked to reply, though the word *yes* echoed loudly in her head.

Matthew's strong arms held her close. 'After what we shared, one truth could hardly make a difference, Duchess.'

Isabelle shook her head, overwhelmed by the strange turn this night was taking. 'I made you a promise,' she repeated.

'And you've certainly kept it.'

Isabelle arched backwards, the better to see his face, and when she met his eyes she was shocked to see her own memories, her own awareness, reflected in their depths.

'What do you want?' she whispered, panicked by the conversation they were having. 'My situation—'

'Your situation is secure, Duchess. I am a man of my word.'

Isabelle didn't know what to do. Every instinct was telling her to politely excuse herself, leave the ball, and remove her family to Moorhen House without delay. She could not be in town with this man; even London was too small. Somehow she knew that they were fated always to intercept one another and that she could not hide from him for ever.

'Matthew...'

His fingers jolted against hers at her use of his first name. His dark head lowered. 'Duchess?'

'There is something I need to tell you...'

She looked up at him again. For a long moment all she could do was stare, trapped by his expectant gaze.

Chapter Five

'May I escort you back to your seat?'

The Duchess didn't even seem aware that they had stopped dancing and were now standing in the middle of the ballroom while other couples skilfully tried to avoid bumping into them. A group of women nearby were watching them closely, their fans covering their mouths—and their undoubtedly speculative words.

She leaned heavily on him, as if she might faint at any moment. Over the music, Matthew became aware of her short, panting breaths. Her eyes were dark with panic, her face contrastingly pale.

Alarm coursed through him. 'Isabelle?'

She eased away from him and slowly raised a hand to her chest. 'I can't…breathe…'

'Duchess?' he urged, keeping his voice low to avoid attracting more attention. 'Look at me.'

She raised her eyes to his, and although she held his gaze her chest heaved with panic and her sharp breaths became more and more pronounced.

'I'm going to take you back to your friends and then escort you to your carriage.'

Without waiting for her reply, he linked her arm through his and led her quickly from the dance floor.

Matthew was aware of all the eyes in the room watching them, watching *her*, with thinly veiled curiosity. 'I am sorry, Duchess,' he murmured, 'to have caused you so much distress. It was not my intention.'

'It's not what you think,' she replied breathlessly. 'There's something I need to tell you… I—'

'Your friend abandoned us at the first opportunity, Lord Ashworth,' Willa said, unknowingly talking over Isabelle in her attempt to move attention away from the fact that he and Isabelle had only managed half a dance together.

Unsure of how to behave, torn between wanting to console the Duchess and grab the lifeline Wilhelmina had thrown him, he replied, 'Leo has never had the ability to stay in one place long.'

'Nor in the company of one woman long,' Willa retorted, eliciting various reactions from the nearby eavesdroppers.

The Dowager Countess Radcliffe gasped dramatically. Lady Pembroke fluttered her fan in a dramatic display of distress. Lord Wickmore, who knew Leo rather well, nodded in agreement.

But as Lady Windhurst's unladylike observation drew nearby attention to her, Matthew looked down at Isabelle. She was staring at him as if she was afraid—as if she wanted to get as far away from him as possible. And, of all the ways he'd imagined she'd react at their reintroduction, he'd never thought that she might be *afraid* of him. Were their memories of that night so different?

'Her Grace is not well,' he said gently, hoping to give her some small relief. 'Mrs Lambert? Perhaps I could escort you both to your carriage?'

Mary immediately took charge of the situation. 'I think that would be best, my lord,' she said.

Willa's eyes narrowed on Isabelle, then widened with concern. 'Izzy, I dare say you *do* look rather pale.'

'It is nothing,' Isabelle replied shakily. 'Only too long since I have been in society. I'm afraid it is all rather overwhelming.'

Willa pushed herself to stand and, instead of politely bidding the Duchess farewell, yanked her into a tight hug. 'Thank you so much for coming, Izzy.'

Although he was certain he was not supposed to hear the next part, Matthew was aware that Lady Windhurst murmured, 'The Earl has departed already, thank God. I shall leave as soon as I have said goodbye to my mother.'

'You will come and visit us soon?' Isabelle managed, still sounding breathless.

'Tomorrow.'

As soon as she had released Isabelle, Matthew exchanged farewells with Lady Windhurst. He led the Duchess and Mary Lambert out of the Russells' ballroom, using his significant height and brawn to part the crowd for the two women who followed close behind.

He waited with them in silence for fifteen minutes as their carriage was called, too conscious of Mrs Lambert's elbow-to-elbow stance next to Isabelle to speak to her as he would have liked. He had so many questions—so many things he wanted to say to her. But most of all he wanted her to stop looking at him out of the corner of her eye, as if he was a predatory cat out to hunt her.

Did she not remember the way they'd fitted so perfectly together? Or the way she'd slotted into his side for the short thirty minutes they'd taken afterwards to come to terms with what they'd done? Had she really not thought of him all this time as he had thought of her—daily? Some nights he'd fallen asleep thinking of her lean, lithe body and her quick-witted mind, only to have her plague him in his dreams too, so that he'd woken up exhausted and angry and yearning for a person he barely knew.

The rumble of an approaching carriage and the Duchess of Everett's palpable relief indicated that their time was up, and Matthew swallowed down his flaring disappointment.

He waited until the carriage was abreast of them, and then, when the Duchess stepped forward, he reached out and grasped her hand, halting her escape. He passed her and held out his other hand for Mary Lambert—something that would have been considered an affront to the Duchess had anyone noticed.

Instead of taking his hand, Mrs Lambert looked at Isabelle, who gave her consent with one curt nod.

He handed Mary into the carriage and then turned his back on her to face the Duchess. 'I am sorry to have distressed you.'

'I know.' She bowed her head, almost as if she were shy or confused. 'Matth—' She caught her breath. 'Lord Ashworth—'

'You may always call me Matthew, Duchess. Surely, after everything, we can remain friends?'

Those words were the furthest thing from the truth—perhaps the greatest lie he'd ever spoken. He could never be friends with this woman. For a martyr he was not. He knew what it was to make love to her, and he found that he would rather end their acquaintance now than see her about and pretend that she had not shaken him to his very core.

'We cannot.'

She raised those dark eyes to his and he saw the way she pulled herself upright, straightening her spine with resolve.

'As you wish,' he replied and, bending over her gloved hand, turned it so that he could kiss the inside of her wrist one last time.

But when he raised his eyes to her face he saw that she was blinking rapidly, her eyes glossy with tears.

'Duchess…' He shook his head, trying to make sense of her odd behaviour.

Before he could say more, Isabelle hurriedly wiped her face and forced her lips into a tight smile. 'Thank you for escorting us to our carriage, Lord Ashworth.'

He held out his hand, ready to help her in, but Isabelle raised her hands to her chest instead and took a single step back, before quickly climbing into the carriage without his assistance.

Matthew's hand curled in on itself as if he were scorched. He stood back as a nearby footman came and closed the door, watching as the carriage started moving, taking the Duchess away from him. With each yard the carriage travelled, his disappointment sank deeper.

Matthew turned on his heel and marched back towards the Russells' ball. All this time he had thought of her, *dreamed* of her, hoping that she thought of him, too…

Growing increasingly frustrated with himself, Matthew pushed all thoughts of the Duchess out of his mind and went in search of a bottle.

He of all people should know that nothing good could ever come of him pursuing the Duchess. Hadn't he told himself that over and over again in the past two years? Hadn't he brought the memory of past scandal, of Christine's frenzied begging, to his mind countless times, in an attempt to remind himself why he avoided attachments altogether?

But it was done now.

It took him only three minutes to get to Lord Russell's study. He had, after all, spent many years visiting Jameson Russell in this very house.

Matthew opened the door—and pulled up short when he saw Leo and Lady Windhurst were in the room. There was nothing scandalous about their situation except the fact that they were alone. They were both kneeling on the floor, on opposite sides of a small table, a chessboard open between them. From what he could see, Willa was giving Leo a thorough fleecing.

'Ah, Lord Ashworth,' Lady Windhurst drawled. 'You have walked in on a most embarrassing situation: your best friend, your closest ally, is being beaten at his best game—by a woman.' She sighed dramatically.

Leo snorted, completely at ease. 'Chess is not my best game. Not by far.'

Wilhelmina tilted her head in agreement. 'Yes. But I don't think we can politely compete in all the other things you are so renowned for.'

Leo choked on the sip of brandy he'd just taken. Matthew did not try to hide his laugh. He stepped into the room, making sure to close and lock the door behind him.

'There's no point in locking us in,' Willa said calmly. 'I seem to get away with quite a lot now that my husband has taken to flaunting his whore.' She refocused on the board and, after a moment's deliberation, moved her last pawn two spaces forward. 'It is rather nice to have such leeway. Don't you think?'

Leo didn't comment, although Matthew would have been a fool not to notice his friend's downcast gaze.

Matthew considered his reply for a brief moment, before settling on the blunt truth. 'I have never for a single moment considered Earl Windhurst an intelligent man, my lady. But his behaviour now proves him the greatest fool that ever lived.'

Lady Windhurst looked up at him in surprise, her serious brown eyes lightening perceptibly.

Matthew held a hand dramatically over his heart. 'Were you mine, I would sail the world to bring you only the best of everything. Spices from India! Dresses from Paris! Caviar from Russia!'

As he'd intended, Lady Windhurst laughed. And, although she hadn't been looking at Leo, Matthew saw his friend's eyes snap to Willa as the sound left her mouth.

'You forget, Lord Ashworth, that I have seen the way you look at Isabelle.'

Matthew's grin faltered, but instead of denying it he shrugged nonchalantly. 'The Duchess is a beautiful woman.'

Willa made that same non-committal sound and went back to the chess game, but she kept on talking as she considered her next move.

'Your taste cannot be faulted. Isabelle is the very best.' She moved a knight expertly, placing Leo's king in check. 'She is cultured and beautiful and rich as sin—her late husband left her a sizeable jointure. She is also *revoltingly* kind and loyal—often towards people such as me, who are entirely underserving of it.'

Having made her move, Willa sat back from the board and frowned.

She turned to him. 'Although she does come with the additional burden of two children.'

Two children.

Time simply stopped.

The sound of his own heart pumping filled his ears as Willa's words registered.

Two children.

'Oh…?' He managed the single word through the block lodged in his throat even as his brain fought to deny it.

Impossible.

It couldn't be…

She would have told me...

And yet even as he thought it, he remembered Isabelle's promise never to contact him again—the very promise she'd reminded him of only tonight. And the look on her face, pale and afraid, as they'd danced. And again as she'd got into her carriage.

Her words, 'It's not what you think', suddenly took on new meaning.

Willa didn't raise her head as she watched Leo try to extricate his king from checkmate. 'Yes. The late Duke of Everett had a son—Luke. He's about nine now. And Isabelle conceived in the few short weeks she was married to the Duke. Seraphina, her daughter, is one and a half.'

Matthew felt the blood drain from his upper extremities. His mind flailed at the calculation even though his heart was constricted by the truth. Because he knew beyond a doubt that Isabelle wouldn't have approached anyone else after she'd accomplished her goal of securing Luke's guardianship.

'Isabelle has a daughter?' he rasped.

'Yes.'

Willa looked up at him. Her smile had died. And maybe it was because Seraphina had just been in Willa's thoughts, but Matthew saw the exact moment that recognition flared in her brown eyes.

He looked away, trying desperately to appear uninterested.

But Wilhelmina wasn't so easily fooled. After a long, drawn-out silence, she said, 'It's so peculiar, though... Sera looks nothing like the late Duke. If I knew less about Izzy, I'd say she'd been thoroughly debauched by someone else before the wedding.'

'Doubtful.' Leo chose that moment to comment. 'The Duchess doesn't have it in her. Too cool. Aloof. Practical.'

Matthew wanted to argue. He wanted to say that she was not cool, but fire in his hands. That she was never aloof, only shy and inexperienced. But practical... He would give Leo 'practical'. The Duchess was perhaps the most practical woman he'd ever met.

He didn't say any of that, though, too overwrought by the sudden certainty that his life had just taken a drastic turn.

'I think I'll retire for the evening,' he said to nobody in particular.

He had to go.

He had to *know*.

Leo waved him off casually. Wilhelmina pushed herself to her feet.

'I'll lock the door after you.' She followed him to the door, lowering her voice significantly as she added, 'I was wondering why she panicked this evening, you know. Before she saw you she was managing her first foray into society since being widowed quite well.'

'Where is she?'

'At home, I imagine.'

'Lady Windhurst,' he said quietly, his tone beseeching. 'Please…'

'She is at Everett Place. In St James's. The house is impossible to miss.' She unlocked and opened the door. 'Had I known I was divulging something I shouldn't have, I would never have said anything.'

'I do not doubt it.'

Wilhelmina stared at him for a long moment. 'If you hurt my friend, there will be hell to pay.'

Matthew didn't reply—what was there to say?

And although she tipped her head in farewell, he felt Wilhelmina's gaze burning into his back as he marched down the corridor.

He didn't let her warning stop him. He exited the house, and the moment he was on the street he started running.

Chapter Six

Everett Place, although technically a townhouse, was probably better described as a town mansion. The six-storey residence had an exterior façade comprised of yellow malm brick. The entrance, offset to the left, was framed by two white Doric pilasters beneath the large Venetian windows that lined the entire front of the house.

It was nearing midnight and, suddenly unsure of himself, unsure of the situation, Matthew leaned against a lamppost on the opposite side of the street and considered his options.

He knew what he *wanted* to do. He *wanted* to storm into Everett Place and demand the truth from Isabelle. But then what? What happened once she'd told him?

Matthew, who was typically so sure of himself, felt new panic at his lack of direction.

I should go home, he thought. *Think this through.*

He even moved off to do just that. But then, just before his eyes left the windows of the house, one of the dark rooms was lit with the warm glow of a candle, and before he could think to move his feet the Duchess herself drew back the lace curtain. She leaned one shoulder against the windowpane and stared out into the night, as if she were searching for someone in the dark…as if she were searching for *him*.

Matthew held his breath as he watched her from the shadows opposite. The Duchess was a beautiful woman, her sable hair still piled atop her head, her skin warmed by the candlelight behind her. She was still dressed in her burgundy gown, and as he watched she wrapped her arms around her waist and looked down on the empty street.

He thought she looked rather sad. And he couldn't help but wonder if she was sad because of him—because of their encounter. The manner in which she'd tried to run from him was indication enough that he had terrified her. Or, maybe, he thought now, he had simply threatened the secret she protected.

The thought that he had scared her shamed him. Had he been less eager to see her again he might have thought his reintroduction through more.

Like now, his mind screamed at him.

He was standing outside her home, spying on her like some deranged madman, and for what? What would he do if the child was his?

Seraphina, Willa had called her. *Seraphina.*

As if his thoughts had somehow conjured her, a second woman approached—a maid. She was carrying a small child who had the same round, cherubic cheeks and dark, riotous curls that Matthew remembered on Eleanor, his youngest sister, at the same age.

The child was crying, her eyes scrunched closed, her tiny hands fisted in frustration.

His heart simply stopped beating for one perfect moment, before resuming at an accelerated pace.

His stomach roiled with nausea.

Sweat broke across his brow.

His mouth watered, and for one long moment all he could do was close his eyes and swallow down the anxiety clogging his throat.

He should turn and walk away. He should leave. Only Matthew couldn't get his feet to move. Instead, he opened his eyes again and stared, in a daze, as Isabelle turned away from the window.

Her sadness simply lifted. Her lips curled into a genuine

smile as she extended her arms for the crying child. Seraphina went to her and immediately nestled her head in her mother's neck, seeking comfort.

The maid left, casting the room into dimmer light as she took her candle with her, silhouetting the Duchess and her child in the window. Together, they looked like one of Raphael's *Madonna and Child* paintings. Isabelle was beautiful—if not virginal. The dress she wore would have evoked purely carnal thoughts in the most decent of men. And Seraphina... She was a cherubic replication of...*him*.

Isabelle brushed Seraphina's curls back from her forehead and placed a single kiss on her cheek. Although he couldn't hear what she said, he saw her lips move as she cooed words of comfort.

Matthew would have given anything at that moment to be standing there with her—with *them*—listening to her maternal chatter. What words did she speak to calm her child? What stories did she weave for her? Or were they not stories at all, but simple nothings measured out in that universal tone reserved for young children?

Hating to leave, but knowing that he was intruding on a private moment, Matthew finally moved to go. He'd go home—for now. At least until he could plan his next steps.

He took a step forward, inadvertently bringing himself out of the shadows—and realised his mistake too late.

In the still, dark night, his movements were amplified. He hesitated as the Duchess saw his brief advance and turned to look out of the window.

Their eyes met.

There was one horrific second in which she recognised him, followed quickly by her terrified retreat—a retreat that left him more certain of the child's identity than her physical appearance ever could have.

He looked up at the dark window for a long moment, daring her to step back into the light and face him.

The Duchess did not.

Of course she did not.

And so, helpless to do anything else just then, Matthew simply turned and walked away.

If he'd imagined that his life would change once he'd returned from his tour, he never could have imagined that it would change so soon—nor so drastically. For there was no doubt in his mind that he had been looking at *his* child, *his* daughter.

Seraphina.

Isabelle had almost managed to convince herself that she had imagined Matthew, Lord Ashworth, standing outside her house and looking up at her bedroom window the night before by the time she went down to breakfast the next morning.

She'd tossed and turned all night—one moment convincing herself that it had certainly been him, and that she would have recognised him anywhere, and the next telling herself that she'd imagined the entire episode and that Matthew had far better things to do with his time than follow her home and wait beneath her bedroom window like some sinister Romeo.

'Good morning, Mary,' she said as she entered the dining room.

Mary, who was sitting at the family dining room table reading a letter, looked up at her and smiled. 'You slept rather late this morning.'

'On the contrary,' Isabelle replied, 'I barely slept at all. And then couldn't find the energy to actually get out of bed once the sun had risen.'

She walked to the sideboard to peruse the breakfast that had been laid out and, sensing that her uneasy stomach wasn't ready for the full English fare, settled on pouring herself a cup of tea instead.

'Is anything the matter?' asked Mary.

Isabelle considered her cousin over the rim of her teacup. 'I don't know,' she admitted finally.

Hearing the uncertainty in Isabelle's tone, Mary put the letter she had been perusing down on the table and turned, giving Isabelle her full attention.

'Last night, once we'd returned from the ball...'

'Yes?'

'Well, I was in my bedroom…' She trailed off, unable to finish.

'And?'

'Well, I could have sworn I saw Lord Ashworth standing on the street below, looking up at me.'

Mary paled. 'Are you certain it was him?'

Yes. Isabelle exhaled a huge breath, but didn't answer the question out loud, settling on 'I had Sera with me' instead.

'Oh.' Mary sat back in her chair, but instead of calming Isabelle, maybe telling her she was delusional, or reminding her that Lord Ashworth probably had no interest in his illegitimate daughter, she asked, 'Do you think he knows?'

Isabelle moved to sit opposite Mary at the table, her worry suddenly amplified by her cousin's. 'If it was him, he most certainly knows—or at least suspects,' she whispered. 'How could he not?'

'What will he demand?'

'Demand?' The idea that Lord Ashworth would demand anything of her hadn't even entered her mind.

He wouldn't…would he?

'Izzy, you are a *duchess*,' Mary replied quickly, leaning across the table. 'One with a considerable fortune and no husband's protection. And Lord Ashworth is a notorious womaniser with a highly questionable character. He could demand anything.' She shook her head rapidly, as if wanting to deny the statement, even as the words 'And you'd have no choice but to give it to him' came out of her mouth. 'Seraphina looks too much like him,' she said.

Isabelle took a deep breath and tried to calm herself. 'As far as I know, the Heather earldom is intact,' she countered, trying desperately to ignore the frantic ticking of her pulse. 'His family fortune is considerable. Why would he need to demand anything from me?'

'Well…' Mary's brows drew together as she considered the question. 'What *else* could he want?'

'I… I have no idea.'

They were saved from having to speculate by a light knock on the door.

Both she and Mary resumed their respective breakfasts, and Isabelle called, 'Enter!'

'Good morning, Your Grace.' The butler came in and bowed, holding out a silver tray with the morning mail.

'Thank you, Gordon.' She took the three letters off the tray. 'Have you seen Luke this morning?'

'Still abed, Your Grace. Though I passed Tess in the hall, on her way to wake him for your walk.'

'Thank you.'

The butler bowed and left the room.

Isabelle flicked through the letters. The first, from her mother, she decided to leave until later in the afternoon, knowing that it wouldn't contain anything urgent—she'd seen her at the ball just last night, and her mother had had nothing to say to her beyond a cursory greeting. The second was from her solicitor, Mr Briggs, who was undoubtedly writing to confirm the monthly estate meeting that she had insisted Luke partake in since her husband had died. The last…

Isabelle stared at her name, written in a neat, masculine hand, for a long moment. There were two parts of her, each vying for control. One wanted to tear open the letter and read what he'd written. The other wanted to throw it into the blazing fire and pretend she'd never received the missive at all.

'Is it from him?' asked Mary.

'I don't know.'

After a long moment, she opened the letter with trembling hands.

Duchess,
Meet me at Hyde Park Corner. Two o'clock. We have much
to discuss.
M

'He wants to meet me,' Isabelle said finally. 'Today.'

She read the note to Mary, making sure to keep her tone neutral despite the heavy dread collecting in her stomach.

'Oh, Izzy, what are you going to do?' Mary's face was still pale, her eyes wide with fear.

'I'm going to meet him,' Isabelle replied matter-of-factly. 'There's no way around this, Mary. Whatever he has to say to me—whatever he wants from me—cannot be ignored.'

She tucked the letter into the long sleeve of her dress so that she could destroy it later.

'You're awfully calm, Isabelle.'

Isabelle didn't feel calm at all. She felt quite ill, actually. However, there was one thing keeping the worst of her panic at bay: the memory of that night. Matthew had been kind and gentle with her. He'd never laughed at her situation nor made her feel scandalised or cheap.

'I don't remember him being cruel,' she said quietly. 'Quite the opposite, in fact. Perhaps he just wants to know the truth? Perhaps he has heard that I have a child and put the pieces together?'

'I suppose there is only one way to find out.'

Isabelle nodded her agreement, and they both lapsed into silence.

Mary finished reading her own letter and soon rose from the table. 'I will be ready to accompany you.'

'Could you tell Luke that we'll delay our walk until then?'

Mary hesitated. 'You think it a good idea to take him?'

'I don't see the harm in it.'

But internally Isabelle thought that the more people between her and Lord Ashworth the better. Last night, when he'd held her in his arms, she'd wanted to rest her head against his chest and breathe in the scent of him—the scent that still haunted her sensory memory two years later. She'd wanted to lean into his touch where it had burned through her clothes...

'And Sera?'

'No,' Isabelle said immediately. 'I... I can't.' She raised one trembling hand to her tired eyes. 'People would talk, Mary. Only weeks out of mourning and spotted gallivanting around the parks with Lord Ashworth—and a child who looks eerily like him? No,' Isabelle repeated, straightening her spine. 'I want to keep Sera away from this. She must stay here with Tess.'

'I think we should have Willa accompany us too.' Mary turned back from where she stood at the door. 'That way it will seem as if we are out together and have just happen upon the Viscount.'

Isabelle considered Mary's suggestion. Not only did Willa know Lord Ashworth, she'd also provide a necessary distraction. After all, he could hardly threaten or expose her in front of two other people and a child—could he?

'Yes. We shall ask her when she arrives.'

'What do we say?'

'That we would love her to join us for a walk in Hyde Park.' Isabelle shrugged, but the gesture did nothing to dispel the heavy weight of guilt sliding through her. 'To be entirely honest, Mary, I… To have done what I did…'

'You didn't have a choice.'

'There is always a choice. And I knew the consequences of mine when I made it. Now there is nothing to do but face Lord Ashworth and reap what I have sown…' The knowledge calmed her. 'There is no way around it. And to be entirely honest… Even if I could take it back, I wouldn't. He gave me Seraphina.'

Suddenly, the door to the dining room burst open and Willa herself strode in, her quick steps filled with anxious energy.

Gordon hurried to keep up with her, bowing quickly before Willa could speak. 'Lady Windhurst, Your Grace,' he wheezed, his breath coming in uneven gasps.

'Heaven knows I don't need an introduction, Gordy,' Willa teased, using the pet name that only she used for Isabelle's elderly butler.

Gordon merely frowned, bowed again, and repeated, 'Your Grace,' before departing.

As soon as the door had clicked shut behind him, Willa spun around to face Isabelle. 'You little hussy!' she declared, her brown eyes wide.

Mary gasped.

Isabelle froze for one perfect second, before a small, hysterical giggle escaped from between her lips. 'I suppose our promise to keep silent won't be necessary after all, Mary.'

'How?' Willa threw her hands in the air. *'When?'*

She began an agitated march around the dining room.

'I mean, I always wondered at Sera's looks, but… *You*. I

would have lost that wager a hundred, nay, a *thousand* times over! You…' she glanced around the room as if to check for eavesdroppers, lowered her voice, and stage whispered '…and *Lord Ashworth*?'

'Wilhelmina, dear,' Isabelle chastised. 'Could you perhaps *actually* whisper instead of *pretending* to whisper?'

Willa hurried over to the seat Mary had just vacated and dragged it out with little grace or ceremony. She plonked into it and rested both elbows on the table. 'Tell me *everything*, Izzy!'

'How did you…?'

'I didn't. Not until you came up in my conversation with the gentleman last night.'

Isabelle listened as Willa explained how she'd put the pieces together.

'I'm sorry to have brought it up,' Willa finished. 'By the time I realised, it was too late.'

'It's not your fault.' Isabelle sighed. She related her own story to Willa, ending with, 'I always had a feeling that there would be a bigger price to pay one day…'

'What do you mean?' Willa asked, looking back and forth between Isabelle and Mary.

'He has asked me to meet him at Hyde Park Corner today at two o'clock.'

'Drat.' Willa raised one hand to her face and tapped her index finger against her lips as she considered. 'Do you know what I would do?'

'What?'

'I wouldn't go.' Willa slammed her palm on the table. 'I would show him that I cannot be cowed. You are a *duchess*, Isabelle!'

'Mmm…' Isabelle mumbled, considering.

'You don't think that would push him to do something rash?' Mary, ever calm and rational.

'Like what?' Willa countered. 'He's hardly going to run around the park shouting his sins for all the world to hear.'

'True.' Mary nodded slowly. 'He wouldn't dare. Not after his last scandal.'

Willa looked back and forth between them. 'What scandal?'

'He was...*involved* with the Marchioness of Dunn—Christine Dalmore—when he was quite a bit younger,' Isabelle offered, feeling vaguely guilty for sharing the gossip. 'It was how he came to be on our list.'

'It didn't end well,' Mary finished.

'Oh, I remember something about that...' Willa tapped her fingers on the table. 'She caused a scene when he broke it off.'

'*Caused a scene* would be putting it lightly.' Mary glanced at Isabelle, as if to make sure she had her approval to talk of such things. When Isabelle nodded, she added, 'The Marchioness went to his club and threatened to kill herself if he did not take her back. Apparently, she had to be sedated before her husband could transport her to the country. Soon afterwards she travelled abroad, and to my knowledge has not returned.'

'How odd. He doesn't *seem* the callous type.' Willa turned back to Isabelle. 'What do you think? You know him best.'

'On the contrary. I do not know him at all.'

Although she did not say it, Isabelle reminded herself that, even if Matthew had been nothing but kind and gentle with her, he had a past that proved him a reprehensible rogue, a man who should not be trusted. She briefly fought an internal battle, pitching the memory of her night with him against her knowledge of his previous scandal, but when she factored Sera into the equation it was an easy decision.

Pointing to the small writing desk in the corner of the room, Isabelle said, 'Mary, pass me that pen and paper.'

Mary hurried to oblige.

Willa grinned wickedly. 'You think he deserves the courtesy of a note?'

'No.'

Fuelled by thoughts of the Marchioness's ruination, by memories of Matthew, and by a new fear for herself and her family, Isabelle hurriedly scrawled a reply. And if, through her determination, the memory of his gentle manner and quiet care flared, Isabelle did her best to ignore it. Her own potential scandal aside, Matthew had the power to ruin Seraphina—and that she would not abide.

'I think *I* deserve the pleasure of refusing him.'

The note was short and borderline rude.

M,
In answer to your request: no. I regret to inform you that
I am otherwise engaged at home for the remainder of the
day. Nonetheless, I hope you have a pleasant walk. The
weather looks promising for a promenade...
D

She didn't know why she signed it 'D' for Duchess, instead of 'I' for Isabelle. Knew only that she rather liked the way he turned her title into an improper endearment.

'What I wouldn't give to see his face when he reads it!' Willa laughed.

Even Mary offered a small smile. 'Hopefully, he doesn't retaliate.'

Chapter Seven

Matthew couldn't help but scowl when he read the Duchess's curt reply—her *refusal*, as it were.

'Taps!' he called, his voice booming through his study and out into the hall.

His butler appeared in the open doorway almost immediately. 'My lord?'

'Have one of the footmen fetch me some flowers.'

Taps's white bushy eyebrows rose high on his forehead at the strange demand—or perhaps at the angry tone it was delivered in. 'Flowers, my lord?'

'Flowers, Taps.'

'Any specific *type* of flower?' he asked, bewildered by the request.

'No. My only requirement is that the arrangement be *very* large.'

'My lord.' Taps bowed, and then left the room in a hurry to complete the task.

Matthew read the note again. He could imagine her, reading his own demanding letter, her dark eyes narrowed in frustration, her pretty lips pursed as she thought of how best to refuse him… But instead of making him angrier, the image cooled his temper.

He raked both hands through his hair and expelled a tired exhale. He didn't quite know what the right thing to do was—not when it came to Seraphina.

And when it came to Isabelle… Oh, to say he didn't know what he *wanted* to do would have been a flagrant lie. He wanted to see her naked breasts again, her rosy nipples peaking with desire. He wanted to run his hands over the petal-soft skin beneath her navel and work his way down to her thighs. He wanted to dip his fingers into her and hear those shocked little sounds she made each time he did.

But what he wanted to do barely seemed like the right or even the *civilised* thing to do, given the circumstances.

Matthew shifted in his seat, trying to dispel the heavy weight of his need. He picked up the ivory letter opener on his desk and restlessly spun the short blade between his fingers.

I should court her—openly and for all of London to see.

Isabelle might be a widow and a duchess, but she was only twenty years old. The *ton* could hardly fault him. And even if they did, Matthew would try not to care. He had been considered a rake since the age of twenty-five, when his ill-advised affair with the Marchioness had imploded. But even with that scandal looming over his head, mothers still tried to foist their daughters upon him at every available opportunity. He was, after all, a viscount, and would one day be an earl—a fact that seemed to override any maternal hesitation regarding the number of scandalous things he was supposed to have done in his past.

But still, the possibility that his past might taint Isabelle—or, God forbid, Seraphina—gave him pause. Despite his restlessness, despite his urge to act, he would have to be careful. Now, more than ever before, he would have to proceed with caution.

Matthew was so lost in thought that he didn't notice the hour slipping by. His correspondence—which included some business that he had intended to conduct on his father's behalf—lay forgotten in front of him as he pondered Isabelle and Seraphina, and when Taps re-entered, saying that the flowers had been procured, Matthew practically jumped to his feet.

'Have them ready for me. I will be out momentarily.'

'May I have the carriage brought round, my lord?'

'No, I'll walk.'

Taps opened his mouth as if to comment, or perhaps to protest, but then seemed to think better of it at the last moment. 'Very well, my lord. Shall I have a footman assist you?'

'No. Thank you, Taps. I believe I can manage flowers.'

'My lord.'

Taps bowed and left the room, leaving Matthew to put on his own coat and gloves.

It was only five minutes later, when he stepped into the hall and saw the monstrous flower arrangement, that he realised he might have been too hasty in refusing the carriage. The blasted thing had to be four feet tall and nearly half as wide, leaving him to wonder how he was going to see his own footfall through the foliage.

He frowned down at the flowers for a long moment, identifying white and red roses, blue forget-me-nots and white daffodils before his floral knowledge ran out. He wondered if Isabelle was as enamoured of floriography as his sisters were—and then hoped to God that none of the flowers included in the arrangement would give offence.

'Is something the matter, my lord?'

'It's rather larger than I expected, Taps,' he drawled in reply.

'Carriage, my lord?'

'Please.'

Willa, Mary and Isabelle all sat in the receiving room, talking and laughing as the day passed languidly by. While Mary sat on the settee, drinking her tenth cup of tea, Willa played a game of chess at a nearby table with Luke, and Isabelle sat on the floor with Seraphina, rolling a ball back and forth on the carpet between them.

They all paused in their conversation when the sound of a mighty crash echoed through the cavernous foyer of Everett Place.

'Goodness!' Willa exclaimed, her eyes wide with curiosity. She pushed herself to her feet. 'What on earth was that?'

'I have no idea.'

Isabelle followed suit, instinctively picking up Seraphina and hurrying towards the receiving room door without hesitation. She opened the door with one hand, pulling up short when she saw the chaos that had been unleashed into her home.

Gordon and Lord Ashworth were both lying on the floor beneath a rather dishevelled mass of flowers. The small Sutherland table in the foyer had been overturned and the vase upon it—a blue French enamel one she'd received as a wedding gift from her cousin—was broken into numerous pieces that were scattered around the pair like jagged confetti.

Matthew was the first to move, heaving the ridiculous arrangement off both himself and the elderly butler before pushing himself to a stand and extending a hand to help Gordon up. As soon as both men were upright, he ran a hand through his hair, scattering tiny leaves and petals about the foyer.

He surveyed the carnage around him. 'Blast.'

Seraphina giggled, and the joyous sound echoed loudly in the otherwise silent foyer.

Matthew's attention snapped to her.

His grey eyes widened perceptibly.

His chest heaved with a shuddering in-out breath, and although his thoughts must have been running rampant he didn't say anything at all—just stared at his daughter in mute shock.

Isabelle, too, was not quite sure what to do or say.

'Apologies, Your Grace.' It was Gordon who broke the silence. The butler was red with embarrassment. 'I was trying to direct Lord Ashworth where to set down the flowers, but there was an…impediment.'

'I see,' Isabelle replied. She cleared her throat, curious as to what 'impediment' Gordon had been referring to, but no further explanation came. 'Please fetch a maid to come and clean this up, Gordon.'

'Yes, Your Grace.' The butler disappeared, his mortification clear in his hurried footsteps as they echoed down the hall.

'Here, let me take her.' Mary took charge and came forward, her arms extended for Seraphina.

Isabelle let her go, knowing that it was best that she spoke to Lord Ashworth alone. 'Thank you, Mary. I'll only be a moment.'

Isabelle took a deep breath and turned to face Matthew again.

Except he wasn't looking at her. He was watching Seraphina, his eyes tracking her intently, as if he were absorbing every detail of her in the finite time he had. Seraphina peered at him from around Mary's shoulder, oblivious to the tense situation, her baby smile wide, her little hand clenching and unclenching in a little wave in his direction.

'I take it you did not receive my reply to your letter?' Isabelle asked, trying desperately to ignore the confusing pull of awareness spreading through her body.

When Willa gently shut the receiving room door behind her, leaving her alone with Lord Ashworth, he finally turned to look at her.

'I did,' he replied. 'But, seeing as you thought to mention you'd be at home, I thought I'd call.' Leaning down, he picked up the flowers off the floor and bowed. 'Though I must admit this is not quite how I imagined it would go.'

'No. I don't suppose so.'

Were it any other man, she might have laughed. The flower arrangement was absurdly oversized, the foyer a mess of over-turned furniture, petals and broken pieces of vase. But it wasn't *any* man. It was Matthew—and they both knew why he'd come.

Isabelle had lost the ability to say more. She just stood there in front of him, speechless in her fear and shame.

'You didn't tell me.'

As if sensing that polite small talk would be wasted, Matthew cut straight to the point. He shook his head, his familiar grey eyes filling with confusion and, surprisingly, pain.

'*Why*, Duchess? I…'

He ran one large palm through his shaggy hair—hair that Isabelle remembered the sliding, silky weight of with absolute clarity.

The scurry of an approaching maid prevented her reply. Isabelle swallowed down the panic clogging her throat and indicated for him to follow her as she walked across the hall to her late husband's study.

Once they were inside, she leaned her weight against the door, supporting herself against the sudden exhaustion that swept through her. Of all the fears and worries that had plagued her since Sera had been born, this had not been included among them. Not necessarily the fear that Matthew would find out—he'd only have had to see Sera once to know that she was his—but that he would *care*.

They were both quiet, each wondering what to say and hoping that the other would fill the heavy silence.

'I made you a promise,' she said eventually. He opened his mouth to speak, but she talked over him, needing to purge herself of the truth after all this time. 'And every time I sat down to write you, to tell you, I remembered how kind you had been. I remembered that you had briefly thought I was trying to trap you, and I couldn't... I thought you'd see it as just that—a... a trap.'

Matthew placed the flowers down on the large desk. He didn't come towards her, just watched her face as if he were gauging her every expression. 'I might have at first. But I would have come home, Duchess.' His sincere eyes bored into hers. 'I would have done the right thing by you. I would have—'

'You didn't *have* to,' she countered. 'I was safe. Nobody knew—nobody *knows*,' she corrected hurriedly. 'Matthew... Seraphina will be raised as a lady, the daughter of a duke. You can have your life free from the burden of us.'

'The *burden* of you?' He took one large step closer, his features darkening with anger. 'Did you ever stop to think that I wouldn't want her raised as someone else's? That I'm not the type of man who'd let my child—irrespective of the circumstances of her birth—walk through life unprotected?'

'No,' she admitted honestly. And even though her heart softened at his possessiveness, she couldn't allow it. 'We could never say anything.' He opened his mouth to argue, but she hurried on. 'Even if you wanted to claim her, you couldn't. She would be *ruined* before her second birthday,' she added desperately. 'Is that really what you want?'

'No.' He frowned down at her. 'Of course not.'

'So, why are you here?' she asked, raising her hands to her heart in a forlorn gesture. 'If people saw you two together, they would know. And even if they couldn't prove it, the rumours would be enough.'

His eyes clouded with regret. 'She looks too much like me.' It wasn't a question. Still, Isabelle could only nod.

'Oh, God.' He collapsed onto the nearby settee as if he'd lost his legs. 'I think it's only dawning on me now,' he whispered. 'I assumed when I saw her last night... But hearing it confirmed...' Leaning forward on the chair, he hung his head and raised his right hand to his face, his index finger and thumb pressing down on his eyes. 'Oh, God,' he repeated, and expelled a shuddering sigh. 'I have a child. A...a *daughter.*'

His words came out laced with blatant shock and fear and wonder.

Isabelle wanted to offer some comfort—some words that might make him feel better. Yet she didn't know where to begin. What words were there? So she stood in silence like a scared schoolgirl—not a grown woman who'd traded her body for a favour from the very man in front of her.

After a long moment, he slowly turned to face her. 'May I assume that you won't marry me?'

Isabelle was so stunned that for a full three seconds she merely stared. But when she replied she did so with the confidence of a woman who knew she would never marry again. 'You may assume so.'

'Still so worried about your title, *Duchess*?' His eyes flashed. His tone oozed bitterness. 'You realise that you outrank me? And that you would keep the title Duchess of Everett even if you married me?'

Isabelle tried to stave off the hurt that lanced through her at his callous words, but the only way she knew how to defend herself against it was to let the rage come.

'I do not think only of myself! Seraphina *and* Luke are mine to protect. If people were to find out I could lose my guardianship of Luke. And you... Matthew, you have a scandalous past—or have you forgotten your marchioness so soon?'

He flinched against the accusation. And his voice was filled with bitterness when he spoke. 'It is rather difficult to forget when it drags behind me like a chain!'

'If you became involved in Sera's life, your past would follow her too. I am saving you, Matthew—from a loveless marriage to someone you would never have considered were the circumstances different.'

Her words were sure, her resolve true. And if Isabelle allowed herself one small moment to imagine what it would be like, to be married to Matthew, she did not linger on it long.

Matthew's eyes snapped with emotion. 'Don't presume to know what I think, Duchess.'

She didn't know what he wanted from her and so, at a loss for the right words, Isabelle fell into a restless silence.

'We won't say anything, then,' he suggested after a long while. 'As far as anyone would know, Seraphina would still be the daughter of a duke. But Duchess, if you married me, I would protect Sera—and Luke. I would treat him as my own. I would love and protect him and ensure that his estate and interests were being sufficiently managed until he was of age.'

'At what cost?' Isabelle cried out, overcome with an emotion that wasn't all fear. It was desperation too. A longing for him to stop painting a picture of a future that could never be practically realised.

Isabelle's life had taught her many hard truths—the first of which was that a woman tied to a man would always be trapped, whether she be wife or daughter or sister. As a daughter, she had been passed on with thought only of the title she would marry into and the benefits that the union would reap. As a wife, irrespective of how short the marriage had been, she had very quickly realised that there would be no escape at all.

But when Matthew talked, when he spoke of hypotheticals that involved them *together*, she couldn't help but become caught up in the possibility.

'Nobody could prove anything.'

Matthew rose off the settee in one fluid movement and rounded the furniture to face her again. He stood so close that she had to crane her neck to meet his eyes.

'It would be a rumour—maybe a minor scandal. And it would eventually die down.'

'Until she comes out and society scorns her! Until what happened between us ruins her chances,' she argued, knowing that she was right in this one instance.

'Chances for *what*?' he demanded, exasperated. 'Duchess, together we have titles, land and more money than we could ever spend! We could give her the dowry of the century. Seraphina could choose anyone she wanted. *Anyone!*'

'That's not true!' Isabelle raised her voice to match his. 'Only a man would think that being raised a bastard wouldn't have consequences!'

'She's not a boy.' He lowered his voice again, his tone growing colder with each point he made. 'She can't inherit. She loses nothing by people merely *suspecting* she is illegitimate.'

'How could you even say that?'

'Because it's true.'

'Rumours will do far more damage than you are able to repair by throwing money at them.'

'How can you—?'

'I won't allow it, Matthew.'

He recoiled as if she'd struck him.

'I'm sorry,' she said.

'So, that's it?' he asked. 'I'm never to meet her, speak to her or know her—my own child—because you are a coward?'

'A coward?' Isabelle whispered as the blood drained from her face. Pain and fury mingled in her chest, stealing her breath. But when she replied, she let it come in a torrent. 'Do you know how afraid and alone I was throughout my confinement? Do you know the pure agony of birthing a child with only a friend and a doctor—a stranger—for comfort?' she demanded.

She felt her anger spiking when he paled.

'Or do you know the fear of being left alone at *nineteen years old* with a new infant and nobody to go to for help or advice except a nursemaid and a few kindly servants who'd had children of their own?'

'Isabelle—'

'No.' She held up a hand, halting him. 'We are done here.'

'And what if I claim her anyway?'

Isabelle took a step back as the horror of his threat hung over them. 'You promised you would never—'

'That was before you had my *child*.'

He closed the space between them again, catching her wrists

in his big hands and pulling her closer, until she was nearly up against him.

'Don't you *dare* touch me,' she warned, braving her own nerves to meet his furious gaze.

'Or *what*, Duchess?' he growled, his breath sawing out of him to strike her forehead.

He was close—so close that Isabelle could feel the rage and heat pouring off him.

Instead of being afraid, she felt a thrill shoot through her. Memories assaulted her. She could remember the matching canter of their beating hearts and the feel of his big hands stroking her skin. She could remember the weight of his body, pinning her down, grounding her to the earth as she shattered. And the way he'd cradled her gently afterwards, as if she were special, as if she were precious—precious *to him*.

Good Lord, she realised with no small amount of horror, she would give a lot to have this man kiss her again. Her eyes tracked to his lips even as her own opened on a shaky exhalation that she was helpless to prevent.

Matthew's hands flexed around her wrists, and when she dared to look up at him she saw that he was no longer angry. He was watching her expression, his hunger blatant. And instead of making her angrier, the fact that he so clearly desired her forced tears into her eyes.

Matthew released her suddenly and took a step back as the last of the fight drained from his eyes.

He sighed tiredly. 'Please don't cry.'

She wiped her face, furious with herself—furious with *him*. 'You are threatening everything that I have,' she replied, despite the cool tears trailing down her face. 'And now you dare tell me not to cry?'

'Duchess—'

'Get out of my house.'

His head snapped up at the command, but instead of the fury she'd expected all she saw in his gaze was a deep sadness punctuated by the flickering flames of his desire—desire for *her*.

He bowed ever so slightly. 'I will send terms, Duchess.'

'You would blackmail me?'

'You would think so little of me?' he countered bitterly.

And before she could issue a retort, he turned and left, closing the door softly behind him.

Chapter Eight

As Isabelle had expected, Lord Ashworth's 'terms' arrived the very next day. However, instead of the mere letter she had been expecting, the missive was accompanied by a beautiful rocking horse, with a large red bow tied around its neck, and a zoetrope.

The rocking horse was crafted from dark mahogany wood and set upon gliders that slid over a stationary base. The bridle and saddle were miniatures, made from real leather, and when Isabelle lost to temptation and touched the horse's mane and tail, she was both shocked and fascinated to find that it was real horsehair.

And that was nothing compared to the name that had been skilfully carved into the glider closest to her: *MATTHEW*.

It had once been his.

The zoetrope was beautiful too. The animation device included a cylindrical tub that looked almost like a hat box, set atop a spinning wheel-like base. A strip of images depicting a horse and rider had been placed inside, and when she turned the wheel rapidly and looked through the side slats the moving reel made it appear as if the horse and rider were galloping round and round. There was a small accompanying box that included different image strips to place in the device.

The receipt of gifts was not something that Isabelle was

comfortable with for two reasons. One, she and Matthew were most certainly *not* courting. And two, the extravagance of the gifts he had sent for the children would certainly raise eyebrows should anyone discover who they'd come from. And, worse, if she returned them she knew he would simply send them back, pointing out that they were for the children—not for her.

Her theory was proved correct when she opened the letter and read:

Duchess,

I know what you're thinking—you've always wanted to be gifted a pony. Unfortunately, said equine is spoken for by another dark-haired beauty. And it would be unfair to gift one child and not the other, don't you think? Should you like to ride a real horse sometime—or, rather, any time— I would gladly accompany you.

In the more likely scenario you never want to see me again, and after our last encounter I find that I cannot fault you. I am sorry, Duchess. While it is no excuse, I was overwhelmed and behaved poorly as a result. Please forgive me.

Though I understand all your reasons for forbidding any contact with S, forgive me again when I say that these are my terms: I want to see her, Isabelle. Twice a week, at a time and location conveniently private and safe to both of you.

Send me a letter indicating when and where and I will be there. If you agree to those meetings I promise never to approach you or S in public or otherwise interfere with her upbringing.

While I don't know exactly how this will end, I hope you believe me when I say that I have no desire to harm you or the children. I merely want to make up for lost time.
Yours,
M

Isabelle found herself alone with her emotions. How could one letter so easily tear down her defences? If he had written and demanded money, or threatened to publicly claim Sera, it almost would have been easier to deal with than the desperate compromise he'd offered. She could have hated him then. But the fact that Matthew demanded nothing but the opportunity to spend time with his child was perhaps the only argument he could have used that would override her common sense—because it would be absolutely reckless to allow such meetings to occur.

But how could she deny him? Even if she wanted to, Matthew had all the power. With only a few negligent words he could start a rumour that would ruin not only Isabelle, but Sera and Luke too.

With one last glance at the toys, she directed Gordon to have them moved upstairs—the rocking horse to the nursery and the zoetrope to Luke's bedroom. Although she tried not to dwell on it, accepting the gifts felt like welcoming a Trojan Horse into her home. What anyone else might have considered innocent children's playthings were, to her, weapons of war—a war that she was already losing.

Isabelle went into the study and closed the door. She sat at the big desk and removed a crisp new sheet of paper.

She had no point of reference for what she was about to do, so she took several minutes to think over her reply before penning it.

M—

Although entirely inappropriate, the children will appreciate your gifts. Thank you.

As to your request, it would seem I have no choice but to accept. Given the unusual circumstances, and our need for discretion, I propose that we meet here, at E Place, every Monday and Friday at midnight.

Although an inconvenient time, my reasoning is two-fold. S has an ingrained clock that seems to chime at the

witching hour. She is always awake then, as you may re-
member from your last midnight visit. Additionally, my
household will be long abed and less likely to interrupt—
or talk of your visits with anyone.

   If that is amendable to you, I shall see you tomorrow.
D

PS Please don't knock or otherwise make your presence
known by tripping over in my hall again. I will leave the
servants' entrance at the back of the house unlocked and
wait in the study for you to let yourself in.

With the letter written and re-read a dozen times, Isabelle sealed it inside an envelope and addressed it to the Viscount.

Before she sent it, she called Gordon into the study and bade him close the door behind him. 'Gordon...' Isabelle trailed off, unsure of how to speak to the elderly butler—especially given the topic of the conversation.

'Your Grace?' he said, concern lacing his tone.

'Gordon,' she tried again, 'I have found myself in a situation that is going to require your particular discretion.'

Gordon tipped into a bow, but the expression on his face remained completely neutral. 'I am at your service, Your Grace. I assure you that I and your entire household would never betray your confidence.' He frowned, his bushy brows almost meeting in the middle. 'Were any of the staff to talk, I would personally see to their dismissal.'

Rather overwhelmed by this passionate speech, Isabelle observed, 'I do believe that is the most I have ever heard you speak, Gordon.'

'A servant should neither be seen nor heard unless required, Your Grace.'

Isabelle's lips turned up in a small smile. 'Your standards are stricter than mine. I rather enjoy hearing you all laughing and talking amongst yourselves; it makes the house feel less lonely.'

Gordon's lips hinted at a smile for a small moment.

Encouraged by the small gesture, Isabelle forged ahead. 'I have renewed my acquaintance with a friend who has recently returned from his tour of the continent. He will be visiting with me every Monday and Friday.'

'Yes, Your Grace.'

'At midnight.'

Gordon did not hesitate. 'Would you like me to attend you and your guest personally, Your Grace?'

'No,' Isabelle replied immediately. She could barely speak to Gordon about the meetings, let alone have him witness them. 'You should take your nights to rest, Gordon. I'm merely letting you know why I shall be unlocking the servants' entrance and wandering about the house on those nights.'

'Yes, Your Grace. If you should need anything prepared ahead of time, you have only to let me know.'

'Thank you.' Isabelle cleared her throat. 'There is one other matter I wish to discuss with you.'

Gordon waited expectantly.

'On those nights I would like Seraphina's cot to be made up in my room. She shall stay with me.'

If he was surprised by her request, he didn't show it. 'And Tess?'

Isabelle considered the nursemaid. 'God knows that Tess would love two nights a week when she didn't have to wake up with Sera, Gordon. I will speak to her and make sure that she knows she's not needed.'

'Yes, Your Grace.' Gordon gave another stiff bow. Then he opened his mouth, closed it, and opened it again as he struggled with his need to add more.

'Please, speak plainly,' she told him.

'Your Grace, I would not presume… That is, I would hate to overstep…'

Isabelle waited patiently.

'Your Grace… Are you in any kind of trouble that I could assist you in resolving?'

Isabelle smiled. The butler stood a little straighter and returned to his infallible self.

'No,' she replied. 'I am not in any trouble. However, I do recognise your concern, Gordon. Your commitment to me and my family is greatly appreciated.'

'Your Grace.' He took a fortifying breath. 'I shall make the necessary arrangements. If that is all?'

'Yes, thank you.'

He bowed one last time and left the room as routinely as he'd entered, leaving Isabelle with no doubt that Gordon had been asked to do far worse in service to her late husband. She felt newly indoctrinated into a world of secrets and scandal that she'd never thought she'd be a part of.

Alone again, she slouched back in the chair, considering what she'd done. Her butler—and potentially her entire household—would now think that she was having an affair. And, worse, they would quickly surmise as to why she was letting her midnight visitor meet with her infant daughter. The servants were not idiots. If they had already suspected that she and the Duke had never consummated their marriage, they would almost certainly be able to confirm it now. Her only consolation was that her servants knew the value of discretion—and the advantage of being employed by a duke. It was a coveted position, and one she suddenly hoped they all took very seriously.

Chapter Nine

Matthew supposed that no true rogue would have felt the way he did, standing outside Everett Place in the middle of the night, staring at the small servants' entrance at the back of the house. It felt indecent. Wrong. As if he were some thief in the night—not a mere man, preparing to meet his infant daughter in secret for the first time.

Even the nerves swirling through his stomach were new and unsettling, as alive and mobile as they were weighted and heavy. It was strange, he thought, but he had not felt this tight-chested fear even when he'd secreted himself in the Marchioness's bedroom on the nights when her elderly husband had not been at home. At twenty-five, he'd barely stopped to think of anything—not impropriety, nor risk or heartbreak. He'd only thought of the woman eagerly waiting for him.

Raising his hand, he placed his palm on the door and pushed, surprised when it gave no resistance. He'd been half expecting that Isabelle wouldn't let him in after all…that maybe she'd come to her senses and bar his entry.

Yesterday, when he'd made his threat to claim Seraphina, he'd seen the Duchess's fear, and although it still shamed him to have scared her, he wouldn't have been surprised if that same fear had prompted her to renege on their compromise.

He stepped into the kitchen and immediately saw the single candle and matches that had been left there. He lit it before making his way through the glistening scullery, past the kitchen, with its faint smoky tang, and up the narrow servants' stairs.

He opened the door at the top of the stairs and turned down the corridor towards the study. The door was slightly ajar, with the faint glow of candlelight beckoning him like a moth to the flame.

Matthew took a cautious step forward, then paused as he became aware of the rapid acceleration of his heart in his chest. For someone who had only ever been superbly fit, he discovered the anxious threshing of that organ was not only surprising, but deeply terrifying. There was no doubt in his mind that this was what a man felt just before his heart simply failed and his soul took flight from this mortal coil—breathless, sick, and filled with fear of the unknown beyond.

Had he been able, he might have laughed at himself. He had faced much worse, and still he didn't think he'd ever been this afraid.

He took a moment to calm himself by taking deep breaths and reminding himself that he was meeting an infant—not walking to the front line or the gallows. Forcing purpose into his footsteps, he strode to the door. He raised his hand to knock and then, remembering the Duchess's warning for discretion, merely placed his shaking palm on the cool surface and pushed.

He wasn't sure what he had been expecting, but seeing Isabelle sitting on the floor in a simple hunter-green dress, her black hair cascading down her back, most certainly wasn't it.

'Duchess,' he murmured quietly, in case she hadn't heard his silent entry.

Isabelle turned, angling her head over her shoulder to glance at him. Her dark eyes took in the whole of him, from his unstyled hair to the tops of his freshly polished shoes.

'You came.'

'Of course.'

'You did not reply to my letter.'

She rocked forward onto her knees with a small grunt of effort, and it wasn't until she stood and affected an ungraceful turn that he realised why.

Seraphina stood in front of her. The child's little arms were stretched upwards, her hands in Isabelle's, as if she were supporting herself—or maybe as if they were supporting each other. Seraphina took two confident steps forward, her laughter-lit eyes—*his* eyes in *her* face—watching him.

He stared at her, unsure of what he was supposed to do— how he was supposed to act, or what he was supposed to say, if anything. He swallowed down the emotions—sadness, fear, awe, excitement—that knotted his throat.

She had a halo of thick, dark curls and grey eyes. She was so *small*, and yet also adorably chubby. She reminded him of a mischievous cupid, lying in wait for the perfect moment to release an arrow and wreak havoc.

Both females stood there, waiting for him to do something— *anything*, really.

'Matthew?' said Isabelle.

'Mmm?' he managed, tearing his eyes away from Seraphina to look at the Duchess.

She was watching him cautiously, almost as if she wasn't sure what to do either. But then, after a barely perceptible pause, she started walking towards him, both hands gently propelling Seraphina forward too.

It was only when they were standing directly in front of him that he managed to admit, 'I... I don't know what to do.'

Her dark eyes softened. 'You could start by introducing yourself.'

'Oh. Um...' Matthew ran one hand through his hair. 'Introduce myself...'

Changing tactics at the last moment, he lowered himself to his haunches and regarded Seraphina at her level.

The child seemed to know that this was no typical introduction. She didn't reach for him, only smiled happily and tilted her head, as if giving him time to sort his jumbled thoughts.

'Hello, Seraphina,' he managed, his voice hoarse with emotion, his heart thick with regret, and confusion, and a strange need to be known by this little person in front of him.

'Hello!' she squeaked.

Matthew, who had not been expecting a reply, let alone such an exuberant one, reared back, falling arse-first onto the carpet, his hands braced behind him.

There was a moment of perfect silence, during which he looked from the Duchess's shocked face to his daughter's. And then Seraphina started laughing, her high-pitched baby giggles filling the moment and pushing the awkwardness out.

A strange effusion of heat spread through Matthew's chest at the sound and, try as he might, he didn't think he'd ever heard anything so pure and joyous. When he chanced another glance at the Duchess he saw she was trying very hard not to laugh, but her pretty mouth trembled visibly with the urge.

'Perhaps we can try that again,' he murmured, and rearranged himself on his knees.

Matthew opened his coat and removed a small sprig of flowers from his inside pocket. He considered the three bright yellow blooms for a long moment before holding the bundle out to Seraphina.

'Daisies?' Isabelle asked as Seraphina released her hand and reached forward to take the offering, her tiny fingers closing around the stems.

Matthew shook his head. 'These are the blooms of the cinquefoil plant,' he explained. 'My sisters are obsessed with that book *Le Langage des Fleurs* by Madame Charlotte de la Tour. I had reason to peruse it once I got home last night.'

'Oh, yes. I believe we have the translated version here somewhere.' There was a brief pause before she asked, 'What does the cinquefoil signify?'

Matthew floundered for a fleeting moment, before clearing his throat and replying, 'Lasting friendship.'

His words came out tight and clipped, and he wondered if the Duchess would sense the lie.

'That's very sweet of you.'

Sweet? Could she not see that he was devastated? That his entire heart, his very life mechanism, was straining on the edge of implosion as he watched his tiny daughter wave the flowers about as if she'd been born to receive them. He was distraught...

broken by the fact that Isabelle hadn't told him—hadn't planned *ever* to tell him. He was tortured, angry at the thought of what the Duchess had suffered alone, when he should have—*would have*—been there. And, perhaps most of all, he was defeated. Because even as he raged against the thought he knew that Seraphina would never truly be his—*could* never truly be his.

Because Isabelle was right. If Matthew's past did not affect Seraphina, the circumstances surrounding her birth most certainly would. It would ruin them, and the only thing he knew to be true any more was the fact that he would never harm either Seraphina or Isabelle. Not like that. Not in any way. They were his to protect. Seraphina as his child. And Isabelle at the very least as the mother of his child.

As if she'd sensed the offence she'd inadvertently caused, the Duchess added, 'I didn't mean to imply—'

'I know.' Matthew tried to meet her eyes and smile, but the attempt fell flat.

When Seraphina released her mother's hand and walked to him, the flowers outstretched in front of her, as if she were going to give them back to him, he raised his hands instinctively.

His daughter walked straight into his bracketed palms, her small ribs pressing against palms that suddenly felt too big… too clumsy. Matthew's entire body went rigid.

'What do I do?' he asked, simultaneously wanting to pick her up and hold her and yank his hands away for fear of scaring her.

He had no experience with children—of any age.

But his inexperience didn't seem to matter to Seraphina. When he didn't move, she simply turned in a plodding semi-circle and plopped into his lap, as if she had no thought to the unfamiliar man in her home, no knowledge of the danger of strangers.

'Is she always so oblivious to potential danger?' he asked, newly terrified.

God, London was one of the most dangerous cities in the world! And Seraphina was so small, so breakable. The possibilities suddenly seemed endless and terrifying.

'Are you a danger to her?' Isabelle inquired, her dark eyes lit with humour.

'No,' Matthew replied, 'but she doesn't know that.'

The Duchess laughed, and the unfamiliar sound reached for him, unspooling some of the new tension in his chest.

'If it brings you any comfort, she's never unsupervised.'

'I have to be completely honest, Duchess. I don't think I'll ever be comfortable again.'

'It is strange, is it not? To want to protect someone you don't know at all?'

He nodded, listening to Isabelle's softly spoken words as he watched Seraphina sit on his lap and deconstruct the flowers one petal at a time.

'From the first moment I held her, I've been terrified in a way I never knew possible.'

He could imagine her holding Seraphina for the first time...

'Was it long—your labour?' he dared to ask, knowing that they had long left propriety behind them.

Isabelle still flushed a brilliant pink at the question, but instead of deferring, as he'd expected, she sat down in front of them and started rearranging the yellow petals on the carpet, as if unable to meet his eye. Her long, slender fingers enchanted him. Her hair spilled haphazardly over her shoulder, making her look like some fantastical nymph.

'Fourteen hours.'

Matthew blanched. 'Fourteen *hours*?'

Was that normal? He had no idea.

'It was terrifying,' she admitted quietly. 'I felt as if I was somehow inside and outside my body at the same time.'

'Who attended you?'

'Mary—you know my cousin Mary. And my physician, Dr Taylor.'

He ignored the twinge in his chest at the knowledge that another man had been there when he had not. 'Your mother...?'

'My mother did not come.'

There was enough said in the simple statement, enough in her unemotional tone, that Matthew didn't push for more.

'I... I wish I could have been there.' He could have held her hand and told her that everything was going to be fine. He could have talked her to distraction. He could have held Sera the moment she'd arrived...

Isabelle shook her head. 'No, you do not—trust me on this. Even *I* did not want to be there.'

He laughed, and Isabelle leaned forward conspiratorially.

'I thought poor Mary would faint away at any moment—and so did Dr Taylor. He made her sit at the side of the bed and hold my hand so that she couldn't see what was happening. She didn't say a word the entire time—only sat there, pale and silent, like a wrongly convicted prisoner in front of the judge. And then Sera came out, screaming for all of England to hear.'

Isabelle reached forward and brushed Sera's hair back from her forehead.

Seraphina leaned against his chest and yawned, making a sound that was close to 'Mary'.

'She doesn't talk much yet?' he asked.

'It depends. I feel as if she picks up a new word every day, but usually her talking is more babbling.'

As if to prove Isabelle's point, Seraphina issued a long sentence that Matthew couldn't decipher. He looked to Isabelle for translation, but she merely shook her head and laughed.

'Your guess is as good as mine.'

'Ma!' Seraphina squawked, and held out her arms in Isabelle's direction.

The Duchess moved as if to take her, and then caught herself. She looked up at Matthew. 'Do you mind?'

'No, of course not.'

She plucked Sera off his lap quickly, only coming close to him for the fraction of a second it took for her rosewater scent to fill his sinuses and flood his mind with memories. But the moment she leaned back with Sera he felt bereft. Alone.

'She usually stays up for an hour or so before I can get her down again.'

'Not your nursemaid?'

'Tess. She used to try for hours, but Sera was not very accommodating of her efforts. I think it's because I let her sleep in my room for too long after she was born—almost six months.'

'For convenience?'

'In part. I…' She hesitated.

'Tell me,' he urged, hearing the desperation in his tone And casually added, 'I want to know.'

'I couldn't bear to be separated from her. My entire body mourned the distance.'

'I understand.' He knew what it was to mourn being physically close to a particular person—albeit in an entirely different way.

Seraphina started to nod off in the Duchess's lap, her eyes blinking closed and then open again, as if she was fighting sleep even as it overtook her.

'She's losing the battle,' he commented quietly.

Isabelle looked down at Sera and smiled. 'I'm not surprised.' She placed an unconscious kiss on their child's head of curls. 'She doesn't usually have additional entertainment.' Her eyes snagged on the petals strewn about the carpet. 'I'm sorry she destroyed your gift.'

'Don't be.'

Matthew pushed himself to his feet and looked down at Isabelle and Sera. Isabelle sat sideways on one thigh, the dark red and gold carpet complementing the deep green of her dress as it pooled around her legs. She looked up at him, her eyes wide, filled with unsaid things.

Reaching down, he gently extricated Seraphina from her lap, immediately struck by the unfamiliar weight of a sleeping child in his arms. He held out a hand to help Isabelle up. The Duchess took it, her small, cool palm sliding into his fiery hot one.

Matthew tugged her to her feet and released her immediately, afraid of what he'd do if he had time to ponder the feeling of her skin on his and the small distance separating them. He gently unlatched Seraphina from his arms and passed her back to Isabelle.

'Thank you,' he said. 'I appreciate you allowing this.'

'You didn't give me much choice.'

His eyes snapped to hers, but there was no anger or judgement in her expression now, only a faint smile. 'I'm sorry, Duchess, for everything I never did for you—for both of you.'

'And I'm sorry I never told you, Matthew,' she replied, her

expression painted with sorrow. 'I almost wrote a thousand times, but...'

'I understand why you didn't. My behaviour that night—'

'Was unimpeachable, all things considered.' She said the words firmly, despite the brilliant blush flooding her cheeks.

Unable to stop himself, Matthew reached out and tucked a long coil of sable hair behind her ear. Isabelle didn't move... she barely breathed.

'Goodnight, Duchess.'

'Goodnight.'

'Friday?'

She nodded once, and although he longed to brush his own palm over Sera's downy head he resisted, somehow knowing it would be too much too soon for the Duchess. Instead, he bowed once and stoically left the room.

It was only once he was back on the dark street that Matthew linked his hands behind his head and took a single deep breath in, filling his lungs with the crisp London air and releasing the anxious breathlessness he'd suffered all through his first meeting with Seraphina. The breath slowly eased the tightness in his chest, filling him with renewed hope.

He could make this work. He *would* make this work.

He had to. For Sera. But also for Isabelle.

He was in awe of her, of what she'd done, young and alone in a world that rarely cared for either of those things.

The Duchess was...well, rather magnificent.

Isabelle waited an entire thirty seconds after Matthew had left the room before gently placing Seraphina down on the nearby settee and hurrying over to the large floor-to-ceiling bookcase against the far wall of the study.

She knew she had the translated *Le Langage des Fleurs* somewhere. The book had been all the rage when she was younger, and she'd bought a copy for herself a year or so ago, when she'd seen it on display in a bookshop—only to realise that one did not need a book on floriography if one did not receive any flowers.

Isabelle found it in minutes, tucked between a book on English horticulture and another on modern agricultural practices. She hastily flipped through page after page, her eyes quickly scanning the text until she found the cinquefoil plant and read the description.

> *Beloved Daughter. In wet weather the leaves of this plant contract and bend over the flower, forming, as it were, a little tent to cover it—an apt emblem of an affectionate mother in protecting a beloved child.*

Isabelle, who had seen the embarrassed flush spread over Matthew's face, had sensed that he hadn't been entirely truthful about the flower's meaning, but she never would have expected such a compliment—for a compliment it most certainly had been.

She wondered why he hadn't been honest with her. Most men she knew—nay, most *people*—would have preened at their own thoughtfulness and inadvertently removed any genuine sentiment in doing so. But Matthew...

She supposed he had always been a contradiction to her. She'd approached him because of his tarnished reputation, and instead of the rake she'd been expecting she'd discovered a man with an immense propensity for honour. He was a man who'd told her he'd never wanted to see her again—and then been devastated when she'd adhered to his wishes. Though she supposed that had more to do with the surprise of Seraphina than with Isabelle herself. He had boxed her into a corner and issued his 'terms', giving her no choice in his introduction to Sera, yet somehow she understood that the action had been born more from his desperation than any literal threat to ruin them.

She didn't know Lord Ashworth well, but she didn't have to know him to recognise that he was not the type to expose a child—*his* child—to the world for his own petty revenge.

The knowledge brought with it a new truth. She should call an end to this madness before it got out of hand—before someone saw him sneaking into her house in the middle of the night, or Seraphina grew old enough to know him. Or, God forbid, became attached to him, only to have him devastate her when he eventually decided it was too much and abandoned her. Abandoned *them*.

For Isabelle already knew that she would not remain unaffected by Matthew either.

With a glance at the settee, to make sure that Sera was safely positioned, she walked around the desk and collapsed into the big chair.

Isabelle's own fear, and her anxiety over Matthew's effect on her, made her want to end their arrangement. But what of Seraphina? What was the best thing for her?

Isabelle leaned back in the chair as she pondered the question. She had no husband. If something happened to her, Sera would have Willa, Mary and the financial means to have a fulfilling life, but surely having one more person to love and protect her would be a good thing?

Matthew was titled and powerful. And if something *did* happen to Isabelle she felt that he *would* look after Sera.

Luke, should he be of age in such a scenario, would too.

But what if it was next year? Or the year after that? Or tomorrow? She'd leave both children alone in the world, with nobody but her solicitor with any real means to oversee them and ensure that they stayed clear of the dangers of the world.

It was a sobering thought—one that, once in her head, Isabelle couldn't ignore. She couldn't push Matthew out of Sera's life. And, although she tried not to dwell on it, it wasn't only because she was certain he would never expose them. She had recognised the awe-struck fear on his face when Sera had first gone to him. He'd said, 'I don't know what to do.' And wasn't that exactly how she'd felt when Dr Taylor had placed Seraphina in her arms for the first time? Hadn't she, in that moment, desperately wished that she'd had someone there—wished she'd had *Matthew* there, taking charge of the situation, telling her that everything was going to be fine?

'I'm probably making a huge mistake,' she said aloud.

She suspected he would be the type of father she wished she'd grown up with…the type of husband she wished she'd had the chance to marry. And she found that she didn't have what it took to deprive him of Sera—or deprive them both of him.

Chapter Ten

She had been expecting Lord Ashworth to stay completely out of her life, with the exception of his bi-weekly meetings with Seraphina, so Isabelle was shocked to see her name penned in his neat hand on a letter that arrived for her the very next evening.

She tore it open without hesitation, drawing a curious look from Mary, who sat across from her in the drawing room, embroidering a small cushion cover.

Duchess,

All of last night, when I should have been sleeping, the questions that scattered from my mind upon meeting S came back to plague me. There's so much I don't know. More even that I want to know. Forgive me for not waiting until Friday, but I am returning to this page every time a new question occurs to me. And even if you choose not to reply, I find that penning them gives me a chance to commit them to memory, so that I may ask them at another time.

Why the name S?

What was her first word?

Last night she said, 'Ma', which leads me to believe it was some variation of that...

When did she take her first steps?

Do she and Luke get on? Or is he like I was at his age—rather uninterested in his little sister?

When did she first sleep through the night?

Are you exhausted all the time?

More to come,

M

Isabelle read and re-read the letter, committing each question to memory, as Matthew said he had. There was a strange burning sensation in her chest—one that was so immense and uncomfortable that she instinctively raised a hand to press down on it.

'Izzy?'

'Mmm?' Isabelle looked up at Mary.

'What is it?'

For some inexplicable reason a hot blush climbed up Isabelle's neck. There wasn't anything personal in the letter, only questions about Seraphina, yet Isabelle didn't think she'd ever felt such an intense sense of intimacy before, and over something as simple as words on paper.

'It is a letter,' she replied finally. 'From Lord Ashworth.'

'And? What did he say?'

Mary, who had been entirely disapproving of Isabelle's decision to let Matthew meet Seraphina, but had not been able to come up with an alternative compromise, stared at the letter as if she might incinerate it with her scorn alone.

'He has questions—about Sera.'

'Questions?'

Isabelle read them aloud, deciding at the last moment not to share the final one.

'You're not going to reply, are you?' Mary asked, horrified. Before Isabelle could comment, her cousin continued, 'Isabelle, these meetings are dangerous enough. But letters—letters that anybody could intercept and read!'

'Neither of us mentions any names, Mary. And I've been destroying them after I've read them.'

'Knowing no names doesn't stop the society pages from exposing their subjects to ridicule—and names aren't going to matter when the correspondence is occurring *between your homes*!'

'You're right. I shall ask him not to write again the next time I see him.' Isabelle pushed herself to stand.

'Where are you going?' asked Mary.

Isabelle tucked the letter into her sleeve. 'To find Seraphina.'

It wasn't exactly a lie. But Isabelle felt Mary's eyes on her back as she left the room.

Inside the nursery, Sera was sitting on the rocking horse while Tess held her steady with one hand and gently moved the horse back and forth with the other. Instead of holding the little reins, Seraphina grasped the horse's mane with her tiny fingers, alternately pushing and pulling at the long hairs with each back-and-forth movement. Her contagious baby giggle filled the room with lightness and joy.

'She's found a new passion, Your Grace,' Tess said, laughing. 'Every time I take her off, she cries as if I've personally wronged her.'

Isabelle's eyes tracked Tess's hand as it pushed the toy, her fingers resting by the name carved into the glider. If the nursemaid had questions about where the toy had come from, she didn't dare ask them. Still, Isabelle fought self-consciousness.

'I've come to relieve you of your rocking duty, Tess,' she said, walking towards the rocking horse. She opened her hands and lifted Sera from the seat.

Instead of fussing, as she'd expected, Sera babbled with pleasure and reached up with one chubby hand to touch Isabelle's hair.

'Would you like me to change her so she's ready to go out, Your Grace?'

'No, thank you.' Isabelle noted the simple white dress Seraphina was wearing. 'I'm just going to write some letters in the study for now.'

Knowing that Isabelle would ring for her when she was

needed, Tess started packing away Seraphina's small mountain of toys.

Isabelle carried Sera from the room and down the stairs, only pausing to reposition her daughter on her hip and mumble, 'You're getting heavy, my love.'

Time was passing indiscriminately. Soon Sera wouldn't want to be carried. Then she'd be too big to carry. Before she knew it, her daughter wouldn't need her at all—and then what was Isabelle to do with herself? She had thrown herself into motherhood with a fervour born from the need to be a better mother than her own had. She had no leisure pursuits, no particular talents that could be exercised. It was a sobering thought, really, that a title could not buy a woman everything.

Inside the study, she settled Seraphina on her lap at the desk and passed the child a piece of paper to tear to shreds as she removed a second sheet for herself.

For those few precious minutes that they sat together Isabelle found comfort in Seraphina's nearness. She could smell her daughter's familiar baby scent. She could feel the way Sera relaxed back against her, with absolute trust that she was safe and loved. It made Isabelle wonder how any mother—her own included—could bear to be deprived of that connection.

Hadn't Jemima Conway felt that first swoop of overwhelming emotion the moment Isabelle had been placed in her arms? Hadn't she been filled with the same awe and fear as Isabelle had the first time she'd held Seraphina, after labouring alone in pain for hours and hours?

All the years she'd lived in her mother's house had already supplied her with an answer. Her mother had only participated in Isabelle's upbringing on the rarest occasions, choosing instead to go about her own life and leave the child-rearing to nursemaids and governesses. Though Isabelle had seen her almost daily growing up, they had only ever spent time together during perfunctory meetings—meetings that had been scheduled and that had never lasted more than thirty minutes before Isabelle had been swept back to the nursery.

It had been the reminder of those short visits to her uninterested parents—the anticipation and excitement, and afterwards the disappointment—that had made Isabelle vow to be different. *Her* children would never question her love. They would never think that they were anything but the centre of her world.

With Sera's comforting weight on her thighs, and a simmering burn of anticipation in her chest, she began her reply to Matthew.

M,

When I was a child my father brought home an angel for the top of the Christmas tree one year. The angel had a white silk dress, a fur-lined coat, gossamer-like wings and blond ringlets that felt like real human hair. It was the most beautiful thing I'd ever seen, and when I asked my father which angel it was, he panicked and replied, 'S—'.

I don't think he even knew about the biblical six-winged angels. But the name held, and that rare gift from my father became my most treasured memory. Until S was born. So when Dr Taylor placed her in my arms it seemed only natural that she replace that happy memory.

It is only in writing this story now that I realise perhaps I wanted the reminder too. A reminder that my child must not have only one fond memory of me. A reminder of the type of parent I wanted to be.

Her first word was not, 'Ma', as you assumed. It was, 'More', and she was pointing at her half-finished blancmange at the time.

She took her first steps just a few months ago—which Mary thought rather delayed, but which I am grateful for now that she is active and impossible to keep up with.

She adores Luke. But, though he loves her, his interest seems born more from a sense of familial duty than a genuine desire to entertain her.

She has yet to sleep through the night.

Yes, I am exhausted. Although I must admit that my fatigue is purely self-inflicted, as I insist on helping the nursemaid when S won't go down and cannot stay abed myself once the sun has risen.

D

PS Given the circumstances, I would ask that any future correspondence be exchanged in person rather than via post, and that you personally destroy my letters once you have read them.

Matthew was transported by the Duchess's letter. He could imagine her, a dark-haired, serious child, asking her father who the angel was. And he could see Seraphina, covered in blancmange, demanding, 'More'. It was no stretch of the imagination to picture Sera walking for the first time—she still had the wobbly confidence of a child who was not proficient but rather practising her bipedal locomotion.

An unfamiliar elation filled his chest as he re-read the letter, and the feeling was only dampened by the last paragraph, which confirmed what he'd suspected when he'd seen the Duchess last: Isabelle was tired.

It didn't matter that she was a duchess, with countless servants to help her. Isabelle would be handling every trial in her life—including a sleepless child—herself. Matthew knew that to be true because her stubborn independence was the first thing he had recognised in her when she'd come to him that night, her mind set on taking control of her life and assuming responsibility for Luke's.

It was no wonder he'd been enraptured—the Duchess was unlike any woman he'd ever met.

Then Matthew read the postscript of her letter and, although it hurt, he tried not to let her request that he destroy her letters grate on his already stretched nerves. Her demand was fair, and her concern well-founded. And yet he still could not escape his own bitter regret and shame.

He wondered how things might have been had he never set eyes on Christine Dalmore. Had he just done one or two things differently. Had he just been a little older, a little more mature…

He knew that regret was futile.

Along with all the questions he'd drawn up about Sera the night before, his mind kept searching for a reasonable solution to their predicament—some way for him to be in Sera's life publicly and regularly, instead of behind closed doors as if he was ashamed of her.

If he were any less of a gentleman he'd force the Duchess to marry him and be done with the whole fiasco...

And then what? he asked himself.

People would talk—they always did. And even if there was no proof of Sera's heritage, everybody knew of Matthew's past. Because of that, they would take one look at Seraphina and they would assume the worst.

'My word—has somebody died?'

Matthew looked up, his frown clearing when he saw his mother standing on the other side of his desk. He'd been so deep in thought he hadn't heard the Countess enter.

'Mother,' he said and, holding out both hands, stood to embrace her.

Diana Blake, the Countess of Heather, was a tall, striking woman from whom he'd inherited his black hair and grey eyes, although his nature was closer to his father the Earl's quiet intensity. Matthew could always trust his mother to loudly cut to the heart of any matter—whether he wanted her to or not.

She returned his greeting with real affection, her eyes narrowed on his face with maternal insight and, upon observing the deep-set fatigue in his eyes, she said with concern, 'You look awful, my dear boy.'

Matthew laughed and released her hands. 'I haven't been sleeping well,' he admitted as he rounded his desk once again.

Since he'd found out about Seraphina he'd found sleep impossible. Every time he closed his eyes he saw her—*his child*.

'Would you like to tell me what has been keeping you from your sleep?' his mother asked as she took a seat in one of the chairs opposite his desk.

'No.'

She arched back, shocked by his blatant reply. 'Well, why on earth not? So long as it's not a mathematics test again... As we both know, I was more a hindrance with that than a help.'

'Because if I tell you, you will worry—and, worse, you will tell Father. Which will bring him here with a reprimand and a lecture. And I don't want to hear it.'

'Because you are in the wrong?'

'No. Because I don't feel in the least bit sorry for what I have done,' he replied immediately.

He stopped as soon as the words had left his mouth, stunned with the realisation that they were true. He could never regret that night with Isabelle—rather, he lived to remember it. Seraphina, though a surprise, was *his*, and for that alone he would cherish her.

'I merely need to find a way to bend circumstances and gain the result I want.'

He'd been thinking aloud. But the Countess considered him for a long moment before stating, 'If your intention is to dissuade me, I'm afraid you are not succeeding. You are only making me more curious.'

Matthew pressed his index finger and thumb over his eyes. 'Mother, though I do enjoy your visits, I must ask… Why are you here?'

The Countess arched one brow. 'Do I need an excuse to visit my only son?'

'No. Of course not.' His pause was barely perceptible. 'Shall we pretend you don't have a reason, then?'

She laughed loudly. 'I don't suppose I am very subtle.'

'When you just want to visit me you send a note, inquiring after my schedule.'

He saw her eyes, so similar to his—and to Sera's—glisten with humour.

'When you want to coerce me into something I'm sure to dread, you arrive with no word or invitation so as to take me off guard.'

'You, my dear, are too much like your father.'

They both lapsed into silence as a maid hovered on the threshold of his study, a tea tray in her hands. Matthew waved her in and waited for her to place the tray down and depart before continuing the conversation.

'So?'

'Contrary to your opinion, I am not here to badger you.'

The Countess moved to pour herself tea without asking Matthew if he'd like any. She knew he hated the stuff.

'I merely wish to ask if there is anyone you'd like to invite to the masquerade ball?' She sat back in her chair. 'Invitations go out tomorrow.'

'Ah…' With everything else on his mind, Matthew had quite forgotten about his mother's annual masquerade ball—an event that most of London wished to be invited to, but for which his mother kept to a deliberately select group of people, totalling about seventy-five guests.

'Well?'

'Leo, of course.'

'He is already coming. Your father and I saw him in St James's Square yesterday and invited him in person.'

'Lord and Lady Windhurst.'

His mother's eyebrows arched. 'I have heard *he* is a philandering nincompoop.'

'He is, most certainly.'

'Good God, Matthew!' she exclaimed as a new idea occurred to her. 'Tell me it's not Lady Windhurst who has you so *déboussolé*?'

Matthew ignored the question. 'And the Duchess of Everett and her companion Mary Lambert.'

His mother was uncharacteristically quiet as she considered him through narrowed eyes, the only sound in the room the whirr of the silver teaspoon against the teacup as she stirred her tea.

'You may speak plainly, Mother.'

She took a dainty sip, all the while watching his face. 'I am merely trying to discover which of the ladies it is that you wish to see.'

'Your imagination is running rampant.' He took a deep breath. 'If you must know, Leo is keeping an eye on Lady Windhurst. Her husband's "philandering", as you call it, is taking its toll on her.'

'Is Leo having an affair with her?'

'No. They are childhood friends.'

'Hmm…' The sound was noncommittal. 'And the other two?'

'Are Lady Windhurst's closest friends. She will attend if she knows that they are going to be there.'

'You know, Matthew, you have become a most proficient liar.' She placed her teacup down in its saucer, the little rattle sounding much too loud in the quiet room. 'I don't know whether that makes me relieved that you are now more able to protect yourself from the world, or deeply sad that you thought you had to lie in the first place.'

She stood, forcing her gloves back onto her fingers with irritated tugs. 'I will invite your friends. But heed my warning: nothing good will come from you carrying on with a married woman—as well you know.'

Matthew let the pain come, used to it after years of people referencing the affair either to tease him, as his friends did, or, as his mother did, to remind him of his past mistakes.

Though his parents had both stood by him throughout the months following the scandal, he had felt the full weight of their disappointment keenly. Looking back now, he supposed he had never let them down before. Rather, he had always strived to be a good son…to make his parents proud. He had done well at school. He hadn't drunk to excess or gambled. When he had sought female company he had done so discreetly. Even his affair with Christine had been carefully orchestrated to avoid attention—until he'd called things off and discovered she'd had other plans.

He watched his mother for a long moment as he considered leaving her to her assumptions. But he didn't. For one reason. It wasn't fair to Wilhelmina, who already had to withstand enough of society's scrutiny.

'It is not what you think, Mother,' he said.

She paused, her eyes coming up to search his face. 'And you cannot confide in me because…?'

'It is not my secret to impart.'

'You are not having an affair with the Lady, then?'

'No. Though I would remind you that, irrespective of my past mistakes, my sex life is none of your concern.'

The Countess linked her gloved hands together. She leaned forward and lowered her voice. 'One day, Matthew, you will have children. And I promise you, not a night will go by when you don't worry about them—their carnal desires and mistakes included.'

If she had only known how close she was to the truth just then, the Countess might have stayed. Instead, she turned around and disappeared through the open door, her back straight, her head held high.

Exhausted, Matthew dropped his forehead to his desk and knocked it gently against the hard wood. He knew that hindsight was useless, but that did not stop the deluge of regret.

As if living with the recurring memory of Christine's tear-streaked face and frenzied begging wasn't enough. Now he not only had to live with the consequences of his actions, he also had to ensure that Isabelle and the children did not.

Chapter Eleven

Much to her own embarrassment, Isabelle eagerly awaited a reply from Lord Ashworth for the remainder of the week. Each time Gordon brought in the post she would casually sort through it, regret settling over her when she realised that he had adhered to her request and not written at all.

'It's your own fault,' she reminded herself aloud as she sat on the floor with Seraphina, awaiting Lord Ashworth's Friday night visit. 'You can hardly blame the man for respecting your request.'

Seraphina nodded and mumbled her agreement from her seat on the red and gold carpet.

'Your father is much too honourable,' she said and, smiling, reached out both hands to help Sera rise to stand. 'Don't you think?'

'Ya!' Seraphina laughed and kicked her little feet, forcing Isabelle's sombre mood away entirely.

Isabelle laughed as Sera strung her arms around her neck. She nestled her face against the child, breathing in her familiar scent. 'Oh, Sera. What on earth am I going to do?'

'Ya!' Sera laughed again.

'You think we should run away?' Isabelle asked.

Seraphina giggled, her high-pitched baby laugh merging with Isabelle's.

'If that isn't the perfect sight to greet a man...'

Isabelle's heart simply stopped beating for one perfect moment. She closed her eyes as Matthew's deep voice reached for her, enveloping her like an embrace. How long had he been standing there, looking at them, *listening to her*? A flush of mortification spread through her when she remembered what she'd been saying.

Seraphina suffered no such embarrassment. She peered over Isabelle's shoulder and immediately started jumping up and down when she recognised Matthew.

'Hello, beautiful girl,' Matthew said, his quiet voice filled with humour.

It was ridiculous that his greeting filled Isabelle with heat—she knew he was talking to Seraphina—but it *did*. It spread through her, starting low in her womb and climbing up through her chest to her neck.

Isabelle shifted Sera off her lap, sending her in Matthew's direction before she dared to turn fully and look up at him.

When she did, her breath caught. Matthew was not so formal tonight. His jacket was slung over one shoulder, revealing a burgundy silk waistcoat with the finest gold thread woven through it at even intervals to form a pinstripe. He'd rolled his sleeves to just below his elbows, and Isabelle's eyes immediately strayed to his large hands and powerful forearms, both dusted with a layer of dark hair. He held a sprig of purple vervain in one of those hands. His grey eyes, tired but silvered with happiness, watched as Sera toddled across the room to him.

Sera extended her arms even before she'd stopped, and Matthew immediately bent to scoop her up, his forearms flexing.

Isabelle sat on the floor and observed the exchange. Seraphina didn't hesitate to raise her hands to Matthew's face, touching his nose, his cheeks, and then his hair, as if he was a favoured toy and not a full-grown male.

'Were you having fun with your mother?' he asked, his deep voice travelling across the room even though he whispered.

Seraphina nodded and, without waiting for an invitation,

reached for the flowers in Matthew's free hand. He grinned and started to pass them to her, but before her hand could close around the stem, he snatched them away, hiding them behind his back and affecting a gasp of bewildered surprise that had Sera's own eyes widening.

'Where did they go?' he asked.

Sera's little mouth hung open as she considered him, and then she leaned her entire body to one side to try and peek around his back.

Matthew grinned and glanced at Isabelle. 'She is not so easily fooled, I see.'

He removed the flowers from behind his back and held them out to Sera once again.

She immediately plopped her entire face into the blooms and gurgled. 'Smow!'

'Smell,' Isabelle corrected, looking up at Matthew. 'She wants you to smell them.'

He complied, lowering his face to the blooms as Sera had done, but keeping his laughter-lit eyes on Isabelle the entire time.

'Vervain?' she asked.

'Enchantment.'

Isabelle sensed that it was the truth, but she knew that she'd check the moment he left anyway.

Matthew turned and closed the study door behind him before carrying Sera over to where Isabelle still sat on the floor. He lowered them both down to the carpet and placed Sera on her feet.

Sera walked to Isabelle, the vervain blooms outstretched. 'Smow!'

Isabelle leaned forward and took an exaggerated inhalation.

Then Sera walked back to Matthew and leaned her entire body against his side as she waved her flowers back and forth.

'She won't bite you!' Isabelle laughed, and then, remembering a rather unfortunate incident with Mr Briggs, she amended, 'At least, I hope she won't.'

Matthew blew out a deep breath. 'It's all so new—so overwhelming.'

'I know.' Isabelle looked at them, their dark heads bent together, and a wave of pleasure tumbled through her. Sera lowered herself to sit on Matthew's thigh. 'It would seem as though she doesn't have the same fears.'

'No. I don't suppose she does.' He raised one large palm and tentatively ran it over Sera's curls.

Sera craned her neck to smile up at him, like a puppy enjoying the attention.

But Isabelle was distracted by Matthew's large, tanned hand, too aware of the memory of those same hands stroking over her bare skin, cupping her breasts, lifting her up...

'How was your week?' he asked.

The question, and the banality of it, took her so off-guard that for a yawning stretch of time all she could do was stare at him like a simpleton.

'Good,' she said at last.

He seemed to be waiting for her to say more but, at a loss for the right words, Isabelle chose to focus on Sera instead. It was so much easier...giving herself to her children.

Matthew tried again. 'My mother says that you have "politely declined" the invitation to her ball?'

'I have.' Isabelle had been surprised by the invitation—surprised and then afraid. 'You haven't told her...?'

'No. I wouldn't make a decision like that without asking you first.' His grey eyes darkened and he raised one hand to run it through his black hair. 'But I would be lying if I said I didn't want to, Duchess. I hate pretending that she's not mine. My family... They would be shocked—' he laughed wryly '—and probably angry with me once they found out how she came to be. But they would love her.'

Her blood froze in her veins. What would his mother, the Countess of Heather, think of her if she knew the truth? If she knew that Isabelle had propositioned her son and then birthed his child?

'I would like to tell them eventually—when you're ready.' Now his laugh was mirthless. 'Grandchildren are the only thing they've talked about for years.'

'And if I am never "ready", as you call it?'

She didn't know why his answer was so important to her—but it was. Isabelle had been handed from man to man without ever having been asked what she wanted.

Matthew was kind, and he was quickly turning into one of the best men she knew—though, admittedly, she knew few. Still, that wouldn't change the fact that once his family knew about Seraphina he'd hold all the cards—including hers. As a man, he'd always have more power than her. And as Sera's father, he'd have the power to destroy her completely.

'Then I won't ever tell them,' he promised. He watched her over their daughter's dark head of hair. 'Did you ever stop to think that I would never deliberately hurt you, Duchess? Or that I would want nothing but to care for you and protect you, the mother of my child?'

She deliberately ignored the pleasure that his words evoked and replied honestly. 'No. I have never seen a man take an active interest in his children—especially his illegitimate ones. If I am wary of you, Matthew, it is because I cannot completely trust that you do not have some ulterior motive.'

'What ulterior motive could I possibly have?' he asked in exasperation. 'Sneaking in through your servants' entrance, denying Sera as my own to my family, pretending nothing ever happened between us—those are not the actions of a man who has an ulterior motive.'

He watched her closely, his eyes narrowed on her face as if she was some strange creature that he could not make sense of.

'Have you ever had a man—*any* man—in your life that you could trust? Is it only me that you are wary of?'

'No, it is not you—or not only you. My experience of men has been limited to my father, who gave me away to one of his friends—my late husband, who practically bought me—and you, who...'

Changed everything.

'Who got you pregnant and left you,' he finished quietly for her.

'No.' Isabelle shook her head. 'That's not even close to what I was going to say.'

'Duchess, you are the mother of my child. You have my

word that I will never do anything to hurt you or scare you or threaten you.'

'Even if that means depriving your family of knowing Seraphina?'

'Even then. You have carried, birthed, loved and protected my child.'

When Sera looked up at him, curious at his angry tone, he softened his voice.

'I would choose your happiness over my family's knowledge of Sera every time.'

'But you don't even know me,' she argued, terrified by what he'd admitted. 'We had one night. That is all.'

Matthew's eyes snapped from his daughter's face to Isabelle's, his anger at her observation dying immediately when he saw the glazed fear in her expression. She looked so afraid.

She *was*, he realised. But he was not a threat to her; in fact, he was certain he'd cut his bleeding heart from his own chest to protect her if the need arose.

'Duchess, I don't have to know you inside out to know that you are brave and strong and kind. You showed me that the first time that we met. You show me still every time we are together.'

She merely tilted her head and frowned.

Needing to lighten the heavy mood his words had conjured, he added, 'Stubborn too.'

Instead of gasping, or looking offended, she surprised him by grinning, the wide smile wrinkling her nose adorably. 'I am terribly stubborn. It is my worst trait.'

'No. It's not your worst trait.'

Her eyes narrowed on him, her kissable lips pursed as if in thought. 'Pray, do tell—what *is* my worst trait?'

Matthew had the strongest urge to run his lips across her mouth until she smiled again. Instead, he said, 'You don't trust anyone except for Mary and Willa, and that limits your experience of the world.'

Her shoulders drooped. 'Oh…' Her eyes, so bright a moment before, had lost their shine. 'I suppose you do know me rather well,' she observed forlornly.

'Well, it's either that or your penchant for throwing things,' he teased, hoping to return to their previous light banter.

Her smile returned, but it did not meet her eyes. 'You remember me telling you that?'

I remember everything, he thought.

But, knowing that the confession would not comfort the Duchess now, he answered, 'It is not your fault that you have had to be strong against all the weak men in your life, Duchess—and I include myself amongst them. I shouldn't have...'

Realising that he couldn't regret their night together, he did not finish the sentence.

'Mistrust is a defence mechanism,' he continued. 'And it's one that is extremely difficult to overcome. And you've had to develop yours from the age of thirteen, when your father first accepted your betrothal to a man he never should have considered. I do not judge you for being mistrustful. But I hurt knowing that I will always be included amongst the people you don't fully take into your confidence. And I am ashamed, because I know that there is nobody to blame but myself.'

He made sure to look into her eyes, so that she could see his sincerity when he finished.

'Despite my past mistakes, I would give a fortune to have your trust. And I would never break it were you to honour me with it.'

Matthew did not make promises lightly. And he had most certainly never made such a promise to a woman before. But he hoped that Isabelle would overlook what she knew of his past to see that he told the truth—that nothing had become more important to him than Seraphina and, by default, Isabelle.

'I...'

She raised a hand to her chest, clearly bewildered. Her eyes filled with tears, and he hated that he had caused them. And then she ruined him.

'You have done nothing to earn my mistrust,' she said. 'Despite your "past mistakes"—' she used his own words to hammer home her point '—you have time and time again proved that I *can* trust you. It's *me*. I'm...so afraid. Of everything. Of *everyone*.'

She bravely met his eyes.

'I apologise for declining your mother's invitation. But I don't do well with so many people—especially those I don't know. I have been largely left on my own for most of my life, so it is overwhelming for me to be confronted with so many strangers, all of whom fawn for my attention. It terrifies me,' she whispered, her dark eyes round with anxious dread at the mere mention of a crowd. 'You were right last time—when you called me a coward.'

'I didn't mean it,' he countered, growing more ashamed by the second. 'I was hurt and angry. I don't think you are a coward. I think you are the bravest person I know.'

'No...' She sent him a wobbly smile. 'I hide behind the children.'

'Which is completely natural, considering.'

Isabelle looked at him with those big, sad eyes. 'That may be, but I would like our daughter to have a better example—to feel comfortable in her skin. Luke will go off to school soon enough, and will be indoctrinated into the world by default. But Sera...'

He wondered if she realised she'd said it—*our* daughter...

Their eyes simultaneously moved to where Seraphina had fallen fast asleep on his lap without either of them noticing. Her head was tilted slightly to one side, her little mouth ajar.

Matthew's chest expanded with a foreign emotion, one as deep as it was soothing, as he watched her tiny chest rise and fall with each peaceful breath. He knew, with absolute clarity, that he was exactly where he was supposed to be.

'I should put her down...'

Matthew was desperate to prolong his time with them, even for a few minutes. 'Let me carry her up for you.'

Isabelle opened her mouth to argue, and then just as quickly closed it. 'Thank you. She's getting too heavy for me.'

He gently untangled Sera's legs and tucked her into his side before pushing himself first to his knees, and then to his feet, his usually agile movements made cumbersome as he tried not to disturb the sleeping child.

As he followed Isabelle out of the room and they walked in silence up the dark stairs, Matthew couldn't help but watch her in front of him, her long, thick hair falling out of its haphazard braid down over her lavender gown, the colours contrasting erotically.

He wanted to reach out and wrap his hand in her hair. He wanted to crane her neck back until her lips met his.

Inside her bedroom, he deliberately avoided looking about her private space. He kept his gaze stoically away from the big bed in the centre of the room and placed Seraphina in a small curtained crib. He paused only to tuck the covers around her and brush one hand over her downy head before quickly turning to make his escape—and almost walking into Isabelle, who had come up behind him to see to Seraphina herself.

Her hands came up instinctively, bracing against his chest even as his own hands reached out to grip her upper arms and steady her.

'Oh, I'm sorr—'

'Apologies,' he said, accidentally talking over her.

Instead of releasing her, his hands tightened on her arms, bringing her a fraction closer. Matthew's body flared to life at her proximity, and though he dared not move he had to actively fight his need to close the distance between them and plaster himself against her.

Isabelle did not move her hands from his chest either. She stared up at him with dark eyes, her breath leaving her lips in a ragged exhalation that tore through the room.

'Resisting you is the single most difficult thing I have ever had to do,' he murmured quietly.

She swallowed. Matthew's eyes tracked the movement. He wanted to place his lips there and feel her hammering pulse reaching for him.

'Matthew, I… I don't know what the right thing to do is.'

He heard the need in her voice as she leaned against him and rested her head on his chest for a long moment. As if she needed the contact too. As if she craved him as much as he did her.

He wondered if she could hear his heart galloping, as she had that first night. And, helpless to resist, he raised one hand to cradle the back of her head. When she sighed, and relaxed more fully against him, Matthew closed his eyes and simply breathed in her rose scent.

He wished he cared for her less so he could seduce her more. Just the thought of kissing those soft lips again had him aching with arousal. But although she had come to him willingly that first time, and although she'd carried and birthed a child, Isabelle was frighteningly innocent. So, even as he felt her yielding, and even as his own body hardened in erotic contrast, Matthew summoned the last of his self-control and stepped back from her.

Isabelle exhaled shakily.

'I want you,' he told her. 'You know that to be true.' She opened her mouth, but before she could admit anything that would crush his resolve, he added, 'But I need your trust more. So, until you are certain of what you want, and can ask me for it without any doubt in your mind, I will not touch you.'

It was a promise to himself as much as it was a promise to her.

She nodded, but didn't say anything else. Matthew strode past her and paused at the door to torture himself with one last look at her. Isabelle had wrapped her arms around herself and was looking after him with such raw, honest need that his entire body tensed with regret and longing.

Still, he managed a stiff bow and, before he could change his mind, said, 'Monday, Duchess.'

Chapter Twelve

In the three weeks leading up to the Countess of Heather's infamous masquerade ball, Isabelle saw Matthew every Monday and Friday, as they'd agreed.

At first, Isabelle had been terrified that he'd be seen sneaking into her house through the servants' entrance. However, as the weeks passed, her own desire to see him, coupled with his obvious discretion, had eased the sharp edge of her fear.

Matthew never came empty-handed. He usually brought flowers—white lilacs for youth, poppies for sleep, in the hope that it would facilitate Seraphina sleeping through the night soon—and once, of all things, a pineapple.

Isabelle had been rather caught off-guard by that offering. The hostile-looking fruit, which had been rarer and more expensive than a white elephant at the beginning of the century, had become mainstream with Britain's expansion through the colonies, and it was a diversion from the usual delicate blooms. It was only once Matthew had taken his leave that night that Isabelle had checked in the *Language of Flowers*. And there it was.

The pineapple. Its meaning: you are perfect.

Isabelle had kept the fruit for days, too enamoured of it to send it straight to the kitchen, and her fondness for it undoubtedly resulted in a few raised eyebrows amongst the servants.

In the month during which they had been communicating, Isabelle had grown not only to enjoy Matthew's company, but to *crave* it. The days between Monday and Friday had never felt so long, and the time he spent with them was always too short. And their short time together was somehow ruined, because even as she tried to enjoy it, Isabelle felt swamped with melancholy over the fact that he would be leaving so soon.

She knew that he came for Sera—she *loved* that he came for Sera—but Isabelle had started to ponder where his obligation to their daughter ended and his interest in her began. Worse, even as she knew nothing could come of him—of *them*—she wanted *something*. Only she didn't know what that something was.

But she remembered what it had been like to be with him, and in remembering she dreamed that they would find each other again. Because, sinner that she was, she still burned for him. Sometimes she even woke in the night, aching for his hands on her skin and his mouth on her breasts.

Her desire for him was nothing new. But before he'd come to London—before he'd started visiting, before he'd almost kissed her again—she'd been able to roll over and will herself back to sleep by convincing herself that she'd never see him again. Now...

Isabelle flushed with shame when she thought about the recent pleasure she'd found in using her own fingers and her secret, lurid memories. But instead of the spreading relief she'd expected it had left her feeling rather desolate. As if she'd been saddled with a life of blancmange after a taste of the finest Parisian desserts.

And Matthew had been true to his word. Not only had he not kissed her, he had not even touched her in the most casual of ways since he'd made his promise to earn her trust. And Isabelle, who still felt like the shy, inexperienced girl who'd first gone to him, could do nothing but wish she'd been more certain, more brazen.

The thought made her grumble aloud.

'Is anything the matter, Izzy?'

Isabelle considered her cousin. Even now, at home with no-body about, Mary was perfectly made up in a light blue day gown, not a hair out of place.

'Mary, may I ask you a dreadfully personal question?'

Mary put down the book she was reading and waited in silent invitation.

Isabelle searched for the correct phrasing before settling on, 'You loved your John dearly—correct?'

Mary's gaze turned wistful almost immediately. 'Yes. Of course.'

'And you...you had a *good* marriage?'

'Yes, for the short time that we were married.' Mary turned to face Isabelle again, her smile dying when she saw the look on Isabelle's face. 'What is this about?'

'Do you miss...? That is to say, do you think about...?' Isabelle covered her eyes with one hand, as mortified by the question as she was desperate for an answer.

'Isabelle...?'

Isabelle took a deep breath, squared her shoulders and, without quite meeting Mary's eyes, asked, 'Do you miss having *relations*? With John?'

Her friend could not have looked more shocked had a horse flown in through the window and laid a golden egg. 'I beg your pardon?'

'I asked if—'

'Oh, I heard you well enough,' Mary said hurriedly, before Isabelle could repeat herself.

Isabelle waited for what seemed an age.

Then Mary pushed herself to her feet and marched to the open door, her back ramrod-straight. She closed them into the study with an impatient snap of her wrist, took a deep breath, and then turned to face Isabelle again, her face set in an unusually stern expression.

'What on earth would prompt you to ask such a question?'

'So, you don't? Miss...*it*?'

Mary ignored Isabelle's question and asked one of her own, demanding, 'Is this about *him*?'

'Does it matter if it is?'

'Izzy!' Mary looked stunned.

'Mary,' Isabelle countered, unsure of how to breach this new awkwardness between them, 'it's a simple yes or no question. I'm hardly asking for the sordid details.'

Mary advanced upon her, her blue skirts trailing behind her like an advancing naval gunboat's wake, her green eyes filled with panic. 'This cannot go on.'

'It was just a question—'

'It was not *just a question*—and you know it.'

Isabelle grew more embarrassed by the second. 'Forget I asked,' she said quietly.

But she couldn't help but wonder if maybe there was something wrong with her—some inner wanton, or a strumpet that whispered the devil's work through her body and made her ache for a man she should not want and could not have.

'Isabelle, you have to reach different terms with Lord Ashworth,' Mary hissed. 'He is dangerous to you. To Seraphina!'

'No.' Isabelle shook her head vehemently at that, and when Mary opened her mouth to speak, she cut off her cousin. 'As my friend, Mary, you may take liberties in speaking your mind. But I'm going to ask you to refrain from passing judgement on a man who has been nothing but a complete gentleman—to me *and* to his daughter.' She took a deep breath in an attempt to calm herself. 'Matthew has made mistakes in the past—'

'He ruined a woman! To the point where she cannot even show her face—'

'Do you think I have not thought about that?' Isabelle demanded. 'Do you think it does not plague me?'

'Izzy...'

Isabelle refused to cry, but she felt the telltale burn of tears. 'Where Sera and I are concerned, he has been *kind* and *gentle* and *protective*.'

Mary paled. 'Izzy...he blackmailed you!'

'He forced my hand in order to meet his child,' she argued immediately, knowing that there was a difference, knowing that *Matthew* was different.

Even though her experience of men had been limited, she

knew Matthew was nothing like her father and the late Duke of Everett. While they had bargained and bartered over her, discussing her worth as if she were a brood mare and not a human being, Matthew had not—and with the leverage he had over her he certainly could have if he'd wished to.

'Until you take the time to actually get to know Lord Ashworth, you will not say another thing about him. You...' She shook her head. 'You don't know him, Mary.' She softened her tone. 'You don't see how he is with Sera.'

With me.

'Need I remind you that he is responsible for this mess in the first place?'

'That is categorically incorrect—and you know it,' Isabelle hurried on before Mary could argue further. 'You are so afraid of the fact that he *did* bed me that you forget I was the one who *begged* him to.'

Isabelle pushed back her chair and with one last look at her friend's pale face and stunned expression left the room.

She needed to get out of the house...perhaps go for a walk. Yes, a walk. She could walk off her anger and her frustration and tire out the children at the same time. She needed to take her temper away from Mary, before either of them said something they would regret.

Isabelle curled her hands into fists and resisted the urge to throw down the new crystal vase on the hall table as she passed—but only barely.

Before she could change her mind, she rang for a maid and asked her to have Tess prepare Seraphina and ask Luke if he'd like to take a break from his lessons to accompany them.

Only twenty minutes later, she exited Everett Place to climb into her awaiting barouche. 'Hyde Park. Thank you, Phillip.'

'Any particular route, Your Grace?'

'If you'd please drop us at Cumberland Gate? I believe we are all in need of exercise.'

The driver bowed and waited for the footman to hand her into the barouche before resuming his seat. And then they were off, gliding through London in the early afternoon.

Isabelle leaned forward and looked out from beneath the

leather canopy as they drove, her eyes tracking the sights and sounds of the city as she tried to forget her argument with Mary.

It was a beautiful day, and the weather seemed to have brought everyone out, giving her the perfect distraction. Oxford Street was bustling. Women in colourful dresses perused the shopfronts, pausing to look in the confectioner's window or enter drapers and silk shops. Men dressed for the day's work hurried about. London was busy and thriving.

In her lap, Seraphina babbled happily and toyed with an errant strand of Isabelle's hair. In the seat across from her, Luke sat quietly, holding the small leather ball he'd brought with him.

'How are your lessons going?' she asked, trying to draw him into conversation.

Luke's green eyes found hers. He smiled and shrugged. 'Mr Watts taught me the phases of the moon by making a new picture strip for my zoetrope.'

'That sounds like fun,' Isabelle commented, unsurprised by the tutor's ingenuity.

Mr Watts, a retired vicar with a love for discovery, was undoubtedly a jewel of the St Claire household. He tried hard to make everything fun for Luke. But Mr Watts was much more than a tutor. In a house full of women and servants, he was Luke's bridge to manhood—something that Isabelle did not take lightly.

It seemed every time she turned around Luke had grown again, with each small spurt bringing big changes. Changes she had no experience in explaining. Changes she had very little knowledge about herself.

Her consolation was that Luke had Mr Watts, and that her stepson would be going off to school in two short years. Boarding school wasn't something Luke had chosen for himself; it was something Isabelle had encouraged. Because there were some things that boys needed to learn from other boys—just as girls needed to learn from other girls.

In theory, her mind corrected, as she reflected on her conversation with Mary.

Isabelle had been expecting Mary to be shy, or even embarrassed—it was, after all, an entirely inappropriate question to have asked. But she had never thought that her friend would immediately see through her. Because although Mary had been wrong in her judgement of Matthew, she had not been wrong in her judgement of Isabelle. And therein lay the problem...

Her thoughts were interrupted by the barouche coming to a gliding stop. Isabelle shifted Seraphina on her lap, welcoming the distraction of the park. While Phillip lowered the leather roof, a footman took Seraphina and then helped Isabelle out of the conveyance. Luke, ever eager, clambered down and ran ahead of them, only slowing when Isabelle called out for him to wait.

After hurried instructions to Phillip to return in an hour, Isabelle set off after Luke, adjusting her pace to Seraphina's little legs. The large footman followed discreetly behind.

She started moving south through Hyde Park, heading towards Rotten Row, keeping Luke in her line of sight and Seraphina's small hand in hers the entire time.

Like the rest of London, the park was bustling. Ladies dressed for display paraded about, hoping to be seen. Several riders trotted by. Barouches and carriages kept to South Carriage Drive, avoiding the footpaths and the dozens of pedestrians.

Isabelle ignored the stares and whispers as several people recognised her and pointed her out to their companions. She must look a fright, dressed in a simple day gown, her hair falling from its pins, her face red from being bent over while hurrying alongside Sera.

She would later blame her own shyness for the fact that she hadn't been watching Luke carefully enough. All she saw, the moment she looked up, was his leather ball careening towards a group of oblivious dark-haired ladies walking with a single man.

Luke watched in horror, frozen to the spot, as the ball flew through the air and hit the gentleman on the back of the head.

With no time to think, Isabelle hiked Seraphina up onto her hip and hurried across the green grass. 'Luke!'

He started back towards her immediately, his face flushed with shame.

As soon as Isabelle caught up with him, she whispered, 'What have I told you about throwing a ball too close to people?'

She stepped in front of him before he could reply, prepared to apologise to the gentleman the ball had hit and to defend Luke against a potential scolding from a stranger.

'I'm so sorry…' she began, looking up—only to trail off when she met a pair of rather amused grey eyes. 'It's you!' she blurted. And then, realising what she'd done, she tried to rectify it with an awkward curtsy and a mumbled, 'Lord Ashworth…'

'Your Grace.'

Matthew's deep voice whispered over her skin.

'I—' Isabelle stopped talking. Because Sera had recognised Matthew and begun squirming, leaning her body forward, her arms outstretched to him. Isabelle instinctively refused to let her go, tightening her arms around the child instead.

When Seraphina cried out in response, kicking her feet in an embarrassing display of temper, Isabelle simply froze. Before she could think what to do—or run away, as she rather felt she might—Matthew plucked Sera from her and settled the child on his own hip.

Isabelle felt as if her shield had been taken away. All around them people seemed to stop what they were doing and watch. And if they thought it strange that her child had reached for Lord Ashworth, they must find it stranger still that Sera instantly stopped fussing the moment she was in his arms.

'No apologies necessary, Your Grace.'

After the smallest pause, in which he seemed to search Isabelle's face, Matthew glanced down at Seraphina.

'And who is this?' he asked in a perfect imitation of polite curiosity.

'My daughter,' Isabelle murmured breathlessly. 'Sera—Seraphina.'

'Hello, Seraphina.'

He greeted his daughter with the same polite smile, but Isabelle saw the warmth snaking through his eyes when he looked at her. And instead of relief that he'd lied for her, she felt the first lick of shame over the fact that he'd always have to. Yes, he had made mistakes. But the man standing in front of her deserved more—so much more than two secret meetings with his daughter a week.

'Matthew?' The eldest of the women standing behind him spoke first. 'Are you going to just stand there, or are you going to introduce us to the Duchess and her family?'

Isabelle's awkward smile tightened as she stared into the woman's familiar grey eyes. Her heart raced, forcing a hot flush of anxiety through her body.

'Forgive me, Mother.'

As if he'd read Isabelle's thoughts, Matthew leaned close.

'Relax, Duchess,' he whispered, before turning around with Seraphina still in his arms. 'Your Graces—' Matthew included Luke in his introduction '—may I introduce my mother, the Countess of Heather, and my two sisters, Lady Caroline Westmoor and Lady Eleanor Blake?'

The ladies curtsied.

Luke bowed politely.

Seraphina hiccupped, causing a round of genuine laughter that momentarily broke through the awkwardness of the moment.

Isabelle turned to her stepson. 'Luke?'

He stepped forward to face Lord Ashworth, looking sufficiently repentant. 'I am sorry for hitting you with my ball, my lord.'

Matthew smiled and gave a small nod in Luke's direction. 'If I may say so, you have a powerful arm, Your Grace.'

Luke flushed, his eyes lighting with a bashful pride that Isabelle had never seen before. 'Thank you, sir.'

'Perhaps we can leave the ladies to get acquainted and put it to good use?'

Luke's green eyes widened and he gave a stammered 'Y-yes', his nervousness at this attention from Lord Ashworth apparent.

Matthew placed Sera on the ground and gave her an elaborate bow. Raising their daughter's hand to his lips, he kissed the back of her tiny fingers.

'Lady Seraphina. It has been an honour.'

Sera laughed happily.

Overcome with emotion, Isabelle could do nothing but move

forward and take Sera's hand, stopping her from walking after Matthew and Luke as they moved away to continue Luke's game.

She watched the first few throws between them before turning back to Matthew's family. 'I apologise for interrupting your walk,' she began awkwardly. 'It—'

'Oh, it is nothing, Your Grace,' Lady Eleanor Blake exclaimed immediately.

The younger lady, who appeared to be around the same age as Isabelle, was dressed in a yellow gown that complemented her black hair. Her sister, similarly attired, but in green, looked just as striking, and Isabelle couldn't help but imagine that this was what Sera might look like when she was grown-up. Tall and fair-skinned, with that striking midnight hair and those expressive storm cloud eyes. Isabelle looked more like her Italian ancestors on her mother's side—her hair dark and heavy, her skin golden, not pale, and her eyes near-black. But these ladies were pure English delicacy.

'We see our brother quite regularly,' Lady Caroline affirmed. She turned to look to where Matthew was throwing the ball with Luke. 'Though I must admit he's not usually this amiable. Is he, Nora?'

'No,' Eleanor replied matter-of-factly, her own gaze tracking where the duo played. 'He is typically quite reserved.'

'If I may ask,' the Countess said, 'how are you acquainted with my son, Your Grace?'

Isabelle turned, a reply ready on her lips. But any words she might have said died as her heart climbed up through her chest and into her throat. Because the Countess was not looking at her. She was staring intently down at Seraphina, and her eyes were wide with equal parts shock and denial.

'Through a mutual friend—Lady Windhurst,' Isabelle managed eventually. 'We were introduced at Lady Russell's ball a month ago.'

She wondered if they could all hear the blatant lie in her words.

'I see,' the Countess replied, and Isabelle thought she rather *did* see.

Noticing their mother's lapse, but perhaps not recognising its reason, both of Matthew's sisters jumped in to further the conversation. 'Are you enjoying the season thus far, Your Grace?' Eleanor asked.

After a strange glance at her mother, Caroline added, 'We love being in London, Your Grace. Don't we, Nora?'

'Please, call me Isabelle,' she replied distractedly, not realising that she hadn't answered the question.

The Countess bent closer to Seraphina and asked, 'How old are you, Seraphina?' in a tone that signalled to her nearby parent that she was the one who was meant to answer.

Isabelle tried to sound calm. 'She is eighteen months.'

'How does a walk sound, child? We are probably close to the same speed.'

The Countess held out her hands, and as Seraphina walked to her grandmother, Isabelle forced herself to let her daughter go, when every instinct was demanding that she take both children and leave.

As the Countess led the toddler down a nearby pathway, Matthew's sisters fell into talking of London and the season. They made observations about recent balls and gave compliments to their hosts, commented on particular dresses of interest that they had noticed, and asked several polite questions regarding Isabelle's own forays into society.

For anyone else, the topics would have been easy small talk. Isabelle nodded and murmured her agreement, but soon ran short of things to say. Mortified beyond reason at her inability to communicate, and desperate to make an effort with Matthew's sisters, she broke a long moment of awkward silence.

'You'll have to forgive me...' A hot blush swept through her at their patient smiles. 'I am recently out of mourning and find that my conversation skills need some practice,' she said honestly. 'With Luke and Seraphina occupying so much of my time, I've grown accustomed to talking predominantly with children.'

Both sisters leapt on the olive branch she had offered, reassuring her that it was entirely natural and that she should not concern herself, but it was only when Matthew wandered back with Luke a few minutes later that Isabelle felt any real relief.

The two were a welcome distraction as they approached, their conversation trailing off naturally once they came abreast of the group again.

Luke looked up at Isabelle. His green eyes were bright with joy, his face flushed with exertion. 'Lord Ashworth has invited us to his family's country seat this September,' he said happily. 'He's going to show me how to fish—and teach me how to hunt.'

'Oh…' she managed. 'That is very kind of him.' She knew her voice sounded too tight, making her seem displeased when in fact the offer was a thoughtful one.

'Oh, you must come!' Nora exclaimed. 'My father and brother host an annual hunting party, but their friends' wives are either too old for Caro and me to enjoy talking with, or—'

'Or non-existent,' Caroline cut in, a teasing glint in her eye. 'Matthew's friends are notoriously single.'

'And proud of it.' Nora grinned.

'They are dropping like flies, and you know it,' Matthew replied. He winked at Isabelle. 'Caro snagged one of my oldest friends from right beneath my nose.'

'I hardly *snagged* Westmoor.' Caro laughed, undeterred. She lowered her voice. 'He came quite willingly.'

Nora and Caroline laughed at Matthew's mock-horrified expression, causing Isabelle to smile too. But she was saved from having to accept or reject the spontaneous invitation by the arrival of the Countess and Seraphina.

While Sera wore a wide grin, the Countess looked grave. 'I dare say,' she observed, 'I haven't had this much exercise in an age.'

'I am told that children keep a person young,' Isabelle replied breathlessly. 'Though I have yet to confirm the hypothesis.'

Everyone laughed, their easy manner unspooling some of the nervous dread still in Isabelle's chest.

The Countess looked at her for a long moment, her eyes missing nothing. 'Forgive my impertinence, Your Grace—'

'Isabelle, please,' she corrected, but she held her breath, terrified of what the Countess might have to say.

'I did receive your apologies regarding my ball, but I do hope you will now reconsider. We shall be eagerly awaiting you.'

Isabelle expelled a long, quiet breath. If the Countess suspected anything it was clear that she would not broach the subject—at least not today. 'I will check with my companion. Perhaps we can attend for a short while.'

'And Lady Windhurst has accepted,' Nora added. 'So you won't have to suffer our company the entire night.'

'Your company is no hardship, Nora,' Isabelle replied—and she meant it.

'You only say that because you do not know her,' Matthew mock-whispered, drawing a dramatic gasp from Nora and chuckles from everybody else.

'I will gladly receive you.' Isabelle turned to the other ladies, including them in the invitation. 'Any time that is convenient for you.' Leaning down, she picked up Sera. 'Unfortunately, I don't get out as often as I should.'

'It's true,' Luke added helpfully.

Matthew's lips quirked. 'We shall have to remedy that, won't we?'

'Yes, sir!'

Isabelle couldn't help but smile. 'Perhaps another day—for now you have lessons you have to get back to.'

Luke hung his head and grumbled his acquiescence.

'Thank you.' She turned to the other women. 'All of you, for including us in your walk.'

Though she didn't say it, Isabelle had found it both unusual and lovely to see how close Matthew's family were to each other, their manner easy, their jokes teasing but light-hearted. It made her wonder about things she shouldn't.

'Thank you, Lord Ashworth,' Luke added.

Matthew bowed, treating the young boy like a peer. 'My pleasure, Your Grace. Perhaps we will see you all at the hunt this year?'

Luke nodded and looked up at Isabelle, fairly begging her to accept the invitation.

Matthew met Isabelle's gaze. 'May I walk you back to your carriage?' he asked, saving her from having to dash Luke's hopes in front of an audience.

'Thank you, but there's no need,' she replied. 'My footman

is here, and my driver should be waiting.' Isabelle tipped her head in farewell. 'Lord Ashworth...'

'Duchess.'

He bowed slightly, but not before she saw the disappointment flash in his eyes.

Isabelle turned to say goodbye to Matthew's family. 'It was lovely to meet you,' she said honestly. 'I hope to see you all again soon.'

'At my ball, perhaps?' the Countess reminded her.

Isabelle nodded, and with one last look, to make sure Luke followed, hurried back in the direction of her barouche.

Chapter Thirteen

Matthew hadn't quite believed it when he'd turned around and bent to pick up that ball, only to come face to face with the Duchess, her heavy hair falling from its pins, her face flushed with embarrassment. In that moment his mind had blanked, words had fled. He'd stood there like a mute until she'd started the conversation.

'Oh, is that Penelope Periwinkle?' Nora asked Caro now, and before he could turn to see where she was pointing both his sisters had walked off to go and talk to their friend.

His mother waited until they were both out of hearing. 'Matthew…'

He turned to find her eyes boring into him. 'Yes, Mother?'

'What have you done?'

Matthew knew what she thought without her having to make the accusation. His own mother believed he'd seduced and abandoned Isabelle. It crushed him. There was a fleeting moment of panic, when he wondered if it would always be like this—if he would always be found lacking because of an affair he'd had when he was *twenty-five*. He even considered denying it, but one look at his mother's face told him that it was too late.

'It's not what you think—'

'Do not lie to me.' She shook her head, closing her eyes in

momentary frustration. 'Not about this. Not about *her*.' She placed a hand over her chest. 'I felt I was back in the past, twenty years ago, staring at my own child. Good God, she is Nora reincarnate!'

'I am not lying, Mother,' he said tightly, trying to hold on to his control. 'I'm merely telling you that I'm not entirely to blame for the circumstances.'

'You expect me to believe that?' she whispered. 'The Duchess is barely twenty years old—and she is *certainly* less responsible than you. Of that I am certain.'

'Yes, Mother,' he replied curtly, frustrated that she should instantly assume the worst of him. He lowered his voice. 'I do expect you to believe me when I say that I did *not* seduce an innocent woman and then abandon her—with a child.' His anger and hurt mingled and leached into his tone. 'You are supposed to be one of the few people who believe the best of me. If you do not, then how am I to convince anybody else?'

How am I to convince Isabelle?

'Are you denying that she is yours?' his mother demanded.

'No.' He turned back in the direction that Isabelle had gone, hoping for one last glimpse of them. 'I'm telling you that if it were my choice I would shout the fact on every street corner in London, the consequences be damned.'

The Countess reared back, clearly struck by the sincerity in his tone. Her grey eyes softened when she saw the hopeless expression on his face.

'The Duchess is afraid of the implications?' she asked.

'Sera looks too much like me,' he confirmed. 'We can't risk people questioning her legitimacy.'

'People will believe what they want to believe anyway. So long as there is no evidence to the contrary...' She paused for a beat, considering. '*Is* there any evidence to the contrary?'

Matthew laughed, hearing the same argument that he'd given Isabelle. 'No. But it's not that simple,' he replied, trying to defend Isabelle's decision. 'She has Luke's guardianship to think of too.'

'Well, look at your sisters.' She pointed to where both his sisters were now engaged in conversation with Penelope. 'They might have been looking in a mirror, and yet they're none the wiser.'

'It's not that simple, Mother.' God, he wished it was.

As if she'd only just realised she had a grandchild, the Countess, overcome by sudden excitement, changed tactic, exclaiming, 'We shall keep it a secret amongst the family, then! Matthew, I'm old. And your father! He could drop dead at any time without knowing he has a *granddaughter*!' she whispered.

'Father is in perfectly good health.'

'For *now.*'

'This is exactly why I didn't tell you,' he insisted, though he couldn't help but be relieved at her obvious excitement.

Whether his mother thought him reprehensible or not, it was clear that she would accept Seraphina. He supposed, given his own past, he hadn't been entirely sure of that. A bungled affair was one thing. But an affair *and* an illegitimate child was another thing entirely.

'I knew you would meddle.'

'Well, someone has to do *something.*'

'Mother…' Matthew took a deep breath in, exhaled, and prayed for patience. 'I know that you and Father stood by me before, even though you were ashamed of what I'd done.'

'You are my child!' she insisted. 'Of course I—'

'But I am begging you now: do not interfere.' He talked over her. 'Not with the Duchess—and not with Sera. I am dealing with it. *When* the Duchess is ready, we will let you into Sera's life. *Please,*' he fairly begged, 'let me fix this on my own. They're mine—my responsibility.'

She regarded him in silence for a long moment. 'I have just realised… She recognised you. Seraphina…'

'Yes.'

'You see her, then?'

'As often as Isabelle will allow,' he confirmed.

Which in his mind wasn't nearly enough. Not enough of Sera. And not enough of the Duchess.

Although he had tried to be the perfect gentleman, leaving as soon as Sera was asleep, not staying a minute past the necessary time, it took conscious physical effort to get his feet moving towards the door and away from them every time.

Matthew would have rather stayed. He *longed* to stay. But more than his own want to linger he wanted Isabelle to feel safe with him. He wanted her trust.

He started off in the direction his sisters had gone. But his mother didn't relent so easily. She followed at his side, her steps matching his easily in her eagerness.

'Did you know? When you left...?'

'No.'

'Oh.' That seemed to throw her. After a brief pause to consider, she hurried after him. 'So, you found out—?'

'A month ago.'

'Good God, Matthew. This is what you were talking about when I visited,' she observed. 'And she...she kept it from you all this time?'

Matthew rounded on her, pulling them both up short. 'The Duchess is not to blame, Mother. She has two children to protect.' Noticing that his voice was too loud, he forced a calm smile that was completely denied by his racing heart. 'Please,' he pleaded quietly, 'leave it be. If you start interfering, she will panic. Isabelle is terrified of how my past might harm Sera, and if you press her she will close me out for good.'

'You care for her, then?'

'She is the mother of my child,' he said gently. 'Of course I care for her.'

But the Countess would not accept half-truths so easily. 'Please, Matthew... When has that ever meant anything? No. That's not the whole of it,' she insisted, placing her hand on his arm. 'You feel something more—'

'My caring for her has to be enough,' he countered. 'For now.'

Chapter Fourteen

The day of the masquerade ball arrived in no time at all. Isabelle, who had spent the past weeks mulling on whether or not to attend, had mostly decided against it by the time the afternoon came. She knew she was far too invested in Matthew's visits than was safe—eagerly waiting for him to arrive and then desperately fighting her need to be touched by him every minute they were together.

She took a small sip of her tea, relieved when it soothed her itchy throat, and glanced at the clock on the mantel. Even if she decided to go, it was quickly approaching the hour when she wouldn't be ready in time to attend the ball anyway.

'I'll stay,' she confirmed to the empty room, ignoring the disappointment that settled within her at the decision.

There was a gentle knock on the door and Mary entered, a large box in her hands. 'Do you have a moment?'

Isabelle put down her teacup. 'Of course. You never have to ask, Mary,' she insisted, hoping that this reminder would be enough to bridge the recent awkwardness between them.

Mary sat on the settee next to her and put the box on the table. She looked down at her folded hands for a moment, as if considering what to say. 'I am sorry, Izzy,' she stated finally. 'For my reaction to your question about…' She cleared her throat. 'About John.'

Isabelle blushed even as she tried to give a nonchalant wave of her hand. 'It is forgotten, Mary.' She took a deep breath. 'You were wrong about Lord Ashworth. But not about me.' Reaching across the space between them, she took Mary's hand in hers. 'Will you forgive me?'

Mary's fingers curled around hers. 'There is nothing to forgive.' Mary looked down at her hands again. 'Izzy, if your past is ever aired it will ruin your life—and possibly Seraphina's too. No excuses accepted. No sympathy allocated. Society will eat you alive and go back to their whores that same night.'

Isabelle stared at her cousin in shock, even as that familiar flicker of panic reared inside her at the thought of people finding out about Seraphina.

'My Lord, Mary,' she managed eventually, 'that is the most unforgiving statement I have ever heard you make.'

'I am being honest.'

'You are worried that Matthew and I shall be found out?'

'I am,' she conceded. 'But I understand that you have thought it through extensively—more so than I have. And I do want you to be happy. It's the very reason I pushed you back into society in the first place—and yet it took you defending Lord Ashworth for me to realise that just because he isn't who I was expecting for you, it doesn't mean that he isn't right for you.'

'Mary, you are getting ahead of yourself.'

'Perhaps…'

Her cousin smiled in a gentle, knowing way that forced a tight fist of fear into Isabelle's stomach.

'But if you're going to do this—see Lord Ashworth and let him be in Seraphina's life—I will not stop you. In fact, I will do everything I can to help ensure that you are not caught.'

'Why?' Isabelle asked. 'I know you aren't fond of the idea.'

'I've had time to think about it,' Mary replied. 'And after some consideration I see that you have two options. The first is that you and Lord Ashworth court openly. People may talk, but so long as everything is above board they will never be able to substantiate the rumours surrounding Seraphina.'

Isabelle ignored the glimmer of excitement at the thought. 'And do you think we should—court openly?'

'Do you plan on marrying him?'

'No.'

The reply came instantly. Isabelle supposed she hadn't considered that courtship must end in one of two ways. And although she hated only seeing Matthew twice a week, she was not ready for another marriage—of that she was sure.

'I have come to care about Matthew, even in the short time he has been back in London. And I've always...*wanted* him. But I... I can't think seriously about marriage.'

The very idea of giving up her independence to another man—even Matthew, whom she was slowly learning to trust— made her chest tighten with panic, for she remembered all too well what it was to be trapped in a marriage she did not want and had not chosen for herself.

'As a widow—and a duchess—you have freedom, Izzy,' Mary affirmed. 'Most of which you would relinquish to your husband were you to marry again.'

Isabelle knew that as keenly as Mary did. 'And my other option?'

'Have an affair,' Mary replied, the bluntness in her tone belied by the embarrassed lowering of her eyes.

'An *affair*?'

'You clearly have an...*affinity* for Lord Ashworth,' Mary said with a small shake of her head. 'An affair would allow you to explore that without compromising your freedom. You are a widow.' Mary shrugged. 'Even if you were discovered there would only be a minor scandal, and then people would move on. But—'

'The children,' Isabelle finished.

Mary nodded. 'Even if society did not care, Gareth St Claire certainly would if he thought he could use it against you...'

Mary didn't have to say any more. Isabelle understood the risk she'd be taking.

'I will help you with whatever you decide, Izzy. Widows take lovers all the time. It's only dangerous to you because of Sera's likeness to Matthew. And if you truly do not want to get mar-

ried again, I see no reason for you to go the rest of your life...'
she cleared her throat, as if searching for the right word, before
settling on '...unsatisfied.'

At the same time Isabelle said, 'Alone.'

They looked at one another—and immediately started laughing.

'I dare say your father would have something to say about
my position as your companion should he ever learn of this,'
Mary teased.

Isabelle tapped the box between them, desperately hoping to
change the subject before Mary could mingle any more topics
as awkward as ruination, carnal desires and her father. 'What
is in here? My curiosity is aflame.'

'It came for you a moment ago.'

Mary reached forward and prised the lid off the box to reveal a beautiful black mask covered in lace and adorned with
a spray of black feathers, and tiny paste diamonds on one side.

Isabelle's resolve softened immediately. 'From Matthew?'

'I'm assuming so. There was no note. Just two boxes—one
with your name on and one with mine.' Mary smiled. 'It was
nice of him to remember me.'

'He is thoughtful,' Isabelle said. 'Do you know he brings
Sera flowers every time he visits?'

'I do,' Mary replied. 'Although I thought they were for you.'

No, the flowers were definitely for Seraphina. *Weren't they?*
Still...

'Mary...' Isabelle looked at her cousin, knowing that she
didn't need permission, but wanting it all the same.

'Promise me you'll be careful' was all Mary said.

'I promise.'

Isabelle's heart stuttered in her chest when the immensity of
her decision dawned on her. She reached into the box to remove
the mask. It was light in her hands. The lace was impossibly delicate. And when she turned it around to fit it over her face, she
saw that the inside was comfortably padded and lined with silk.

Mary reached over to pull the black ribbon around Isabelle's
head and fasten it. 'We'll have to get Meg to pin the ribbon in
your hair.'

Isabelle raised her fingers to touch the mask. 'How does it look?'

'Beautiful. Although it does not even begin to hide your identity.' Mary adjusted the mask slightly. 'Your hair gives you away—so be cautious.'

Losing herself in her excitement, Isabelle flung her arms around Mary.

Mary laughed.

'Thank you, Mary. For...everything.'

'You're welcome.'

'I just want to be *with* him. He makes me feel...' Isabelle waved her hands, searching for the right word. '*Excited*. Happy. And, though it shames me to admit it, Sera is not all of it...'

Mary nodded, perhaps not understanding Isabelle's infatuation, but not doubting it either. 'What you asked me...the other day...'

Isabelle tried to defer. 'You do not have to—'

'I miss it every day,' Mary said quietly, though her eyes remained dry. 'And that is my curse—to always want what I have had and lost and will never find again.'

'I'm sorry, Mary. I wouldn't have asked...'

'I know.' Mary cleared her throat. With one final maternal pat on Isabelle's hand, she rose from the settee. 'We should go and change if we're going to attend.'

Isabelle took a deep, fortifying breath. 'Yes,' she replied firmly. 'Yes, we should.'

'You came.'

Matthew's rather blunt observation caused a few raised eyebrows in proximity to where he was standing by the door, bowing over the Duchess's gloved hand, as the guests behind them waited patiently to be greeted.

He didn't care.

The Duchess was a vision, dressed in a silk emerald gown that bared the smooth skin of her slender shoulders and emphasised the shape of her narrow waist and hips. Her mass of hair had been expertly lifted and pinned in place. Other than the black mask he'd sent her, she wore no other adornment.

His mother greeted the Duchess enthusiastically. 'Your Grace. Welcome!'

A few curious murmurs travelled through the assembled crowd. He saw Isabelle's spine stiffen perceptibly at the sound, but she lifted her chin, as if bracing herself against the attention.

She curtsied gracefully. 'Lord Ashworth. Countess. May I introduce my cousin, Mrs Mary Lambert?'

The Countess and Mary exchanged pleasantries. 'Your Grace, Mrs Lambert—please allow my son to escort you inside.'

Matthew barely refrained from rolling his eyes at his mother's public favouritism, but he did not delay in leading Isabelle and Mary into the ballroom and away from the curious crowd.

'Please forgive my mother,' he murmured as soon as they were alone, 'she is eager to know you.'

Even with her mask on, Matthew saw the questions in Isabelle's eyes. But after the briefest hesitation she stopped to look out over his mother's ballroom, which had been decorated decadently for the evening with colourful silk bows, huge profusions of flowers and strategically placed oil lamps.

'Your mother has outdone herself, Lord Ashworth.'

The comment was issued politely, and with good intentions—Matthew hated it. At least when they were alone with Sera the Duchess didn't waste time on small talk.

'She will undoubtedly enjoy your praise,' he said, trying to remain coolly polite. 'Though Caro and Nora have been working tirelessly alongside her to ensure the evening's success.'

Isabelle smiled at that. 'How are your sisters?'

Mary, who had been watching this polite back and forth between them, interrupted before he could reply.

'Excuse me. I am going to go and talk with Lady Windhurst.'

She walked off before either of them could reply, disappearing into the crowded room like a sparrow to its flock.

Matthew turned back to find Isabelle smiling at him. 'I believe that is Mary's way of telling me that I have no need of a chaperone.'

'Perhaps that's for the best,' he teased, 'considering what I know of Mary's chaperoning.'

Isabelle lowered her head shyly, but Matthew saw the smile

on her lips. His heart ticked impatiently in his chest, reminding him that his time with her tonight was limited.

'Would you dance with me, Duchess?'

He didn't really want to dance, but he needed her in his arms, as close to him as possible, and dancing was the only way he could guarantee that without breaking his promise and carrying her off to some dark corner of the house.

She looked to where couples were lining up for a quadrille, and when she met his eyes again he saw that she was unsure. 'Matthew...'

'You do not wish to dance with me?' he said for her, seeing the look in her eyes.

'No—'

'Oh?'

'It's only that I do not wish...'

'You do not wish...?' he repeated, holding his breath against her reply.

'I do not wish to share you,' she said quietly—so quietly that Matthew found himself leaning forward to hear her. 'In fact, I would rather leave here altogether and be alone...with you.' She took a deep breath. 'That is to say...' She closed her eyes as a flush of embarrassment rose up her chest and neck. 'Oh, God...'

'Duchess...'

Matthew paused again, falling silent as a couple walked past them. He tried to make sense of her words, running them over and over in his head. And even though there was no mistaking the desperate need pouring off her, for it mirrored his own, he had to ask.

'Are you saying that you...?'

Isabelle looked at him in silence for so long that he thought he might have imagined it.

But then she nodded, just one small dip of her head, and whispered, 'Yes. I want...you.'

Chapter Fifteen

⟨⟨⟨⟩⟩⟩

They stayed an hour to avoid comment, but after they'd each made polite small talk with their acquaintances, and danced a single dance together, Isabelle feigned a headache and took her leave.

The Countess of Heather, in her concern, kindly offered her own carriage, so that Isabelle could get home safely and Mary could remain at the ball. And so, less than ten minutes after she'd first said she was feeling indisposed, Isabelle was off, moving through the dark streets of London in the Earl's smart black conveyance.

For minutes, the motion of the carriage seemed to wind her nerves tighter and tighter, each turn of the massive wheels reminding her of what she was risking. This wasn't simply wearing breeches at home or sitting on the floor with her child. This was the stuff of ruin.

'What *are* you doing, Isabelle?' she murmured to herself, overcome with panic.

Alone in the carriage now, she wasn't sure of the wild spirit that had possessed her. She'd only seen Matthew, standing in the hall, dressed in formal black. She'd seen the look in his eyes when he'd greeted her, and in that single moment in time she'd known with absolute certainty that she could not deny him any longer. As he'd escorted her through his parents' house Mary's suggestion had run in circles through her head until the words had simply spilled from her mouth—and not eloquently at all.

But now, with distance, she couldn't help but panic. 'This is a terrible idea,' she said aloud. 'People will find out. And you will be cast out of society.' Leaning forward, she rested her masked face in her hands. 'And you will have nobody to blame but yourself.'

'And me, technically.'

Isabelle gasped and sat up in her seat at the sound of Matthew's voice. She had been so consumed with her thoughts that she hadn't felt the carriage slowing once it had turned the first corner, nor heard the door quietly opening.

Matthew stepped into the carriage, his large body forcing her to move backwards to make space for him.

He closed them in and sat down as the carriage started on its way again. His eyes found Isabelle's immediately, and softened when he read the fear on her face. 'You are afraid?'

'Not of you,' she insisted. 'I want you. I've thought about this for…for weeks.' It was a lie, of course. She had thought of him for far longer than a few weeks. 'But the situation is…*risqué.*'

'To say the least.'

He didn't approach her, as she'd expected—didn't reach out and touch her as she wished he would.

'Isabelle,' he started, his deep voice gliding over her, 'if you are uncertain of me in any way—'

'No.' She shook her head vehemently. 'It's not that. Though I know of your past, I am certain that you would never deliberately hurt me. I've watched you with Seraphina, Matthew. I see the way you look at her—as if you're shocked and terrified and halfway in love already. And I know you'd never do anything that could harm her. In fact, I have never been more certain of anything…'

She had also seen the way Matthew looked at *her*, but Isabelle did not dare bring it up. And as she sat across from him she wondered what it would be like to touch him again, to have him touch *her* again. Her entire being ached to be touched by him again.

'Would you like me to tell you about Christine—the Marchioness?'

Isabelle hated her own insecurity…hated that it mattered to her. But after a long pause, she nodded.

He tried to smile. Isabelle saw the attempt, and she saw what it cost him, and she hated that she had caused him even a moment's pain.

'I want you to understand that an affair, especially one that I intend to be long-term, is no small commitment for me either,' he said.

'I know.'

He tipped his head gravely, but he did not meet her eyes as he started to explain.

'Christine and I began our affair with the mutual understanding that it would one day end. We liked each other. We were… *compatible*. But she was married, and I was an heir who would one day have to take a bride of my own. I was young and arrogant. I thought there would be no consequences for two adults who enjoyed each other's company.'

'Her husband was older, if I remember correctly?'

'She was twenty-two and he sixty-four when they married,' Matthew replied. 'When we started the affair I was twenty-five. She was thirty. For a year, we saw each other when it was convenient for both of us. And, as immoral as it was to have an affair with a married woman, I was not with anyone else while I was with her.'

He was quiet for a long moment, the only sound the roll of the carriage wheels on the cobbled streets.

'For a long time—*months*—I didn't know that she had developed stronger feelings for me. I should have. Looking back now, I can see that the signs were all there. The moment I realised her affections ran deeper than mine, I ended things. It seemed like the right thing to do. I knew I would never feel the same way. I liked her. I cared for her. But…'

'You did not love her?'

'No. And even now I cannot take blame for that. But I can accept responsibility for how poorly I handled everything afterwards.'

Matthew shifted, moving closer, as if he wanted her to see the truth on his face.

'I assumed that because she was married she would not cause a scene. I was young and immature. I ignored her attempts to write to me. I refused to admit her when she tried to visit. And then, after a few weeks, she...'

Isabelle saw the words stick in his throat as the memory rose.

'She came to your club?'

He exhaled a forceful breath, and although she knew he wasn't conscious of doing it, his hand found the back of his neck and pulled.

'I still see her in my sleep sometimes,' he whispered. 'She was...frenzied. Mad... Crying and begging me to take her back in front of a half-dozen people.'

Isabelle's heart went out to the Marchioness—but also to Matthew. She could see what it had done to him. Moreover, she could see the genuine shame pouring from him.

'What did you do?'

She knew the answer before he replied. Matthew's eyes spilled anguish and self-loathing.

'I walked away. I left her there for her husband to come and collect her.'

Isabelle took a steadying breath and, placing one hand on his muscular thigh, braced herself against him so that she could manoeuvre herself and her skirts closer to him in the confines of the carriage.

When she would have sat down next to him, Matthew tugged her, overbalancing her so that she toppled into his lap instead.

'Duchess...' He sighed when she did not move to get off him. His muscles slowly relaxed beneath her. 'I have made mistakes. But I would never let anybody hurt you or the children,' he said.

She could hear the certainty in his voice.

She *believed* him.

'I know.' She shifted so that she could meet his eyes when she said, 'Thank you for telling me—about Christine. I'm sorry. For both of you. But I... I don't want to pretend that knowing the truth of it would have made a difference. I would have come with you anyway.'

'Irrespective, I promise that I will do everything in my power to keep our secrets safe.' His arms caged her, holding her securely on his lap. 'They are my secrets too, Duchess. But you need to be sure that I am what you want, because...'

'Because?'

'Because if I step inside your house I'm not leaving until morning.' His voice lowered. 'I am going to keep you in bed for hours, debauching you in ways that you could not have imagined.'

The warning should have terrified her. She was no inamorata. She was a twenty-year-old widow who had been bedded just once in her life. She should have demanded that he drive her home and then refused to see him ever again. And yet that very fact made her bold. For she had tasted what it was to be loved by this man, and she so desperately wanted to be loved by him again.

Summoning the fragments of her courage, she replied, 'We are decided, then.'

Her tone did not come out sounding confident, like his. It wavered, sounding meek and uncertain. Inexperienced...

Matthew tensed. 'Are we?'

'Yes,' Isabelle managed breathlessly.

She reached up to yank the mask off, suddenly feeling hot and flustered with the fabric over her face.

'No.' He caught her hand in his. 'I want you naked in bed with nothing but that mask on.'

Isabelle slowly lowered her hands. 'You...?'

She couldn't even repeat the words. But a hot flush of awareness seeped through her as they trailed through her thoughts, and the word 'naked' coming from the beautiful man beneath her compounded her nerves.

Did he know what carrying a child did to a woman's body? Was he expecting her to look the same? Isabelle was not a vain woman; however, her eyesight was perfectly fine. She felt the physical differences in herself as viscerally as she had felt Seraphina growing inside her. And although she was still gawkishly slender, motherhood had left its mark on her body.

'Matthew, I'm not...'

He waited patiently, his eyes focused on her face.

'That is to say, I'm no longer...' She took a deep breath. 'Having a child has...' She closed her eyes, mortified at her inability to say the words.

'You are trying to tell me that your body is different from what I remember?' he offered quietly.

'Yes.'

She hadn't realised that she had turned her face away from him until he tipped her chin up. 'Isabelle, look at me.'

He yanked off his own mask then, and Isabelle wasn't sure if it was so he could see her better or if he wanted her to see his face when he spoke.

'You carried and birthed my child. For that alone, your body is something I will always cherish and adore.'

'You are saying that because you have yet to see it,' she pointed out matter-of-factly.

Matthew made a sound deep in the back of his throat. It threaded through Isabelle, soothing her nerves with desire. She felt him already...the hard length of him pressing into her right thigh even through her layers of clothing.

'You feel me, Duchess?'

Isabelle nodded shyly, and resisted the urge to slide over him so that he was positioned closer to her aching centre. The memories came, and with them anticipation. It heated her blood with lust, so that her body throbbed intimately and her breasts ached.

'We have yet to do anything. We have not kissed, nor removed a scrap of clothing, and still my body yearns for yours. The mere *thought* of you is enough to get me hard as iron. These last weeks in your company...so close to you and yet unable to touch you... It has been the worst kind of torture—a hell specifically designed for me.'

One large hand moved to cradle her face.

'In the last month I have found my own release with nothing but my hand and the thought of you.'

'You *have*?'

The image his confession evoked was... Well, she supposed it was lurid and improper—and exceptionally erotic.

Matthew released her face to nip playfully at her ear. 'I have thought of you naked beneath me and on top of me. I have thought of you swollen with my child, your breasts heavy in my hands. I have thought of you in every way you could possibly imagine.'

Isabelle swallowed as slick heat gathered between her thighs. 'You have thought of me with child?'

'If I had been there...'

He sighed, and although she didn't think he was conscious of doing it, he placed one large palm on her corseted stomach. 'I would have worshipped you.'

The admission brought with it an unfamiliar pang of loss. She had hated being pregnant, her body limited and clumsy, her feet painfully swollen. But Matthew's words made her wonder what it would have been like to have had him there with her, whispering delicious confessions in her ear, making her feel beautiful and desired despite her waddling gait and aching back.

'Forgive me,' she whispered, suddenly sad. 'I am sorry I never wrote to you. I didn't know you then. I thought I was doing what any man would have wanted...'

'There's nothing to forgive.' His arms wrapped around her again, holding her close. 'I have revisited every scenario over this last month,' he admitted, 'and there was no way we could have been together without scandal. You did what you had to: you protected your children. You protected *my* child. And you did it largely alone. Do not apologise for it,' he repeated.

'I wish I'd had you with me,' Isabelle offered. 'I think I would not have been so afraid if I'd had you by my side.'

'You have me now,' Matthew promised.

'And that is enough,' she told him, her tone leaving no room for doubt.

'It is everything,' he corrected and, raising his palm to her masked face again, guided her lips to his.

The kiss was soft and sweet and filled with longing. It was as if they both needed the delayed moment of contact to finally relax into being together again.

Isabelle's lips were so soft under his. Her rose scent wrapped around him like the familiar smell of home after a long journey.

Her gloved hands found his face, her thumbs stroking over his jaw in a caress that was loving and familiar, as if she had done it a thousand times before.

Matthew held her close, using both hands to steady her on his legs, and when she sighed, opening her lips for him, he slid his tongue into her warm, wet mouth and took her, gently stroking her, encouraging her to take her own pleasure in return.

And she did. Isabelle's tongue eagerly sought his, taking his gentle caresses and turning them into something deliciously sinful. Her innocent eagerness drove her to be bold. He felt her hands shift from his face to his neck, as if she would bring him closer still. She pressed her body against his in a completely unconscious plea.

Matthew broke the kiss to trail his lips over her bare shoulders, down to the dip in the bodice of her gown where her chest heaved with every in-out breath. He ran his tongue gently over the faint swell of her breasts above her bodice, not stopping until she was writhing in his arms.

'Matthew...' she moaned.

His name on her lips tore him in two. His aching cock became painfully hard, a testament to the years in which he had imagined this very moment.

'You are my every fantasy come to life, Duchess.'

He dipped one hand into her bodice, freeing her breast to his gaze. Her rosy nipple was pebbled with desire, straining up towards him as if begging to be tasted. Several faint white lines that had not been there before ran from her nipples outwards. He trailed his finger over one.

Isabelle instinctively raised a hand to cover these remnant signs of how much her breasts had grown during pregnancy, but Matthew caught her hand in his and held it. Leaning down, he followed the path his finger had trailed with his tongue.

'These lines, Duchess... They drive me wild.'

Matthew smiled to himself, vowing that he would be the last man ever to see her like this. He swirled his tongue around her peaked nipple once before sucking it into his mouth.

'Oh...' Isabelle moaned.

He released her. 'Do you like that, Duchess?'

She shuddered and buried her face in his neck. 'God, Matthew,' she panted. 'I feel as though I'm going to burst into flame. I… My body is so hot.'

'Where do you ache, love?'

She breathed heavily into his neck, refusing to answer.

Undeterred, Matthew slid his free hand beneath her heavy dress and chemise, moving up her stockinged leg to her drawers.

He cupped her over the fabric. 'Here? Is it here where you ache for me?'

'Yes…' she groaned in reply, and pressed herself boldly into his hand. 'Please, Matthew. It's been so long.'

Her plea broke him. Did she know how many times he had imagined losing himself in her again?

'In a minute,' he said gently, feeling the carriage slow. 'We're about to stop.'

He gently lifted her bodice, covering her, and when the carriage stopped had to ask, 'Isabelle, are you certain this is what you want?'

She didn't reply. Instead, she raised her hand and opened the carriage door before the footman reached it, telling him everything he needed to know.

'I'll go around the back.'

He nodded to the footman and waited inside the carriage as Isabelle was escorted to her own front door.

Though it was nearing ten o'clock at night, Matthew knew, perhaps more keenly than Isabelle herself, that only one person had to witness a scandal for news of it to spread like a forest fire. He understood the risk she was taking. And his past experience had taught him that the risk would always be far greater for a woman than any man. Perhaps if he had stopped to think about that at twenty-five he would have been more careful, more sensitive to Christine's deepening emotions and his inability to reciprocate them. He might have spared them both a lifetime of pain and regret.

So he waited now. And when the carriage had dropped him at a darkened corner of the street, he navigated his way to the back of the house and used the familiar servants' entrance without a blush of shame.

He made his way through the house to the hall, where Isabelle stood with her elderly butler, Gordon.

'If you could send up some water for a bath,' she was saying to him.

'Yes, Your Grace.' Gordon took Matthew's coat and gloves from him and then bowed, passing Isabelle a lit candle before leaving them alone together.

'It is shocking how blasé he is about all this,' she commented.

'He undoubtedly did far worse for the Duke while he was alive,' Matthew replied, knowing that Isabelle, for all her freedom, was still relatively naive.

'It doesn't worry you?' she asked seriously as she walked towards the study. 'That people will know...?'

Matthew followed, closing the study door behind him. 'Being in service to a duke is no laughing matter. I'd wager that not a single person in your household would risk their position without a serious financial incentive to do so.'

'I know you're right,' she murmured as she placed the candle on the desk, casting the room in a warm, sensual glow. 'It just feels dangerous...'

Isabelle walked to the whisky decanter on the sideboard and poured two drinks. She handed one to Matthew before taking a small, fortifying sip from her own glass.

He looked at her then, noticing the way her eyes lowered shyly and the way she curled the glass against her chest, as if she were an anxious warrior holding a shield to her breast before a battle.

'Why are you nervous?' he asked gently. 'We have been here before.'

'I know,' she replied breathlessly. 'It's silly. It's just... Well, then there was no...no choice. I needed a favour—and you provided it. But now it's come down to choosing what I want and taking it for myself...' She took a deep breath. 'I guess it seems more... I don't know, really. Just *more*.'

That she wanted him—*trusted* him—enough to be with him

was no small thing, especially considering he'd told her about Christine. She humbled him.

'If there was a promise I could make to erase your nerves I would make it in a heartbeat. My discretion—it is already yours. My fidelity—you have it from this moment on.'

'You do not have to promise me your fidelity.'

'Yes, I do,' he insisted, and it was no hardship. It was important to him that she knew him to be capable of faithfulness. 'Duchess...' Matthew closed the distance between them, coming to stand close enough that Isabelle had to tip her head back to meet his eyes. 'As long as we're together, there's nobody else—for either of us.'

Isabelle cleared her throat daintily. 'I... That is to say, there has been no one before.'

'Nobody?' He dared to ask what he'd only assumed before.

'Only you.'

The admission raged through him, sending fire to his veins. He groaned and closed his eyes against the torrent of heat. He fought to regain control, trying his best to calm his body. After a long moment he opened his eyes and found her watching him, a faint smile on her lips.

Unable to wait any longer, he took her glass from her and placed it on a nearby table with his. 'I should reward you.'

'*Reward* me?'

'For not letting anybody else touch what is mine,' he clarified.

Isabelle's mouth dropped open at his possessiveness, but Matthew didn't let that stop him.

'Would you like that, Duchess?'

She nodded slowly, as if she were a little stunned by her own admission.

'Tell me.'

'I would like that,' she said, and he saw her swallow deeply against her nerves.

'And what reward would you like?'

He led her to the settee and waited for her to sit.

'I... I suppose I don't know.'

Matthew saw her self-consciousness and quickly changed

tactics—wanting her to be comfortable, wanting her to be wanton, wanting her to take her pleasure from him.

'Why don't we start, and you can tell me as we go?'

And with that he knelt on the floor in front of her and lifted her skirts.

Chapter Sixteen

Matthew ran his hands up her stockinged calves, his big palms stroking and kneading as he moved slowly higher. 'What about this, Duchess?' he asked, his voice sinfully low. 'Do you like this?'

Frozen with equal parts nervousness and anticipation, Isabelle was helpless to do anything but nod.

When no response came, Matthew looked up at her from his position on the floor. His grey eyes, dark with lust, studied her face. 'Talk to me.' His hands moved higher, settling on her upper thighs over the fabric of her drawers. 'Tell me where you want me.'

Isabelle remembered those skilful fingers parting her most private flesh and stroking deep inside her, but she found that she could not make the request—could not beg him to touch her *there*.

'I want you everywhere,' she murmured.

Matthew smiled knowingly, but he did not laugh at her shy avoidance. He watched her masked face as he slid one hand through the slit in her drawers, finding her bare thigh. His fingers trailed over her, leaving a fire of sensation in their wake.

'Do you want me here, Duchess?' he asked, keeping his hand on her, mere inches away from where she ached for him.

'No...' she found the courage to say.

'Hmm...' Matthew's hand slid to her inner thigh, edging an inch closer. 'Here?'

Isabelle shook her head and held her breath as he finally stroked over the damp, downy patch between her legs.

He didn't ask again, but Isabelle sighed, 'Yes...' as his thumb ran up and down her seam, threading molten pleasure through her entire body.

'Hold your skirts, Duchess,' he whispered, bunching the fabric of her gown around her waist. 'I want to taste you,' he said, placing his thumb on the small knot of nerves at her apex. 'Here.'

Isabelle froze at the scandalous words, even as her body involuntarily shuddered with the pleasure his touch there wrought. 'Is that...*done*?' she asked, shocked. 'We did not...'

Matthew groaned as he slid a single finger into her. 'We didn't have time for a lot of what I'm going to show you, Duchess.'

Isabelle's head fell back against the settee as pleasure coursed through her, seeming to be concentrated in the spot that he claimed. Her muscles relaxed and her legs fell open in invitation as he thrust deeper inside her, his finger sliding against a particularly pleasurable point each time he withdrew.

Matthew shifted suddenly, leaving her aching and empty. But before she could object, he'd lifted her legs and strung them over his shoulders. He tugged her forward, exposing her to his gaze.

Isabelle should have been horrified, but instead she brazenly gathered her skirts with both hands, as he'd instructed, too desperate for him to touch her again to be coy. From her position on the settee she watched as his dark head lowered, disappearing beneath the mound of her skirts. There was a small, heavy moment when he didn't touch her at all, and the anticipation made her moan in frustration. But then he was spreading her with both thumbs...opening her folds.

Isabelle held her breath.

Matthew cursed. 'You're so wet for me,' he whispered.

And then he curled his tongue through her heat.

Isabelle's hips rose off the settee as her body followed the unusual wet touch. She cried out, digging her heeled slippers into his back to try and find purchase against the impossible sensations raging through her.

Matthew's husky chuckle grazed her inner thigh. 'Did you like that, Duchess?'

'Again,' Isabelle replied, shifting her hips forward. 'Please, Matthew.'

Her request was all it took for his control to snap. With a few deft tugs and several curses he divested her of her shoes and drawers and then settled back between her thighs, his mouth finding her instantly, his lips and tongue winding ecstasy through her as he alternately lapped and suckled.

'Your smell was made for me, Duchess,' he murmured. 'I could stay here for hours…tasting you.' He slid his finger back inside her, thrusting the digit in and out as he leaned forward and tortured her with his mouth.

'Matthew!'

Isabelle panted as her pleasure crested, eradicating her remaining embarrassment. Her body began to draw in, contracting around his finger in time with her ragged breaths.

'Matthew…' she moaned again, while her mind and her body screamed that this was so much more than she remembered.

'Relax, Duchess. Let go,' he whispered, and inserted a second finger inside her channel, stretching her wide.

Isabelle shattered on a loud moan that she would be embarrassed by later. Her body tensed, her back arched and her legs closed around his head, instinctively keeping him with her as the orgasm rippled through her again and again.

His tongue slowed, helping her to ride out the waves of sensation.

Isabelle's thighs trembled. Her breaths strained against the tight cinch of her corset.

Matthew slowly slid his fingers out of her. He kissed each of her thighs before lowering her feet back to the floor and righting her skirts.

His face was flushed. His eyes gleamed with a strange male pride that brought a smile to Isabelle's lips.

'You don't have to look so pleased with yourself,' she pointed out shyly.

'Duchess...' he shook his head, as if searching for the right words '...it pleases me to pleasure you.'

He stood, and Isabelle's eyes widened when she saw the heavy protrusion in his trousers. That same low ache started again between her thighs. She had the strangest urge to reach out and touch him. Her hand even hovered in front of her for a moment—before she realised where they were.

'We should go upstairs,' she said. 'I don't know what time Mary will be home, but I'd rather she didn't walk into the study while we're...'

'In the act?' Matthew offered.

'Yes.' She walked to the desk to pick up the candle, pausing to pick up her drawers and slide her slippers back onto her feet.

When she turned round, Matthew was watching her, his eyes warm with emotion, his person uncharacteristically dishevelled. He looked at her as nobody else had before—as if she was the sun and the moon somehow wrapped in one.

'You are exquisite.'

His words caused a strange sensation in her chest...something that felt like pleasure and panic vying for the upper hand.

'You make me feel...different,' she said, admitting more than she'd planned to. 'As if I'm not alone.' She flushed. 'That must sound silly—'

'No,' he said instantly. 'You make me remember what the point of all this is.'

She frowned, not quite sure what he was saying.

'Life, Duchess. You make me realise what the point of life is. When you're with the right person, at the right time, life changes from an aimless wandering into a *terrifying* adventure. Everything is amplified. The highs are higher...the lows so much lower.' He expelled a huge, shaky breath. 'When I'm with you, I know with absolute certainty that I'm exactly where I'm supposed to be.'

His words hit her like a runaway horse, galloping through her and leaving fear in their wake. She had been expecting him to say something funny or light-hearted; instead, he had deci-mated her with his answer.

Because wasn't that exactly how she felt too?

Wasn't that why she was risking so much to be with him?

She opened her mouth to say something, but no words came. Matthew came to her. He nipped her bottom lip.

'Don't panic.' He held out his hand, waiting until she slid her fingers through his. 'I won't ever ask for more than you're pre-pared to give,' he said, and led her out of the study.

As he guided her up the stairs to her bedroom, Isabelle had the terrible realisation that he wouldn't have to. It was already too late. She would have given him anything—she already had.

He'd said too much. Matthew knew it the moment the words left his mouth, and yet he could not regret them. It was true. From the moment he had found out about Seraphina he had dis-covered new purpose.

He was consumed by them—by Sera's quick smile and her instant acceptance of him, by Isabelle's shy, mistrustful ap-proach when it came to him, and her ferocious stubbornness when it came to their daughter's well-being.

He wanted them, he realised with alarm. And not in the way he'd thought—because of a gentleman's honour-bound duty to take his role in their circumstances. He wanted them to be his because suddenly he couldn't bear the thought that they might not be. He wanted them because the idea of being *without* them brought physical panic to his chest. And because he was hope-lessly besotted—with both of them.

The truth settled low in the pit of his stomach. Loving Seraphina came naturally. Loving Isabelle was a frightening revelation. Because the things he cherished most about her—her bravery, courage and independence—would be the very things that kept them apart.

Isabelle would be fine without him. She had no need for him. She was a wealthy widow, a duchess. She could live her entire life in the safety of her title, with no need to marry again. In fact, he couldn't think of a single reason why she would *want* to marry again.

Love, perhaps?

The thought left him oddly unhinged. Irrespective of how deeply he searched, he could not see enough within himself for her ever to come to love him. Everything that made him eligible—his title, his money, his family name—were things that Isabelle did not need. And the only other thing he was known for was scandal.

'Matthew?'

'Mmm?' He looked up to see her standing outside her bedroom.

'Are you all right?'

'Yes. I'm…happy.'

And he was. He told himself that just being with her again was enough. It had to be. And if one day she realised she needed more than what he had…what he *was*… Matthew supposed he'd deal with that then.

Isabelle opened her bedroom door. Though he had been in her bedroom several times, to put Seraphina in her crib, he had deliberately avoided looking around or staying longer than he needed. Now Matthew took the time to study the room. There were few pastels and frills, and none of the delicate, spindly furniture upholstered in floral print that he'd come to expect in any feminine domain. Instead, Isabelle's mahogany furniture was heavy and sturdy, the rug on the floor a deep red that contrasted with her white bedding.

Her entire domain was just like her: as luxurious as it was practical.

Isabelle stood only a few feet away, resplendent in her emerald gown and mask. She had appeared like some fantastical fairy, promising him ruin, and Matthew was helpless but to take every minute that she offered.

'Matthew,' she said quietly, 'I have to take this mask off. My face is itching.'

He closed the distance between them. 'May I help you?' he asked, one hand reaching up and hovering by her face, waiting for permission.

'Please.' She angled her head to one side. 'Meg has pinned it into my hair, so you're going to have to undo everything.'

Pleasure rumbled through his chest and caught in his throat. He started pulling at the dozens of pins in her coiffure. Her heavy locks slid between his fingers, the silky tresses falling by degrees as he worked to free her. With each long coil of ebony hair that fell, Matthew's lust grew.

'You are so beautiful,' he whispered reverently, running a particularly long strand between his fingers.

Isabelle shifted her head slightly so that she could see him. 'You make me feel beautiful,' she said.

Matthew lost all words as he slid the last of the pins from her hair and un-wove the mask's ribbon. He turned her gently to face him and lifted the mask from her face, untangling the last few strands of her hair as he removed it.

He moved to throw it down, but Isabelle saw the movement and reached out, catching his hand in hers. 'Wait!'

He froze.

She gently tugged the mask from him and, once he'd relinquished it, turned to place it gently on a table. 'I want to keep it—to remember.'

He knew what she meant—that she wanted to remember this night with him, not necessarily the ball—and knowing it soothed some of his panic. He traced the angry splotches that the mask had left beneath her eyes.

'I will buy you more—some that do not do this to you.'

Isabelle laughed. 'I blame Meg's expert fastening rather than the quality of the mask—'

Her breath caught as he smoothed her skin with both thumbs, his fingers gently cradling her head. Her eyes fluttered closed with pleasure.

'Do you like that, Duchess?' he asked, reminding her of their earlier game.

Her eyes opened and she nodded. But instead of letting him lead, she turned her back to him and asked, 'Will you help me out of this dress?'

'With pleasure.'

Matthew wasted no time. He deftly unwound the ribbons at her back and then unbuttoned the gown to expose her corset and chemise. Instead of stepping out of her skirts, Isabelle raised her arms and ducked, forcing him to lift the heavy dress over her head.

He held the garment in both hands as he took his fill of her, standing in the centre of the room wearing nothing but a corset, a chemise and stockings, her long black hair trailing down to her hips.

She blushed and lowered her gaze, and although her corset laced at the front, the Duchess did not move to take it off.

Reminded of her inexperience, Matthew vowed to be gentle, to give her pleasure and to show her how much power she had.

He draped the dress over a nearby chair and went to her. Taking her hands in his, he placed them on his chest and then reached for the hooks that ran down the front of her corset. 'May I?'

'Yes.'

He made quick work of the structural garment, too aware of Isabelle's self-consciousness to linger as he would have liked. As soon as it was off, leaving her in only a chemise and stockings, he took her hand and led her to the big bed in the centre of the room. He didn't lift her onto the pillowed top; he reached for the hem of her chemise and raised it over her head, taking it off.

He dropped the garment on the floor, and before she could cover her nakedness, Matthew wrapped his arms around her and pulled her into his chest. 'Do not be shy. Not with me. I assure you...you are more beautiful to me than any woman I could imagine.'

She did not reply, but he felt her nod against his chest.

Matthew released her and took a step back, desperate to see her, desperate to touch her.

She tensed at his perusal, then softened slowly as she watched him watching her. He was giving everything away—he knew he was. And he didn't care. He wanted her to know what she did to him.

'Matthew, I...'

'Tell me,' he urged.

'I don't want another baby...' She flushed and lowered her eyes. 'I'm...'

He waited patiently for her to continue. Isabelle in the candle-glow was divine: her golden skin flushed with awareness, contrasting with her long, jet hair and the small thatch between her thighs. Her breasts were small and rose-tipped, her nipples pebbled for him. Her waist was tiny. The front of her stomach was no longer flat, but beautifully curved where it had housed his child. Those same faint lines that he'd traced on her breasts climbed up her sides like roots that had once nurtured.

Sensing that she couldn't finish voicing what she'd wanted to say, he knelt in front of her and placed his lips against her bare stomach, before resting his forehead against the same spot.

'I will be more careful going forward,' he promised. 'I won't put you in that position again, Duchess.'

He felt her body yield as she relaxed. They stayed like that for a long moment... Matthew on his knees in front of her, and Isabelle sifting his hair through her fingers.

'Matthew...?'

He rested his chin on her stomach and looked up into her beautiful eyes.

She brushed his hair back from his forehead. 'I don't regret you.' She frowned. 'Do you know, now that I think on it, I never have? Even when I first realised I was pregnant... I never regretted that night. Even when I thought I would never see you again... I knew that I would cherish the memory of you, of the short time we had together.'

Matthew exhaled a deep breath at her confession, knowing that it was more than he could ever have hoped for. He stayed on his knees, his head against her stomach, loving how far they'd come in such a short time and yet lamenting their impossible situation. For impossible it was. Even if Isabelle chose him, they could never be together. Not openly—and not if they were going to protect Seraphina.

He rose slowly to his feet. Cradling her face with one hand, he kissed her gently. 'I have never regretted you either. Not for a single moment.'

Isabelle smiled and, rising up on her toes, returned his kiss. She slid her tongue boldly into his mouth. Her anxious hands fumbled with the buttons at his waistband. Desperate to press his naked flesh against hers, he broke the kiss and hurried to help her, stripping off his clothes in no time at all while Isabelle removed her stockings, clambered onto the bed and slid beneath the covers.

Leaving his own garments in a pile on the floor, Matthew followed. He climbed between the sheets and reached across the mattress to pull her to him.

She laughed loudly and gazed up at him, her dark eyes bright and happy.

Matthew levered himself up onto one elbow so that he could watch her as he trailed his fingers from her collarbone down to her breast. He circled her nipple, teasing the bud into tightening, before he bent down and sucked it into his mouth.

Isabelle moaned and pressed her chest upwards in offering. Her hands found his hair and tugged, as if she would bring him closer still. And when he used his teeth to nip her gently, before moving to worship her other breast, she panted his name.

His hand brushed over her stomach as his mouth worked on her breasts, moving slowly lower and lower until it found her soft, wet centre. He slid his fingers between her seam, stroking them up and down over her damp inner flesh without penetrating her. Her smell…that unique scent of salt and sin and sex…reached for him.

Isabelle's hands floundered before finding his head again, her fingers sliding through his hair and gripping it as if she needed something to hold on to. Her breaths came fast and irregularly, so unused was she to her mingled excitement and urgency.

'Matthew, please…' she moaned when he pressed his thumb against her.

'Please what, Duchess?'

She blushed, but she did not cower. She flattened her chest against his and reached one hand down between them to find his iron-hard length. She gripped him firmly and Matthew closed his eyes, steeling himself against the urge to thrust against her hand.

She brought her lips to his ear. 'Please take me,' she pleaded. 'I need you…inside…'

'Shh, my love…' he whispered, trying to calm her urgency. He rolled them both so that he was on top of her, supporting his substantially larger weight with his elbows. His cock came to rest on top of that triangle of hair—close, but not close enough for Isabelle.

She shifted her hips, trying to angle herself to take him, and Matthew obliged, guiding the swollen head of his cock to her entrance and gently easing into her.

He stopped when she tensed against the intrusion, and with a quiet 'Relax, Duchess...' lowered his head to suckle her nipple into his mouth.

Isabelle's body slowly yielded. Matthew felt her inner muscles loosen, making it easier for him to press deeper. Her thighs dropped to either side even as her feet pressed into the mattress, and she pushed against him, taking him in all the way.

He cursed quietly as her tight, wet heat enveloped him. He held still for a long moment as he tried to regain control. 'Does it hurt?' he asked, his voice hoarse as he steeled himself against the urge to thrust.

'No. I feel...fulfilled...'

She sighed and contracted her inner muscles, causing him to groan and drop his forehead to her chest.

'Matthew?' she asked, her hands finding his hair again. 'Are you quite well?'

Matthew grinned. He nudged his hips slightly, sinking further into her heat. 'I am perfect,' he replied, and began to move.

He braced himself, his elbows by her head, conscious of his weight, and the movement brought them eye to eye. Isabelle was flushed, her huge eyes dark with lust. Her skin was aflame beneath his. She raised her palm to his face and guided his lips down to hers as he moved inside her.

The kiss tore through him. Matthew was lost to her...to her softness and her smell and the quiet little sounds she made. And when he felt her body tightening, drawing him in, he lowered one hand between them to touch her.

Isabelle's moans grew louder as she closed her eyes against the pleasure.

'Look at me, Duchess,' he demanded. He wanted to watch as she unravelled beneath him.

She opened her eyes and struggled to focus on his face. Her

panted breaths brushed against his neck as her body cinched around him. 'Matthew...'

'I know.'

'I can't...' she panted.

'You can,' he promised, increasing the speed of his thrusts. Leaning down, he brought his lips close to her ear. 'Be a good girl.'

She moaned at his words.

'Take your reward,' he rasped as his own body drew inwards, preparing for release. 'Come on my cock, Duchess,' he demanded.

Whether it was his demand or his foul language that she found appealing didn't matter. Isabelle exploded, her body rising off the bed, her loud cry pealing through the room. Her body gripped him mercilessly, and it took every ounce of willpower he had to pull out of her in time. He caught his cock in one hand, and with two quick pumps and a loud groan spilled onto Isabelle's stomach, marking her with his seed.

He collapsed onto the bed beside her, his chest heaving, but when Isabelle tried to move, he stopped her with one heavy hand. 'No.'

'No?' She arched one brow.

'I need one minute,' he said, and buried his face in her rose-scented pillow as he regained his breath.

Chapter Seventeen

Isabelle looked at the beautiful man beside her, his muscular back golden in the candlelight, his shaggy black hair falling over his forehead. Her eyes traced the side of his face from one arched dark brow to his straight nose and sinfully full lips.

She supposed he didn't have the classic handsomeness so valued by the *ton*. Matthew was unfashionably large, with shoulders rivalling any dockworker's, and his rakishly long hair was borderline indecent.

Still, he was quite perfect in Isabelle's eyes.

He cracked one eye open as if he sensed her gaze. He sighed. 'Duchess…'

She smiled at the way he made it a sensual endearment, at the way he murmured it as if he had no adequate words to describe what they'd done.

'You didn't spend yourself inside me that time,' she remarked with a blush, remembering the way he had withdrawn from her, his eyes closed, his throat working on a deep growl, his stomach muscles tensed as he stroked himself to completion.

'Most men are able to pull out before—to prevent the chance of a child,' he told her.

'Oh, but…'

He slowly levered himself up onto his elbows, his shoulders

and arms flexing with the movement. 'I was planning to that night...' he told her.

He pushed off the bed, walked around to her side and lifted her easily into his arms. He carried her through to the dressing room and lowered her gently into the bath, even though the water the maid had brought up was now lukewarm.

'That night you came to me, I wasn't going to... But then I was inside you, and—' he shook his head incredulously '—I lost control. There's no excuse. It should not have happened. It had never happened to me before. And although I cannot regret Seraphina, I am sorry that my actions took that choice from you. It was not my intention.'

Isabelle believed him. 'I knew the risk I was taking,' she said quietly, thinking of all the ways that night might have gone differently. They could have stopped before... He could have withdrawn...

But instead of filling her with regret, the thought terrified her.

If things had gone differently, she would not have had Sera. She may not ever have had a child *at all*.

She stilled as a new thought assaulted her. She might never have seen Matthew again.

Confused by the punch of terror that swept through her at the thought, Isabelle began to panic. She thought of her wedding to the Duke and the terrifying weeks after. She thought of Luke and of Sera. And she thought of Matthew's scandal. Not, as everyone else did, of what he'd done, but rather how it had followed him through life, haunting him.

If the same thing were to happen to Seraphina because of *them*...

'Matthew?'

'Duchess?'

'I want...'

Perhaps sensing her fear, he raised a hand and placed it on her face, turning her gaze to his. 'You can always be honest with me, Isabelle.'

But she could not.

Isabelle smiled despite her inner struggle. *I should take him while I have him*, she thought. Because, despite what he'd said about his fidelity, Matthew was an heir. He would be an earl one day, and he would want heirs of his own to continue his family's legacy. But tonight…

Matthew was on his knees, his muscular forearms pressed against the rolled lip of the tub. She scooted forward, making space for him behind her.

'I want you to come in here with me,' she dared to say.

He pushed himself up to stand, his powerful body rising above her like some marble statue, all corded sleek muscle covered with the black hair that marked him as a man in his prime.

Isabelle tried her very best to be dignified, only sneaking a quick glance at his manhood as it came into view, but Matthew caught the discreet peek.

He held his arms out to his sides, comfortable with his nakedness. 'Look all you want, Duchess.'

His words spread liquid fire through her. Before she could overthink it she turned to look at him, taking her time as she ran her gaze over the golden skin, taut over wide, muscular shoulders, down to his tensed abdominals and the straining length of him. He was beautiful…raw power. He was thick…harder than he had been moments before.

Isabelle's stomach dropped low. 'You are…' She waved in the general direction of his crotch. *'Again?'*

Matthew gave himself one long stroke, his fingers cinching at his base and sliding upward. 'It would seem my body will not stop wanting you, Duchess.'

And with that he climbed into the tub behind her and sat down, his long legs bracketing either side of her.

When Isabelle didn't move, he reached for her, pulling her back against his chest so that she could feel the hard weight of him at her lower back. She thought it odd that something so uncomfortable should also be so comforting, so familiar.

Matthew's hands ran through the water beside her, lifting it so that he could gently rinse the signs of their lovemaking from her. When she was wet and gleaming, he reached for the cake of soap on a nearby stool, lathering it in his hands until his palms were slippery with suds.

Isabelle stared as he worked, fascinated by his broad palms

and strong fingers as they travelled to her chest and began to knead and massage her sensitised breasts.

Her head fell back against his chest, allowing him more room for his ministrations.

Matthew made that now familiar pleased sound deep in the back of his throat as his fingers tugged gently at her aching nipples. Isabelle moaned wantonly as sensation after sensation rolled through her.

He trailed kisses down the side of her neck as one large hand lowered between her legs, his fingers expertly parting her to his touch and the warm water.

Isabelle couldn't help but open her eyes and look down. She watched...embarrassed, heated and utterly wanton...as his index and middle fingers slid over her inner flesh.

'Matth—'

Whatever she had been about to say died on her lips as a knock sounded on the door.

Isabelle was moving in seconds, pushing up from the water and climbing out of the tub before Matthew had even realised that someone was outside. He moved to get out too, but Isabelle held one hand out, stopping him.

'Wait here.'

She waited for him to nod, before hurriedly wrapping a strip of linen around herself and hurrying through to her bedroom. She threw her nightgown over the towel, took a deep breath to try and calm her racing heart, then reached out and opened the door.

Tess stood outside, holding Sera. The child was red in the face, her eyes wet with tears, her little hands scrunched up angrily.

The nursemaid bobbed a quick curtsey. 'Excuse me, Your Grace. I saw the light...'

'What is—?'

Before she could finish her question, Tess started crying too. 'Something's wrong! She's burning up and she won't stop crying.'

'It's all right, Tess.'

Isabelle reached for Seraphina, alarm coursing through her

when the baby's hot skin touched hers. Warmed by the bath as she was, *she* should have been far hotter to the touch than Sera.

Keeping her voice calm, despite her panic, she said, 'Wake Gordon. Have a footman send for Dr Taylor immediately. If the doctor's out, have him keep looking until he finds another.'

'Yes, Your Grace.' Tess turned to fulfil the request.

'And Tess!' Isabelle called. 'Bring up some cold water. Ice too—if we have it.'

Tess didn't waste time replying. She hurried off.

Isabelle closed her bedroom door. As if sensing her mother's worry, Seraphina started crying again—first quietly, and then with loud wails that echoed in the small room.

'What's wrong?'

She turned from the door to find Matthew, already dressed in his trousers and shirt, sans waistcoat and shoes.

'I don't know. She has a fever...'

She lifted Seraphina away from her body, noting that everywhere Sera's bare skin had been pressed to hers was already sticky with the baby's sweat.

'God, Matthew. She's so hot.'

He came forward instantly, placing one huge palm on Seraphina's forehead. 'How long has she been like this?' he asked.

His voice was devoid of emotion, but when she looked up at him she saw the sliver of fear in his eyes before he managed to bank it down.

'I don't know.' Isabelle searched her mind. 'She seemed fine this morning. And with the ball, I didn't... Oh, God...'

'Don't. Don't do that, Duchess.' Matthew held out his hands. 'May I?'

At a loss as to what to do, Isabelle complied, passing Sera to him.

Seraphina's wails turned into quiet sobs the moment she was in her father's arms. The child looked at Matthew for a long moment before plonking her head against his neck and taking a deep, shuddering breath. She fisted her little hand in his shirt, as if she wanted to be as close to him as possible.

Matthew crooned to her. 'Hello, beautiful,' he whispered, and kissed her cheek. When Seraphina started crying loudly again, he brushed his hand over her head. 'Shh... You're going to be well, darling.'

Isabelle's own eyes flooded with tears at the sight of them. Seraphina, unwell and feverish, and Matthew, so calm and reassuring. This, she realised as she watched him take charge, was how it was supposed to be. Not father and daughter seeing each other twice a week, for the hour Sera stayed awake, with Isabelle and Matthew sneaking about as if they were both ashamed of what they'd done, when really neither of them was in the least.

Matthew rocked gently, comforting Sera even as his free hand lifted the tiny white nightdress.

Isabelle was watching his face, and she knew the moment he looked down at Seraphina's back that something was terribly wrong.

'Matthew...'

He turned then, angling Sera's back in her direction and showing her the angry red splotches spreading over the toddler's skin.

Isabelle's heart simply stopped beating. Fear, new in its intensity, sank through her to her very bones. And when she looked into Matthew's eyes she saw the same fear reflected there.

'Measles.'

Chapter Eighteen

Isabelle paled, one slender hand coming up to cover her mouth. Her enormous eyes had turned glossy with tears, and even though she didn't speak, Matthew could see her thoughts running rampant.

'It's a common enough, disease, Duchess,' he said quietly, refusing to acknowledge his own fear. 'She'll be fine.'

His words, although true, left so much unsaid. Measles was particularly dangerous to small children, whose little bodies often succumbed to secondary symptoms, like fever or pneumonia. There was so much that could go wrong, and in one as young as Seraphina those potential risks were twofold.

But his words seemed to be enough to pull Isabelle from her panic. Matthew watched as she slowly straightened her spine, her hands hurriedly wiping away the tears running down her cheeks.

'Yes,' she said firmly, 'she will be.'

'The doctor?'

'He's coming.'

Matthew could feel Seraphina's little body burning against his, her skin so hot that he felt overheated just by his proximity to her. And yet for some absurd reason he couldn't bear to put her down.

'Is he any good?' he asked.

'Dr Taylor?'

He nodded. 'Our family doctor is elderly, but he's been with us almost twenty years…' His mind raced with thoughts of everything he could do, and before Isabelle could reply, he added, 'I'll send for him anyway.'

'Dr Taylor is young, but he has not let us down yet. From what I understand, his services are quite sought-after.'

Matthew shifted his weight from one foot to the other, not stopping his rocking as he attempted to comfort Sera. 'How long will he take to get here?'

Isabelle smiled briefly. 'I have only just sent for him—maybe an hour…'

'That's not soon enough.' Matthew suddenly shifted, passing Sera to Isabelle. 'Here—take her.'

As soon as Sera was out of his arms her cries grew louder, and it took every ounce of willpower that he had to keep moving, to put his waistcoat on without reaching out to comfort her.

'I'm going to fetch my mother to stay with us until the doctors get here.'

'Matthew, the ball… Your mother can't just leave—not without raising suspicions.'

He looked across the room at her. In that moment he knew he would have done anything to protect her from the days to come.

She turned to kiss Seraphina's red cheek, where the rash was already becoming visible, and Matthew forced a half-hearted smile in an attempt not to scare her further.

'My mother nursed me and Caro through it when we caught it at the same time. She's more equipped than we are. Quite frankly, I'm calling in all the reinforcements we have. My sisters are perfectly able to act as hostesses for the rest of the evening.'

'What will the Countess say? About Seraphina?'

Matthew heard the dread in Isabelle's voice and braced himself against it when he admitted, 'She already knows. When she saw Sera at Hyde Park…'

But Isabelle did not seem surprised, as he'd expected. 'I assumed as much.' She rocked back and forth unconsciously, trying to calm Sera. 'Was she angry with me?'

'No. She was shocked. Then ecstatic. And she immediately started scheming—it took everything I had to convince her to stay out of it.'

He watched his words sink in, watched Isabelle's brows dip together in confusion.

'Why would she be angry with *you*?' he asked gently, trying to understand.

'Well, for starters, maybe she thought I was a strumpet who'd had my way with you. And I'm sure that discovering her first grandchild is illegitimate probably came as a huge shock.'

Matthew couldn't help but laugh quietly. 'I assure you that my mother's first inclination was to immediately assume that *I* was entirely to blame.'

Her dark eyes met his. 'Because of the Marchioness?'

Swamped with regret, all he could do was nod and tug on his boots. He still felt that familiar nausea low in his stomach when he remembered Christine's fevered panic and frantic voice as she'd begged him to take her back. But for the first time, instead of bitter anger towards her, he also felt understanding—and a deep, deep shame for his role in her heartbreak.

Because if Isabelle cut him out of her life, he realised, he would probably feel as frantic, as hopeless, as lost as Christine had. And it was the strangest thing to realise that love could be as much of a curse for some as a blessing for others.

'Matthew...' Isabelle waited for him to look at her. 'Even though you were involved in a scandal, you've only ever been a gentleman to us.' She smiled gently. 'And the Marchioness scandal was the reason you came to be on our list.'

That gave Matthew the courage to say, 'It was a mistake—or I used to think it was, until just now. Because if it had not happened you would not have come to me, and for that alone I can no longer regret it. But my mother—and everyone else—has used it to measure my every action for years. When she found out about Sera, she thought that I had ruined you.'

'It is strange, is it not, how the people who are supposed to know us best often don't know us at all?'

Matthew shook his head vehemently. 'Don't forgive me my sins, Duchess. I was to blame for the Marchioness's scandal.'

'Yes, but only as much as she was,' Isabelle insisted.

Seraphina rested her head against Isabelle's collarbone, and Isabelle responded by rubbing her cheek against their daughter's head.

'And in this you are only as much to blame—less so, even—as I am.'

He opened his mouth to argue, to remind her of her innocence, but she wouldn't have it. She spoke over him.

'Do not take that away from me, Matthew. The decision to go to you was mine to make—and I *did* make it. It took an immense amount of courage, but I would make it again if I were given the choice to go back—I would make the same decision every time. I went to you expecting a rake, and I found…you. And you are honourable and loving and kind.'

'No.' Matthew kept his voice low, so as not to alarm Sera, who had finally settled into a restless silence. 'You did come to me, Duchess. But I was not honourable in the least. I wanted you from the moment you spoke to me—before I even saw your face. And even if I had sent you home that night I would have found my way back to you eventually. I would have been powerless to resist you. Do not paint me a gentleman.'

'Fine. But then do not paint me an innocent either. It was *I* who came for *you*, my lord.'

He felt something shift inside him at her words—as if some part of himself that he'd closed off long ago had been released, filling him with an immensity of emotion that nearly overwhelmed him.

He knew, perhaps more than Isabelle, that society had been far harder in its judgement of Christine than of him, but for the first time he accepted that Christine herself had been an equal and eager participant in the affair—and the primary cause of the ensuing scandal. The difference between her and Isabelle was that Isabelle not only made her own decisions, she also accepted the consequences of them. She was truly independent.

Isabelle ran her hand over Sera's head, leaving it on her forehead for a few seconds. 'I can't tell if her fever's getting worse or if I've simply adjusted to her temperature.'

The reminder snapped Matthew from his reminiscing. 'We're

going to have to establish a schedule…have someone always monitoring her fever and her other symptoms over the next few days.'

He was mostly talking to himself as he planned.

'Leo has had it—he had it while we were at school.' He paused to look at her. 'He will be discreet, Duchess. But it is your decision to make.'

Isabelle didn't even reply, knowing that she'd take all the help she could get when it came to the health of her child.

'And Willa,' Isabelle said. 'I know she's had it. She'll come, if Windhurst allows it.'

'I'll speak to her if she's still at the ball.'

A new and terrible thought occurred to Matthew. His gaze snapped to Isabelle, and he knew the truth by the stubborn glint in her eyes before he even asked.

'And you?'

'Will it make you feel better if I lie?' she asked, her body growing rigid.

'Duchess…'

'Matthew, you could bodily remove me from this room and have me shipped to India and I would still slit the throats of my captors and come straight back.' She stared at him, daring him to argue. 'I am an adult, capable of making my own decisions.' When he still didn't reply, too consumed by the thought of both his girls being ill, she added, 'If you even try, I will never forgive you.'

'Duchess…'

'It's probably too late anyway,' she added. 'If the rash is showing already it's too late for me to leave—and you know it.'

Infuriated, helpless, and raging with inadequacy, he paced the room. 'And what of me?' he demanded. 'Am I to stand idly by while you are both ill?'

His very heart flailed at the thought.

'No.' Her mouth turned up in a tired smile. 'I hardly expect you to be idle, Matthew.'

He groaned his frustration. 'Duchess…'

'I need you here,' she said softly, but with not a hint of acquiescence in her voice. 'Matthew, I *want* you here. But if you try to come between me and Seraphina, I will have you removed from my house.'

His eyes snapped to hers even as he paced like a caged animal. But even though he was angry—no, *infuriated* by her—his chest swelled with a strange pride that was equally born from love and admiration.

God, she was magnificent. So strong-willed and brave.

'Fine. Have it your way,' he acquiesced. 'But if you become ill, I'll...'

'You'll what?' She smiled gently.

Matthew couldn't help the exhausted laugh that rumbled out of his throat. 'I will be exceptionally angry with you.'

Instead of laughing, or jesting, Isabelle came to him, tucking herself and Sera against his chest.

'Thank you,' she whispered. 'It makes me feel safer knowing you're here.'

Her words made Matthew feel equal parts happy and devastated. For as much as he craved her confidence in him, he knew that there was nothing he could do to help. Measles was a waiting game—and Sera's tiny little heart, the one he could feel pounding angrily against his own chest now, as Isabelle held their child between them, was the clock.

'I've got to go. I'll be back with my mother and the doctor soon.' He kissed Sera's head of curls.

'What do I do?'

'Try to cool her down.'

'Tess is bringing ice.'

'Once she's brought it, have her wake the rest of the servants. Send anyone who hasn't had it before home until it passes—we'll pay for their leave.'

'You don't think it's too late?'

'I don't know...but it would be impossible to know everyone who's had contact with her recently.'

'Matthew...?'

'What is it, Duchess?'

'If they are already unwell and they leave...'

He cursed. 'They will take the disease home with them.'

'We have the resources to care for anyone who becomes ill

here. At their homes they might not have that—and, worse, they might infect their own families.'

'What do you want to do?' he asked.

'We give them the choice but encourage them to stay here. I know Mary and Tess have definitely had it. They can conduct any outside business until the rest of us know that it has passed.'

'It's your household, Duchess.'

She tilted her chin up. 'I value your opinion.'

'I hate it that you must risk keeping ill people in proximity to you,' he said honestly. 'But we cannot let the servants face this alone—especially if they contracted the disease here.'

'Perhaps we shall be exceedingly lucky and everyone has had it already?' she suggested, her overly bright tone carrying a false humour that he tried to smile at.

Matthew was less optimistic. 'And Luke?'

'He had it as a young child—I was not permitted to see him or tend to him.'

'Well, that's something.'

Leaning down, he took her mouth in one last fierce kiss, pouring everything—all his love and terror and frustration—into it. And then he pulled back, knowing that if he didn't leave soon he'd be too afraid to leave at all.

'I'll be back soon, Isabelle.'

'We'll be waiting,' she replied as he let himself out into the corridor and, without looking back, ran for the stairs.

Diana Blake, the Countess of Heather, arrived before anyone else—including Dr Taylor. The Countess's elaborate gown and coiffure told Isabelle that she had come straight from the ball, pausing only to remove her mask.

'Your Grace.' The older woman dipped into a hasty curtsey in the hall.

Isabelle reached for the woman's hands, halting her mid-rise. 'Please,' she begged. 'No honorifics. Not any more.'

She flushed, unable to say more.

'Isabelle, then.' The Countess smiled kindly and bypassed any further awkwardness by asking, 'How is Seraphina?'

'She is sleeping; her nursemaid is keeping her cool while I

check on my servants.' Isabelle blinked back the burn of self-pitying tears. 'Six of them have not had measles before. Four of them are already showing symptoms.'

The Countess did not seem concerned. She plucked her gloves from her hands in a businesslike fashion and passed them to Gordon, who was hovering nearby.

'Let me see Seraphina first. Then we shall have the servants' beds moved into the same room—it will be easier to tend them in one place. They should rest until the doctor has been to see them and given us further instructions.'

Her confident manner instantly put Isabelle at ease. 'May I have a room prepared for you?' she asked.

'Yes, please.' The Countess turned to Gordon. 'Your name?'

'Gordon, my lady.'

'Gordon,' the Countess repeated, committing the name to memory. 'I have three footmen with me who have all had the measles before. They are here to help. I expect you are able to instruct them to go where you need them?'

Gordon's chest puffed out ever so slightly. 'Yes, my lady. I will see that they're settled.' He bowed. 'Thank you.'

The Countess smiled as Gordon walked away. 'What a dignified fellow.'

She took a deep breath and started up the stairs, leaving Isabelle to follow or be left behind in her own house.

'My son tells me that you have not had the disease yet?'

'No,' Isabelle replied honestly, omitting the fact that her throat had been scratchy for days and, although she had put Seraphina down over thirty minutes earlier, she now felt as if she were heating from the inside out.

'And you will risk yourself to tend Seraphina even though Matthew and I will be here?'

'Definitely.'

Diana Blake did not scold her; instead, she nodded matter-of-factly. 'Very well, then.'

Isabelle wasn't quite sure how she was supposed to react to this powerful woman now marching up her stairs as if she owned the house. The Countess seemed strangely unfazed by the scandalous circumstances, and her calm indifference confused Isabelle to no end.

It was only when they came to her bedroom door that she dared to ask, 'You do not have any questions for me?'

The Countess paused, one hand raised to the handle. 'Oh, I am *aflame* with curiosity,' she admitted, one brow raised in the same haughty gesture Isabelle had seen Matthew replicate. 'But I have the strangest feeling we're going to have a long time to get to know one another.'

'It's not what you think—'

'It rarely is.'

Needing to defend Matthew against his mother's assumption that he'd ruined her, she started trying to explain. 'Matthew... He...he helped me to protect my title so that I could keep the guardianship of my stepson. He did not know me before I approached him. He—at least in my mind—is free from judgement.'

'Yes...' the Countess drawled. 'I'm sure he found *helping* you a great difficulty.'

Isabelle couldn't help but smile, even as she lowered her eyes, mortified by the conversation.

'Perhaps not a *great* difficulty,' she said. 'But he did refuse me at first—until I threatened to go to someone else.'

Diana Blake's eyes widened at that. 'You...?'

'I had a list.'

'A *list*?' The Countess paused. 'Well, when this is all over I definitely want to hear that story.' She leaned forward conspiratorially. 'Matthew is being very close-lipped about the entire situation.'

'He is a good man.'

'He is in love with you,' the Countess countered bluntly. 'He may not realise it yet, but I know my son rather too well. Seeing him watching you in the park that day...' She shook her head, a wistful smile on her lips. 'It made me remember what it is to be young and in love.'

The words slammed through Isabelle. 'No,' she said, denying it to herself as much as to the Countess. 'He is merely concerned for Seraphina.'

The Countess reached out and clasped Isabelle's hand. 'Don't fret, child. How about we call it a problem for us to solve another day?'

Isabelle nodded eagerly, grateful for the compromise.

'Now, let me see my granddaughter,' she demanded, and opened the door herself.

As the Countess set about quietly feeling Seraphina's temperature and asking Tess questions about her symptoms, Isabelle couldn't help but ponder the Countess's words.

Though he had not said it specifically, Matthew had admitted enough for her to understand that he cared. Moreover, he had *shown* her. His every action was a promise to protect her—not, as she'd once feared, to possess her or control her.

To no advantage to himself, he had kept his word and not told anyone about Seraphina. And he had promised her his fidelity. And, although the neglected little girl she had once been would have been too afraid to believe that a man like Matthew could love her, the woman she had become desperately wanted to.

Because as she watched Matthew's mother tend their child… as she thought about him out looking for his own family doctor and calling their friends to assist them…she finally understood what marriage should be like.

It was not a trade—a young woman's flesh for the hope of healthy offspring—but a partnership. Marriage was having someone to share the burden when everything fell apart. Marriage was having someone step in and help when you didn't know what to do. And it worked both ways, with each supporting the other. Marriage was a constant when the world was not—or at least it *should* be.

Isabelle fleetingly wished that things could be different—that she and Matthew could be together openly without the potential for scandal. Still, knowing that such thinking was futile, and that neither she nor Matthew would jeopardise Sera's standing in the world, she pushed it from her mind and refocused her attention on what needed to be done.

Chapter Nineteen

By the time Matthew got back to Everett Place with Leo, whom he had fetched from their club with a request for help and a promise to explain everything as soon as possible, Dr Taylor was in Isabelle's bedroom, holding a stethoscope against Seraphina's chest as the child slept. Isabelle stood nearby with his mother, Mary and Willa, all of whom had left the ball immediately upon hearing the news.

Dr Taylor looked up when Matthew entered the room, but did not comment as he moved to stand by Isabelle's side.

'Sorry I took so long,' he whispered, just for her. 'I had to track down Leo at the club.'

'He is here?'

'I have left him in the drawing room for now.'

'And your doctor?' she asked.

'He is away. Travelling for—'

'She is in the worst of it now,' Dr Taylor interrupted quietly, trying not to wake Sera.

The doctor was a small, thin man with a youthful face that almost looked too young to shave, but when he spoke he did so in a calm, practical manner that put some of Matthew's unease at bay.

'As difficult as it is going to be, try to keep her as cool as possible until the fever passes. It should only be a day or two, but in one as young as Seraphina fever can be extremely dangerous. Try to wake her every two hours, to drink some milk or water. If she can eat, that's good, but she may not feel like it.'

'Is there nothing else we can do?' Matthew asked, feeling helpless and frustrated.

'At this point keeping her hydrated and combating the fever are crucial. If need be, bathe her in cold water every few hours, but ensure that she is dried well and changed into clean, dry clothes each time. I can leave an iodine solution for the worst of the rash to reduce itching.'

'So, that is it?' Matthew ran his hand through his hair. 'We just wait and hope she gets better?'

'Matthew...' Isabelle linked her fingers through his, and he felt her hot palm sliding against his cooler one. 'The doctor is doing everything he can.'

'There is an outbreak,' Dr Taylor added. 'I will be with many other patients—probably for weeks—but I will come back to check on her every morning and evening, Your Grace.' Then he bowed in Matthew's direction. 'My lord, your daughter is healthy and strong. Her chances are good.'

Matthew didn't even try to deny his claim to Sera. If their physical similarities weren't enough, then the fact that he was seemingly losing his mind in her sickroom most assuredly was.

'Dr Taylor—'

Matthew braced himself for Isabelle's denial—waited for her to deny that he was Sera's father.

'May I offer you some refreshment? Maybe something to take with you if you're going to be out all night?'

Dr Taylor bowed. 'Thank you, Your Grace. I would appreciate that.'

Isabelle nodded, but it was Mary who quickly left the room to see that something was prepared for the doctor.

'My lord?' The young man started putting his stethoscope back into his bag. 'If I may offer one last word of advice?'

Matthew nodded once.

'Should you need a second opinion, then, please, seek one. But do not let any doctor give her an emetic or prescribe blood-letting. There is new scientific evidence that neither method works for measles, and in one as young as Seraphina they could cause irreparable damage by stressing her body further. She is too small to attempt such practices.'

'You are awfully young to be so confident,' Matthew observed.

Dr Taylor did not seem offended. Instead, he smiled, as if he knew exactly how good he was. 'If any doctor insists on either, ask him how many of his patients have succumbed to measles.' He snapped the top of his medical bag closed. 'In my ten years of practice I have not yet lost any patient to this particular disease.' He started for the door, Isabelle following. 'And I'll be damned if my first is going to be a duchess's daughter.'

'Thank you for coming so quickly, Dr Taylor,' Isabelle said at the door. 'And for your discretion, as always.'

Perhaps Matthew should be more concerned, but he knew that secrecy was not an insignificant part of the doctor's profession in his treatment of members of high society.

'I'll check on your staff before I leave,' said the doctor.

'I will show you downstairs.' Willa moved to escort him.

'Thank you, Lady Windhurst.' Dr Taylor paused one last time before leaving. 'Your Grace, if I may be so bold… You should be resting and hydrating too.'

The door clicked shut behind him, leaving them momentarily alone with the Countess.

Isabelle exhaled deeply and turned to rest her back against the door. Her eyes were tired, the worry in them clear. Her typically straight posture was rounded, as if she were carrying an immense weight. Her hair had been loosely braided, leaving several long strands to escape. They were plastered to her face, and although he had not looked closely before, while he'd been focused on Sera's diagnosis, his eyes narrowed on the telltale redness spreading around her eyes and up her neck.

'You are unwell.'

She nodded tiredly. 'I thought it was from the mask,' she said. 'But it's the measles rash.' She shook her head. 'I've had a scratchy throat for days and I didn't—'

Matthew swore. He went to her, covering the space between

them in two large steps. His hands moved to her face, tilting her chin up so that he could see the rash even as he gauged the severity of her fever with his touch.

'I am fine,' Isabelle insisted.

'The doctor checked her before you arrived, Matthew,' his mother said from her position by Seraphina's crib.

He didn't know what to say. He had no idea how to express the crippling fear that suddenly consumed him.

Isabelle caught his wrists, holding his hands against her fevered cheeks. 'I'm going to be fine. But Sera... Matthew, I need you...'

'Tell me what to do,' he begged.

Isabelle looked to his mother. 'I think it's time we woke her up and tried to get her to take some milk. Maybe a cold bath?'

The Countess nodded her confirmation and walked to the corner of the room to the bell-pull as if it were her own house.

'The doctor knew?' his mother asked. 'That Matthew is Seraphina's father?'

Matthew glanced at his mother in surprise. He had assumed that the doctor had put two and two together—not that he had known all along.

Isabelle took one look at his face and started laughing, her tired chuckles forcing tears to her eyes. 'Well, I had to curse *someone* during my labour,' she said. 'It hardly seemed fair to the poor Duke, given that he was dead—and not responsible for my condition in the first place.'

Matthew smiled, despite his fatigue and worry. His mother laughed. And even though they all knew it was going to be a long few days in Everett Place, the brief flash of humour seemed to breathe a moment of calm, of hope.

But the moment ended too soon—the second his mother leaned into the crib and picked up Seraphina.

Sera opened her eyes, scrunched her little fists together and let out a loud, self-pitying wail. 'Oh, I know, child,' his mother crooned. 'You must feel horrid.'

Seraphina screamed louder in response and Matthew itched to go to her, to take her in his arms and rock her back to sleep. He resisted. Despite her infallible appearance, he knew his mother needed to be useful or she'd go mad with worry—they had that in common.

So he went to Isabelle instead, taking her hand in his and leading her to the bed they'd vacated only hours before. 'You need to rest. My mother and I will look after Seraphina.'

Isabelle's glazed eyes widened as he turned her and started undoing the buttons down the back of her simple gown. 'Matthew—'

'She knows we've had a child,' he teased gently. 'She hardly thinks we did it with our clothes on.'

His mother laughed quietly as she continued to comfort Seraphina, but she turned her back, giving them some privacy.

Isabelle didn't try to stop him as he stripped off her dress, leaving her only in her thin chemise, and while he turned away to lay the gown over a nearby chair she climbed into her bed. By the time he was back at her side, she had closed her eyes.

'I'm so tired,' she murmured.

'Sleep, my love. We'll wake you if there's any change with Sera.'

He covered her with the comforter just as four maids carried in buckets of icy water to pour into the tub. The moment they left, he used the ice block and some strips of fabric to keep Isabelle cool, alternately pressing a cold one to her forehead and rinsing and wringing out the one he'd used previously. In only minutes, she was fast asleep.

Mary knocked quietly and entered the room. 'Willa and Leo have left,' she said. 'I didn't think there was any point in us all being up at the same time. They are going to return in the morning, to help where they can.' She placed her hand on Isabelle's cheek. 'She's not as hot as Sera…'

'I think she's as exhausted as she is unwell,' Matthew said. 'It's been a stressful month for her—and that's without her being up every night with Sera. We should let her sleep.'

'Matthew,' his mother interrupted, 'why don't you leave Mary to cool Isabelle while you help me with Sera's bath?'

He looked to Mary.

'I can manage, my lord.'

'Matthew? Please,' said his mother.

Mary nodded, her eyes fixed intently on his face. 'I was wrong about you,' she said. 'But I had no reason to believe you loved them.'

Matthew opened his mouth, the denial coming instinctively, if not truthfully, but Mary only patted his hand in a gesture that was surprisingly maternal for a woman so young.

'I'm sorry for thinking ill of you. I shall endeavour to be more supportive.'

He exhaled tiredly, sensing that there was no point in pretending that he did not love them when everybody clearly saw how he felt.

'As long as you continue to care for my girls, I don't mind if you don't like me.'

'Nonetheless, it is a beneficial side benefit.' Mary waved him away with a small flick of her fingers. 'Go and see to your daughter, my lord. I shall stay with Izzy.'

Matthew rose off the bed and walked to where his mother held a sobbing Seraphina. The moment she saw him approach Sera unstuck her face from the Countess's neck and held out both arms to him.

'Hello, my princess.' He took her familiar weight, felt his own panic settle slightly once she was in his arms. He kissed her fever-flushed face. 'Do you feel terrible, darling?' he crooned, lowering his voice for her.

'Ya!' Sera cried and nodded, her lower lip wobbling.

He rubbed her back for a long moment, rocking from side to side in a rhythm that was as instinctual as eating or sleeping. 'You're going to be fine...'

'Matthew?'

He looked up to find both his mother and Mary Lambert staring at him, their faces showing equal surprise. 'Yes?'

'We need to get her into the cold bath.'

A shiver ran through his own body at the thought of the chilly water. Still, he shifted Sera to his hip and took off his shoes, then passed her back to his mother for a moment, so that he could remove his jacket and waistcoat.

He walked through to the dressing room with Seraphina and gently lowered her into the tub. The moment she felt the cold water she started screaming, her little hands reaching for him as she tensed her chubby legs and tried to lever herself out of the uncomfortable situation.

'I know... I know, beautiful...'

Seraphina didn't calm—if anything, she screamed louder. Unsure of what to do, or how to help her, Matthew supported her tiny back with one hand and climbed, fully dressed, into the frigid water with her.

Seraphina's shock at this untoward situation stopped her screams. She watched him, her sad grey eyes huge in her face, as he spread his trousered legs either side of her, making sure she was stable in the slippery bathtub.

His own breath came out in a stuttering exhalation as his body grew acclimatised to the cold.

'This is bloody awful, isn't it?' he asked as the water soaked through the layers of his clothes.

Seraphina nodded and reached for his leg in reply, her discomfort momentarily forgotten by this strange turn of events. While she was distracted, he cupped the cold water in his palms and let it fall down her nightdress, where he knew her skin was angry with red splotches. She shivered like a wet cat and turned to look up at him, her face set in an expression of horrified betrayal.

'Sorry, my love,' he murmured, not quite able to hide his grin.

'Try splashing,' his mother commented from the door, holding a towel in her hands.

Matthew obliged, using one large palm to splash water in Seraphina's direction, turning the uncomfortably cold bath into a game that had the child squealing with delight—and leaving the dressing room in a puddle of water.

They played for only a few minutes, alternately splashing one another and laughing, but once Sera started shivering with cold, Matthew picked her up and handed her to his mother, who was waiting nearby with the towel.

She wrapped Seraphina in it, leaving a corner of fabric loose to rub over his daughter's downy head. Matthew stood up in the tub. He was soaked through, his clothes dripping with what seemed like buckets of water.

'I'll have Mary find some clothes for you until one of the footmen can go to the house and fetch fresh garments.' His mother turned to leave, only pausing to add, 'You know, despite your past mistakes I've always been proud of you, Matthew. You are a remarkable son.'

Surprised by the compliment, Matthew simply replied, 'Thank you, Mother.'

'I am sorry for the way I reacted when I first saw Seraphina. To assume that you were entirely to blame was unfair of me. Regardless, I've never been prouder of you than I am now. Having a remarkable son is easy—in fact, I'm sure most women think their sons are remarkable, even when they are not. But knowing that I have raised a man who has turned into a remarkable father... Well, if this wasn't all so secretive, I would find myself rather braggadocious about my own parenting abilities.'

Unable to contain his amusement, Matthew raised a single brow. 'Should I say congratulations?'

His mother laughed, making Seraphina giggle too. 'One day he will know how I feel,' she told Sera, and exited the room, her granddaughter in her arms.

Chapter Twenty

True to his word, Dr Taylor came back every morning and evening to check on the household, only staying long enough to update his care instructions and leave additional iodine solutions before hurrying off to the other affected London families in his care.

Willa and Leo came each morning too, and stayed all through the day to help with Sera and the servants, so that the others could rest and try to recuperate for the long night ahead.

While Isabelle slept on and off through her raging fever, Matthew, his mother and Mary, with help from Meg, Tess and Gordon, took turns tending to their eight patients.

On the third morning the doctor took one look at Matthew and Isabelle—the former sitting in a chair by the bed, the latter propped upright on a mountain of pillows—and declared, 'You both need to sleep. Seraphina will be fine without you for a few hours.' Dr Taylor merely raised one sardonic brow when they both nodded tiredly and asked, 'And how are my patients this morning?'

'We bathed Sera three times last night.'

Matthew, who had got into the tub each time with his daughter over the past three nights, had been as miserable as she had by their last soaking. Just the thought of it now had a shiver of dread passing through his entire body.

'The last time was just after midnight. By then her fever seemed to have subsided, so we let her sleep through the rest of the night.'

Dr Taylor chafed his hands together, warming them, and then bent over the crib where Seraphina was fast asleep. He placed his hand on her forehead. 'Her fever has broken. That's good; she's through the worst of it.' He placed his stethoscope against her tiny chest, falling quiet as he listened to her heartbeat. 'She is going to be fine.'

Isabelle closed her eyes in relief. Although he wasn't sure she was aware of having done it, Matthew felt her hand seek his on the bed and hold on.

Matthew returned the squeeze, too relieved to do anything except ask, 'So that's it?'

'Continue to monitor her. Let her sleep as much as she can. When she wakes make sure she stays hydrated and eats. The rash will last another seven to ten days. It will look unsightly,' he warned, 'but it won't do her any harm so long as you keep her clean and apply the iodine to reduce irritation. Try not to let her scratch, and keep her indoors until the rash has gone.'

Dr Taylor approached the bed.

'If I may examine you, Your Grace?'

Isabelle smiled tiredly at him. 'Of course, Dr Taylor,' she replied, her words punctuated by a hacking cough that Matthew felt in his own chest.

The doctor asked her to lean forward, and once she'd complied, placed the stethoscope on her back. He kept his expression neutral, but Matthew was watching the doctor's face, and he saw the man's eyes dampen.

'What is it?' he asked.

Dr Taylor ignored him. 'Your Grace, when did the cough start?'

'Early this morning,' Matthew replied for her.

He'd been lying next to her, listening to her ragged breathing the entire night, so he knew exactly when she'd started coughing—that was why he'd propped her on the pillows.

'Why?'

'There is fluid in your lungs, Your Grace,' Dr Taylor replied, and gently leaned Isabelle back onto the pillows.

Isabelle did not seem surprised at all. She nodded and closed her eyes. 'I do feel rather the worse for wear.' She inhaled a deep breath once she'd finished talking, as if even that short sentence had exhausted her.

'What does that mean?' Matthew demanded, growing increasingly frustrated.

'The Duchess has pneumonia,' the doctor stated blandly.

'No!' The word was out of his mouth before he could think.

'I assure you, my lord—'

'How is that possible?' he asked, his voice rising in his fear. 'She was feeling better just yesterday!'

'It's a common secondary symptom of the measles disease. Your Grace…?' Dr Taylor cleared his throat. 'This will get a lot worse before it gets better.'

'I understand,' Isabelle replied calmly.

Matthew pushed back his chair and stood, unable to sit still, unable to keep silent while they talked as if nothing was the matter. He paced to the window, stopped, turned, and then paced to the other side of the room.

'Matthew?'

He raised one hand to the back of his neck, pulling it down as if he might relieve his fear if he only placed enough pressure there.

'Matthew!' Isabelle rasped again.

He took one deep breath to try and calm himself and turned to face her. 'Duchess?'

'You need to have Mary fetch Mr Briggs—my solicitor.'

He frowned. 'No.' He shook his head. 'We're not even close to having to think about…'

He couldn't even say the word—couldn't even think about Isabelle without any life in her.

Isabelle looked to the doctor.

He shrugged. 'You are young and strong. There is no reason that you shouldn't live through this.' The doctor paused, his eyes finding Matthew's. 'But—'

'Don't!' Matthew said immediately.

'Healthier people have succumbed,' the doctor said gravely. 'One third of all patients who catch a contagious disease die— not from the illness itself, but from pneumonia. My lord, it is never too early to have one's affairs in order.'

'Matthew,' Isabelle wheezed, clearly growing agitated, 'if I die, Luke and Seraphina will be left as wards of the Chancery Court. I can't let that happen...'

Matthew's blood chilled at the thought.

'We need to have Briggs organise everything—even if it's just a precaution.' Isabelle drew in a deep breath that rattled through her chest. 'I should have done it before, only... I've never been sick—not seriously. But I of all people should know how quickly...' She didn't finish the sentence.

Matthew was torn between wanting to deny the possibility that Isabelle would succumb and doing what he knew was best for Luke and Sera. His soul rebelled at the idea of the Duchess gone, her chest unmoving, her beautiful big eyes blank, her smile silent. She was *his*, goddammit. She couldn't leave now that he'd finally found her again.

'I'll ask Mary to send for him.'

Matthew left the room before either Isabelle or the doctor could see how much this diagnosis had affected him. He needed to be strong for Isabelle, for the children, but the moment he was alone outside the bedroom he slumped against the wall and closed his eyes.

Just for a moment, he thought, exhausted from the last few minutes—from the last few days.

Last night he'd finally thought that things were turning to the good. He'd felt Seraphina's fever receding each time he'd checked on her, and he'd sensed she was out of the worst of it. But this... Isabelle catching lung fever... This was something he had not expected and was not prepared for.

'Matthew?'

He opened his eyes to find his mother standing further down the corridor with Luke at her side. Both of them were watching him cautiously, as if they knew he would not be collapsed against the wall for any small reason.

He tried to smile. 'You can send word to Father that Seraphina will be fine,' he stated, knowing that his father and his sisters had been confused by the turn of events even as they had been worried about the Duchess and her family.

His mother nodded, but, sensing his dread, did not smile. 'And Isabelle?' she asked.

Matthew's eyes flickered to Luke as he wondered what to do. The boy was nine. He was old enough to do so many things, but Matthew had no idea how honest he should be with him—if at all. There was nothing either of them could do for Isabelle except wait, and it seemed futile to have the boy worrying.

'She is not feeling very well, but she's strong,' he said, settling on a deliberate half-truth that somehow still felt like a lie.

Luke nodded, his relief obvious. 'May I see them?'

'Of course.' Matthew reached out a hand and gave Luke's shoulder a reassuring squeeze. 'Your sister is sleeping, but Izzy is awake. She is with the doctor.'

Matthew waited until Luke had knocked on the door and entered before turning back to his mother. Unlike Luke, whose childish faith made him believe what Matthew had told him, his mother looked drawn and pale.

'What is it?' she asked.

'Pneumonia.'

She inhaled a sharp breath. 'What does the doctor say?'

'It is going to get worse before it gets better.'

He closed his eyes and pinched the bridge of his nose with his thumb and forefinger, staving off what felt like the unfamiliar burn of tears.

'Isabelle has asked for her solicitor to...' He couldn't finish the sentence.

He didn't have to, either. His mother came to him.

She placed her palm on his cheek. 'Preparing for the worst is what any good mother would do, Matthew. It does not mean that she has any intention of dying.'

'I don't know what to do,' he countered restlessly. 'I feel so useless.'

'Sometimes there is nothing you can do except love a person and be with them.' She slowly lowered her hand, glancing towards the closed door of the bedroom. 'Have you told her how you feel?'

He shook his head. 'She's not ready to hear it.'

'Matthew, if you do not tell her and something happens, you will regret it for ever. It's important to tell people that you cherish them when you have the chance.' Her grey eyes, so similar to his, tracked his face. 'Why are you so afraid? It's not like you...'

'I've never had *cause* to be afraid before,' he said honestly. 'I never even knew this type of fear existed before this week.' He unconsciously raised his fisted hand to rub it over his aching heart. 'I haven't been able to sleep for the constant need to look into Sera's crib and count her tiny breaths, or stare at Isabelle's chest as it rises and falls. I feel like a madman. If anything were to happen to either of them...' he said, and shook his head suddenly, rebelling at even the thought of everything that could go wrong. 'No. I can't even consider it.'

Feeling panicked by the possibility, and by what Isabelle had asked him to do, he turned and walked blindly away from the Countess without further explanation.

Despite Matthew's insistence, Isabelle absolutely refused to see her solicitor in her bedchamber. She would not lie abed while she discussed the future of her children with Mr Briggs, irrespective of how comfortable she felt with the man.

'You are aging me, Duchess,' Matthew murmured as he helped her down the stairs, one arm around her waist to support her.

Isabelle laughed—and regretted the action immediately when she started coughing. Pain lanced through her chest with each expulsion of air, and although she'd just washed, using a basin and a cloth, sweat dampened her back and chest with the small exercise.

She paused halfway down the stairs to take a break, exhausted from the coughing jag.

Matthew grunted and then, without a word, leaned down and picked her up.

'Matthew...' She sighed tiredly. 'I'm perfectly capable of walking.'

'I like carrying you,' he countered, stealing any further argument from her. He tightened his arms slightly. 'I like the way you fit perfectly against me.'

At a loss for what to say, Isabelle merely rested her head on his shoulder as he carried her to the study.

Gordon opened the door for them, revealing Leo, Willa, Mary, the Countess and Mr Briggs. And as Matthew carried her gently to the settee, Isabelle tried her best not to flush with mortification at the scene she was creating.

But any awkwardness over the situation did not have time to grow as Wilhelmina exclaimed, 'Good God, Izzy! You look positively awful!'

Leo snorted.

Mary smiled and shook her head.

'I must be honest,' Isabelle rasped as Matthew placed her down, 'I have felt better.'

She wheezed, and the sound sawed through the room, adding a gravitas to her voice that she wished could have been avoided.

Matthew sat down next to her, and it was Isabelle who took his hand in hers, needing to be the one to acknowledge what it was they were doing. He looked at her for a long moment, but it was only once she nodded that he turned back to the room and began.

'Thank you all for coming...'

As if sensing that this was no ordinary occasion, everyone hurried to find a seat. Mr Briggs sat down opposite Isabelle, giving her his full attention. He was a tall, thin man, with kind eyes and a wide smile that instantly eased some of the sick dread collecting in her stomach.

'Your Grace,' he began, 'I am so sorry to hear that you have been ill.'

'I have pneumonia,' Isabelle said matter-of-factly. 'And while I am certain that I will be fine, it has made me realise that my affairs are not in order, Mr Briggs.'

'Hogwash!' Willa exclaimed. 'You have years to mull over any dreary business.'

Willa opened her mouth to say more, but before she could

Leo gently placed his hand over hers and shook his head, stopping her.

Isabelle replied gently, 'Willa, it's just a precaution. I have no intention of dying. But we cannot ignore the possibility.' She turned back to the solicitor. 'Mr Briggs?'

Simon Briggs stood immediately, bowing for the second time. 'Your Grace... If I may use your desk?'

Isabelle nodded, and the solicitor took his leather case to the large surface.

'You have only to tell me what you would like and I shall draft a document within a day and have it returned for your signature tomorrow.'

'Today,' Isabelle insisted tiredly. 'I will sign the draft today— just in case.'

Briggs nodded cautiously. 'Very well.' He removed a paper and pen from his case. 'Whenever you are ready.'

'It's simple, really. I have only three requests. Upon my *eventual* death, I transfer full guardianship rights of my daughter, Seraphina, to Lord Ashworth and his family.'

'That may be difficult, Your Grace. As a woman, you cannot assign guardianship in your will—'

Isabelle smiled at the solicitor, taking any sting out of her next words. 'He is her father.'

Briggs's eyes rounded with surprise. 'I see.'

'It is not what you think, Mr Briggs...' Isabelle began.

'It is not my concern, Your Grace. My loyalty lies with the Dukedom, to the current Duke of Everett, and to you, as the person whom I believe cares for him most in the world. The rest...' he leaned forward, lowering his voice '...is perhaps best kept confidential.'

Isabelle nodded, but the man's loyalty had brought the burn of tears to her eyes. 'Mr Briggs, if I am not here to look after Luke, I would like you to approach the Chancery Court and request to serve as his guardian. Gareth St Claire surely could not intervene if Luke was legally bound to the executor of the Dukedom. While I cannot legally assign his guardianship, I would like you to include this as my wish, so that the Chancery may consider it above granting guardianship to a stranger.'

'Your Grace…' Briggs shook his head.

'I trust you to do your best by my children, Mr Briggs, as you have done by the Dukedom these past twenty-two years.'

'I am honoured, Your Grace. Truly,' the elderly man insisted. 'However, as only a father can name guardians in a will, perhaps I could make a few suggestions?'

'Please do.'

'Common law states that the next closest relative who cannot inherit should be named guardian.' His astute gaze landed on her hand, which remained linked with Matthew's.

'So, Gareth St Claire, next in line for the Dukedom after Luke, cannot become Luke's guardian,' Isabelle confirmed, remembering when she and Matthew had first discussed the possibility two years ago.

'He cannot,' the solicitor confirmed. 'However, the next closest relatives—'

'My parents?' Isabelle shook her head, thinking back not only on her own lonely childhood, but on her parents' complete lack of interest in Luke and Seraphina. To them, children were not to be seen or heard until they could behave and converse like adults. 'They wouldn't be my first choi—'

Mr Briggs smoothly took over. 'But if you were to remarry, Your Grace, your *husband* would be the most likely candidate to petition for guardianship.'

The room became eerily quiet. Nobody talked as his implication sank in. Isabelle's mind raced, her thoughts a jumbled mix of confused longing and calm realisation.

'Mr Briggs, are you saying that were I to remarry, upon my death, my husband would likely become guardian not only to Seraphina, but Luke as well?'

Briggs nodded. 'Given that they would to all appearances be his stepchildren, and not his blood relatives, he would still have to petition, Your Grace. But with your express wishes and my recommendation, and considering the children's welfare, it would be a logical approval. Lord Ashworth's family estate is notoriously lucrative. Unlike any other guardian, he would have no financial motive for tampering with the Duke's estate. Coupled with the fact that I manage the Duke's finances separately…it would be difficult for the Chancery to deny that Lord Ashworth would be the best candidate for guardianship—at least until the Duke turns fourteen and may choose his guardian himself.'

As if aware of the enormity of what he was suggesting, Briggs added, 'I understand that the timing is a concern, Your Grace. But if you could arrange a special licence in the next few days—'

'Hours,' the Countess of Heather interjected. 'The Earl plays bridge with William… I mean, the archbishop. We could have a licence within hours.'

'And if you *wanted* to remarry, of course,' Briggs continued, 'it would be one way to keep the children together in the unlikely event of your death.'

'We have some concerns.' It was Matthew who spoke now. 'About how our marriage would affect Seraphina. Her resemblance to me is not insignificant.'

Isabelle's heart clenched with fear at the reminder, and yet for the first time she also felt a conflicting warmth spreading over the fear, taking the edge of panic away. Because as she watched Matthew talking to Mr Briggs, trying to find a solution to their predicament, she understood that he would do everything within his power to protect the children, even if that meant denying Seraphina as his own.

'Undoubtedly.' Mr Briggs nodded. 'However, to my way of thinking your options are twofold. You could do as the Duchess suggests, and guarantee a separate legal guardian for each child, or alternatively you could try to keep them together. Of course in the first instance, and in the unlikely event of the Duchess's death, people would assume they knew why Seraphina had been left in your legal care and Luke had not, my lord. My suggestion may result in the same rumours, but the children would most likely be kept together and raised in your care.'

'To clarify: you are saying that, either way, we are not going to avoid a scandal.' Isabelle spoke the words nobody else seemed to want to, and although her voice was clear and calm, her heart pounded with fury.

To be ruined was to be a social pariah. Despite being legally perceived as the Duke's daughter, Seraphina would never escape the whispers. Her peers would use it against her. Many suitors would not even consider her. Sera would grow up in a shame that should not be hers to carry.

Isabelle wondered how it was that a child—*any* child, completely innocent in its circumstances—could be condemned for the way they had been brought into the world? Sera was cherished and loved. She would grow up to be good and kind. She should not have to suffer because of the manner in which she had been conceived.

Mr Briggs's nod was barely perceptible. 'There will be some whispers, undoubtedly. However, so long as the rumours could not be substantiated, and along with my recommendation, they would bear little influence with the Chancery Court.'

'Do we have any other options?' Matthew asked. 'Any way to protect Sera?'

'None that I can think of, given the uncertainty of the Duchess's health and the urgency with which we must act.'

'Are we all forgetting that this may be entirely unnecessary?' Willa interjected.

'I cannot have things undecided and risk leaving the children unprotected,' Isabelle countered immediately.

The fever she could feel raging through her body made her decision easy. She knew that she must decide, and decide soon. And she believed in the deepest corner of her heart that Matthew would do right by both children should she succumb.

Although she had tried to do the right thing by Sera, although she had denied Matthew and his right to claim his daughter, Fate had intervened, and it was Fate that had decided the consequences they all must live with. For consequences there would be.

Moreover, Isabelle *wanted* to be his.

Swallowing the fear that brought tears to her eyes, she turned to face the man who had become integral to her family in such a short period of time. 'Matthew?'

'Yes,' he said immediately.

Keeping their hands linked, he moved to kneel in front of her.

His intense grey eyes bored into hers, and in them she could see her own need, conflict and confusion reflected.

'Isabelle, I've been yours for a long time,' he said. 'And although this isn't how I imagined it, and although I would rather cut my heart out than see you or the children hurt, I can't pretend to be anything but overjoyed that you'll be mine. Marry me—and not just for me. Marry me for our children.' He sighed deeply, his grey eyes filled with emotion. 'Marry me because you *want* to.'

Isabelle heard both her friends' wistful sighs, but she did not turn to look at them. She didn't need anybody else's advice on this one decision. She knew what she wanted. She knew what was right. Right for her and for the children. Moreover, she knew that Matthew, who had lived with his own scandal for years, was willingly subjecting himself to society's judgement once again—for them. And his certainty solidified her own.

'Yes,' she said, her voice hoarse with fever and emotion.

Her words spurred a flurry of activity into the room. The Countess of Heather clapped her hands excitedly. 'I'll see to it immediately,' she said. She paused on her way to the door to ask, 'Isabelle? You don't mind if I organise things for tonight—here? And invite the rest of the family?'

Isabelle shook her head, her eyes finding Matthew's. 'I don't mind.'

He smiled up at her from his position, kneeling on the floor. 'Isabelle...' He shook his head as if he were undone, as if he had no words.

'I trust you,' she said simply.

But her heart leapt in her chest at this half-truth, because trust was the least of it. If she had struggled to admit her love for him before, she had been forced to confront it while she'd watched him care for her family. She loved him, this man who had time and time again been with her when he didn't have to—but wanted to. This man whom she might have for one day, one week, one lifetime...

'I am sorry that it has happened this way.' His thumbs stroked over the backs of her hands. 'I wanted you to choose me on your own—not because you had no choice. But even so, and even with the scandal, I cannot be anything but overjoyed.'

The statement brought a raspy chuckle to Isabelle's throat. 'I don't doubt it,' she said.

And in that moment, in that still second of time when what they were doing sank in, she felt the same happiness spread through her own heart.

'It is strange,' she whispered, just for his ears, 'that I am the happiest I have ever been when I am also the closest to death I have ever come.'

'Don't,' he insisted vehemently. 'Don't say that.'

Mr Briggs cleared his throat, breaking the tender moment. 'Was that all, Your Grace?' he asked. 'I should get this document drawn up.'

'No, I have one more request,' she said.

Matthew hauled himself up onto the settee next to her.

Isabelle looked across the room to her two best friends. 'Should I die, I would like my personal funds distributed thus. One thousand pounds to each of my servants, irrespective of their rank, two thousand pounds each to my butler, Gordon, my maid, Meg, and my nursemaid, Tess. And the remainder to be split equally between my two closest friends: Mary Lambert and Wilhelmina Windhurst.'

'That can be arranged, Your—'

'I refuse.' This absurd statement came from Wilhelmina, of course. 'I don't want your money, Isabelle!' her friend exclaimed. 'I want your company for many years to come.'

'It's just—'

'Yes, we know,' Willa drawled. 'Just a *precaution*.'

'You two have been my best friends. You have supported me even when your own lives were far from ideal. I'll have no use of my money when I'm dead, and Matthew will make sure that the children are taken care of. This is important to me, Willa.'

'Drat!' Willa replied, her tears spilling over for the first time. 'I don't suppose we have a choice but to keep you alive, then?'

'You will stay tonight? I would like you to be here.' Isabelle turned to Mary. 'Both of you.'

'Of course,' Willa stated.

Mary could not voice her consent through the tears in her eyes, but she nodded her promise anyway.

And now their business was concluded there was nothing for Isabelle to do but rest—and wait to be married.

Chapter Twenty-One

By the time evening came, Isabelle could barely talk for fear of falling into one of the coughing fits that left her short of breath and gasping for air. Her entire body was ablaze. Every time she stood too fast the blood in her head seemed to rush to her feet, leaving her light-headed and weak.

She was feeling worse. And even though she was aware that she should be in bed, resting, she was too anxious to complete her wedding to relax. She could not rest until she knew the children would be taken care of.

Isabelle sat patiently next to Willa as Mary put the finishing touches to her hair, adding a single red rose to the simple chignon that Isabelle had insisted upon, given the simple ceremony—and the fact that she would be back in her bed almost as soon as it was over.

'Are you positive this is what you want?' Mary asked quietly, her eyes finding Isabelle's as she moved around the dressing table to speak to her.

Willa and Mary were both watching her face, their worry amplified by their twin looks of concern.

'I'm certain,' she replied, and her voiced was laced with wonder. 'This whole time...even when I didn't know him... I missed him. I thought about him every day for the years that he was gone. Every time I looked at Sera, or got lonely…' She released a wheezing laugh. 'I know it's impossible to love someone after meeting them only once…but I don't think it's impossible to *want* to love someone you've only ever met once. And once was enough for me to know that Matthew was the type of man I wished I had married—the type of man I would want to love. I think I can be afraid—afraid of marriage and of losing my independence—while still recognising that he is what I need to be happy.'

'And love?' Mary asked quietly.

'I do love him.' Isabelle admitted it aloud for the first time. 'He's the only man who's ever adhered to my wishes, who's treated me as an intelligent woman who knows her own mind, instead of someone to be purchased and shelved—and he didn't have to. He's an impossibly good father to Seraphina. And although he hasn't had as much time with Luke, I know in my heart that he would only ever treat both children equally. He makes me feel safe—as if I don't have to worry about everything myself because I trust that he'll be there to share the burden.'

Willa cleared her throat. 'Um… I beg your pardon?'

Isabelle wheezed again as her laugh climbed free. 'It's different. You two…' She took her friends' hands, one in each of hers, and looked at them in turn. 'You two have become so much more than friends. You're the sisters I never had.'

Willa sniffled.

Mary dabbed daintily at her eyes.

'If I die, will you promise to help him?' she asked shakily, knowing it was a momentous burden he would be taking on.

When tears burned her eyes at the thought of losing them, of never seeing the children grow up, of never experiencing life with Matthew by her side, she let them fall unashamedly.

'Matthew has his family, but the children know you. They will need you. Especially Sera… You two know how devastating even a single rumour can be, and now…'

She did not have to finish the sentence. They all knew that the whispers had started already.

Mary replied, 'Of course,' without hesitation. She knew what it was to fear the worst and have those fears realised.

Willa shrugged. 'If it makes you feel better. However, I do not anticipate needing to. You shall be fine.'

'Yes, she will.'

They all turned to see Matthew. He was standing on the threshold, dressed smartly in contrast to Isabelle's well-worn hunter-green day gown, which was the only dress she could bear to have against her feverish skin. His hair was contrastingly dishevelled, as if he had been running his hands through it constantly. His grey eyes were dark with fatigue and worry.

Isabelle tried to smile, but she couldn't quite bank down the overwhelming fear that this might be it—this could be the end of everything she'd only just found. Her lips wobbled with the realisation.

Matthew looked to Mary and Willa. 'May I have a moment?' he asked. 'I will help her down.'

'I don't see why not,' Willa said. 'It's not as if we've adhered to a single tradition anyway.' She paused in front of Matthew and pulled him into a spontaneous hug. 'We're glad to have you, you know.'

Matthew smiled and returned the hug. 'I am glad to be had, Willa.'

Mary followed Willa out of the room, and although she did not hug Matthew, as Willa had done, Isabelle saw the kind smile she shared with him.

The door closed, leaving them alone together. If she'd thought she would be nervous, Isabelle was surprised to find that she was perfectly calm. Content. She looked at Matthew for a long time, taking in the broad shoulders that had held so much the past few days, and the strong hands that had reached out to help without being asked.

He came to her, lifting her easily off the chair and carrying her to the bed before sitting down with her on his lap.

'How are you feeling?' he asked, his hand rising to feel her face. He hissed out a breath before she could reply, the moment he touched her bare skin.

'The fever is coming on in full force now,' she stated, knowing that lying was futile. 'We need to hurry. You already have a blotchy bride; it won't do to have a sweaty one too.'

He didn't argue or try to deny it. And he didn't shrug away from her clammy skin either. 'Okay. But first...' He shifted slightly, making space between them so that he could reach into his jacket pocket. 'There is a tradition in my family,' he began as he pulled out a velvet ring box, 'that the first son receives this ring from the Countess of Heather for his bride.'

He opened the box to reveal a halo ring. A large oval ruby was centred atop the band, surrounded by ten tiny European-cut diamonds that gave the ring the appearance of a flower. It was beautiful.

'It is your mother's?' Isabelle asked uncertainly.

'It *was* my mother's,' he corrected. 'Now it is yours. Until, one day, Luke asks you for it.'

Isabelle understood what he was promising her—that he would treat Luke as his own though they would never share a name or a title. 'The Countess—'

'Has her wedding band,' he said, 'and she has given us her blessing.'

He slid the ring onto her finger.

Isabelle swallowed down the dry lump in her throat and raised her hand between them so that they could both look at the ring. It was slightly too large on Isabelle's finger, but she didn't care.

'Thank you,' she whispered and, placing her hand on his cheek, guided his mouth to hers for a quick kiss. 'I love it.'

'But not nearly as much as you love me,' he said, his arms tightening around her as if he was expecting her to run away at the declaration.

Isabelle tensed on his lap. 'You heard?'

He nodded, his grey eyes dark with emotion. 'I did.'

'I was hoping to tell you in person...' She began to explain, embarrassed that he had heard her tell her two friends how much she loved him before she'd had the chance to tell him herself.

Matthew rested his forehead against hers for a moment. 'How about I go first?'

She nodded.

'After the scandal with Christine, I avoided even the most casual of attachments. I was too afraid to trust myself, let alone anyone else. Until you, Duchess… I've thought about you every day since that night you came to me, sometimes even dreaming of you, so that I would wake in the night, yearning for you. I was with one other woman between you then and you now and it felt wrong—so wrong that I promised myself I would find my way back to you, even if only to prove that it was all a figment of my imagination.'

Isabelle pulled back to look at his face, surprised by the confession.

'I extended my tour so the end of it would coincide with your mourning ending, because I knew that once I was on British soil again I would not be able to resist seeking you out.'

Isabelle was struck speechless by the confession. She stared at him, her heart pounding in her chest.

'I was lucky enough to run into Willa, who invited me to Lady Russell's ball, but even in the days before then I was seeking out our mutual acquaintances—who are surprisingly few—in the hope of an official introduction.'

'Matthew…' She didn't know where to begin.

'I wanted you before I found out about Sera. But from the moment I realised she was my daughter, I knew I would wait a lifetime to make you—all three of you—mine.'

He touched the ruby ring with one finger.

'Duchess, you're going to get through this, and then we're going to have a lifetime together. But I want you to know before we get married that I love you. I have for a while. At least since you threatened to kick me out of your house—the first time. And I would have waited for you.' He kissed her forehead gently. 'I would have waited for ever for you.'

Isabelle closed her eyes, basking in the certainty of his love. 'I've been so afraid for so long,' she whispered, her fingers rising to stroke his face. 'I was afraid of being a widow and afraid of being remarried…afraid of being a mother…afraid of… Well, *everything*. And then you came back. And instead of exposing me or blackmailing me, as I expected, you took some of my burden and stepped into a role you didn't ask for. You put our daughter first. If I wasn't already in love with you as a man, I would love you for being the father that you've become.'

She pulled back so that he could see her eyes when she continued.

'You understand that the fact that I'm leaving my children to your care is all the proof you'll ever need? They have been my entire world for a very long time. If I did not love you with my whole heart, I would not entrust them to you.'

'I know, Duchess. They're mine now too,' he said. 'And if it eases your mind at all,' he said, laughing suddenly, surprising her, 'I have asked Luke for his permission to marry you.'

'Oh...' Isabelle sighed.

'He did not let me off lightly,' he added, grinning. 'He asked me why I wanted to marry you, and then, after I'd convinced him I loved you, he made me promise that I would never let you leave him and Seraphina.' Matthew's deep voice settled over the room. 'He went as far as to insist I move to Everett Place if I could not afford a house big enough for the entire family.'

Isabelle shook her head sadly, even as she smiled at Luke's demands. 'He's always been afraid of being left behind,' she observed. 'It's part of the reason I didn't run from marrying the Duke. I couldn't leave Luke—not when he was so clearly an afterthought for everyone else.'

'Not any more,' Matthew promised, and took her mouth, sealing the vow with a fierce kiss.

Isabelle melted against him, sank into him, drawing from his strength as she deepened the kiss, making it last as long as possible while she still could. She didn't want this moment to end—didn't want to face what she could feel blazing through her.

She groaned when Matthew broke the kiss to nuzzle her neck. His breath came as rapidly as hers as he trailed his lips across her feverish skin. 'Christ, Duchess... Your skin is aflame.'

Isabelle didn't reply. Instead, she pushed herself off his lap, self-conscious of the sweat that was starting to seep through her clothes, and held out one clammy hand for his.

'Shall we?'

Matthew took it and raised it to his lips. 'Yes.'

* * *

By the time he'd placed Isabelle on her feet by the study door, she was glistening with sweat.

'You should be in bed,' he commented.

'The clergyman is hardly going to let you marry someone who cannot get out of her sickbed,' she replied quietly, smiling despite her fatigue.

Her humour did nothing to calm Matthew, who pushed open the study door to find his family, friends and an unfamiliar clergyman his mother had undoubtedly bribed and browbeaten to be there waiting patiently inside for their arrival.

His sisters sat on the settee, with a splotchy red Seraphina between them, acting as if they hadn't discovered they had a niece only hours before. His father and mother were watching the scene, looking somehow smug despite the scandalous circumstances. Willa and Mary were fussing over an enormous flower arrangement that looked eerily familiar, and Leo stood by the fireplace with Caro's husband, Michael Westmoor, talking animatedly with Luke.

All activity stopped as he and Isabelle walked into the room, their hands clasped together. Instead of happy chatter, he heard the room fall quiet. Matthew tensed against it, knowing what they saw: Isabelle was not well—and she was getting worse by the minute.

His mother, thankfully, broke the moment, coming forward with his father in tow. 'We'll save introductions for later,' she said, cutting off the Earl, who had opened his mouth to formally introduce himself. With an impatient wave of her hand and a quick wink in Isabelle's direction, his mother called the clergyman forward.

The ceremony was blessedly quick, with none of the typical prayers or sermonising. Matthew and Isabelle exchanged vows along with the rings that Matthew had given Luke for safekeeping earlier in the day, and even though it was not customary, he couldn't resist kissing his bride the moment they were pronounced husband and wife.

For such a small group, their friends and family raised a significant racket when Matthew gently cupped Isabelle's fevered face in his hands and placed his lips on hers. They clapped and cheered loudly, while Willa released a shrill whistle that had Leo covering his ears despite his grin.

Gordon passed around glasses of champagne, but it was only once the vicar's registry had been signed by both he and Isabelle, and the clergyman had left, that Matthew called for everyone's attention.

He picked up Seraphina from the settee and waited for all eyes to turn to him before starting. 'Thank you all for being here…'

He passed a glass of champagne to Isabelle, before reaching for his own, unconsciously moving it out of Sera's reach when she tried to make a grab for it from her position on his hip.

'We understand that this wedding did not occur under ideal circumstances, but Isabelle and I are grateful to each of you for your love and support. Luke?' He called his new stepson to where they stood. 'Thank you for allowing me the honour of making Izzy my wife. I promise that I will love and cherish all three of you until my dying breath.'

Luke smiled shyly, but Matthew didn't press him to say anything, sensing that the boy was rather overwhelmed by all the attention. Instead, he turned to Isabelle, and the emotions on his face were clear for everyone to see.

'As soon as *my wife*—' he exaggerated the words, drawing another round of laughter from their guests and a blush from Isabelle '—is well, we will celebrate properly. But until then…' He held up his glass. 'Please raise your glasses to Isabelle, the Duchess of Everett and Viscountess Ashworth.'

'To Isabelle!' everyone parroted, and sipped their champagne.

Matthew couldn't resist leaning down to kiss Isabelle again, only pausing when Sera reached up and tapped his face, wanting his attention. He released his wife with a small laugh and turned to give his daughter his attention.

'So impatient,' he said, and placed a kiss on Sera's lips when she pursed them in demand for one.

'No fever?'

He looked down into Isabelle's glazed eyes, his heart softening when he saw the worry in them. 'No, Duchess. She is fine. Worry about yourself now; we're all here to look after Sera.'

The group slowly disbanded, forming clusters of twos and threes around the room as they ate, drank and celebrated the hurried nuptials.

Matthew watched Isabelle closely, and when she grew paler, her breath coming in painful-sounding rattles, he lifted her in his arms and without a single word carried her from the room.

He knew she was truly ill when she did not object, only nestled against him as he carried her up the stairs to her bedroom.

He gently sat her on the edge of the bed as he removed her shoes, stockings and dress. He tried not to show his worry when the dress came away damp in his hands, or when he saw the aggressive red splotches spreading over her beautiful skin. But when she suffered a coughing fit that left her doubled over and gasping for breath, Matthew's blood ran cold with fear.

The past three days had already weakened her considerably, turning her naturally slender frame alarmingly thin. Though her rash was not as bad as Seraphina's, it was still scattered over Isabelle's face and neck, before disappearing beneath her chemise.

Matthew tried not to think about the looming night ahead, focusing instead on each minute that Isabelle remained cognizant.

He propped her against her pillows, leaving the clean bedcovers off her entirely. 'Can you try and drink something, my love?' he asked. 'Dr Taylor should be here soon.'

Isabelle nodded tiredly, but she did not open her eyes again. She managed to drink a half-glass of water before falling asleep, and by the time the doctor arrived, thirty minutes later, she would not wake up at all.

Chapter Twenty-Two

Isabelle slept for three days, not waking when the doctor came to check on her nor when Matthew tried to lever her up to pour some broth down her throat. She tossed and turned, often mumbling nonsensically and clutching the bed-linen agitatedly in her hands. Her breathing was laboured, as if she were running for her life even in her dreams. Her skin, once so golden and healthy, had paled, with her face taking on a blue tinge that put the fear of God into Matthew's very soul. Sweat poured off her small frame, dampening the sheets every few hours as the fever raged through her.

Matthew was helpless to do anything except try to cool her, and cradle her in his arms while his mother, Mary and the maids changed her sheets, talking to her when everyone else retired for a few hours of rest.

Almost seventy hours into her fever dream, Matthew still sat in a chair by Isabelle's bed, watching her chest rise and fall with each breath, despite his itchy, tired eyes and bone-weary body. He counted her breaths, collecting each one with equal parts gratitude and dread.

In another chair in the corner of the room, the doctor dozed. He had come to check on Isabelle earlier in the night and, seeing her condition, had promptly decided to stay and tend her himself—and it was that decision that had confirmed Matthew's worst fear: Isabelle was fading.

There was a gentle knock on the door, and when whoever stood outside did not immediately enter, Matthew pushed himself to his feet and went to open it. He was surprised to find the nursemaid, Tess, standing outside, with Seraphina in her arms and Luke at her side.

Both children were dressed in their nightshirts, reminding him that it was nearing midnight and that they were supposed to be in bed—though they were wide awake.

'Forgive me, my lord,' Tess began, curtseying awkwardly under her burden. 'His Grace wanted to see the Duchess, and I could not dissuade him...'

Matthew's eyes sought Luke. The boy stood at Tess's side, trying to see past Matthew's large frame to where Isabelle slept.

Matthew stepped aside immediately, making space for Luke to come into the room. 'Thank you, Tess.' He held out his arms for Sera, sighing deeply when his daughter's familiar weight was transferred to him. 'I'll make sure they get to bed.'

'My lord?' she queried, as if preparing to argue.

'Sleep, Tess. There's no point in us both being awake.'

Matthew sat down again by Isabelle's bed, with Seraphina cuddled against his chest and Luke hovering at the bedside, unsure of himself or what to do.

'Will she die?' the boy asked quietly.

Matthew's head snapped up at the question. The young Duke's green eyes were wide with fear and brimming with tears—tears that the child immediately tried to knuckle away.

'Luke,' Matthew said softly, 'come here.'

Luke walked around the bed to stand in front of Matthew, his entire body rigid with uncertainty.

Matthew raised one hand and placed it on Luke's bony shoulder, forcing the young Duke to meet his gaze. If he had thought that lying to the boy to protect him had been difficult, then telling him the truth in order to prepare him was ten times more so.

'I don't know,' he said honestly after a long moment. 'Izzy is very sick.'

Luke's tears started falling more rapidly, his lips wobbling even as he fought to stay composed.

'But we're doing everything that we can to make her better.' Matthew nodded in the doctor's direction. 'The doctor is staying nearby in case we need him.' He gave the boy's shoulder a squeeze.

Luke nodded and lowered his eyes. His voice, when he spoke, was quiet and full of dread. 'I'm sorry I hit you with my ball,' the child whispered.

Matthew, who had always thought the boy's aim truer than anyone else had imagined, smiled tiredly. 'That's of no matter. I know that you love Izzy, Luke. And that you were protecting her and your sister.'

'She's not my sister.'

Matthew drew back in surprise, frowning. 'Who told you that?'

'I'm not a baby,' Luke said, growing petulant. 'People think I am—but I know things! I know that my father forced Izzy to marry him, and that she never wanted to. She married him because she didn't want to leave *me*. And I know that you come and visit Sera at night—'

'Luke, I have never thought you a baby.' Realising that the Duke knew far more than he'd ever have guessed, Matthew looked into the boy's eyes.

'Everybody treats me like I'm one.'

Matthew nodded seriously. 'We don't mean to. I think it's just because we don't have any experience,' he admitted. 'Both me and Izzy, we… We're learning as we go.' Matthew searched for the right words through his exhaustion. 'Luke, you are a remarkably clever young man—nobody doubts that. And you're clever enough to know that blood doesn't make a family. Izzy is not your mother—she is your stepmother—and yet you love her as if she *were* your mother.'

'I love Sera too,' the boy said. 'But I know she's not my sister.'

'Okay. But you have to love her and protect her as if she were your sister,' Matthew said. 'Because that's what we do. We love and protect the people in our family—even if we don't share their blood.'

Luke straightened his thin shoulders. 'I know.'

'And I need your help.' Matthew ran his palm over Sera's head. 'Because I don't know what I'm doing.'

It felt strange to admit his biggest fear to someone so young, but Matthew knew that it was important for Luke to understand that some fears did not subside, no matter how grown-up you were.

The Duke seemed surprised by the admission. He considered Matthew in silence for a long moment, before nodding. 'I will help,' he said. 'But if Izzy dies, you cannot take Seraphina away.'

'I can,' Matthew countered. 'But I will take you with me too.' He watched the emotions flit over Luke's face—fear, then realisation, and along with it hope and finally, relief—and he promised himself that this boy would never feel anything but entirely wanted, completely belonging.

Luke looked at him, then nodded. 'I suppose if my solicitor says it's fine, then I *could* come with you.'

Matthew bit his cheek to stop himself from grinning. Behind him, the doctor's subtle throat-clearing told him that the man was fighting the urge to laugh too. But Matthew smiled at Luke and finished their serious discussion by saying, 'But for now, we're going to focus on getting Izzy better.'

'Yes.' Luke nodded, and turned back to face the bed, his shoulders rounding with a very adult fear when he saw Isabelle, so small in the centre of the large bed. 'Can I sit next to her?'

'Of course.'

Luke climbed onto the bed and lay down next to Isabelle, making sure not to jostle her. He kept his back to Matthew and Sera, but Matthew saw the way Luke linked his fingers with Isabelle's, holding her hand even though she did not return the pressure.

Luke was asleep in minutes, his body only slightly smaller than Isabelle's. Keeping Seraphina against his chest as she dozed, Matthew pushed himself to stand and went to fetch one of the clean blankets that was lying in wait for the next bed-change rotation. Using one arm, he unfolded the blanket and draped it over Luke, pausing only to sigh tiredly and run one hand through the boy's hair.

'You seem to be going through a baptism by fire,' the doctor commented.

'You have children?' asked Matthew.

'Two,' Dr Taylor confirmed.

'Please…' Matthew laughed tiredly '…tell me it gets easier.'

Samuel Taylor tucked his hands into his pockets and smiled. 'Each age has it challenges. Although this—this sickness,' he clarified, 'is always difficult, irrespective of what age a child is.' He paused for a moment. Then, 'If I may say so, my lord, you are doing rather well, all things considered. I dare say you will be fine.'

Even though Matthew did not have the doctor's confidence, he did not have the energy to argue. Instead, he said, 'Thank you, Doctor,' and sat back down with Seraphina to wait.

Matthew woke with a start to someone shaking him roughly. He came to immediately, his eyes finding the bed for fear that Isabelle had worsened. She was fast asleep, her chest rising and falling evenly, but Luke was awake and watching her face in silence.

'Matthew!'

He turned to find Mary at his side, her green eyes wild with panic. 'He's here—Gareth St Claire. He's demanding to speak with Isabelle. Something about the wedding…'

Exhausted from the long battle with measles and pneumonia, frustrated by his own helplessness, and furious at the gall of the bastard, showing up now of all times, Matthew slowly stood, ready for a fight.

He gently extricated Seraphina from where she slept against his chest and, walking around the bed, placed his daughter on Isabelle's other side. 'Could you watch her?' he asked the doctor. 'I'll send her nursemaid up in a minute.'

Dr Taylor nodded.

'What are you going to do?' Mary whispered fervently.

'Get rid of the bastard,' Matthew replied. 'Once and for all.'

'Should I call the solicitor?'

'No.' He tipped his shoulders arrogantly, considered the question again, and then corrected himself. 'Only if I kill the man.'

Mary paled. 'Matthew…'

He marched for the door without replying, too angry to modulate his mood, too enraged even to attempt to be rational. Gareth St Claire had been a thorn in Isabelle's side for long enough. Well, not any more.

He descended the stairs two at a time, his heavy footfall echoing through the cavernous hall of Everett Place.

At the bottom of the stairs stood Gordon, barring Gareth St Claire's entry to the house. The old butler's back was straight, his hands fisted at his sides as he went head to head with the unwelcome guest.

'Her Grace is ill,' the butler was saying. 'You may come back when she is recovered—'

'Who are *you* to talk to *me* like that?' Gareth St Claire demanded.

The man had the same small, round frame and blue eyes as Matthew remembered the late Duke having. His clothes were finely tailored. His hair neatly trimmed. But his manner was rotten to the core.

Before the butler could reply, Matthew took a deep breath to regulate his fury, and said, 'Gordon runs this household on behalf of the Duke and my wife, the Duchess of Everett.'

His statement, and the ice-cold tone with which he had delivered it, travelled down the stairs and through the hall, causing both men to turn and peer up at him.

Before either could move, Matthew continued, 'And who, might I ask, are *you*, storming into a house that is not yours when half its inhabitants are in their sickbeds?'

'I am Gareth St Claire!' he replied, puffing out his chest like a peacock.

It was a pity, though, that Matthew was on the hunt. 'I'm sorry—*who*?'

'The late Duke of Everett's cousin,' Mr St Claire clarified, the first hint of a blush working its way up his neck.

'Ah, so you are Luke's *second* cousin?' Matthew calmed his voice, affecting surprise. 'Apologies… Had I known we were receiving distant relations I would have been more prepared.' He turned to Gordon, who stood completely still, awaiting instruction. 'Gordon, please have some tea brought into the study for me and Mr St Claire.'

'My lord.' Gordon bowed and left to complete his task, his head held high.

Matthew led the way to the study, knowing that Gareth St Claire would follow without prompting. Once they were inside he sat down at the late Duke's desk and, resting his elbows on the surface, steepled his fingers and waited for the man to speak.

'I have heard that you and Isabelle are married?' Gareth began, wasting no time at all.

'You have heard correctly.'

'This entire situation reeks of scandal,' he wheezed, dropping his significant girth into a nearby chair. 'First, Isabelle is conveniently with child, only weeks after my cousin died—'

'I think you will find that she was with child while he was still alive,' Matthew drawled. His eyes snapped to Gareth's face, and he purposely let his rage show. 'Unless… I do beg your pardon,' he said, keeping his voice contrastingly devoid of emotion. 'Are you implying that the Duchess—my wife—miraculously fell pregnant at eighteen years of age by someone else in the mere two weeks she was married to your cousin?'

Gareth had the grace to blush. 'No. Not at all. I am prepared to admit that the child—'

'Seraphina.'

'Yes… That *Seraphina* was a happy coincidence. But the situation surrounding Isabelle's illness and your urgent marriage, on the other hand, is questionable.'

'In what way?' Matthew held up one hand, halting the man from replying as he added, 'And before you answer that, consider your situation, *cousin*. You are in the Duke's house, accusing his stepmother, the Duchess of Everett, and his stepfather, the Viscount Ashworth, future *Earl* of Heather, of…?' He stopped abruptly. Frowned. 'I apologise… What are you accusing us of, exactly?'

'The situation—'

'A love-match between a widowed duchess and a titled peer?'

'It was rather hasty...'

'What reason had we to wait?' Matthew countered. 'The Duchess has had one white wedding and did not care for another, and *I* certainly did not want one.'

'But—'

'Your coming here, at a time when my wife is *bedridden*, not to congratulate her on her wedding or to check how your young cousins are faring in the wake of the measles epidemic... Well, it shows your true colours, *Mr* St Claire.'

Gareth huffed out an indignant breath. 'Well, I never—'

'You are a vile, greedy man who would suck the life out of a woman and her children like a leech at the first opportunity.' Matthew leaned forward in his chair, lowering his voice ominously when he added, 'Let me be perfectly clear when I say that the Duke of Everett has the full support of the Heather earldom.'

'And that of Lord Russell and Lord Windhurst,' said Willa.

'And that of Lord Westmoor,' Caro added, fortifying Willa's statement.

Matthew looked up to see Willa and Mary standing in the doorway. His father, mother and two sisters were standing behind them, forming a small but mighty army.

Gareth St Claire balked, his face whitening with rage.

'While my family, and my *connections*, span continents,' Matthew continued, 'you—a middling country squire—would dare to insult my *wife* and her children. Your own cousin's progeny,' he added, though it burned to deny Seraphina.

'I did not mean to cause offence...' Gareth St Claire started backtracking immediately. 'I only thought that, g-given the hasty nuptials, it was my familial obligation to e-ensure that Isabelle was not being taken advantage of.'

'Mr St Claire, given that you have met my wife, I find it difficult to believe that you would ever think her capable of being taken advantage of.' Matthew paused, letting the silence build. 'No. The only reason you come here at such a time is that you believe the situation might be extorted to suit your own base needs.' He leaned back in the Duke's chair. 'Let me assure you, I have married the Duchess because I love her, and because every second I was apart from her was torture. I married her *quickly* because once I found her I wanted no possibility of giving her any time to discover how completely above me she is in every way.'

Gareth mumbled a nonsensical reply to that.

'If there is nothing else, I believe I should be getting back to my wife now.' Matthew pushed his chair back and rounded the desk, only pausing to wait for Gareth to catch up so that he could show the man out—for good.

As soon as the aggrieved relative was on the outside steps, Matthew closed the door in his face and leaned his back against it.

His friends and family crowded into the hall, watching him in stunned silence like a crowd watching a mercurial tiger at the zoo.

Matthew felt mad with fatigue and worry and anger. He raked his hands through his hair.

'Good lad!' His father raised his fist in victory.

'Hear, hear!' Willa seconded.

'*That's* going to come back and bite me on the arse,' Matthew muttered, unable to feel quite as triumphant as the others.

'It's doubtful,' his father stated. 'Bullies are notorious for only advancing when they perceive an easy target.'

'If the rumours break, and a scandal—'

'Matthew.' His mother cut him off. 'Whatever comes now is unavoidable.' When he didn't reply, she advanced, her brows raised. 'You knew that this would happen when you married Isabelle. You have dealt with it to the best of your ability. And now it is done—at least for the time being. So? Do you regret your decision?'

'No. Never.'

'Well, then.' She stepped past him and started climbing the stairs, essentially ending the conversation.

The Earl clapped him on the shoulder. 'If and when, my boy... We'll worry about it if and when we have to. For now, show me where I can find a drink.'

'Mary, could you show my family to the parlour?' he asked, even knowing that his wife's friend had had only as much sleep as him the last few weeks. 'I have to get back to Isabelle.'

'Of course.'

'We shall regale you with our scintillating company,' Willa added, opening her arms and ushering his father and his sisters towards the parlour like a mother hen with her chicks.

'Consider me regaled already,' he heard his father say, before they all disappeared into the room, the door clicking shut behind them.

Left alone in the hall, Matthew exhaled a deep breath and turned to face the stairs. Climbing them seemed momentous in his exhaustion, each small step some great feat of energy instead of a minor impediment. Still, he climbed them, placing one foot in front of the other as he made his way back to his wife's bedside.

Despite his mother's blasé attitude, and his father's confidence that Gareth was too much of a coward to cause a stir, Matthew could not quite stem his foreboding. But he would protect Luke indefinitely. Of course he would.

And now Gareth knew that.

Still, his mother was right about one thing: there was nothing else he could do for now.

Matthew was so lost in thought that he didn't recognise the happy chatter for an entire five seconds after he'd walked into Isabelle's bedchamber. It came to him by degrees—the sound of Luke's laughter, his mother's tired chuckle…

And there, through them all, he heard Isabelle rasp, 'There he is.'

Chapter Twenty-Three

Isabelle opened her eyes slowly, wincing when her head pounded in protest. She tried to swallow, her dry throat fighting her efforts.

The first thing she saw was a familiar pair of green eyes. Luke was lying next to her, his head on her wrist, looking up at her as if he wasn't quite sure that she was really awake.

'Luke…' she murmured.

'Izzy?' His reply was whispered through tears.

'What's wrong?' she asked, confused.

Why was Luke sleeping in her bed? And where were Seraphina and Matthew?

'I thought you were going to die,' Luke said, sniffling.

Alarmed by the declaration, Isabelle croaked, 'What?'

'Try to stay calm, Your Grace.'

She tipped her head forward to find the source of the voice and saw Dr Taylor standing at the foot of the bed. The doctor smiled at her and walked to her side.

'What happened?' she asked. 'The last thing I remember is…the wedding.' She turned to look at the doctor. 'I *did* get married?'

'Yes. Congratulations, Your Grace.'

'Lord Ashworth asked my permission,' Luke stated seriously.

Isabelle remembered Matthew telling her that quite clearly now. 'Yes, I know.' She lifted her hand from under him and ran it through Luke's hair, alarmed by how much effort the small gesture took out of her. 'Thank you.'

'He said he loves you.'

'He loves *us*,' Isabelle amended, knowing it to be true.

'May I examine you, Your Grace?' Dr Taylor asked. 'I should be on my way soon.'

Isabelle nodded her consent, and the doctor helped her lean forward so that he could place his stethoscope on her back. The only sound in the room as he examined her were her own laboured breaths.

After a long moment, he said, 'There is still fluid in your lungs…though that is to be expected.'

'I feel better,' Isabelle said, not wanting to alarm Luke. 'Tired. But better.'

'Your Grace…' the doctor's voice was grave '…though your fever has broken, the pneumonia will persist for weeks— *months*. It is of the utmost importance that you do not overtax or exert yourself until your lungs fully recover. If you do, you run the risk of regressing.'

Isabelle nodded. 'I will be careful.'

Dr Taylor strung his stethoscope around his neck and looked at her for a long moment. 'I will give instructions to your husband too. Although God knows the man will not let you raise a finger for years to come.'

The words 'your husband' echoed through her head. Isabelle wheezed in pain as a laugh climbed from deep in her chest. 'He has been here?'

'He has never left. The man hasn't slept in three days—'

'Three days?'

'You were very ill, Your Grace,' the doctor replied gravely. 'Lord Ashworth is going to be very relieved to see you awake.'

'Where is he?'

'I believe there was a…situation that needed to be resolved.'

'My cousin came,' Luke clarified, his nose wrinkling with displeasure. The boy leaned forward, green eyes twinkling. 'I heard Lord Ashworth tell Mary to call Mr Briggs should he kill him.' Luke started laughing, his boyish giggle filling the room.

'He...?' Isabelle looked to Dr Taylor for confirmation.

'I wouldn't worry about it, Your Grace. I believe Lord Ashworth was jesting.' Dr Taylor turned to Luke and winked, adding, 'Probably,' causing the boy to dissolve into another round of laughter.

Isabelle tried not to laugh, not wanting to encourage Luke's questionable behaviour, but her lips threatened a smile anyway. 'I suppose I shall need to be updated in full once I'm up and dressed.'

'I recommend another week—maybe two—of bed-rest,' Dr Taylor countered severely.

'But—'

Isabelle's argument was cut off by a loud exclamation at the door. She turned to see the Countess of Heather standing on the threshold. 'Isabelle!' the Countess exclaimed. 'You're awake!' She marched across to the bed and felt Isabelle's face with her hand. 'The fever has broken?'

'Yes,' Dr Taylor replied.

Isabelle, stunned by the genuine display of affection, sat completely still.

The Countess lowered herself to sit on the bed, not bothering to rearrange her skirts before taking both Isabelle's hands in hers. 'You scared us to death, child.'

Isabelle didn't know what to say, overwhelmed by the glossy tears in the older woman's eyes.

The Countess didn't seem to mind. She laughed happily and, without releasing Isabelle's hands, turned to the doctor. 'Thank you so much, Doctor. We were all quite sick with worry.'

Isabelle heard the truth in the words and it settled through her entire body, filling her with warmth. In that moment she felt a connection with the Countess that she had never felt with her own mother. Because here was a woman who loved her children as much as Isabelle did—who understood what it was to constantly worry and fret over their health and happiness and, by default, the health and happiness of their chosen partners.

'Thank you, Countess. For staying.'

The Countess waved her hand in a nonchalant gesture. 'We are one family now, my girl. You couldn't get rid of us if you tried—though Lord knows Matthew is probably going to need a few weeks alone with you to recover from the scare.'

'Where is he?' Isabelle asked. 'And Gareth…?' The words died on her lips as Matthew's large frame filled the doorway, to be immediately replaced with, 'There he is.'

Matthew didn't move or speak. He didn't even appear to be breathing. He stared at her as if he wasn't sure whether or not he was hallucinating.

Isabelle took in his dishevelled appearance. His eyes were dark with fatigue. His face looked gaunt, as if he had not slept or eaten in days. His hair fell past the collar of his shirt, and Isabelle's fingers itched to run through the unruly mass.

The Countess was the first to speak. She rose to stand and held out one hand towards Luke. 'Perhaps we should give them a moment.'

Luke went willingly, not even pausing to look back as he started chatting to the Countess.

Dr Taylor, bag in hand, paused by Matthew's side on his way out. 'She must stay in bed for a week. Maybe longer. I will come every few days to check on her. My instructions remain the same. She must rest and try to resume regular eating and drinking as soon as possible. Warm broth will help soothe her throat. Use the eucalyptus and camphor salve twice daily. Keep her warm, dry and well rested.'

Matthew nodded, but his eyes never left Isabelle.

'It is important that she does not strain herself. Any exertion could cause her to regress.'

'I'll make sure she rests,' Matthew affirmed. He reached out his hand for the doctor's. 'Thank you, Dr Taylor.'

Dr Taylor returned the handshake and left the room.

Matthew came to her immediately, sitting on the edge of her bed when all she wanted was to be in his arms. 'Isabelle…'

She looked up into his eyes, saw the worry and relief and love there, and marvelled at it. 'Matthew.'

Needing the contact, she reached out and touched his face. He bowed his head and, raising both his hands, pressed her palm hard against his flushed cheek, as if he was afraid she would disappear at any moment. His breath came in one huge shuddering sigh.

'I—I thought you were going to...'

Isabelle's heart swelled with love. Leaving her hand in his, she moved inelegantly from beneath the covers and slid onto his lap, nestling against him as his arms wrapped around her.

'I would never leave you willingly,' she said, meaning every word. She would fight for this man. Not just for herself, but for Luke and Sera too. 'I love you, Matthew.'

He buried his face against her neck, even as his arms tightened around her. 'Christ, Isabelle, I love you so much.'

A ragged sob tore from his chest, shocking Isabelle into silence. Unsure of what to say, but wanting to comfort him, she ran her hand repetitively through his hair as he fought to regain the control that she knew he so cherished. She didn't move away. She didn't speak. She just let herself be held, knowing that Matthew needed it as much as she did.

It dawned on her as they sat there, wrapped up in one another, that this man was her husband. *Hers.* For the rest of her life she would have this—this comfort and joy. And, yes, this fear. For loving someone was no guarantee that there would be no hardship—in fact, if anything, it was a guarantee that there *would* be. Because you had so much more to lose when you truly loved someone. If misfortune struck, the consequences were so much greater.

The feeling of Isabelle's hand in his hair was like a dream—one he never wanted to wake up from. Her body, nestled as closely as possible against him, was so small and frail, so light, that he was immediately worried about the weeks ahead.

He raised his head to look at her, his beautiful wife. 'Please, don't ever do that to me again.'

She smiled tiredly. 'I intend to live a long time yet, my lord.'

She placed her hand on his cheek, drawing his mouth down to hers, and Matthew sighed into the kiss. For one long moment he allowed himself to taste her, sliding his tongue between her lips to gently stroke hers. But when she wrapped her arms around his neck and pulled him closer, her breath wheezing, he pulled back.

'Matthew…?'

'No exerting yourself, love.'

'I hardly think that's what he meant,' she replied, but the words lost any force because of the way she rasped them.

He lifted her easily, repositioning her in the centre of the bed. 'We have a lifetime. There's no rush.'

Matthew started to move away, all too conscious of his body's response to Isabelle, but she caught his hand in hers, stopping him. 'Please…' she patted the space beside her '…stay with me.'

'I don't think—'

'I want to sleep with my husband,' she countered. She yawned once and curled into the covers. 'I think I am allowed that much, considering I was deprived of my wedding night.'

Matthew, wanting nothing more than to hold her, took off his shoes and climbed onto the bed fully clothed. Isabelle moved over, making room for him, and the moment he lay down beside her shimmied closer again, snuggling against him as if she needed his body heat. She closed her eyes.

Matthew repositioned himself, shifting onto his side so that he could hold her as close as possible and touch her, his fingers trailing down her arm and the soft fabric of her nightdress.

'I don't want separate rooms,' she said suddenly.

'Hmm?'

'Wherever we end up living, I want to sleep in your bed every night,' Isabelle clarified. 'I don't want separate rooms.'

'All right.'

It was the easiest demand she'd ever make of him. He'd give anything to have her like this, soft and cuddly and pressed up against him every night.

'And I want more babies. Not until Sera is a little older, but maybe in a year or two…'

Matthew froze, even as he began to harden at the thought of her pregnant with another one of his children. 'As many as you want,' he promised.

She nodded sleepily. Matthew was watching her face, so he saw the frown pucker her brow right before she opened her eyes.

'What did Gareth want?'

'To fulfil his "familial obligation" and ensure that you had not been taken advantage of,' he said drily. 'Duchess…?'

She opened her eyes and turned to face him. Her hand found his face, immediately soothing.

'What is it?' she asked.

'The scandal is coming,' he said honestly, hating to alarm her, but wanting her to be prepared. 'The gossip columns were already speculating. And now, with your cousin…'

She nodded seriously, but she did not seem as alarmed as he'd expected. 'We are prepared for the possibility, Matthew. All that's left to do is protect the children as much as possible.'

'I agree. I don't want Luke and Sera subjected to specula- tion,' he admitted. 'I think we should close up Everett Place and remove the household to my family's country estate. My father and Briggs can handle your business from here until the season ends.'

'We should let the rumours die down?'

Matthew nodded. 'In a few years, nobody will care. We can return to London once some time has passed—when Luke goes to school, perhaps? I would like to be nearby for his first year. But until then we can remain separate from the *ton*. I can man- age my family's land and estate. We can choose those friends we would like to come and visit us…spend time with family…' He ran his hand down to her stomach. 'Add to our own family…'

'Yes.'

'You must think about it.'

'I don't need to. I trust your judgement. And Sera… We will protect her for as long as we can. At least until she's old enough to understand.'

'She will carry our sins,' Matthew murmured regretfully.

'But she will carry them knowing that she is loved uncon- ditionally. And one day she will meet a man who sees her for who she is and not for how she was born, and he will love her fiercely and love her regardless.'

'But not for many years,' Matthew said, sounding less en- amoured of the idea than Isabelle was.

Isabelle laughed. 'I think I would rather enjoy living solely in the country for a few years.'

'You are known to be quite reclusive,' he teased. 'But I should warn you that living with my family coming and going all the time is hardly going to be what you're used to.'

Isabelle sighed happily. 'No, I don't suppose it will be. But I am glad nonetheless.' She kissed him. 'I rather adore your family.'

'Me too,' he admitted.

Isabelle repositioned her head on his arm. 'I suppose I should pay a visit to my parents soon and inform them of our marriage.'

'I wrote to them.' Matthew didn't want to hurt her, but he couldn't hide the truth from her. 'Yesterday, when I thought...'

'And?'

'Your father replied, asking me to keep them apprised of your condition.'

Matthew had not penned a reply to that, knowing that her parents did not deserve one.

'Thank you for doing that.'

'You do not seem surprised.'

In fact, he thought, she did not seem affected by their negligence at all.

'My parents are not like yours,' she said simply. 'How could I be surprised or upset when I have never known or expected anything different from them? I was a disappointing alternative to the son my father wanted, but never sired. In their minds they are excellent parents, for no other reason than that they raised me to be a fit wife for a duke.'

'My parents are yours now too,' he pointed out, feeling angry and sad for her. 'You have an entire family you never bargained for. And you will probably be sick of their attention within a fortnight.'

'I know—and I couldn't be happier.' She burrowed against him. 'I can't wait to get started on the rest of my life with you,' she murmured sleepily. 'It still feels like a wonderful dream I might wake up from at any moment.'

Matthew kissed the side of her face.

'I'm so tired...' Isabelle mumbled, yawning again. 'I know

I've slept for three days, but I rather feel I could sleep for three more.'

Matthew brushed her hair back from her face, revelling in the silky strands between his fingers, memorising the gentle weight of his wife's head on his arm and her body curled against his.

'Sleep, my love.'

'Don't leave.'

'Never.'

Matthew waited for Isabelle to fall into a deep sleep before finally closing his own eyes after almost a week of wakefulness. And as his body gave way to exhaustion and his mind began to shut down, he had one last singular thought: *I don't deserve to be this happy.*

Epilogue

London, 1844—two years later

Isabelle gripped her hands together to stop herself from reaching out and smoothing Luke's hair, aware that he would be humiliated by any maternal gesture in front of his school friends.

'You will write if you need anything?'

Luke smiled nervously. 'I will.'

'We will see you at half term,' she reminded him.

Matthew, perhaps sensing her struggle, took over. 'You are going to be fine,' he said quietly. 'But any time you need us you will write and we will come. And, Luke, if you hate it here, we will bring you home.'

Luke expelled a tight breath. 'I know. I'll be fine,' he insisted bravely.

'Ashworth!'

Isabelle turned to greet the approaching stranger as Matthew came to stand beside her. The man was tall and thin, with an elaborate moustache that Isabelle instinctively knew his wife must hate. A young boy trailed behind him.

'Talbot.' Matthew returned the greeting, shaking the man's hand. 'Allow me to introduce my wife—'

'Ah, yes! The Duchess of Everett,' Talbot replied, pointedly ignoring her pregnant belly, which had already attracted a few scandalised glances. 'I heard your marriage caused quite a stir, Your Grace.'

Isabelle smiled indulgently. 'I prefer to be known as Lady Ashworth, Lord Talbot.' She curtsied. 'It is a pleasure to make your acquaintance.'

'Yes. Quite.' Lord Talbot smiled kindly before dismissing her to talk to Matthew.

Isabelle, sensing the two young boys' awkwardness, stepped in to make introductions. 'May I introduce you to our son, Luke, the Duke of Everett?'

Luke stepped forward, his hand outstretched towards the Talbot boy. 'It's a pleasure to make your acquaintance.'

'Graham,' the boy replied informally, and returned the handshake.

The boys assessed each other for a long moment, as if deciding whether or not to strike up an alliance. Isabelle held her breath as the silence stretched, only expelling it when Graham nodded his head in the direction of a small group of students standing nearby.

'Come on. I'll introduce you to my friends.'

Luke nodded, smiling brightly at the possibility of meeting more people. 'Let me just say goodbye to my parents.'

Isabelle's throat burned with unexpected tears. It wasn't the first time he had referred to them as such, but hearing it still affected her as much it had the very first time.

Matthew had started it—introducing them to his acquaintances as his wife and children as naturally as if it were complete fact. But it had taken Luke over a year to overcome his self-consciousness enough to reciprocate.

The first time he'd actually said, 'Perhaps we should ask my father,' had been in response to a question that Mr Briggs had asked regarding the estate, during one of their monthly meetings. Matthew had cleared his throat and attempted to answer the question casually, despite his emotion. Isabelle had excused herself to go and cry in the corridor.

Since that first awkward acceptance they'd fallen easily into their roles, and now it was strange to think that there had been a time when they had not been such a close-knit family.

Isabelle pulled Luke into a brief hug. 'Be good,' she whispered, and released him almost immediately.

Matthew shook Luke's hand. Neither of her boys said anything, but Isabelle saw and read the silent messages conveyed between them before Luke took one last big breath and turned away too.

She watched him for only a moment, not wanting to embarrass him. But turning and walking away was one of the more difficult things she'd ever had to do, made easier only by Matthew's supportive arm around her.

Matthew handed his emotional wife into their carriage and pulled himself into the conveyance after her. He sat down and, reaching over, lifted her onto his lap and into his arms immediately.

'He'll be fine,' he promised when she sniffled.

'I know,' she replied as the carriage began to move towards their London home, where Seraphina was waiting with Tess. Isabelle rested her head against his chest, her hand coming to fidget with the buttons on his waistcoat. 'It's just... He's still so young.'

Matthew's own heart clenched in his chest. 'He is. But he's clever, Duchess. He'll be fine. And if he's not he'll come home, and we'll find an alternative.'

He kissed her face, pulling a shiver over her skin.

'Luke is a duke,' he went on. 'His path will be a lot easier than that of most of the other boys there by default.'

When a single tear trailed down her cheek, Matthew placed a hand over the swell of her stomach—which, although partially hidden by her dress, was still clearly visible in contrast to her tiny figure.

'Don't fret, my love.'

'I'm not usually this nonsensical,' she insisted, wiping her face. 'It's the baby. I'm hot and bothered *all the time*. Which makes me waspish. I can't sleep.' She slouched against him. 'I feel so *lumpy*.'

Matthew sounded his disapproval deep in the back of his throat. 'You're not "lumpy"; you're beautiful,' he whispered. 'Maybe you just need a distraction.'

His hand reached beneath her skirts to trail up her stockinged calf and—to his absolute delight—straight beneath her chemise to her soft centre.

'You're not wearing drawers, love,' he observed huskily.

'I can't stand them against my skin,' she replied breathlessly. 'So many layers...'

Matthew took her mouth in a gentle kiss as his fingers parted her damp flesh, running over her repeatedly until she arched her back, pressing herself wantonly against his hand.

He groaned his approval. 'Do you like that, Duchess?'

She panted her reply. 'You know I do.'

He laughed and dipped his head to lick the top of her breasts, which seemed to grow heavier each day in her pregnancy. 'I want these in my hands,' he murmured, breathless in his excitement.

'Yes...' Isabelle ground her bottom over the hard length of him in reply. *'Yes.'*

He quickly unlaced the ribbons at her bodice, thanking God that her condition made corsets ill-advised and unnecessary. He spread her dress open to reveal her chemise and, too impatient to remove the last garment, sucked her hard nipple gently into his mouth through the fabric, making sure to be careful with her sensitive breasts.

Isabelle moaned her pleasure. Her hands sank into his hair and tugged, trying to pull him closer, and when Matthew reached beneath her dress again, sliding a single finger into her wet core, she moaned and ground herself against his hand.

'Please, Matthew...'

Matthew complied, shifting his mouth to her other breast as his fingers thrust in and out of her and his thumb found that little bud of nerves.

Isabelle's body clung to him, pulsing and drawing him in as she moved closer and closer to orgasm.

Mad with lust, crazed with the smell of his wife filling the carriage, Matthew released her breast with a small pop. He brought his lips to her ear. 'I love your body, Duchess,' he crooned, his fingers never stopping. 'When we get home, I'm going to strip you naked and let you ride me, so that I can watch you on top of me.'

'Yes…' she hissed, enjoying the fantasy she knew they'd play out as soon as they got home. It was no secret that he loved to watch her, full of life, pregnant with his child.

'I'm going to squeeze your full breasts and suckle your nipples until you are screaming my name.' Her body tensed for one perfect second. 'I'm going to worship you,' he whispered, just before she shattered.

Isabelle's back arched. Her hands tightened in his hair. Her body took his fingers greedily, as if she might prolong the sensation if she could only hold on to them for longer.

He kissed the side of her head as she collapsed against him, her breaths heavy and ragged.

Isabelle was quiet for a long moment as she regained her composure, but as soon as she became aware of his hard length pressing into her she shifted on his lap, making space for her hand to find him beneath his trousers.

Matthew hissed out a sharp breath. 'Not here, my love. I want you in bed. Naked.'

Isabelle raised her eyebrows. 'Anyone would think you quite debauched, my lord. Lusting after a pregnant lady.'

'Perhaps,' he conceded. 'Although lusting after one's pregnant *wife* seems the gentlemanly thing to do.'

She laughed and shifted again, moving to the seat to begin fastening her dress. 'I still don't understand why you find my condition so appealing,' she said off-handedly.

Matthew gently swatted her hands away and began helping her, deftly re-lacing the front of her gown as he had hundreds of times before.

'It's not only your condition, Duchess, though I *do* find the idea of my child growing in you sinfully delightful.' He watched the blush spread over her face, enamoured of the fact that he could still embarrass her. 'It's you,' he said simply. 'It's only ever been you.'

Isabelle sighed and rested her head against his shoulder. 'Who would have thought that a simple favour could lead to this?'

Matthew leaned down to kiss her. 'Not me,' he replied. 'Though I am exceptionally glad I was first on your list.'

* * * * *

Author Note

Thank you so much for reading *One Night with the Duchess*! Researching and writing this book was so much fun, and I can't wait to continue this journey with you.

If you have ten seconds to spare, I would be eternally grateful if you left a review of *One Night with the Duchess* on Goodreads. It could be only a few words, but every review helps spread the word!

If you enjoyed *One Night with the Duchess* and would like to stay in touch with the Widows of West End, Willa and Leo's book is coming soon! Follow along on Instagram (@author. maggie) for updates, promotions, and sneak peeks.

Warm regards,
Maggie Weston